Claire's love affair with Greece started more years ago than she cares to remember. Corfu was her first destination as a teenager, and since then she has travelled extensively around the country, particularly the islands, and is even learning Greek, very slowly.

The sunshine, the culture, and the warmth of the Greek people, not to mention the food, inspired her to write this, her second novel.

Claire is a long-time journalist and TV producer, who has worked in features, showbiz, and interiors. She is married with two grown-up children and lives in southwest London.

⬛ instagram.com/clairecarverauthor
⬛ facebook.com/clairecarverauthor

Also by Claire Carver

Still Got It

TOO GLAM TO GIVE A DAMN

CLAIRE CARVER

One More Chapter
a division of HarperCollins*Publishers* Ltd
1 London Bridge Street
London SE1 9GF
www.harpercollins.co.uk
HarperCollins*Publishers*
Macken House, 39/40 Mayor Street Upper,
Dublin 1, D01 C9W8, Ireland

This paperback edition 2026
1
First published in Great Britain in ebook format
by HarperCollins*Publishers* 2026
Copyright © Claire Carver 2026
Claire Carver asserts the moral right to
be identified as the author of this work

A catalogue record of this book is available from the British Library
ISBN: 978-0-00-880116-8

This novel is entirely a work of fiction. The names, characters and incidents portrayed in it are the work of the author's imagination. Any resemblance to actual persons, living or dead, events or localities is entirely coincidental.

Printed and bound in the UK using 100% Renewable Electricity
by CPI Group (UK) Ltd

All rights reserved. No part of this publication may be reproduced, stored in a retrieval system, or transmitted, in any form or by any means, electronic, mechanical, photocopying, recording or otherwise, without the prior permission of the publishers.

Without limiting the exclusive rights of any author, contributor or the publisher of this publication, any unauthorised use of this publication to train generative artificial intelligence (AI) technologies is expressly prohibited. HarperCollins also exercise their rights under Article 4(3) of the Digital Single Market Directive 2019/790 and expressly reserve this publication from the text and data mining exception.

*To my childhood friends, Alison, Lynn, Katy and Sharon.
We've still got each other's backs, and, even better,
still like each other!*

Chapter One

Sofia Barnes lay back on her sunbed and stretched her arms out wide, wide enough to hold hands with the two women on the beds either side of her.

The view of the infinity pool and the glittering blue sea beyond was breathtaking. From behind her designer sunglasses Sofia watched a yacht with billowing white sails slowly make its way across the horizon. To her left a whitewashed town rose up in the distance like an elaborate wedding cake, dotted around with the turquoise roofs of churches clinging to the hillside.

Sofia squeezed both the hands she held hard, very hard.

'Wake up, you two. What a view! Can you believe we've made it? We've finally started out on our very own Greek odyssey. We get to explore three gorgeous islands together in all their glory. This is the life!'

'Ow!'

The woman to her left, Maddie Stevens, sat up abruptly,

knocking her pink crocheted sunhat to the floor, and rubbed her palm.

'Sof, careful, that hurt.'

Charlotte Trent, lying on the other side of Sofia, just murmured and shimmied down the sunbed a little more, the toes of her long, curvaceous body, in its low-cut red costume, almost over the edge of the bed.

'Yes, leave us alone, Sof. Let us sleep if we want. You forced us to have two Aperol Spritzes the second we arrived at the hotel, one after the other. We're not twenty anymore. What did you think would happen? And what's wrong with a little snooze anyway? We've been travelling most of the day.'

Sofia leapt up off the sunbed and stood in front of her friends, blocking their view. She pointed up at the castle that stood atop the white icing houses. She couldn't keep still a moment longer.

'Boring! We're here to celebrate fifty years of knowing each other. Fifty years! How many friends can say that? We've got to make the most of our time together. We need to go into that town up there and check it out as soon as we can.'

Maddie reached over, picked up her hat from the sun-warmed tiles and plonked it back on her head, stuffing her flame-coloured hair underneath as best she could. She'd made the hat herself and been stunned to learn that crocheted hats and even dresses were all the rage now. There'd been plenty on sale at the hotel boutique, at ridiculous prices. Perhaps she should change jobs, leave the care home and its lovely but demanding residents far behind, and go into fashion design. She stared up at her friend.

'Calm down, Sof, for God's sake. I'd forgotten for a

moment what it's like spending more than a couple of hours with you. You're manic. You were like this at school, bloody exhausting.'

Sofia drew herself up to her full height of five foot two, tiny gold string bikini glinting in the sun.

'Charming, both of you. Is this the thanks I get for single-handedly organising the whole trip? Three weeks of bliss, without either of you having to lift a finger?'

Maddie smiled at the woman who'd been part of her life for so long.

'Yeah, sorry, Sof. It's a fabulous idea, and you got us a such a great deal. I still can't believe it's costing so little. Especially when we're staying in places like this. I know June's not high season for Greece, but even so…'

Sofia clocked Charlotte's frown at the comment, shook her head in her friend's direction and put her finger to her lips. Luckily, Maddie was applying yet more suncream to her pale skin and didn't notice. Eventually, Maddie settled back down on her sunbed, sequinned kaftan billowing around her, and sighed.

'You can call me naïve if you like, but I just thought I might have a few moments to relax occasionally. I'm quite keen to do some snoozing in the sun.'

Maddie glanced up at the town, the blinding sun reflecting off the white of the houses.

'There's no way I'm trekking up all those steps in this heat anyway, especially with my skin. I'd be a leathery old prune in minutes.'

Sofia tutted.

'Less of the old. That's a banned word on this holiday. Sixty is the new forty you know. We're still in our prime.'

Maddie snorted.

'Well, you may be... Not sure I am.'

'Of course you are.'

Sofia sat at the foot of her friend's sunbed and tickled her feet.

'Get off!'

'I know you've had a truly horrible time, Mads, the worst, but we're here to help you. Tony wouldn't want you to sit around moping for the rest of your life, would he? He was always so full of fun, the—'

'Please don't say life and soul of the party.'

Maddie's voice was sharper than she'd intended. She really didn't want to hear any more tributes to her late husband, Saint Tony, as she called him in her head. He'd selfishly upped and left her fifteen months ago. One minute smiling his smile that pulled everyone in, the next breathing his last, laid out on the kitchen floor. A massive heart attack, they said; nothing that could have been done, they said. Her mind flooded with images of his handsome face, robbed of life. He'd left her to cope alone, but there was more, so much more.

At the gathering to mark a year since his death, she'd lost her temper and messed up so badly she was now estranged from her son and her gorgeous little baby granddaughter. The shame and guilt at her actions ambushed her at odd moments during the day and often woke her at night, stabbing the images of being told to get out of her son's house into her brain over and over again.

She hadn't even been able to tell the two women in front of

her, her oldest and closest friends, what she'd done. They'd never look at her the same way again.

When she raised her head again, she caught the look of concern that passed between Sofia and Charlotte. She mustn't spoil the mood. They all deserved a break. Sofia worked far too hard, and Charlotte was wound tight as a coil most of the time.

'Let's all go into town a bit later, when it's cooled down. You know what they say about mad dogs and Englishwomen going out in the midday sun.'

Charlotte coughed.

'Er, I think it's Englishmen…'

'Whatever.'

Charlotte sat up under her fringed umbrella, almost hitting her head on its wicker roof, long blonde hair escaping from its messy ponytail.

'Did you know that it was also Noel Coward who wrote that wonderful Patsy Cline song, 'Mad About the Boy'? About an actual boy? Or hopefully a young man.'

It was an obvious attempt to change the subject away from Tony, but Maddie played along.

'Yeah, of course. Everyone knows that.'

'Did you really?'

'No … but you always were the school swot.'

Maddie's smile showed her comment was without malice.

'Hmmm. Not sure what good it did me.'

'How can you say that? You've got your art hanging in galleries around the world; you've got a nice house, lovely kids, loads of friends… And *your* husband's still alive.'

She hadn't meant to say those last whispered words out loud. Two drinks and no food hadn't helped. She mustn't get bitter and twisted. Since Tony died, it was like she'd lost whatever filter she had, and she'd never had much of one to begin with. But it was hard to sit there and listen to her friend feeling sorry for herself. Charlotte had no idea. Not that Maddie wanted her friend to know what it was like to live without her husband, but still.

'Sorry. Just slipped out.'

Maddie was shocked to see Charlotte's blue eyes glitter with unshed tears.

'Things aren't always what they seem, Mads.'

Charlotte took a deep breath and gulped back a sob. She mustn't break down. Not this early in the holiday. Just the word husband was enough to set her off. She couldn't let what she'd seen that night overwhelm her yet again. Just the thought of opening that door and seeing them together was enough to make her feel nauseous. Doug had betrayed her big time, there was no doubt about that, but what was she going to do about it, that was the question?

She had three precious weeks to try to work out the answer.

Maddie reached out to stroke her friend's arm. She'd rarely seen Charlotte get emotional at the drop of a hat. Cool, calm, collected Charlotte was usually the sensible one. The giver of advice, on everything from recipes to relationships.

The three of them hadn't seen quite as much of each other as they usually did over the past year. Although they lived in different parts of the country, their aim had always been to meet once a month in person. But the aftermath of Tony's death and Sofia's ridiculous workload had meant more WhatsApp group calls than meeting up. It wasn't the same. She wasn't going to feel guilty about it – she had more than enough guilt on her plate – but she had to admit she'd dropped the ball on both her friends' lives recently. There was obviously something big going on in Charlotte's life that she didn't know about.

'You're right, Char. Things are never what they seem, lovely.'

Maddie really did care deeply about both these women, but her ability to deal with other people's problems had been severely weakened since Tony's death. She had to get out of her own head. She wasn't the only one with problems. Charlotte deserved her help too.

'Do you want to talk about it?'

A screen came down over her friend's eyes before she'd even replaced her sunglasses.

'Not at the moment, but thanks.'

Sofia had moved her pink and white striped towel to sit in the full glare of the sun.

'OK, whatever you two are talking about looks a bit heavy. That's enough of that. That sounds like late night stuff, to be discussed at length when we've downed a few.'

Maddie mouthed '*bossy cow*' at Charlotte, which at least raised a smile.

Sofia raised her hand.

'And before anyone says it, yes, I know I'm sitting directly in the sun. Being half Spanish has its advantages, and one of them is the ability to tan easily. Believe me, after sitting in that office day in day out for what seems like ever, I'm desperate to feel the sun on my body.'

Sofia stretched her arms up into the air and pushed out her chest.

'Apparently, there's a nudist beach on the other side of the town. Anyone else up for it?'

Maddie pulled her hat down even further and hugged her knees under her pink floral kaftan, another number she'd knocked up herself.

'Not me, that's for sure.'

Charlotte shook her head.

'Me neither. No interest in showing the world my stretch marks and Caesarean scar. Not that I'd ever swap my kids, but not having any has certainly helped you keep your fabulous figure, Sof. No more bikinis for me. But if I had your body, perhaps even I'd be tempted.'

Charlotte was confident that Sofia would take this as the compliment it was. That was the advantage of knowing someone for so long. They knew everything, or as near to everything as it was possible to, about each other. Which wasn't quite the case at the moment, but she was working on it.

In the early years, they'd shared everything, from starting their periods to the stress of exams to the joy and despair of boyfriends. She'd met Maddie and Sofia a couple of weeks after they all started at secondary school, and the three of them had remained tight to this day.

They'd never been the popular girls, in fact Charlotte smiled remembering how downright awkward they'd been back in the day. Three only children, without any siblings to pave the way at a sprawling comprehensive. Sofia had been teased for her braces and the trace of a Spanish accent, she for having a posh voice and being tall and skinny, and Maddie for her flattened northern vowels and blushing the same colour as her hair if anyone even spoke to her.

They'd improved with age, like fine wine, or that's what they liked to believe. The combination of a petite brunette, a gangly blonde and a redhead with a temper to match always reminded her of a selection box. Dressed up in their finery, they were convinced they'd still got it.

Sofia had said way back in school that she never wanted children and stuck to it. She'd been a favourite, if sometimes overindulgent, aunty to her and Maddie's children, but she'd never shown the slightest inkling to change her mind. Obviously, it was far too late now anyway.

Sofia wagged her finger at the two of them.

'We'll see. Swimming naked is one of life's true pleasures. Maybe later on in the trip when you're both a bit more relaxed, I can gently persuade you.'

Charlotte snorted.

'Force us into it, you mean, with your special set of lawyer-talk tools?'

'Oh, I didn't know that was a thing. Where can I buy some? Is there a B&Q near the Old Bailey?'

'Very funny.' Charlotte eyed her friend. 'How did you manage to get three weeks off in one go anyway? Normally we have to push you to even take a long weekend away from that office. What have you promised to do?'

Sofia fiddled with one of the tassels on her hammam towel.

'Nothing. It just came … at the right time.'

Not that it had been her choice. It was true that such a long trip was unheard of at her company. The words permanent holiday flashed into her mind, but she blinked to get rid of them.

'Speak up, Sof. I can see there's more to this than meets the eye.'

Sofia touched her nose and spread out some imaginary suncream.

'Are you planning a new career as a private detective?'

'No, but I'm very good at knowing when you're lying, Pinocchio. I've watched you in action with our old headmaster, Mr Turner, remember, who you persuaded that it was a case of mistaken identity when we were caught smoking with the naughty boys round the back of the bike sheds.'

'That did you a favour too. He was going to call our parents in. Yours would have gone ballistic.'

'True. Anyway, that's not the point. You may have been able to bamboozle him, but you haven't answered my question.'

'I'm asking for a lunch recess, m'lud. Shall we order a couple of club sandwiches with chips between us to keep us going until dinner?'

Charlotte conceded defeat this time round, much to Sofia's relief.

'Don't know where you put it all, but why not?'

Maddie put her book down.

'Sounds great. Let's throw in a couple of those Greek beers you introduced me to at the airport, as well. What were they called? Mythos?'

Charlotte raised her eyebrows and shot a look at Sofia.

'Not for me. I'd never be able to climb those steps later.

And I really want to see the monastery set into the cliff. Apparently, it has some lovely paintings and exquisite religious icons.'

Maddie grunted under her umbrella.

'You sound like you're fronting a travel show, Char.'

'Well, art is how I make my living.'

No one spoke. Charlotte had long suspected that her friends thought what she did was some sort of hobby. Not a real job. They assumed that it was Doug's business that kept their lifestyle going. Little did they know. Another secret she was keeping from her friends.

Maddie wasn't giving up.

'Sof? Beer?'

'No, not for me either, thanks. I'm going to save myself for this evening.'

'Spoilsports. OK, just one for me then.'

Sofia flagged down the pool guy, who they'd discovered was called Dimitris.

Maddie watched to see if he could keep his eyes off Sofia's body. Men really did adore her friend, and she did plenty of adoring back. Younger guys were her thing, with no ties, no long-term relationships.

Sofia had been badly burned by her parents' divorce and her father's betrayal, something she hid from most people. But they'd been there; they'd seen the devastation first hand; they'd held her as she sobbed. The experience had made their friend fiercely independent, and the steady stream of gorgeous guys who paraded through her life never lasted, even if they thought they were in with a chance.

Maddie couldn't imagine being with someone so much younger. She couldn't imagine being with anyone else, full stop. But especially not with the way she felt about her own body at the moment. She'd bought two swimsuits with tummy control panels, but she was planning to wear her kaftans over the top most of the time.

Ironically, of the three of them, she'd always been the fitness freak, the one constantly in the gym, walking for miles, watching what she ate and drank. Until… Tony's smiling face flashed before her eyes, but she couldn't give him a seat at the table right now.

The ice-cold beer was placed on the table, its green bottle dripping with condensation, a very welcome distraction. The glass to accompany it was iced on the outside, turning it opaque. Maddie nodded her thanks and poured out a full glass, desperate to get her hands on the liquid gold and feel it cooling her throat and snaking its way down to her stomach to give it a hug. It certainly helped take the edge off.

Sofia tried not to watch Maddie drinking with such relish as she washed off her suntan oil in the open-air shower at the side of the pool. The woman was entitled to drink what she liked after what she'd been through, and they were on holiday after all.

She forced herself to look away and stared down at the shower tray inlaid with grey and white pebbles in star shapes, which matched the floors and terraces throughout the hotel, while all the doors and woodwork were painted a pastel blue.

It was the same décor in their rooms. The three of them were next to each other in a row on the second floor, with their own little terraces complete with concrete bench seats and plunge pools. It was major luxury, and although she thought Charlotte had worked it out for herself, she'd confess to her later that she'd told a little white lie to Maddie about the price and subbed it herself.

Charlotte was like a bloodhound. Once she got a sniff of something, she wouldn't let it go. Sofia pulled her dark bob into a ball on top of her head with the band she wore round her wrist.

'Time for a swim. The food'll take ages. I know that from bitter experience after staying with my friend Grace on her island in the Cyclades. It's the same all over Greece. They prepare everything properly with fresh ingredients, but the one thing it isn't is quick.'

She turned and dived into the deep end with a flourish, kicking up spray that managed to splatter both of the others.

'Urgh! You monster. Go away.' Charlotte stirred on her super thick grey sunbed cushion, tastefully edged in cream, before closing her eyes again and turning onto her stomach.

The cool water enveloped Sofia as she dived deeper. She opened her eyes to stare at the dolphin painted on the bottom of the pool.

Hopefully Charlotte, or Sherlock as she'd be calling her from now on, wouldn't dig any deeper into why she was suddenly so flush with money and able to take such a large chunk of time off.

The truth was too painful to voice to her friends. She'd been cruelly tossed aside by the law firm she'd helped to build, leaving a big black hole in her life. The words redundancy agreement in black and white at the top of the letter delivered to her house by a courier had left her breathless. She might have more money in her bank account than she'd ever had in her life, but what the hell would she do next?

That, she wasn't ready to talk about.

Chapter Two

Sofia turned and shut the bedroom door quietly behind her, in case anyone else on their corridor was still having a snooze. Between three and five in the afternoon were the golden hours in Greece, when many of the shops shut and nearly everyone took a break, either at home, dozing, meeting friends in a café, or having a long leisurely lunch. Even the workmen were supposed to down tools.

She'd agreed to meet the others downstairs in the pool bar bang on five, for their trip into town.

The door to her left opened too, and Charlotte stepped out into the corridor. Sofia held her finger to her lips. Like her, Charlotte was in a flowing floral maxi dress, pale green to her pale pink, and they walked silently past Maddie's door and down the stairs to the covered bar area. Charlotte popped up onto a white-painted high stool with ease and nodded her head at the neighbouring one.

'Do you need a hand up?'

'Bloody cheek. Just because you're a giant. I'm petite, not a dwarf.' Sofia looked around her. 'Not that I have a problem with dwarves of course, but I can manage to get onto a bar stool myself, thanks.'

Charlotte put her hands in the air in a gesture of surrender and failed to stifle a grin at Sofia's ungainly ascent.

'Fair enough. This giant's just asking.'

She indicated at Sofia's dress.

'I'm pleased you listened to what I was saying about the dress code in the monastery. It's no bare legs and covered arms. I know we're both wearing elbow-length sleeves, but I'm taking a scarf as well just to be on the safe side. It would be terrible to climb all the way up there and be turned away, wouldn't it?'

Sofia rolled her eyes.

'Yeah, terrible. Not sure how I'd cope.'

'OK, no need to be sarky. We agreed there should be something for everyone on this holiday, didn't we? And this is very definitely something for me.'

Dimitris the pool guy moved in their direction from the other end of the bar.

'Oh look, here's something for you…'

Sofia smiled a tight smile. Her love life had long been a hot topic of conversation. Going for younger guys who didn't expect any commitment had worked out well for her over the years. If you didn't get close to people, they couldn't leave you. Just the thought of her mother's anguished face, hoping against hope that her husband would leave his mistress and come back to her someday, was enough to put her off anything more serious. Her friends got a vicarious thrill out of her dates too, loathe though they'd be to admit it.

'You're hilarious.'

Dimitris was indeed a sight to behold, one made up of a tanned, ripped, body with a full head of dark curls and eyes the colour of the sea on a cloudless day, and normally she'd waste no time going into flirt mode. But she was on a very special holiday with her friends. Not on the lookout for men. Not this early on, anyway. It was only day one.

'What can I do for you, ladies?'

Sofia hated being called a lady and it was even worse to be lumped in with a group of them. That was unnecessarily ageing in her opinion. Being called girls was way preferable.

'A coffee for me please, *dipló cappuccino skéto zestó, parakaló.*'

'Ooh flash.' Charlotte turned to her. 'What exactly is that?'

'A hot double cappuccino, without sugar. They often whack loads in unless you ask them not to. The Greeks are sweet-toothed by nature. Also, once the sun comes out, they assume everyone wants their coffee cold with ice, which is a *freddo espresso* or a *freddo cappuccino*. You're considered strange if you still want it hot.'

'I'm strange too then. And don't say it! How do I ask for the same?'

'*To ídio, parakaló.*'

Charlotte tried out the strange words, rolling them round her mouth.

Dimitris smiled, showing brilliant white teeth, and went behind the bar.

Sofia turned to Charlotte.

'OK, a quick lesson. *Parakaló* is please and *efcharistó* is thank you. And you might as well take in *kaliméra*, good morning, *kalispéra*, good afternoon or evening, and *kalinýchta*, goodnight.'

Charlotte repeated the words while they waited for their coffees.

'Oh yes, I'm going to use these later. Teach me some more.'

'Hey, you're pushing me to my limits already. I only know a few words and phrases that Grace taught me.'

'Ah yes, will we get to catch up with Grace again when we arrive at our final island, *her island, the one that's only a short plane hop to Athens*? I haven't seen her for years.'

'It's not *"her island"*, but yes, you certainly will, Grace and her partner, Will. See what I did there?'

'You talk about her a lot.'

Sofia stroked Charlotte's leg.

'Ah, how cute, you're not jealous are you? I've known you and Maddie a whole six years longer than Grace. You get first dibs.'

Charlotte let out the breath she'd been holding. Doug's cheating had affected her in ways she'd not expected. Obviously, she was beyond furious with him, but the past month had made her question everything and everyone she thought she knew. Her world had been tilted on its axis, and she wasn't sure if it could be righted again. She'd needed that reassurance that she still held top spot in Sofia's list of friends, albeit shared with Maddie.

'Good.'

Charlotte put her finger to her chin and pulled a face. It was time to lighten things up.

'And is there any other reason why we're all being dragged back to that particular island? I seem to remember a guy you mentioned meeting there last year, "a real Greek god", you said. Apollo, was it? No, not Apollo, Adonis. That's it! Adonis. You said he was amazing in bed. And you've been back there since, I know you have, from your Insta pics.'

Sofia grabbed the coffees that Dimitris had put on the counter and nodded her thanks. She handed one to Charlotte.

'You're right.'

'I knew it!'

'About the stools. I'm not keen on the stools. Let's move to that table over there underneath the umbrella.'

She wasn't keen on the topic of conversation either. The men in her life weren't meant to be anything other than transient. She'd already broken her own rules by spending time with Adonis over the last twelve months; a couple of weekends on the island and one in Athens. She'd persuaded herself that she was missing Grace and had to see her, but she needed to shut down this idea that Adonis was something special, to herself as much as the others. He was just one guy in a long line. They had fun, but she couldn't let it become anything more. Before losing her job, the possibility of spending any more time with him hadn't been on the table, and that's the way it had to stay.

Seated at a sea-themed mosaic-topped table, Charlotte took a large gulp of her coffee.

'OK, I've got the message on Adonis. We'll park that for a while. But before sleepyhead gets here, would you like to explain why she thinks this hotel's some sort of cut-price break? One step up from Butlin's?'

Sofia's face was that of a naughty child.

'I knew you'd clocked it. I was planning to tell you as soon as I got you on your own, honest. I was so keen for us all to be here together, that I might have discounted the price a bit.'

'A lot…'

'OK, a lot. But I didn't want to embarrass her into saying she couldn't afford it. She obviously needs a holiday more than any of us.'

'It's a bit sneaky, but I agree with you on this one. She looks completely knackered. Obviously, I won't mention it.'

Charlotte finished her coffee in record time and checked her phone again.

'She's fifteen minutes late already. Do you think one of us ought to go up there?'

Sofia leaned back in the chair and crossed her legs.

'No, leave her a bit longer. The amount of alcohol she's knocked back today already, she's probably slept through any alarm. Let's just enjoy the view.'

Sofia focussed on the cloudless sapphire sky and the dark shapes of islands crouching in the distance, trying to work out which one it was they'd be taking the ferry to next.

Charlotte leaned in closer.

'Yeah, I was going to mention that to you too.'

'What, the view?'

Charlotte had her *'we've got to talk about this, and I won't take no for an answer'* voice on. Sofia knew it was useless to resist, but the few moments of peace had been welcome.

'No, Maddie's drinking. She's hitting the booze pretty hard, isn't she? Should we be worried?'

Sofia shrugged her shoulders.

'It's only the first day, so maybe it's just the novelty.'

Charlotte frowned at her old friend. Maddie seemed even

more unhappy than the last time she'd seen her. She was snappy and ready to take offence at the slightest remark. It was no surprise she was missing Tony like mad, but Charlotte had a gut feeling there was something else going on as well. It was frankly a relief to be worrying about someone else's problems for a while.

'Really? You're not bothered?'

'Look, I agree we should keep an eye on it. I don't like to judge, but it does seem a bit over the top.'

Charlotte leaned in so close Sofia could smell her floral perfume.

'Also, I'm not being a bitch, honestly, and I'm in no position to talk, but don't you think she's put on quite a bit of weight since we last saw her? I'm not sure she's coping that well.'

Sofia pinching her arm put an immediate stop to the conversation.

'Mads! We're over here.'

A figure in a white kaftan which almost touched her ankles, complete with a wide brimmed straw hat, made her way towards them.

Sofia threw down the last dregs of her coffee.

'I don't think she's going to offend or inflame any monks in that gear, is she?'

'Miaow.'

The taxi deposited them at the foot of the cliff, and all three women just stood for a moment, shocked into silence as they caught their first glimpse of the spectacular white monastery clinging for dear life to the sheer grey stone, like a stray chess piece.

Charlotte recovered her voice first.

'That is truly something, isn't it? It looks like it's hanging in the air, suspended above the sea. You know it dates back to the eleventh century?'

Maddie nodded in Charlotte's direction.

'She's off. But on this occasion, I have to agree that it's bloody spectacular.'

Her gaze went all the way up the steep cliff to the church.

'How many steps did you say it was?'

Charlotte appeared to mumble an answer.

'Speak up, Char.'

'Three hundred.'

'Great. Just throw me in the sea if I don't make it.'

Charlotte ignored Maddie's outburst and glanced at her guidebook. She still preferred to buy one as soon as she got to any holiday destination rather than rely solely on her phone. What if the battery died? The thought of not being prepared brought her out in a cold sweat. Even more so, now. Any problem she could eliminate before it hit her was a win.

'Apparently the view from the top is even more amazing. We'd better get a move on. It shuts at seven, and there's lots to look at.'

Maddie and Sofia raised their eyes to the heavens behind their friend's back.

'I know what you're doing.'

Charlotte whipped out her phone.

'OK, quick selfie of us in front of the monastery for the blog first. Smile. Say cheese!'

Maddie's sigh told Sofia that she wasn't the only one who wasn't keen on the idea of endless photo opportunities. They were here to relax, not pose on their sunloungers like twentysomethings. Charlotte had decided she was going to document their trip, but they didn't seem to have much of a say in it. She'd have to devise ways of keeping that to a minimum, especially if it was going to upset Maddie.

Photo over, the three of them set off together up the steps, but it soon became obvious they'd need regular stops to allow Maddie to catch up. By unspoken agreement, Charlotte and Sofia made a big show of drinking from their water bottles every few minutes and exclaiming about how hot they were. Sofia hoped there'd be toilets in the monastery; at this rate she'd need one the moment she reached the top.

She was close enough to Charlotte to hear her tut every now and again at their progress, but luckily Maddie was too far away.

'Not far now! One last push.'

Charlotte's voice rang around the stone, bouncing off the cliff and out to sea.

Maddie, bent double, raised her head.

'Give it a rest, Char. We're not on a school trip. Or about to give birth. Please cut out that *"head of the PTA tone"*.'

'But I was head of the PTA.'

'Yes, and don't we know it. Don't let me lose my place. I'm counting the steps. Two hundred and eighty bloody eight... Two hundred and eighty bloody nine...'

At the top, Charlotte clapped loudly as the three of them reached the entrance.

'Well done us.'

The sight of old skirts, trousers and shirts hung over railings greeted them, next to a notice translated into many languages. Sofia read it with care.

'Hang on. We could have borrowed the stuff here to make ourselves decent enough to get inside and just worn shorts and t-shirts on the climb, rather than suffering in these hot dresses.'

Charlotte's look of surprise was a bit too animated for Sofia's liking. She pointed a finger at her friend.

'You knew, didn't you? You always do your research.'

Charlotte looked the other way.

'I've got it! You just didn't want to put on old clothes that other tourists have worn. You've always had a thing about clothes from charity shops.'

Maddie put her hand up to touch a floral elasticated skirt billowing in the breeze.

'Is that true, Char? If so, you should be ashamed on both counts. I love charity shops. Most things I own are from them. And they provide a big chunk of funding for the care home. We couldn't cope without it.'

Charlotte sighed and put her hands in the air.

'OK, sorry, you've got me. Look, I regularly give money to charity too. It's not charity shops per se that I don't like or buying stuff from them.'

Sofia screwed up her nose.

'So, what is it then?'

'It's imagining the backstory about where they've come from and who donated them that I can't cope with.'

Maddie and Sofia raised their eyebrows in unison.

'I know it sounds mad, and I probably should have told

you both earlier that you could borrow stuff. That was wicked of me. But don't we all look nice and elegant?'

Maddie's grunt was reply enough.

At the door they were greeted by an elderly monk and offered shot glasses of *psimeni raki*, which he explained was a local brew made with fermented grapes and herbs and was traditionally offered to travellers who'd made the long trip here. To accompany it were little sweets, *loukoumi*, liberally sprinkled with sugar. OK, being dropped off by a taxi didn't actually qualify as a pilgrimage, thought Sofia, but it was very welcome anyway.

Everyone nibbled on something that tasted very similar to Turkish delight, but while Charlotte and Sofia sipped their drinks and tried not to cough at the strength of the spirit, Maddie knocked it back in one.

'*Efcharistó*. That's hit the spot.'

The monk nodded and motioned to them to carry on walking.

The intricate paintings, icons and old photos dating back hundreds of years, grouped on the white plaster walls, had Charlotte in raptures. Her rapid-fire questions to the elderly priest were answered in stuttering English. Charlotte stared intently into the frames, her blue eyes in their pale-pink framed glasses reflected in the pictures.

'Do you think she should have brought a magnifying glass?' Maddie whispered to Sofia now she'd got her breath back. 'I know none of us have perfect eyesight these days, but she's virtually got her eye up against the frames.'

'I've certainly not seen her this excited about anything since we arrived on the island.' Sofia stifled a yawn. 'Admittedly it was only this morning, but it seems ages ago. It's like we've all pressed pause for a while.'

Sofia strained to hear Maddie say *'good job'*. Her friend hung back a moment to stare at the memorial candles at a little altar in the corner. To Sofia's knowledge, Maddie had never been in the least bit religious, but she turned away to give her some privacy anyway. Sofia herself had been brought up Catholic, and although somewhat lapsed, she was still a highdays and holidays attendee. If Maddie could get some comfort here, who was she to judge?

Maddie put a coin in the donation box, lit one of the thin tapering candles from another already burning and placed it in the holder. She closed her eyes and put her hands together in prayer. It was a desperate move, given her previous aversion to religion, but she had nothing to lose anymore. She'd try anything. Tony was gone for good, far beyond her reach, but she had to find a way to reconnect with her son and granddaughter before she lost them too.

Sofia was waiting when she opened her eyes again, but she just smiled and took her hand. Maddie was grateful that her friend wasn't going to push her to reveal what she'd been praying for. They moved in Charlotte's wake on to the next room, which, to Sofia's delight, was manned by a much younger priest.

Even the flowing black robes couldn't hide his broad shoulders, and when he turned to greet Charlotte, his cheekbones and melting brown eyes wouldn't have looked out of place on a male model.

Sofia covered her mouth with her hand.

'Now that is what I call a work of art.'

Maddie's giggle had Charlotte looking back and frowning.

'What's the matter with her? Has she not seen *Fleabag*?' Sofia continued. 'The hot priest vibe is still huge. That guy could give Andrew Scott a run for his money.'

Maddie's barely stifled laugh elicited another stare.

Sofia grabbed her friend's hand.

'We'd better get outside before she comes over and gives us a good telling off.'

If they'd thought the view looking up at the monastery was stunning, Charlotte was right: the view from the monastery looking back at the sea was breathtaking. Maddie marvelled at the sheer mechanics of building such a structure back in the eleventh century. A pool of crystal-clear turquoise water beneath them lapped at the rocks as the warm air caressed their faces, and there was even a white sand beach a few metres further along.

'Do you think they climb down there for a swim when we've all gone home?'

Sofia shut her eyes and imagined the scene.

'I'd certainly pay to see that if the hot priest was swimming ... naked.'

'Sof! Stop it.'

Maddie put her hand on the wall and stroked the rough white brick.

'Do you think Char's even more uptight than usual? She said something weird to me back at the hotel, about things not being as they seem. And I swear she had tears in her eyes.'

Sofia put her head on one side.

'That doesn't sound good. I'll try and get her on her own

for a chat too. We love her dearly, but I do agree she's being a bit Hyacinth Bucket.'

'Most of the people back there'—Maddie pointed into the tiny church—'wouldn't have a clue who we were talking about.'

'Shame. They're missing out.'

Charlotte wandered out of the monastery door at that very moment and stood looking out to sea, oblivious to them standing at the end of the narrow pathway.

'Char! Over here.'

Sofia took a deep breath at the unguarded sadness in her friend's eyes when she turned round, before she plastered on a smile. Maddie was worried about Charlotte and in turn Charlotte was worried about Maddie. She was concerned about both of them. And Charlotte had undoubtably, and correctly, picked up that there was stuff going on with her too. All three of them were hiding things they didn't want the others to know. It wasn't their usual way of communicating, but the traumatic events of the past year or so had contributed to them being a little bit distant from each other, rather than pulling them ever closer together.

Also, she suspected no one, herself included, wanted to ruin this precious holiday together in Greece with tales of woe. As far as proof went, she could only really speak for herself, but she'd put good money on it being true for each one of them. She'd have to find a way of gently teasing out the secrets and maybe revealing her own if the time was right.

Chapter Three

The main town – or *chora*, as Charlotte informed them all main towns on the islands were referred to as a matter of course – was splayed out below, white houses tumbling down the hillside like building blocks.

They'd come in at the top of the town, after leaving the monastery behind, and it felt to Sofia like the narrow lanes bound on either side by whitewashed stone walls were beckoning them in, inviting them to wander among the shops and cafés.

Charlotte set off determinedly down the nearest one on the right.

'We can take any one of these. They'll all lead to the main square eventually.'

Sofia and Maddie followed in her wake, but Maddie halted after only a few steps.

'Stop! Wait a second. Look at these. Aren't they pretty?'

She pointed down at the basic flower shapes outlined in

white paint every couple of metres on the grey stone pathways.

'And look, up that way there's a different shape... Little boats! And the one over there has cats.'

Maddie looked back down at her feet.

'It seems a shame to walk on them.'

Charlotte whipped out her phone and snapped away.

'Well spotted. They're cute, and great for the blog.'

The blog was something she'd devised on the plane over to try to take her mind off Doug and his mistress. Giving herself something to work on would have to take the place of painting or drawing, her usual ways of losing herself and escaping her own thoughts.

It was yet another thing Doug had taken from her, the ability to paint, to do her job, the job she loved with a passion. Since she'd fled from the scene in that office a month ago, and ordered Doug into the spare bedroom, the muse had completely deserted her.

Every time she walked into her studio at home, her pulse raced, and when she sat down at the hand-made easel and looked at the selection of paints in front of her, her mind went blank.

Even squeezing some paint from a couple of tubes and touching it onto the paper with her favourite brushes failed to ignite anything beyond a series of blobs of colour, blurring as the tears fell onto her lap. Luckily, she'd already finished and delivered everything necessary for a prestigious gallery exhibition in a few months' time. But the thought that she might not be able to paint again scared her almost as much as the situation with Doug.

She supposed she should have discussed the idea of the blog with the others beforehand, but she needed it so badly, she couldn't bear one or both of them kicking up a fuss and making her stop.

Sofia nudging her brought her back to the present.

'Char? You've been on the same shot for ages.'

'Sorry. I wonder if they mean anything?'

Sofia gave her a sly smile.

'You mean you don't know?'

Charlotte smiled back.

'I don't know everything. But I know how to find out most things. Google is your friend, remember.'

'Not mine,' replied Sofia. 'I'd rather discover things first hand and explore without knowing exactly where I'm going or what I'm going to find.'

'Me too,' said Maddie.

They both witnessed Charlotte's shudder.

The trio wandered further into the maze of streets, in some places almost able to touch the rough painted walls on both sides if they put their arms out.

The shops all had their wares displayed outside, racks of scarves in pretty pastels, arranged on white wooden ladders, and bowls of jewellery, keyrings and purses on tables and windowsills, many of them printed with the bright blue *'mati'* or evil eye symbol.

Charlotte picked up a keyring with a ceramic eye attached to it and held it tight in her palm.

'They're supposed to protect you from evil spirits and negative energy,' she said in a quiet voice.

Maddie reached for one too.

'Well, I think we all need one of those. Let's buy three and hang them from our bags.'

Sofia grabbed the third.

'I'm in.' Her attention was caught by a cotton scarf in swirling pinks, which she pulled off the rack.

'Ooh, that's gorgeous. You could put it round your neck or use it as a beach towel, couldn't you?'

Charlotte and Maddie exchanged a look of dread but kept quiet.

'Let's go in and have a good look round. I'll buy us the keyrings as a present.'

The other two followed, dragging their feet. Sofia's shopping addiction was well known and something they'd learned how to manage like a military operation if they didn't want to be stuck in shops for hours. It was fruitless to try and stop her this early on. They'd just have to hope that a tiny taste of purchasing power would satisfy her craving.

Through the window, they could see that Sofia had already reached the dresses and was thumbing through the racks with a big smile on her face. Maddie's stomach rumbled loudly as they crossed the threshold.

'I'm starving. We're going to have to be tough with her. She's going cold turkey after one trip to the changing room.'

'Agreed.'

A white linen shift dress edged with gold, and two others in navy and sage green decorated with strips of silver and bronze were being whisked away by a delighted store owner. The scarf and the keyrings were already on the counter waiting to be wrapped and paid for.

Sofia handed over her bag to Charlotte. 'Please look after

this for a minute. I'll come out and show you everything, I promise.'

'Great.'

Maddie wandered over to the nearest rack and flipped through a few of the price tags before returning to Charlotte's side.

'It's not cheap, is it?' she said under her breath. 'Even if we are in the back streets of a tiny island.'

'No, Sofia did admit that herself. But she loves'—Charlotte put her fingers up to form air quotes and added in the tiniest hint of the Spanish accent that Sofia had inherited from her mother—'"The soft fabrics and bits of bling that make Greek clothes so special."'

Maddie laughed. 'That wasn't a bad impression. Perhaps you've missed your vocation. Stand-up comedy, here we come.'

'Hardly.'

'It's her money. She works hard enough for it. Thank goodness we haven't had all those urgent work calls interrupting everything like we usually do.'

Charlotte crossed her fingers.

'No calls yet… But it's still only the first day, remember.'

'True.'

Charlotte stroked the fringing on a green crocheted handbag and held it against her side.

'This is nice.'

'Put that back. Don't waste your money. I can make you one for free.' Maddie's whisper was loud enough to attract the attention of the store owner who stared with sad eyes as

Charlotte put the bag down and flicked through the clothes rack again.

'I'm probably a bit sour because there's nothing, absolutely nothing, here that would fit me. It's all made for Greek women who tend to be on the short side.'

'Don't let Sof hear you say that. She'd go bonkers.' Maddie lowered her voice to a whisper again. 'Even if anything did fit me, it's far too rich for my pocket.'

Sofia emerged from the back in the white linen dress.

'I love it! I'm definitely going to get it.'

Charlotte and Maddie just nodded as she ducked back in.

Sofia's phone buzzed with a message. Another one five seconds later. And another one five seconds after that.

Maddie eyed the bag slung over Charlotte's shoulder as the sequence started again.

'It sounds like some sort of code… Dare we?'

Charlotte's face gave her the answer.

'Absolutely not. We are not looking at her messages. I can't believe you even suggested it.'

'You want to though, don't you? There's something going on with her. It would give us a clue.'

'Oh yeah, but it's not happening.'

Sofia emerged in the navy dress, but as she did another twirl, the buzzing phone halted her in her tracks. She ran and grabbed her bag off Charlotte's shoulder.

The stop start code was Adonis's way of letting her know he had a few minutes' break from his busy job as the newly promoted manager and co-owner of the best hotel on his island.

Unfortunately, he had a knack of ringing at exactly the wrong time. He couldn't be available when she was resting in her room, could he? No, he had to ring when she was in a tiny changing room with her friends standing the other side of the flimsy curtain.

Deep down, she knew it wasn't his fault. He could hardly whisper sweet nothings in her ear while he was dealing with hotel guests.

'Hello?'

'It's me. Is it a good time to talk?'

'No, it's a terrible time. I'm standing here in my underwear.'

'That sounds interesting... But why are you speaking so quietly?'

'Because I'm in a shop changing room.'

'Ah, I see.'

'It's impossible to talk now. Can we speak later?'

'Sadly, I don't think so. We have a function in the restaurant. But I will try again tomorrow.'

'OK.'

Sofia put the phone in her bag with a sigh.

Maddie had moved a few steps towards the curtain under the watchful eye of the store owner and pretended to examine the jewellery.

'Anything?'

'Not any actual words sadly.'

The ending of the call prompted Maddie to move swiftly back to her previous position, and seconds later Sofia stepped out in the sage green.

'This one's perfect, too! Don't you agree?'

'Lovely.' Maddie shot her a stare. 'But aren't you going to tell us who the hell that was on the phone?'

Sofia ignored the question and went back to the sanctuary of the dressing room. She wasn't going to try and explain her relationship with Adonis while she was in a shop, if it was even possible. Her friends would probably accuse her of being a cougar again, given the age gap between them.

She slung all three dresses over her arm and approached the counter. The store owner's excitement was palpable from several feet away.

'I'll take the lot please, plus the scarf and the keyrings.'

'Of course, madam.'

Madam was worse than lady in Sofia's opinion, but she'd committed to buying them now.

She doled out the keyrings, and after they'd fixed them to their bags, they merged with the gaggle of people making their way through the streets, walking towards the sound of live music and the smell of frying meat and herbs in the air.

Moments later, another brightly lit shop façade attracted Sofia's attention, but the others were ready. They put an arm through hers on either side and Maddie reached out and gently turned her friend's head to the front.

'Sof, we're desperate for food. Eat first, shops later.'

'OK, fine.'

Sofia's lingering glance back at the shop had all the pathos of the heroine in a French tragedy watching her lover go off to war, and Maddie and Charlotte couldn't look at each other as they knew they'd lose it.

The street led directly into the main square, now abuzz with noise. Tables with pastel-painted chairs in different colours to denote the separate establishments were arranged around the edges under trees providing plenty of shade. Fairy lights twinkled in their branches, and the centre of the square boasted a statue of an unknown man surrounded by stone benches. Children darted hither and thither, and babies dozed in pushchairs while their parents ate, drank and talked loudly.

Charlotte marched them towards a restaurant in the top left-hand corner.

'Always go for the one which looks the most popular. And listen out for people speaking Greek, rather than tourist languages.'

'But we're tourists.' Maddie's puzzled look made Sofia smile.

'Oh no, Char likes to think of herself as a traveller rather than a tourist, don't you, dear?'

Charlotte held up her middle finger, and then quickly added two others to the gesture as a waiter approached them.

'A table for three please.'

They were shown to one on the edge of the restaurant with a view right across the square.

Settled with a large vat of rosé wine, bread and an interesting bright green dip made from parsley which Charlotte informed them was called *maidanosaláta*, Sofia poured them all a large measure and handed out the menus.

'And breathe…'

The three women took big swigs of the wine and sat back in their seats. Sofia reached over to clink their glasses.

'*Yamas!*'

'*Yamas!*' Maddie responded with gusto and took another swig.

Charlotte was already head down in the menu.

'Shall we do it the Greek way and just order some dishes to share?'

Sofia and Maddie nodded.

'I could read it out and we could all pick a starter and a main course?'

Only Sofia replied.

'Fine. I really don't mind. Surprise us.'

Maddie's attention was focussed on a couple with a baby sitting a few feet away, as a toddler played around the parents' feet.

The baby reminded her so much of Elsie that it squeezed Maddie's heart. Just the Greek baby's little face laughing as her dad played peekaboo with her was enough to make her stomach knot into a ball. When was she going to hold her precious granddaughter in her arms again?

'Mads? Thoughts?'

Sofia's eyes were on Maddie again as she watched the baby like a hawk.

Maddie's appetite had disappeared, along with her sense of ease.

'Anything's fine with me.'

Charlotte put the menu down on the table with a bang, which made Sofia look up.

'OK, I'll just make the decisions then. Any allergies?'

'Not that we've developed over the past year, Char. Calm down. You sound like the flight attendant on the way over.'

Charlotte turned to summon a waiter.

'OK, don't blame me if there's something that makes you ill.'

'We won't.'

While Charlotte talked to the waiter and tried out some fairly tortuous Greek, Sofia laid her hand on Maddie's shoulder and pulled her gaze away from the little family a few feet away.

'Have you got any more pictures of your gorgeous granddaughter to show us?'

'What?'

Why was Sofia asking her this now? Had she somehow worked it out? Maddie dismissed this as impossible. She hadn't told a living soul about what had happened, and she'd made sure not to mention it to Tony either in their occasional, one-sided chats.

'Well, I'm no expert, but Elsie will have grown so much since the last shots you showed us. It must be at least three months ago.'

Maddie returned from somewhere that looked very far away to Sofia and scrabbled for her phone.

'Yeah, here she is.'

Several up-to-date photos of Elsie smiling in the arms of Maddie's daughter, Becca, were exclaimed over.

'Becca looks like a very happy aunty. She'll want one soon.'

'Mmmm, probably.'

In fact, her daughter had been trying for a while, but Maddie didn't think it was her place to reveal Becca's secret sadness each month when she failed to conceive.

Sofia tried to make her voice sound as calm as possible.

'Is there one with you holding the baby?'

Maddie put her phone back in her bag and snapped it closed.

'No, sorry.'

'Ah, that's a shame.'

'Can't be helped.'

Maddie glanced over at the baby again, now sleeping in its mother's arms.

'Maybe next time you see them?'

'Yes, I must remember to get someone to take one.'

There was something off about her friend's reaction, Sofia was sure of it. It needed further investigation.

Oblivious to the undertone at the table, Charlotte poured them all another glass.

'The starters are here. Let's tuck in.'

A parade of colourful dishes arrived at the table, and Charlotte pointed at each in turn.

'We've got *fava*, a dip made with split peas, onion and garlic, *kolokithokeftédes*, courgette fritters served with a ramekin of yoghurt, and *karpoúzi saláta*, a large green salad with watermelon and local cheese. Haven't I done well?'

Sofia did a thumbs up sign as she tucked into the dishes. A moan escaped her mouth as the separate flavours vied for attention.

'Full marks, Char.'

Maddie forked up a mouthful of salad although eating was the last thing she felt like doing. But she was going to have to force herself, otherwise the others would know there was something seriously up.

'Mmmm, this is gorgeous. I think there's some honey in there as well.'

Charlotte waved her hands.

'And there's more to come.' Charlotte looked at her phone.

'I've ordered *giouvétsi thalassinón*, which looks like seafood risotto, but is in fact made with orzo pasta, and *kotópoulo lemonáto*, chicken with lemon sauce and rice. I think that will be enough.'

Maddie mimed falling off her chair.

'Crikey. I don't think I'm going to able to walk after this.'

Sofia beckoned the waiter over.

'More wine will help us wash it down.'

Two hours later, with all the food eaten, mini ice creams in chocolate, vanilla and strawberry flavours were brought to the table.

Maddie groaned as soon as the waiter left.

'Who ordered those? I can't manage another thing.'

Sofia grabbed the chocolate one and ripped off the packaging.

'It's a tradition in Greece. If you've eaten a meal at the restaurant, they offer you a free dessert, and sometimes a liqueur as well. I think it's offensive to turn it down.'

Charlotte picked up the vanilla.

'Well, I don't want to offend anyone. Mads, you're left with strawberry.'

'Fine. I'll find a tiny corner somewhere.'

The waiter returned with three shot glasses and two bottles.

'*Raki* or *mastika*?'

Both Charlotte and Maddie waved away the *raki* and all three of them opted for the mysterious sounding *mastika*, which Sofia didn't have the heart to tell them was actually made from tree bark resin. Some things were better kept to herself.

'Down in one! *Yamas*!'

Sofia's voice in her ear shocked Charlotte into gulping it down before putting a hand on the table to steady herself. She'd tried to keep up with her friends, who had knocked it back with abandon. It meant she'd drunk more in one night that she usually did in a week, probably more like a month.

The music in the square had been getting steadily louder, and one table had already risen en masse and started dancing, arm over arm and feet crossing in a series of steps that looked far too complicated to master in a week, let alone a night.

Maddie threw out her arms and looked at Charlotte.

'Look at that scene! Doesn't it make you want to paint it? Believe me, I'm no artist and even I want to paint it.'

Charlotte spoke without thinking.

'I haven't painted anything in a month! Nothing. I'm not sure I can even paint anymore.'

Tears sprung into her eyes, and one tumbled out onto the tablecloth. She tried to cover it up by putting her hand over her face and lowered her head to the table.

But a gentle stroking of her hair on both sides told her that her friends had left their seats and were standing over her.

'Shhhh. It's fine.' Sofia put a tissue in her hand.

Charlotte wiped her eyes and managed to sit back up in the chair.

It was Maddie who reached over to stroke her leg.

'Your poor thing. Is it like writer's block?'

'Not exactly…'

They were both waiting for her to speak, to explain. She

couldn't tell them the truth, but she'd have to come up with something. As she tried to form the words in her head, a middle-aged woman at the end of a very long line of dancers approached her and attempted to pull her to her feet.

'Dance, please. All of you. Feel the music of Greece.'

The three women looked at each other, nodded, and linked hands. Charlotte could have kissed her unknown saviour.

'Try to follow me,' the woman shouted above the music, which was speeding up considerably. 'But if you can't, *den peirázei*, it doesn't matter, let the music guide you.'

After a few stumbles, Sofia and Maddie started to get the hang of the steps and the beat, although Charlotte wasn't anywhere near. She was never going to be a dancer, but it really didn't matter as the atmosphere was so welcoming. Men, women and children moved like one giant snake.

As the music built to a crescendo and more and more people joined the line which wound itself into a series of circles, Charlotte gave up any attempt to master the steps and just let herself be dragged along.

She glanced up at the faces of her friends, glowing with exertion but wreathed in smiles. It struck her anew that she loved these women, heart and soul. After her sons, they were the closest thing she'd get to unconditional love from another human being, now her parents were long gone. Her husband had sunk right to the bottom of the pile, not that she'd ever been under any illusion that his love was unconditional. But she couldn't give him headspace right now. Staying in the present was the important thing, feeling the music making its way through her body from the toes up.

Her heartrate soared and when the climax of the music

came, the roar of the crowd was deafening. The circles within circles pulled apart and the woman who'd invited them to dance bowed extravagantly and put her hands together in thanks.

They flopped back down onto the chairs, too exhausted to even attempt to speak. Sofia topped up their glasses one last time and was pleased to see Charlotte looking way more relaxed.

She'd been about to tell them something significant earlier, Sofia was sure, but it could wait. It was only their first night together. They had plenty of time. Whatever it was stopping Charlotte from painting must be serious, but they'd had such a fun night it would be a shame to spoil the mood.

Chapter Four

Something or someone was pulsing bright light into her eye. Over and over again. And it hurt, big time. Finally, Sofia managed to open the eye that wasn't being blasted, but the same thing happened again. Where the hell was she?

When she finally managed to raise her head from the pillow, it all came back in one big rush. The endless rosé, the free liqueurs and the dancing. Even the thought of being twirled around now could bring on a migraine, she was sure of it.

The tiny gap in the curtains she'd haphazardly pulled together in the early hours of the morning solved the mystery of the light torture. It was the sun sneaking its way in. But she wasn't in a John Donne poem where the sun stroked lovers in bed with its playful touch; she was in hangover hell.

Her head ached like she'd been kicked by a mule and her stomach churned ominously. Sofia reached for her phone. Eleven thirty already. They'd missed breakfast. Not that she was in a state to eat any, but still, it was included in the price, and she hated to miss out on the extras.

A message from Adonis made her smile.

I hope you had a good night with your friends. Talk soon.

It had been a bit too good.

In the shower, tiled in hundreds of tiny turquoise mosaics, she turned the dial to cold and the power on full blast, and let it run all over her, including her open mouth. She remembered a second too late they'd been told not to drink the water. A few mouthfuls wouldn't hurt, surely.

Feeling slightly better, she took some painkillers with the cold bottled water from the fridge and picked out a turquoise bikini and a hot pink broderie anglaise mini dress, with matching fuchsia flip flops. Sunglasses firmly in place and her hair scraped back into a ponytail, she spared a thought for how the others were faring.

A gentle knock at the door told her at least one of them was up.

Maddie stood on the threshold in a dressing gown, dark rings under her eyes, her red hair in a wild halo around her head.

'Morning. I feel like shit. Why did we drink so much?'

Sofia turned out her hands.

'Pass. But it was fun, I do remember that.'

'Suppose we've missed breakfast?'

'Can you seriously think about food now?'

A grumble from Maddie's stomach told Sofia in no uncertain terms that the answer was yes.

'We can probably get something from the bar.'

Sofia nodded her head in the direction of Charlotte's room.

'Did you knock for her too?'

'Yeah, nothing. She was definitely the worst of the three of us. She never normally drinks that much.'

Sofia shoved her phone into her silver cross-body bag along with the room key.

'Well, we'd better go and check she's OK. You know what a lightweight she is.'

Repeated knocking and gentle calling had no effect. Sofia put her hand on Maddie's arm.

'You stay here. I'd better go down to reception and see if they've got a master key. She could be choking on her own vomit or something.'

Maddie snorted.

'That's a bit OTT. She's a middle-aged woman who's had a few too many, not Jimi Hendrix.'

Sofia failed to hide a smile as she made the sign of the cross.

'God rest his soul. This is serious.'

Maddie put her finger to her lips as very slowly the door opened in front of them. A figure in a white nightie, looking like an understudy for the part of Miss Haversham in a very out of town production of *Great Expectations*, appeared at the door.

Sofia put her hands together in prayer.

'Holy crap, Char. You look truly awful.'

The wraith-like figure put her hand on the door to steady herself.

'I feel truly awful. Come in.'

The effort of getting to the door had obviously taken it out of her and Charlotte collapsed down on the bed, head in hands.

'I think it's food poisoning.'

Maddie sat down next to her and patted her on the shoulder.

'Is that what they're calling drinking your own bodyweight in wine nowadays?'

Charlotte attempted to lift her head.

'How can you make a joke of it?'

Sofia stayed standing, warily gauging the exact green of Charlotte's face on a posh paint chart. Somewhere around Minty Pallor, with a touch of Leaf Mould around the edges and definitely a hint of the Parsley Dip they'd consumed many hours ago.

A sudden attempt by Charlotte to sit up was followed by a low groan.

Maddie pulled her hair back from her friend's face and gathered it in one hand.

'Quick, Sof, she's going to be sick. Get towels from the bathroom and wet them if you can.'

'Can't she make it in there?'

'No time.'

Sofia rushed into the bathroom just as she heard the unmistakeable sound of someone being sick.

She glanced back to see that Maddie had managed to pull Charlotte forward so that there was now a multicoloured mess on the tiled floor.

Charlotte's head was between her knees.

'Nooo. Nooo. I'm sorry. I'm sorry.'

Maddie still had hold of her hair with one hand and was stroking her back with the other.

'Shhhh. Don't worry. Better out than in.'

Maddie beckoned to Sofia to lay the towels down.

'Can you help me get her into the shower?'

Sofia nodded, but kept her head turned away and tried not to breathe in. If she caught a hint of the smell, she'd be off herself. Maddie seemed oblivious. She supposed endless exposure to elderly people and grandchildren could do that to you.

Once inside the bathroom, Maddie pulled Charlotte's nightie over her head and coaxed her under the shower while Sofia hung back.

'Don't worry, I can take it from here. I know it's not your thing. Go downstairs and explain that we need new towels urgently. And can you put the 'Do Not Disturb' sign on the door when you leave, please.'

Sofia caught a glimpse of Maddie gently soaping Charlotte's body under the shower as she closed the door.

It was the owner Maria on the desk, a jolly dark-haired woman of around her own age. Sofia was glad that it wasn't the trendy young receptionist, Elina, she had to explain it all to.

Maria threw her hands up in the air the moment she saw her.

'Oh no. You have missed breakfast. You and your friends.'

This was obviously a serious issue. Not eating for more than a few hours in Greece was seen as a problem akin to getting stopped by the police or having your wallet stolen, as she'd observed before on her visits to the country.

Sofia leaned over the desk to whisper as a couple of guests were milling about.

'It's fine. We've got a bit of a situation upstairs. Charlotte in room one has got food poisoning...' Sofia mimed a spectacular vomit. 'And unfortunately we need some clean towels.'

Maria fixed her with a stare.

'Food poisoning is very rare in Greece as we use only the best and freshest ingredients.'

Dissing the food hygiene obviously wasn't going to get her very far. The Greeks were justifiably proud of their cuisine as well as their beaches and history and weren't shy in coming forward to praise every single aspect.

Maria leant over the desk.

'Maybe it's not food poisoning?'

The hotel owner was giving her a chance to wriggle out of it, which Sofia grabbed with both hands.

'No, you're right, Maria. I think it's too much sun.'

Maria winked.

'Or maybe too much…'

Maria mimed knocking back glass after glass of something. Sofia met her eye and both of them had a little giggle.

'It's no problem. I will call Dimitris at the pool and send him up with fresh towels, a bag to put the dirty stuff in and a couple of cleaning bits.'

'Thank you. So much.'

'I'll tell my son to leave it all outside rather than barge in.'

Sofia took a step back.

'Dimitris is your son?'

Sofia was aware this wasn't the takeaway from the sentence she should be focussing on, but it brought her up short. He was a lot younger than she'd thought. She could quite possibly be a mother to a son the same age. It was a sobering thought.

'Yes, my baby. Youngest of three, and the most difficult.'

Sofia forced out a smile as Maria took out her phone.

'We're very grateful to you.'

'*Den peirázei*. It doesn't matter. You're welcome.'

While Maria spoke in rapid Greek, Sofia fired off a text to Maddie letting her know the plan.

Her phone pinged with a message seconds later.

> She's over the worst. Sleeping it off in bed. Stay where you are. I'll be down as soon as I've cleared up. Mads x

She didn't need telling twice. Clearing up sick really wasn't on her list of preferred activities. She wasn't sure it would be on anyone's, but she'd much rather deal with the admin side.

Maria had finished the call. Like most conversations in Greek, it had sounded like a shouting match, but Sofia had learned to accept that ninety-nine times out of a hundred it was just a friendly chat.

'That's all sorted.'

'Thank you again…'

Maria put up her hand.

'Stop with the thanks. Now, you go and sit outside under an umbrella, and I will bring you a coffee.'

'If you're sure. That would be lovely.'

She could certainly do with one.

'Pah. This is my job. Off you go.'

Twenty minutes later she was joined by Maddie, and as soon as Maria spotted them together, she came out with more coffees and a laden plate.

'We had some pastries left over from breakfast. They are all *spitikó*, home-made. I made them myself. You cannot go all morning without food.'

Sofia shook her head.

'Oh no, Maria, it's really not necessary. Coffee is fine.'

But Maddie already had her hand on the plate.

Her shock at seeing Elsie's doppelganger last night had put her off her stride, and she'd eaten a lot less than the others, carefully concealing food and only taking tiny amounts. But her appetite was back with a vengeance.

'This looks fantastic. I could eat a horse.'

Maria's smile at Maddie's enthusiasm lit up her whole face.

'Let me explain.' She held up a large cigar shaped tube, dusted with icing sugar. 'These are *bougatsa*, filo pastry filled with a sweet custard, these, *kourabiedes*, cookies made with almonds, and these'—Maria puffed out her chest and pointed to the large squares—'are pieces of *portokalópita*, an orange pie, or cake really. Try… try.'

The slight stare that accompanied the food poisoning comment earlier was back in play.

'My *portokalópita* is said to be the best on the island.'

Maddie put a piece in her mouth and groaned with pleasure. Both women turned to look at Sofia. Maria had spoken the last sentence like they were about to argue and stick up for the cakes of women called Despina or Anna up the road. Sofia really didn't fancy any food the state her stomach was in, but she could see she had no choice.

She put the square of cake dripping with syrup into her mouth and let out an involuntary groan identical to Maddie's, as the fresh orange cut through the sweetness.

'Oh my God. That is absolutely stunning.'

Finally satisfied, Maria strode off back to reception with a wave.

Sofia turned to Maddie.

'She's lovely, but a little scary, isn't she?'

'Sorry, mouth full.'

Maddie eventually swallowed and drank a glug of coffee.

'I can't believe everyone's not the size of a house, if all this is on offer every day. They are fantastic.'

'Good.' Sofia reached for Maddie's arm.

'By the way, you were amazing back there, looking after Char. I know I was useless.'

Maddie smiled and flicked away any suggestion that she might have done anything praiseworthy. Sofia had noticed this tendency in Maddie before, to belittle her own achievements. She'd have to work on it.

'I'm used to anticipating the needs of the residents. Knowing when someone's going to puke has become second nature.'

'But you're so gentle and kind. You must have the patience of a saint. Don't they irritate you at times with their constant demands?'

Sofia had never really done old people. Her mother, Isabella, had returned to her native Spain after the messy divorce from Sofia's father, Patrick. Isabella had then spent the next forty years caring for her own mother, Lucia, who as far as Sofia could see had been a mean and bitter old hag. Her grandmother had lived to a hundred and one and only released her daughter from the burden of looking after her a couple of years ago, having scuppered any chance Isabella had for another romance.

Her father's parents were already dead when Sofia was born, as indeed Patrick was now, felled by a huge stroke while in bed with his second wife, which was fittingly ironic. She conjured up his big handsome face in her mind, along with memories of days out as a child, she on her father's shoulders, while her mother gazed adoringly at him. It had been a picture book childhood, full of trips to the zoo and holidays abroad. Until he'd taken a big hammer and smashed it all apart. He'd have been ninety-four this year, this very month in fact, had he lived. Why was she suddenly giving him headspace? He had barely figured in her thoughts for years.

Maddie's coffee cup was halfway to her mouth.

'The residents irritate me? Of course not. I care about each and every one of them. Do you seriously think I could do this as a job if they *irritated* me? I'm missing some of my favourites already. I've never had three weeks away from them before.'

'Sorry. That was a bit crass of me. I was just thinking about my grumpy grandmother and the way she treated my mother.'

'Apology accepted.' Maddie reached over. 'Try the *bougatsa*. They're amazing.'

Sofia had to admit that the custard filling was dreamy. But she hadn't finished. She'd not had a chance to talk to Maddie about her work for ages. And it would keep them off the subject of her own job, somewhere she didn't want to go quite yet.

'Can I ask you a sensitive question?'

'Fire away.'

'How do you cope with the death of the residents? Given the very nature of your job, it must happen fairly regularly.'

Sofia was genuinely interested. She couldn't imagine being

surrounded by all that death and decay every day. Just the thought of her mother departing this world was enough to throw her into a panic.

Maddie swallowed the last of the orange cake.

'It does happen regularly, as you say, and you are always sad. You have a little tear and move on. But because you're one step removed, it doesn't hit you anyone near as hard as when it's personal.'

Maddie staring into space made Sofia determined not to let her dwell on Tony again.

'And can you honestly say you know them all? Everyone in the home?'

Maddie's eyes were back in focus.

'Of course not. It's not school. You get to know some residents better than others, but they all have such interesting stories to tell when you sit and listen. People tend to forget that they had full lives before going into a care home, and it's usually a last resort, and always a difficult decision for the relatives. We understand that, and the relatives need support as well. There's so much guilt when someone can no longer cope with a parent or a partner.'

'My mother would have been a lot better off putting my grandmother in a home when she became frail. She's still fit and well, thankfully, but it's too late for her to start over.'

'Is it? Is it ever too late to change your life?'

The intensity of Maddie's gaze made Sofia look away.

'Is that aimed at me?'

'Only if you want it to be.'

'I'm fine with my life, thanks.'

'If you say so. And you've got to remember, it was your

mother's choice to look after your grandmother. She's a staunch Catholic, isn't she? In some cultures, putting someone in a home is seen as a terrible thing to do, but it's not easy either way. And don't get me started on the ridiculous cost of private care homes. It's scandalous.'

Sofia wasn't ready for a full-on political debate before lunch and with a pounding head.

'I won't. I know everyone's asked me how I managed to get so much time off, but how did *you* get three weeks off in a row as well?'

Maddie licked the icing sugar off her fingers.

'Not that you gave us a straight answer to that one… As for me, my boss virtually pushed me out of the door. I hadn't taken any holiday since'—Maddie looked out to sea—'Tony died.'

'What, over a year?'

'Well, I took a few lieu days, but no paid holiday. It was easier to be at work, to cover other people's shifts, rather than sit in on my own and stare at the walls of an evening.'

Sofia took her friend's hand.

'Oh Mads, I didn't realise things were that bad. You should have told us.'

'You've both got busy lives, and we hardly live round the corner from each other. I didn't want people to feel sorry for me, the pathetic widow, desperate for company.'

'No one would have thought that!'

'Maybe not, but when you go from being part of a couple to being on your own, people see you differently.'

'I'm nearly always on my own.'

'With respect, that's different. You've chosen your lifestyle.

You never wanted to be tied down. I didn't choose this. I thought we'd be together till the end. Once Tony retired, we had such plans…' Sofia ached at the break in Maddie's voice. 'Gone, all gone in an instant.'

Sofia leant over to give her friend a big hug.

'Can't you still carry out some of those plans, in his memory? Go somewhere that the two of you wanted to go to? Get a group of his friends together? He was such a popular guy.'

The tears that had been threatening started to drip down Maddie's face.

'Oh yes, he was popular. Bloody popular. Everyone loved Tony. I sometimes think people would rather I'd have gone in his place. Dull, reliable Maddie that hardly anyone would miss.'

Sofia wiped away her friend's tears with a tissue.

'Now, you stop that at once. Of course nobody thinks that. Tony was a lovely guy; you don't need me you to tell you that. And I'll admit he was once the hottest boy in the sixth form. But he chose you, Mads. He loved you. And you loved him. It must be hell to live without him, even for one day. But you've got to find a way to carry on.'

Maddie's voice was barely above a whisper.

'Why?'

Her friend's tear-stained face broke Sofia's heart.

'For your kids, for your granddaughter, for your friends, but most of all, for yourself. I know I'm making it sound simple, but please don't waste the years you have left. Tony wouldn't have wanted that, would he?'

Maddie's shake of the head reminded Sofia of a small child being asked to eat a vegetable they hated.

The shock of hearing just how lonely her friend was had made her realise she should have done more over the past year. Just because Maddie said she was fine on the phone each time the three of them spoke didn't mean anything. She'd been guilty of accepting her assurances at face value, and if she was being honest, relieved that Maddie was doing OK. Her friend had put on a great front, but they should have dug deeper.

'What about your kids? Aren't they being supportive?'

'My daughter makes sure to visit as often as she can, but she's rushed off her feet. She runs two businesses now with her husband and, between us, she's been trying to get pregnant for a couple of years as well.'

Maddie's plan to keep that one quiet had gone out of the window, but sometimes she couldn't stop herself blurting things out. Perhaps it would throw Sofia off the scent.

'I hope she gets what she wants. And your son? He only lives up the road.'

The bleak look in Maddie's eyes told Sofia more than words ever could.

'He blames me for Tony's death.'

'How the hell did he come to that conclusion?'

'He says I should have made him go to the doctor's more regularly for check-ups. And that I shouldn't have made him cooked breakfasts and given him bacon.'

Maddie put her hand on Sofia's.

'It was our treat at the weekends. He loved my fry-ups. We'd sit and eat in the garden whenever we could, with big mugs of builders' tea.'

The light came back into Maddie's eyes as her memories gave her a precious moment of peace.

Sofia tutted.

'It's ridiculous to blame Tony's death on a few fry-ups. It would have been a hugely complicated picture that led to his heart giving out.'

'Deep down, I know that, and Dan does too. But he's hurting. He was so close to his dad. He needs someone to blame. I didn't even tell him about coming here to Greece. His sister knows of course. So, he can phone her if he's bothered.'

'Of course, he's bothered about where you are in the world.'

Maddie shrugged her shoulders.

'Don't know, don't care.'

Sofia held her friend's hand again.

'You know that's not true.'

A change of subject was sorely needed. Sofia pointed at a three-masted sailing ship anchored out at sea. People were diving and jumping off the sides into the azure water.

'That's so gorgeous. We ought to think about going out on one. It looks like fun. Let's move to the sunloungers and just have a lazy afternoon by the pool. We've got to wait for madam to wake up anyway.'

Maddie let herself be led away. She reached back for the plate at the last moment.

'Let's order more coffee. There's no point wasting these last few bits.'

Maddie flopped down on the nearest sunlounger. She'd let part of the truth out, and it felt good. It was only a drop in the ocean of her shame and sadness, but it was enough for now.

Chapter Five

Charlotte crept out of her room before dawn the next morning and shut the door carefully behind her. She'd already been awake for a couple of hours, but she couldn't stay still a moment longer. She'd had way too much sleep the previous day after decorating the bedroom floor, leaving her friends on their own until well into the afternoon. The burst of heat that came over her when she remembered Sofia's shocked face after she'd vomited and Maddie's soft hands pushing her naked into the shower, halted her in her tracks for a moment, until it passed.

The garden on the level below the hotel's swimming pool was somewhere she could go and sit and not disturb anyone. She had a torch on her phone, and a bottle of water, and she would wait for the sun to rise. The air was already warm, and as she brushed by the pink and white oleander bushes, they released a delicate scent which told her their flowers were getting ready to open themselves up once the sun touched their petals.

The stone seat she chose was decorated with the same grey and white pebbles in star shapes as the pathways, but the padded cushion on top was a tiny touch of comfort.

Not that she deserved it. She was as shocked as Sofia that she'd let herself get in such a state. Her dreams afterwards had been full of tables groaning with food and wine, with red-faced women drinking straight from bottles and lying in stupors on the ground. A bit like Hogarth's scenes of London's gin drinkers, women careless with their babies, but instead of being in black and white, these were full colour. She often found herself dreaming in well-known paintings, which would sound incredibly pretentious if she said it out loud. Maddie would be on her in a flash.

She probably worried a bit too much about what other people thought, full stop. For the past thirty years, her life had run along the same tram lines – Charlotte the artist, wife and mother – lines that she was terrified to move out of, lest she get hit by a passing car.

A month ago, a great big car had strayed inside the lines of her tidy life and knocked her off her feet, but she wasn't ready to inspect her internal injuries quite yet, let alone announce them to the world. She smiled at her own fanciful images.

Maybe she should buy some paper and pencils and try and draw her pain. She deliberately hadn't brought any art materials in her case like she usually would, as she couldn't face trying and failing yet again.

As a well-known artist, she'd once been asked to judge a local competition for migraine sufferers painting how it felt while they were in the grip of one. Never having had a migraine, she'd been astonished by the ferocity of pictures of heads split in two and one of a dagger going into an oversized eye. There were lots of stars and kaleidoscopes as well as half views to represent one eye not working.

It had given her an understanding of what it must feel like, more than any words ever could. The winner had been a portrait of a woman lying in bed in total darkness, with just a sliver of light penetrating through a gap in the curtains and illuminating her face twisted in agony.

Her sudden inability to paint after all these years was hard for other people to understand. She'd been about to try and explain it to her friends the other evening, but she wasn't sure what she'd have said without revealing everything, which she was nowhere near ready to do.

Most people assumed that she could just set up her easel, like she was in an office, and paint away on a nine-to-five basis. Maybe it worked like that for some artists, but not for her. She needed to feel inspired before she could start a new painting. She didn't work to commission, to someone else's wishes; it had to come from within. And there was nothing, absolutely nothing, inside her right now.

The images of that fateful night, of planning to surprise Doug at work, flooded her mind yet again. She'd been the one who got the surprise all right. Charlotte closed her eyes to chase the pictures away.

When she opened them again, the sun was just peeping over the edge of the sea, turning the sky around it a pale orange, which deepened into tangerine as the minutes ticked by. The glow it cast on the water was truly magical, and with her painter's eye, she started counting all the variations of blue and orange she could see.

A sound behind her caught her attention and she turned to see a door opening at the bottom of the hotel, one of the rooms with only a view of the courtyard, which she assumed were staff accommodation as she'd seen buckets and mops piled up outside. From her vantage point, she had a clear view of the man who emerged into the early morning light. She bit back a gasp when she realised it was none other than the hot priest from the monastery. And standing in the doorway waving and blowing a kiss was Dimitris, who she'd been told by Sofia was the hotel owner's son, as well as being the pool boy.

At the last moment, the priest turned back and planted a kiss on Dimitris's lips before he walked away, up the steps at the side of the hotel, and out of sight. It was a curiously intimate moment to witness. Charlotte hunkered down further into the bench and just prayed that neither of them had seen her.

When she sat up straight again, Dimitris was standing at her side. She covered her mouth with her hand to stop the scream. He put his finger to his lips and indicated at the bench.

'May I?'

'Of course.'

The boy, he'd probably describe himself as a man, but he was around the same age as her youngest son, was shaking. He grabbed her hand and spoke to her in a croaky whisper.

'Please, please do not tell my mother what you have seen.'

There was real fear in his eyes, and Charlotte put her hand on his to reassure him.

'Of course I wouldn't do that. It's none of my business, and anyway'—she tried out a wink—'I didn't see anything.'

Charlotte turned her head in the direction of the garden. 'I was totally focussed on the cute kittens playing over there.'

The air seemed to settle around them.

'Thank you.'

One of the kittens chose that moment to dart out onto the path and was ushered back to safety by its watchful mother.

Dimitris pointed over to some empty dishes at the edge of the garden.

'I feed the mother and leave water out for her. She is very protective of her kittens.'

Charlotte smiled.

'We mothers tend to be.'

The young man was quiet for a moment, but Charlotte wanted to remove any doubt for him. Her youngest son, Rueben, was gay, and after a few turbulent years in his teens had found a lovely partner, George, who everyone adored.

'I honestly would never say anything to your mother, but can I just ask why telling her is such a problem?'

'In Greece, being gay is not so accepted as somewhere like Britain, and while no one would turn a blind eye in Athens or Thessaloniki, on the islands it's more difficult. Island life is intense; everyone knows everyone, or is related to them. They're always in each other's business.'

Charlotte smiled and patted his shoulder.

'Yes, it's a little bit like that in the village where I live in Surrey.'

Dimitris took a deep breath.

'And I have been stupid enough to fall in love with a priest. Although he is thinking of leaving the Church anyway. And please don't mention that to anyone either.'

'You're not stupid. You're in love. I can see it's not an ideal situation...' Charlotte almost laughed at her own understatement. 'But your mother might surprise you if you can work up the courage to tell her.'

'Maybe...'

The sad young man next to her didn't seem convinced. The full light of a new day illuminated his expressive blue eyes, framed against the background of the sea.

She kept her voice low.

'Sometimes you just need to be brave, rather than live in fear of the consequences of your actions.'

She was talking to herself as much as him.

They both stared out at the ocean as the sun rose higher, turning everything golden.

Dimitris rose slowly from the bench.

'I must go now; it will soon be time to start work. Thank you for your advice. I'm not sure when or if I'll be able to take it, but it was good to talk to someone.'

'You're welcome. Your secret is safe with me.'

Charlotte took a moment to practise the deep breathing she'd been taught in yoga class.

Who was she to advise him on anything? She could certainly dish it out, but could she take her own advice about being brave? It wasn't like she had a clue what she was going to do next about her own relationship. It was hanging by a thread, that was the only thing she was sure about, but any decisions she made could be life changing.

It had been one strange morning, and it wasn't even six o'clock. The others wouldn't be up for hours.

Chapter Six

They'd all agreed at breakfast to spend the morning on the beach, chilling, followed by an afternoon activity. Paddleboarding had come first in the vote, much to Maddie's annoyance. She sighed as she got up from her sunlounger and followed the others heading for the shoreline. They'd outvoted her two to one. It wasn't the sort of afternoon activity she'd had in mind. She'd have been perfectly happy to stay under her umbrella ordering cocktails and possibly strolling up and down the beach a couple of times. But no, Sofia and Charlotte were determined to 'do something physical' after sunning themselves for a few hours and dipping in and out of the sea.

Maddie had forced herself to go in earlier up to her waist but returned to her sunlounger sharpish. It wasn't quite as warm as she'd hoped, still being June, but she'd given it a go. She wasn't the world's greatest swimmer and preferred to stay well within her depth. Tony had been the swimmer. She'd been the one waiting on the beach towel with the picnic and the Thermos of coffee. She mused a moment on why couples insisted on assigning roles to themselves. It was almost as if she hadn't dared to improve her swimming when Tony was alive, so that his position as the Mark Spitz of the north wasn't challenged.

And she had to admit she'd have found it strange if Tony had taken singing lessons and started belting out her beloved soul classics, or any songs at all. That was her thing, and she'd thoroughly enjoyed being in her choir, especially when they performed at care homes, including her own, and got all the residents clapping along to the oldies.

For the past hour she'd been content to watch Sofia use her stylish front crawl, going so far out to sea she could barely make out who it was, and imagining for a moment it was Tony, about to turn round and swim back to her.

'Keep up, Mads!'

Charlotte and Sofia had already reached the three paddleboards laid out on the sand, one red, one blue and one yellow, presumably so they could work out who was drowning in an emergency. Not that she was being negative or anything.

Big black double-ended paddles lay beside each one, and Maddie was pleased to see life jackets as well. Health and safety didn't always seem to be at the top of the average Greek's agenda, if their driving was anything to go by.

'Bagsy the blue one!'

Charlotte had already stationed herself by the paddleboard at the far end.

Sofia turned to her.

'Mads? Any preference?'

'Not doing it and going back to my sunlounger?'

'Hilarious. We've signed up now.'

Sofia twirled her finger around in what she probably thought was a cool move.

'There's no getting out of it. It's happening, girl.'

'Then I really don't care if I make a fool of myself on the red one or the yellow one.'

'OK, I'll take yellow then.' Sofia stared down at her floral bikini. 'It goes a lot better with this.'

Maddie was still in one of the two swimsuits she'd been rinsing out in the shower each night. Just how many bikinis did Sofia own? She'd counted at least five and they were only on day four.

'OK, I'll take the red paddleboard and do my best Pamela Anderson in Baywatch impression then.'

'Looking forward to that.'

The arrival of their instructor stopped Maddie's slow-motion run along the beach towards the board.

They all stopped what they were doing for a moment to stand and stare.

'Hello. I am Giannis, here to help you.'

Even she, who was convinced she'd never look at another man in her lifetime, let alone sleep with one, could appreciate that Giannis was a bit of all right. Unlike the pretty boy, Dimitris, at the pool, this was no callow youth. There was no doubt that Giannis was a grown-up.

Knocking forty, 'tall, dark and handsome' didn't do justice to his six pack, muscly legs and tousled sun-bleached hair, coupled with green eyes the colour at the very edge of the sea. Crikey, she needed to get a grip.

'So, have any of you been paddleboarding before?'

Charlotte's hand shot up.

Giannis fixed his sea-glass-coloured eyes on her and smiled.

'You don't need to put your hand up.'

'Right, sorry. Yes, I've done it a couple of times on the Thames.'

'OK. And you?'

Maddie could see his eyes roving over Sofia's body before returning to her face. Like every other man who came within a few feet of her friend, he was about to feel the full force of the Sofia effect.

'Me? Yeah, a few times in the South of France.'

Sofia kept her voice low and smooth, like she was auditioning for an M&S food ad. It was nothing like her usual clipped tones. Maddie, who'd seen the performance many times before, knew it meant Sofia was interested, but damned if she'd show it.

'Excellent, that is excellent.'

Finally, Giannis swung his eyes round to her, reluctantly it seemed.

'And you?'

'Nope. Never. Not much call for it on the Manchester Ship Canal.'

His furrowed brow made her want to laugh.

'Where is this place?'

'Don't worry. Forget it. No experience at all. I'm a paddleboard virgin'—Maddie pointed a finger at her friends—'but these two tell me it's easy.'

'For most people, it is.'

His wince was a bit unnecessary. Giannis was giving her the once-over too, but in a very different way from Sofia.

Solemn faced, it was like he was assessing her body for a structural survey and wondering if there was some rusty iron or dodgy concrete in there.

'We will give it a try.'

'So good of you to give me a chance.'

The megawatt smile was back.

'You're welcome.'

She wasn't sure if Greeks did sarcasm, but on this evidence, probably not.

'OK, lifejackets on. And into the water. Just up to our'—he pointed halfway up his leg—'How you say? Cows?'

Sofia lowered her voice to a whisper.

'He means calves.'

Maddie snorted.

'Yeah, I think I got that.'

Giannis strode ahead with Sofia's board and paddle tucked under one arm, while the others had to scramble to pick up their equipment with Sofia looking on, smiling smugly.

After dropping her paddle for the second time, Maddie's patience was shot.

'Sof, can't you at least take this? Just till we get out there, please.'

'Fine.'

After ten minutes on what to do and how to attach the cord to their ankle so their paddleboard wouldn't float away, they were finally allowed to stand on the board to practise balancing.

Maddie could tell straightaway that it wasn't going to work, as she was in the sea more than she was on the board. Not that it mattered if she was upside down with her head in the sand, as Giannis was only interested in helping Sofia with the correct stance, which involved lots of body contact and giggling, mainly on Giannis's part. Neither she nor Charlotte got a look in.

She exchanged an eye roll with Charlotte, as Giannis finally detached from Sofia and spoke.

'Let's go a little deeper. And now, I need you to kneel on your boards.'

That, she could just about manage.

'Then, push yourself up to a standing position with your hands.'

He must be joking. After falling in yet again, Giannis appeared next to her board. The disappointment was writ large on his handsome face.

'OK, for you sitting down will be best, like this.'

He mimicked climbing aboard and lowering his bottom, all the while keeping his eyes on Sofia. It was hardly subtle.

'Now, let's try for real in the sea.' Giannis pointed into the distance. 'Don't go beyond those yellow buoys and call out if you feel you're in danger. I will be keeping a close eye on you all.'

Maddie caught Charlotte's eye.

'I think we all know who he'll be keeping a close eye on,' she mouthed.

Sofia and Charlotte were up on their feet and off in moments, followed closely by Giannis.

Staying in the shallows astride the paddleboard and learning how to turn the paddle to decide the direction wasn't a bad way to spend the next half an hour, Maddie thought. The sun was warm on her shoulders, and the water was cooling on her legs. She congratulated herself on managing to avoid careering into any small children and even spotted some tiny fish below her darting around. Shadowing one small shoal had her staring deep into the turquoise water, but a sudden tug at her paddleboard made her look up again. She was almost on top of a group of rocks at one end of the beach, and her frantic attempts to outsmart the current were failing miserably. She was moving, or being forced, forward at a rapid rate.

Sucked into a channel between two rocks, the sea pushed her from behind like an overenthusiastic Boy Scout. Not that she was in any real danger, but she'd noticed earlier that there wasn't a lifeguard on the beach. Maybe it was too early in the season.

The little pushes became big shoves as the paddleboard bucked beneath her like she was a competitor in a watery rodeo. Soon she'd be eyeballing the rocks from a geologist's viewpoint. How was she ever going to reverse her way out? There was no point asking for Giannis's assistance. He'd probably fixed Sofia's safety cord to his own ankle by now, if not another part of his anatomy.

Embarrassing though it was, it would have to be the girls to the rescue.

'Help! Sof! Char! Over here.'

When she craned her neck to look behind her, her two friends were paddling towards her like maniacs, no sign of Giannis anywhere.

She'd finally come to a halt with the nose of the paddleboard against the rock face, and she was stuck fast. The water was only up to her knees, but the channel was narrow, and it was a tight squeeze.

A scrabbling noise behind her told her that her rescuers had arrived.

'I can't move. Can you pull me out?'

The sound of barely smothered giggling reached her ears as inch by inch the paddleboard was eased away from the rock. How very dare they!

'You're not laughing at me, are you?'

'No ... not really.'

Charlotte's voice sounded like she was being strangled. Sofia didn't speak at all.

'I know you are. That's so mean.'

Without warning, the paddleboard whooshed backwards out of the channel like a cork out of a bottle and Maddie gasped as she parted company with the board and hit the seabed with a thump.

Before she could react, two strong sets of arms pulled her upright again.

After she'd shaken the water from every part of her body, including her eyelids, Maddie twisted her hair into a rope and wrung that out too. She wasn't injured, thank goodness; it was just her dignity that had taken a hit.

When her friends came back into full focus, it was obvious Sofia and Charlotte were trying desperately hard not to catch each other's eye, and she could swear that Sofia was pinching her own hand to stop herself losing it.

While she could appreciate that the whole episode must have looked like something out of one of those programmes where they paid people hundreds of pounds for funny videos, it wasn't quite so amusing to be the star.

But her friends' desperate attempts not to laugh were ridiculous, and Maddie found her mouth twisting into a grin too, much as she tried to stop it. Charlotte clamping both hands over her own mouth was the final straw, and Maddie was powerless not to join the others as the tears streamed down their faces.

The three of them hung on to each other, barely able to breathe, as the laughter ripped through their bodies, bending them double.

'Sorry for laughing. But when you shot out…'

Sofia couldn't even complete the sentence, as the domino effect started again and all three of them fought to gulp down enough lungfuls of air to survive.

Maddie put up a hand.

'Stop! We've got to stop. I may not have laughed like this for a very long time, but I can't cope with much more.'

The others nodded, but their shaking bodies told Maddie they were far from finished.

Giannis finally rocked up as the next bout of laughter took all three of them down again. He turned to Sofia.

'Is everything OK? Shall I call a doctor? Is your friend having a fit?'

Sofia shook her head as the three friends clung to each other, helpless in the grip of another wave of giggles.

They'd got into this state at school on several occasions, much to the irritation of the teachers, but it had been a very long time since it had last happened. Maddie certainly wasn't going to be taking up paddleboarding any time soon, but it was wonderful to see her friends' faces lit up with laughter for a change.

Sofia checked the address on her phone one more time. It was a flat at the top of the old town, away from the hustle and bustle of the port and its string of restaurants. She'd eaten at one of the tavernas overlooking the sea earlier with her friends after their paddleboard outing.

It had given them all a fierce appetite, and they'd enjoyed plenty of *kalamarákia tiganitá*, squid cooked in a delicate batter until just brown and smothered with lemon juice, accompanied by a simple *horiátiki*, the traditional Greek salad that varied slightly from village to village and town to town. The combination of ripe tomatoes, slices of fresh cucumber and peppers, plump black olives and chunks of feta cheese liberally drizzled with olive oil and sprinkled with herbs never disappointed. She'd tried to make it many times at home, but it was never quite the same.

Pleasantly full, she'd suggested an early night for the others after their busy day at the beach, and they'd gone off quite happily. Her excuse for not joining them was that she was restless and needed a good walk to get rid of some of her energy, which was partially true, the energy bit anyway. Maddie had given her an old-fashioned look when she kissed them both goodnight and wished them *kalinýchta*.

The streets she was walking through narrowed as she climbed higher with every step. A WhatsApp message from Adonis earlier had told her that the hotel restaurant had another party on and he wasn't free to speak until the following evening.

He was harder to get hold of than the Pope. She'd

somehow thought that being in the same country and time zone would make it easier to chat. He was only a couple of hours away by boat. Work appeared to be his greatest love, but he could be lying for all she knew, and staring into one of the waitress's eyes right now, or worse.

There was one woman who always seemed to be at his side in all the hotel's social media pics. Attractive, a lot younger than her, and definitely Greek, she was called Aphrodite, a goddess for his god. She'd hate for anyone to know that she'd gone to the trouble of looking this woman up on the hotel's website, but she wouldn't let it get to her. She and Adonis weren't joined at the hip, and they definitely weren't a couple. They both had their own lives to lead.

Darkness was falling fast, but the white painted walls helped with navigation as they threw what light there was back at her. The red dot on her phone told her she'd arrived.

Chapter Seven

A steep set of stairs led up to a pale blue door, and on each step was a painted oil can containing a geranium, their red petals still bursting with colour in the gloom. The plants matched her red halter neck dress perfectly. Charlotte would love the arty touch on the steps, and maybe it was the sort of thing that would break her painting drought, not that she'd be bringing Charlotte, or indeed anyone else, up here.

The door was opened before she reached the top of the stairs, and a smiling Giannis, barefoot and dressed in a white linen shirt and jeans, ushered her in. He must have been watching out for her, which was a bit freaky.

There were a couple too many shirt buttons undone for her liking – she'd seen plenty of his chest during the day – but it felt good to be enfolded in his arms, and his slightly too powerful aftershave was a wonderful mix of lemons, salt and basil.

'Sofia. Welcome.'

He beckoned to her to follow him through the living space,

painted a simple white, with a single sofa and couple of blue rugs on the rough tiled floor. She caught a fleeting glimpse of a big wooden bed through a partly opened door, but he swiftly led her away from the bedroom and up a few stairs to a roof terrace.

Sofia took a moment to appreciate the view spread out below them, clusters of pulsating lights dancing all along the coast, lit-up boats in the harbour swaying in the breeze and the sound of a guitarist somewhere picking out a mournful tune. There were fairy lights all around the railings that enclosed the terrace, and a tiny blue metal table was set with a bottle of wine, two glasses and a bowl of olives. Luckily, she'd already eaten, but she hadn't come here for food, and they both knew it. A burning candle gave out the fragrance of a whole orange grove. As a seduction scene, she had a very strong feeling it had been used more than once.

Giannis took her hand and escorted her to the table. He insisted on pulling out her chair with a theatrical flourish and made sure she was seated before he took his own seat. His hand grasped the wine bottle like it was an extra-large paddle, his long brown fingers almost reaching all the way round the glass.

'Shall we?'

'Shall we what?'

All the attention was a bit overwhelming. A small frown messed up his perfect smile.

'Have some wine.'

'Oh yes, of course.'

Two glasses in, and conversation was flagging. She really didn't want to hear any more about paddleboarding, kite surfing or parasending as long as she lived. Things needed to move on a bit.

She took his hand this time and gave him her best sultry smile, which did the trick. It was almost too easy. He gathered up the bottle and glasses and virtually pushed her down the stairs.

'We can finish this somewhere more comfortable.'

'Super.'

After a deep, hard kiss in the living room he carefully untied the bow at her neck and let her dress fall to the floor, leaving her in just tiny white briefs and a pair of red espadrilles.

'Wow, Sofia, you really are gorgeous.'

His own clothes come off in seconds, and she wondered if he'd been a stripper in a previous life. Or maybe he still managed to alternate it with paddleboard instructing. They both required a certain amount of balance. He obviously didn't bother with underwear, but a quick glance told her he was primed and ready to go.

She hadn't expected to be picked up and carried the couple of feet to the bedroom, but it wasn't an unpleasant sensation. He laid her on his bed with a reverence she'd only previously seen him use when talking about a topflight paddleboard he'd imported from America. The whole thing felt surreal. It was like it was happening to someone else.

Untying the ankle straps of her espadrilles took him mere seconds and as her shoes hit the floor with a bang she tried not to think about how many euros they'd cost. Her pants he pulled down with his teeth, which made her wonder if it was one of his signature moves. If so, it needed a little practice.

It took quite a while for him to finally get them over her feet. She needed to banish the vision of him as a naughty puppy, who had raided the laundry basket, and focus.

But his body in the low light was everything she knew it would be, and his toned, tanned skin up close was warm to the touch.

Round one of the sex was good, very good, verging on excellent in fact, hard and intense, with no talking, just as she liked it. But although her body responded all the way to the end goal, her mind was still somewhere else. In the final seconds before she went over the edge, Sofia imagined looking down at herself from the ceiling, one of two anonymous tanned bodies writhing on white sheets beneath her. A wave of sadness washed over her, so intense and unexpected that she cried out into the night.

'Oh baby. Yeah, that's it. Make all the noise you want.'

Back in the moment, Sofia knew that round two was out of the question, for her anyway. Usually with younger guys, and she only really dated younger guys, she'd expect to move on to rounds two and three fairly quickly, but it wasn't going to happen this time. Giannis peeled himself off her and lay on his back, a fine sheen of sweat glazing his hair free chest and reminding her of an oven ready chicken. His punch into the air caused her to look away, lest she burst out laughing.

'That was fantastic. You really inspire me.'

He leaned over to kiss her just as she rolled onto her side, so his wet lips landed on her back and his voice was muffled.

'The night has only just begun, Sofia. We have all the time in the world… Time to explore each other properly.'

Giannis's wink when she turned back to face him, coupled with his clichéd conversation put the seal on it.

'Just need the loo. Back in a second.'

'OK, sweetheart. I'll be waiting…'

Sweetheart! She certainly wasn't his sweetheart. Thank goodness that her dress was in the other room. Spying her shoes on her side of the bed, Sofia gathered them up and hid them in front of her as she tiptoed out of the room. Her pants he could keep. He probably had a whole drawer full.

The thought of her underwear as part of a collection was on her mind as she crept out of the apartment and escaped into the street. She'd agreed to the meet-up, and while she insisted any man she slept with wore a condom, the whole thing had left her feeling a tiny bit grubby.

Breakfast next morning was a lively affair. Both her friends chatted away ten to the dozen after all that sleep. Despite her physical workout, Sofia herself had tossed and turned all night, dreaming of being late for important meetings in far-flung rooms.

'Enjoy your walk last night?'

Maddie's query had far too much emphasis on the word walk for her liking.

'Yes, lovely. I really enjoyed exploring all the little backstreets.'

Well, that at least was true. In the past they'd often had a good laugh about some of the men Sofia had hooked up with, but this was one she didn't particularly want to share.

Thankfully, the hotel owner, Maria, bustled over at that point to take them through the breakfast specials, carrying a full plate.

'Today, for our guests, we have *spanakópita*, the king of pies.'

She put her fingers to her lips and kissed the air.

'The fresh spinach and the salty feta filling go so well together.'

A coquettish smile appeared on Maria's face, and Sofia could see instantly what she'd looked like as a girl. She served them all a big piece before they could accept or refuse.

'It's been said that my *spanakópita* is the best on the island. Obviously, you must judge for yourselves. Eat, please.'

Sofia wondered what else in Maria's repertoire was *'the best on the island'*. She'd already used that line about the orange cake. Did it include everything she cooked? Dutifully she put the piece of pie in her mouth. Used to just a takeaway coffee on the go in London, all this early morning eating was totally alien, but she could get used to it. Having been the same weight her whole adult life, she'd definitely put on a few pounds since arriving in Greece, but that was the least of her worries. She wouldn't be going into court in her smart black suits anymore. Who would care if they no longer fitted?

As advertised, the pie was indeed delicious, the crunchy filo pastry making way for a savoury explosion in her mouth, and all three of them hoovered up every last bite.

Maria smiled at the empty plates. As she went to walk away, she turned back for a moment as if she'd forgotten something.

'Oh yes. I'm supposed to tell you we also have *strapatsáda* today, scrambled eggs with tomatoes and feta.'

A theatrical shrug of the shoulders followed.

'Sadly, for you it wasn't made by me, but by our chef, Panos. You might want to try it I guess, if you are not too full after more *spanakópita*.'

Maria left for the reception area as a guest was waiting to check out.

The three of them locked eyes.

Charlotte smiled.

'Dare we try the *strapatsáda*?'

Maddie got up from the table.

'Don't be ridiculous. We're three women in our sixties. We're not going to be cowed by all this competitive cooking malarkey. I'm getting in there.'

Sofia put her hands up.

'I'm full, honestly.'

Charlotte nodded.

'So am I.'

Maddie pursed her lips at her blonde friend.

'Liar. You're just scared of Maria.'

Charlotte held up her hand and squeezed her thumb and forefinger together to leave a tiny gap.

'Just a teeny bit.'

Sofia shouted at Maddie's rapidly departing back.

'Don't go bonkers. Remember we've got lunch in a few hours.'

It was their last full day on the island before leaving for their next destination on the ferry the following evening. Maria had arranged for them to go on a tour of a goat farm up in the hills, run by some relative, which included 'a simple lunch' with wine. Sofia had come to understand that no lunch in Greece could be described as simple. It was best to be prepared. Maria wouldn't tell them exactly what they'd be getting as she wanted it to be a surprise, but it wouldn't be a just a sandwich and a bag of crisps, that was for sure.

A text from Adonis came into her phone.

Sorry about last night. Hope you found something nice to do.

Sofia looked down at the table. Probably best not to be honest about her evening. She had nothing to hide – they were both free and single – but in the end, it hadn't been quite as nice as she'd hoped.

She looked up again just in time to see a secret smile pass between Charlotte and Maria's son, Dimitris, who was walking through the breakfast room on his way to the terrace. He even gave her friend a little wave.

Surely not? She blinked to make sure her eyes weren't deceiving her. Charlotte's relationship with her husband Doug had always made her a tiny bit envious. The man had a wicked sense of humour as well as being more than passably good-looking. He and her friend were often to be found giggling away in corners together at social events.

Sofia found it hard to believe you could retain that level of interest in someone over such a long period of time. They must have been married more than thirty years. Thirty years with the same person sounded like a prison sentence. Her usual cut-off point was around thirty days.

She'd managed to massage her ill-advised starter marriage to fellow lawyer, Rupert, into limping on for a year, but in reality, she'd checked out mentally after six months, the twenty-five-year age-gap proving too big to bridge on both sides. No one blinked an eyelid when it was that way round, older men with young women.

He was a lovely guy, a bit like a more charming version of her father, which a psychologist would have had a field day with, but she'd been desperate to progress in her career and see as much of the world as she could, while he'd been happy to stay out late most nights drinking whiskey in gentlemen's clubs with his cigar-smoking cronies, forcing her to seek other amusements.

She'd been the one to leave, but neither of their hearts was really in it. The divorce had left her with a little mews house in Chelsea, where she still lived, plus an in-depth knowledge of the legal system, and some lovely jewellery. At least she and Rupert had parted as friends. Sofia crossed herself and blew a kiss to the sky to his dear departed memory, hoping Charlotte wouldn't notice. But her friend's eyes were still firmly on Dimitris.

Of the three of them, Charlotte had always liked to keep things closest to her chest, and worried the most about what other people thought of her. Maddie couldn't give a toss about other people's opinions, particularly now Tony had gone. Sofia considered herself somewhere in the middle.

Dimitris grabbed a croissant from the display with one hand and stuffed it into his mouth. With the other, he picked up a banana to go. Sofia would have put money on Charlotte being the least likely person she knew to have a holiday fling with a guy young enough to be her son.

Still, her friend had seemed out of sorts at times over the past few days, and the thing about not being able to paint was plain weird. Charlotte had painted for as long as she'd known her and had never mentioned the muse vanishing before. Charlotte not painting was shocking, like Charlotte stopping breathing. It meant something was seriously wrong.

But she was probably putting two and two together and making seventy-five. She was hardly in a position to make any negative comments about being attracted to younger guys. But the big difference was that she was single. She'd never had to worry about betraying anyone. Perhaps it was just lack of sleep sending her mind off in crazy directions.

The flush that appeared on Charlotte's cheeks when she realised Sofia had clocked the exchange was hardly proof of her innocence. Sofia raised her eyebrows towards a departing Dimitris.

Charlotte's voice came out in a hiss.

'You can't be serious, Sof. We don't all have our minds below the belt!'

'Just saying…'

'For goodness's sake. He's a nice young man that I happened to bump into early one morning when he was about to start his shift. He's the same age as Rueben. And a guy young enough to be my son is absolutely not who I'd chose if I was going to be unfaithful to Doug.'

If? Since when had it become an if?

Charlotte was still in full flow and Sofia didn't bother to interrupt.

'Look, we had a little chat and watched the sun rise. That is *it*.'

Maddie returned to the table with a full plate of *strapatsáda* garnished with cucumber and olives.

'What is *it*?'

Charlotte put her coffee cup in its saucer so violently that some of the brown liquid spilled over the side.

'Oh nothing. Sof was just accusing me of copping off with Dimitris, the pool boy.'

Sofia looked around her.

'Keep your voice down. Maria's only over there. I wasn't accusing you of anything.'

'Sounded like it.'

Maddie forked up the first mouthful of her second course.

'Mmmm, yummy. Now, you two. Play nicely. Calm down. Calm down.'

The calm down was a pretty good impression of Harry Enfield's character in *The Scousers* and had all three of them smiling again, although Charlotte's smile looked somewhat forced to Sofia.

She put her hand on Charlotte's arm.

'OK, I'm sorry if I implied you were up for jumping on Dimitris.'

Charlotte's tight smile remained.

'And I didn't mean to give the impression you were a sex-crazed nymphomaniac only after young flesh.'

Maddie was making good headway with her plate of scrambled eggs.

'That's better, isn't it?'

Sofia wasn't entirely convinced, but there was no point pushing it now. Charlotte's over-the-top reaction to her suggestion had been totally out of character. There was definitely something else lurking behind it.

Maria's tut as she passed their table at Maddie's food choice was more than loud enough for them all to hear.

'Woah.' Sofia wagged her finger at her friend.

'You're for it now.'

'Lucky we're leaving tomorrow then.' Maddie pushed her empty plate into the middle of the table. 'I rather like this idea of island hopping. I'd never done it before you suggested it, Sof, but leaving your mistakes … or triumphs … behind you and moving on to pastures new is starting to really appeal to me.'

Me too, thought Sofia. The thought of bumping into Giannis again was excruciating.

'It's like a blank slate.'

Maddie put a napkin on her head and twirled her hand in front of her face like a low rent fortune teller.

'We can reinvent ourselves on each island if we like, change our names, our appearances, our very souls.'

A confused frown appeared on Charlotte's face, which made Sofia smile. For an artist, her imagination was sometimes on the limited side.

'I don't think we need to go quite that far.'

Charlotte's colour had at least returned to normal after her outburst, thought Sofia, as her friend stared at a map on her phone.

'OK, let's meet down here at eleven for our taxi. Don't be late. Wear suitable shoes, and don't forget suncream, hats and insect repellent.'

Sofia saluted.

That was more like the Charlotte she knew and loved.

Chapter Eight

Charlotte screamed as three goats ran across the road in front of them without warning, forcing their taxi driver to slam on his brakes.

'I don't think they learned the Green Cross Code at goat school,' observed Maddie. 'None of them Stopped, Looked or Listened.'

Sofia exchanged a look in the rear mirror with the driver who had lovely green eyes.

'At least we managed to avoid them. You'll be talking about Tufty the Squirrel next, Mads. You're really ageing us here.'

Maddie shook her head.

'You're wrong. The Green Cross Code was big when we were kids in the seventies, but apparently, it's still used today. My daughter told me.'

'Interesting.'

Sofia hoped the driver's English wasn't good enough to translate Maddie's whole sentence, particularly the bit about being kids in the seventies. Not that she was planning anything with this guy, one man per island was enough. But she liked to think that people, well mainly men, thought she was in her early fifties at most, preferably late forties at a pinch. Mentally, she was forever twenty-eight, but that didn't count, unfortunately.

Her local pharmacy had unexpectedly come up trumps on the flattery meter recently when she'd had to pick up some antibiotics for a throat infection.

The guy had looked at the prescription and back up at her several times before saying 'This can't possibly be for you. It says you're sixty-two. There's obviously been some mistake.' She could have jumped over the counter and kissed him, there and then.

Not that she was ashamed of her age; she just didn't feel the need to broadcast it. She didn't feel sixty-two, so why should she go around admitting it? If it was fine for men to quote the Groucho Marx line about *'only being as old as the woman you feel'*, then the same was true in reverse. Younger men kept her young too.

'Oh look! There are more of them.'

Charlotte's voice in her ear was very loud.

'And there are some baby goats too. They're so cute.'

'You mean kids.'

Charlotte pulled her phone out.

'Whatever. I've got to capture this. Look at that tiny brown and white one trying to keep up. Oh, I hope he won't get separated from the rest. Look, he's trying to feed from his mum as she's going along, but the mother's not keen. She's pushing him away, poor little thing.'

Sofia opened her window to see better, only to be assailed by the sour smell of goats en masse. She quickly closed it again.

'Not surprised.'

At least her friend had perked up after their row at breakfast. It felt like they were edging closer to finding out what was really going on. But Charlotte would spill when she was ready and not before.

'The colours of the goats against the rocks are spectacular. Blacks, greys, browns and whites in all shades, like a patchwork. The subtle contrasts would give such texture and depth to any picture. It would have to be in oils.'

Sofia had considered the landscape a bit dull after the vibrant blues of the sea and the pinks of the bougainvillea down by the coast, but what did she know? At least Charlotte seemed to be talking about painting, if not actually doing it.

Maddie sighed as yet more goats wandered out into the road and eyeballed them through the windscreen, the bells round their necks tinkling away merrily.

'Haven't they got vegetation to munch on? We've got a lunch to get to.'

The driver started to move slowly through the goat gathering, and its members finally accepted the impromptu road party was over. Charlotte continued snapping away at their departing backs. Sofia waved goodbye to their animal friends and turned to face Maddie.

'Have you got worms? Surely, you're not hungry already?'

Maddie waggled her hand.

'Ish.'

Charlotte held up her phone.

'We're nearly there! It's a tour of the farm first, remember.'

'Can't wait,' Maddie whispered to Sofia.

A younger version of Maria, named Alexa, was already waiting by the entrance with a group of around a dozen others and welcomed them at the gate.

'Ah, our stragglers are here at last! Let's carry on with the tour.'

Alexa herded them sheep dog style straight over to a field where the animals were having their daily feed.

'Not more bloody goats,' Sofia managed to say to Maddie under her breath.

'I'm not interested in them either, per se, just what they produce. Goat's cheese is one of my very favourite things in the world.'

Sofia picked her way delicately through the dirt, avoiding the many olive-sized black droppings. She hadn't worn her new and extremely expensive gold espadrilles to impress some smelly animals. They probably wouldn't come under Charlotte's definition of 'suitable shoes', but she was damned well going to get as much wear out of them as possible.

The goats were munching away at big metal troughs of food raised up to head height. Sofia poked Maddie in the side to alert her to Charlotte's continued interest in the animals, as she continued to photograph their every move, even crouching down to get close-ups of their faces eating.

'At least she's happy,' Maddie whispered in her ear.

'Manic more like,' she whispered back, which earned her a strong stare from Alexa, who was giving them the detailed lowdown on goat behaviour.

Sofia pretended she had something in her shoe and pulled Maddie to the side, away from Alexa's watchful gaze.

'Char really went off on one at breakfast.'

'Yeah, I wondered what that was about.'

'Aside from me accusing her of fancying Dimitris she made an odd comment about Doug. Are things OK there?'

'As far as I know, but she's not mentioned him much, has she? And she doesn't seem to get any phone calls or messages from him. Not that I'm Mrs Popular, but on our previous trips away I often used to hear her chatting to him most evenings.'

Chatting to Adonis once a week would do her right now, thought Sofia, but this wasn't about her.

'There's something weird going on. We need to get on it.'

'Agreed.'

'Everyone! Gather round.'

Alexa swept her arm in an arc around the farm.

'Now we will show you how farming used to be, before modern machinery. Please make your way into the barn.'

Maddie and Sofia hung back while Charlotte rushed to the front.

'It's like a school trip,' Maddie said behind her hand, 'with Good Charlotte as our poster girl.'

'Isn't that a band?'

'What?'

'Oh, nothing.'

Crammed into a tiny timber-beamed space with a dirt floor and lots of large wooden equipment, the others had fallen silent.

Sofia tripped over a rake in the gloom and pitched forward.

'Shit!'

Alexa raised her head.

'So, if we're ready at the back there.'

'So ready.'

Sofia held back a giggle at Maddie's reply. At school they'd been sent to the headmaster for giggling in assembly more than once, and things hadn't moved on hugely in the following fifty years.

Charlotte had always been up the front at all school events, surrounded by her fellow senior prefects. It still rankled with Sofia that she'd never been made a prefect, although Charlotte had allowed her and Maddie to sneak into the cupboard-sized senior prefects room at breaktimes and share their one jar of Nescafé.

When she'd asked Charlotte to look into the prefect oversight, her friend had somewhat too gleefully reported back that she and Maddie were considered subversive, and it was never going to happen. Bloody cheek.

'So, any questions?'

Sofia hadn't listened to a word the woman had said about how the goat's cheese was made in the olden days and what the various wooden barrels and paddles did. She was too busy worrying about Charlotte and whether Adonis could finally take a break to speak to her.

After a few queries from the American contingent about how the islanders managed to do all this without electricity and running water, and one from Charlotte about hygiene, Alexa looked around the room.

'Any last questions?'

Maddie put up her hand.

'Are we going for lunch now?'

Alexa's face fell.

'Yes, follow me.'

The covered terrace with its rough stone floor, gleaming farm machinery and tools placed at apparently random points, had been cleverly put together, thought Sofia. Tables covered in blue and white checked tablecloths, with vases of fresh greenery were matched with white painted chairs and there was even the odd chicken clucking in between the tables. Sofia wondered if they'd been let out only five minutes earlier solely for their pleasure. Since when had she become quite so cynical?

The Americans were oohing and aahing away like crazy, cameras at the ready.

Alexa beckoned them all in out of the sun.

'Choose a table, please, and sit down.'

Sofia made for one laid for three in the corner, next to a large terracotta pot overflowing with blue flowers and a view of the hills behind. There was bread on the table along with a jug of wine. It was a loaf of the yellow corn bread that they'd had at quite a few of the local restaurants.

She'd already broken her no bread rule for the good stuff several times. There was bread and then there was Greek *psomi*. So fresh and springy. Maddie broke off the end of the loaf and stuffed it in her mouth as Alexa spoke again.

'In a moment you will each be given an individual cheeseboard, which has on it three different goat's cheeses, all made here with milk from our own goats. One has been matured for a year, another for two years and another for five years, and it will be very interesting for you to taste the difference.'

Alexa raised her voice a notch.

'Accompanying the cheeses will be three different types of honey, again from our own hives. It has been said that our thyme honey…'

'…is the best on the island,' the three friends chorused together in time with Alexa, confident she couldn't hear them from where she was.

'Definitely related to Maria,' said Maddie as she poured out three large glasses of the white wine and clinked glasses with both of them.

'*Yamas!*'

Charlotte looked in Alexa's direction.

'Aren't we supposed to wait for the food?'

'Bollocks to that.'

Maddie was already on her second glass by the time the rectangular wooden boards were brought out and laid before them.

The three selections of cheese were cut into triangles, fanned out and placed at regular intervals along the wooden board, interspersed with little white china dishes of honey as well as grapes, apricots and nuts, with big bowls of diced tomatoes and olives to share on the side.

Charlotte whipped out her phone.

'Oh, isn't it pretty, like a still life. This is great for the blog. You can see the variations in colour in the cheeses. The older one is darker and creamier and has a rougher surface.'

'Gold star for the blonde in the corner,' said Maddie, breaking off another hunk of bread.

'Are you finished, Char? I don't know about you, but I've had enough of just looking at it.'

Everything else was forgotten for an hour or so as they nibbled away at the various cheeses, discussed the different intensities of flavour, took guesses at what the bees had been feeding on when they made the honeys, and refreshed their palates with the sweet juicy tomatoes and plump olives.

Maddie's call for another jug of wine and more bread was treated with slight surprise by their waitress who nevertheless recovered herself quickly and went off to fetch them.

'That was absolutely stunning.' Charlotte put down her napkin. 'But I'm beat. I really can't manage those last few bits of cheese.'

'Hand them over.' Maddie rubbed her stomach. 'I've still got a little corner left I can tuck them into.'

Sofia leant back in her chair.

'I've eaten more today than the whole of the past week. There's no way that could be described as a simple lunch.'

A glance over at the entrance told Sofia that hunky taxi guy was back.

'Who fancies an afternoon at the pool with Dimitris waiting on us hand and foot?'

'Me!'

Maddie's voice was a little too loud in the still air and people at the other tables turned in their direction. She'd drunk most of the second jug of wine herself. Drinking in the daytime never ended well. Sofia had suggested the pool so her friend could sleep it off.

'Char?'

'What?'

Her friend seemed far away again.

'Are you up for an afternoon with Dimitris tending to our every need?'

Sofia tried to keep any hint of suggestion out of her voice, but she needn't have worried as Charlotte just looked blankly ahead.

'Fine.'

Chapter Nine

The following evening, the wind took their hair and whipped it up around their heads as the three friends stood at the back of the boat and held on to the railings. The engines churned the turquoise water below them to a frenzy as the ferry started to pull out of the harbour, and the whistles of the Greek port police gradually faded into the distance, while the friends and relatives frantically waving to passengers reduced in size until they were miniature figures on the dock.

Maria and Dimitris had accompanied them to the harbour and there'd been plenty of hugging and kissing. The week had gone by in a flash. Sofia had agreed with the others that she was sad to say goodbye, and there was lots of talk of returning the following year. She'd refrained from saying anything when she saw Charlotte and Dimitris exchanging contact details. There was no way she was going to light the touchpaper on that one again.

The evening sun was warm on their faces, and the breeze had lulled to a soft caress as the boat edged further and further from the port. The essence of the island was laid out in front of them as if on a platter. Behind the harbour the rows and rows of white cubed houses rose up and up with the ruined castle standing proud against the sky. On the other side of the port the hills loomed large on the horizon, slumbering brown shapes crisscrossed with paths and roads. The sun glinted off the windscreens of toy-sized cars crawling across the landscape like ants, and the sound of laughter floated through the air like old perfume.

Maddie climbed up and spreadeagled herself against the railings to do a quick Kate Winslet in *Titanic*, earning her a grin from Charlotte. There'd been precious few of those on offer this week, mused Sofia.

Her friend's curly red hair was even more unruly than usual after the wind had messed with it, reminding Sofia of how she'd been the one to spend hours brushing and styling it in Maddie's bedroom after school, trying to coax it into one of the trendy styles that the other girls at school were sporting.

She'd been there to witness Maddie's joy, when her friend's single mum had paid for a birthday blow-dry that she could ill afford, to give her daughter straight shiny hair for the first time ever, and then Maddie's sadness a week later that it was back to its usual copper curls. Deep down her friend must have known that it wouldn't last, but she'd wanted to believe in it so badly.

The light tan than Maddie had acquired over the past week and the smattering of freckles across her nose really suited her. They couldn't wave a magic wand and bring Tony back to life, but Sofia hoped and prayed that this holiday was at least allowing her funny, brave friend to relax a little.

The noise of the engines straining told Sofia, who'd been on a few Greek ferries, that the boat was turning, ready to pull out into the open sea. They had three hours to kill before they reached the next island, and she had something special in mind.

Maddie climbed down from the first rung of the railings, slipped on the deck and was caught by Charlotte.

'Thanks, lovely. What's the plan now then? Are we going to go to the bar?

Sofia clapped her hands together.

'No, we are not. Fanfare please…'

Maddie played an imaginary trumpet.

'We're going for a three-course meal with wine thrown in at the boat's restaurant.'

Maddie frowned.

'Sounds pricy.'

Sofia held hands with her friends.

'I am treating you both.'

Maddie opened her mouth to protest.

'And I'm not taking no for an answer.'

Sofia fought to keep the emotion out of her voice.

'I've got something I want to tell you both … but first we eat.'

'You're not ill or anything, are you?'

Maddie's worried little face almost undid her. She should have thought before she opened her mouth. For Maddie, *something to tell you* was always going to be linked with Tony and illness, major illness.

'Oh God, no, sorry. It's nothing like that. This is a good thing, honestly.'

It didn't feel like a good thing at the moment, and she wasn't sure it ever would, but she didn't want Maddie worrying all through the meal.

The restaurant was on the next floor down. They were shown to a table next to the lovely picture windows overlooking the sea by a waiter in a blue and white striped waistcoat echoing the colours of the ferry company, and indeed of Greece itself. Sofia idly wondered if their uniforms had been made up out of a job lot of leftover flags.

Crisp white tablecloths and a carpeted floor were a world away from the cafeteria they'd passed on the way, with weary travellers slumped in their chairs over half-drunk coffees, or fast asleep on bench seats. The final destination of the ferry was Piraeus, Athens' port, but it wouldn't arrive there until early the next morning. Happily, they were getting off at the next stop, just the right amount of time for a decent dinner and a confession.

Sofia shooed Charlotte and Maddie into the seats right next to the window. She wanted her friends to have the best possible experience.

Charlotte's animated face proved she'd done a good thing.

'What a view! We should be able to see the sunset from here as well, and watch it go down over the sea in a blaze of glory.'

'Yes, I'm determined to hang out here until it's time to get off, so we don't need to move anywhere else. There's no rush.'

Charlotte picked up her knife and fork and inspected it for marks.

'Clean as a whistle. It's like a proper restaurant. I didn't expect that on a ferry.'

Sofia picked up the wine list.

'It looks so much better than it did on the website. Now, wine. White or rosé?'

Maddie twisted the ring on her wedding finger round. Sofia had noticed she often did it when she was nervous. She hadn't yet dared to suggest to her friend that it was time to take it off completely.

'I was quite fancying a red tonight for a change, if that's OK.'

'Of course it's OK. You have what you want. Char?'

'Rosé for me please.'

'Me too. So, let's get a bottle of each. Here's the waiter with the menus.'

With their food choices settled, and the wine opened, a basket of warm hand-made rolls was delivered to their table, wrapped in more crisp white linen and accompanied by a black olive dip.

Maddie raised a glass at the other two and took a big swig of her red.

'Cheers! I bet those meatballs…'

She picked up the menu again.

'I mean those *keftédes* you chose, Char, are nothing like the Swedish meatballs we had to make for home economics that time. Do you remember?

'God, yes, what were they called? Kot-something?'

'*Kotbuller*! That's it.'

'After we'd spent all lesson moulding that grey meat with our hands, I didn't fancy them at all. I think I put them in the bin.'

Maddie's mouth turned down.

'We weren't allowed to waste food in our house. Everything I made in that class my mum made us eat for tea.'

Charlotte wrinkled her nose at the thought.

'What I most remember about the whole experience was those two brothers we were paired up with. Irish boys from the estate next to the school. What were they called?'

'Keiron, and … Dennis! He was known as Dennis the Menace.'

'He had lovely green eyes though. They spent the whole lesson giving us tips on how to shoplift. Do you remember?'

'It's coming back to me.'

'It was in the days before plastic packaging. Dennis's top tip was to shove things in the central well of toilet rolls and cover it over with something else.'

Maddie let out a snort.

'Yes, I do remember. We just stood there listening, like the good girls from the villages that we were, bussed into the big town on a school coach every day. We nodded sagely as if it was something we were planning to rush out and do.'

The laughter in Charlotte's voice cheered Sofia no end. But she had to say it.

'But you did have a little go at it, didn't you, Char?'

Her friend rolled her eyes.

'I knew you'd bring that up. It was my one and only time, and yes … I got caught red-handed.'

'It's because you've got such an honest face.'

'Mmmm. I was with that snotty girl … Camilla, was it?'

'Yep, that's her.'

'I think her parents thought that sending her to a comprehensive was some sort of social experiment. Do you remember we all used to meet in town at the Wimpy on a Saturday afternoon? We'd spend hours in there, nursing a single coffee and waiting for certain boys to come in.'

Maddie's confused face stared between them both.

'Surely there wasn't anything to shoplift in the Wimpy? Unless you had a yearning for those red plastic tomato sauce containers with the moulded leaves on top?'

Charlotte shook her head.

'No! Although they were very kitsch. We were in that awful department store in town, Fogeys, or something like that.'

Sofia laughed. This was nicely taking her mind off what was about to come.

'Hardly. I think it was called Fingles.'

'Well, it was full of people our parents' age and older.'

'You mean our age now?'

'Shut it. Things were different back then. Sixty-year-olds were considered old. Anyway, do you want to hear the story or not, since you've brought it up?'

'Yes, Miss.'

'Camilla told me to take a pair of tights to prove I was hard.'

Sofia let out a giggle.

'You? Hard?'

'Look, I was a bit scared of her. For some strange reason I picked a horrible pack of really thick old lady flesh-coloured ones that I wouldn't be seen dead in, and put them in my bag. Next thing I know, there's a tap on the shoulder and a *"Come with me young lady."*'

Maddie put her hand over her mouth.

'Did they call your parents?'

'Oh yes, I had the full works. They allowed me to go with a telling off because I wasn't a *known face*.'

'And they didn't even have CCTV in those days. So, it wasn't like they were monitoring you from afar.'

'No, they must have been watching us. Camilla strode past me and out of the entrance with half the lingerie department stuffed up her top, so I learnt my lesson there. No more trips to town with Camilla.'

'What a bitch!'

Maddie put her head on one side.

'I think she had a few problems of her own. She disappeared in the end, didn't she, and was homeschooled?'

Sofia nodded.

'You're right. She certainly had a problem keeping her hands in her pockets. She once told me she'd nicked the complete range of Miss Selfridge eye shadows and lipsticks.'

'Yes, but that's sad because her parents would probably have bought them for her if she'd asked.'

'I know you love a lame duck, Mads, but I think she needed professional help. Although … she did have great parties. And a swimming pool. Do you remember her seventeenth? When we all stripped off and dived in?'

Charlotte pursed her lips.

'Not all of us, Sof.'

Maddie put up her hands.

'Count me out as well. I was necking with Tony somewhere in the garden.'

'Just me in my birthday suit then.'

'Who would have thought it?' Charlotte's comment was accompanied by a smile.

'OK, no need to go on.' Sofia shifted in her seat. 'Where was I when all this cooking was going on?'

'You volunteered for DT and metalwork instead, don't you remember?' Charlotte poked her in the arm. 'You said it would be much better for meeting boys, as hardly any girls would volunteer, and you'd have your pick.'

'Did I actually say that?' Sofia sipped her wine. 'I was a calculating little madam, wasn't I?'

Charlotte smiled again.

'You said it—'

'I mean, it was true. There were only two girls in that class, so it worked a treat. I met my first'—Sofia counted on her fingers—'second and third boyfriend there.'

'I'd have been happy with just one boyfriend at that stage.' Charlotte turned down her mouth.

'You were far too picky, Char. I think the guys were a bit scared of you. Doug must have worked extremely hard to cut down all those thorns, climb the tower and claim his princess.'

Charlotte ignored her comment completely and carried on talking.

'Who was that tall, dark, dreamy guy with the black curly hair? He was two years above us and lived right opposite the school. You used to go over there at lunchtimes *"for a sandwich"*'—Charlotte managed to get all flavours of suggestion into her words—'while we went down the Chinese to buy spring rolls with our dinner money.'

Sofia trawled her memory banks.

'Ah yes, Jon. Both his parents were out all day working, which was extremely useful. Believe me, I learnt a lot more in an hour there than I ever did in biology.'

'I bet you did.' Maddie looked down at her plate. 'There was only one boy at school I was interested in, and I think you both know who it was.'

Sofia hoped the food would arrive before Maddie drank anymore and got melancholy. Her friend had never been a good drunk, and an early experiment with Pernod, which the next morning had her convinced she'd gone blind, had elicited a promise that she'd never try it again. She'd not experienced Maddie on red wine, so they were in uncharted territory.

'Lovely Tony.' Charlotte raised her glass. 'Your gorgeous, *loyal*, husband and our wonderful friend.'

Maddie caught Sofia's eye and raised an eyebrow at Charlotte's emphasis on the word loyal. Sofia gave a tiny shake of the head.

'Tony always had time to listen and would give you an honest opinion. He stayed the same generous boy we knew in the sixth form for the rest of his life. He put you first every time, Mads. Whatever you wanted, he made it happen. You even managed to make him leave his beloved Surrey behind and move back up north with you. You had the best, no wonder you're hurting so badly.'

As soon as the words were out of her mouth, Charlotte saw the confusion on her friends' faces and regretted her choice of words. She'd let her anger at Doug infect what she'd said and turned things weird. Shutting up now was the best plan, before she started something she couldn't stop.

'To Tony!'

Her friends raised their glasses too.

'Tony!'

Maddie took another large gulp of red wine before she spoke in a voice overlaid with sadness.

'He was happy to move to Manchester too, Char, honestly. I didn't force him. There were more job opportunities up there and we thought it was a better place to bring up the kids. My mum had gone back up north years before, and it's nice to have your mum around when you've got small children.'

Charlotte wiped a tear from her eye with the linen napkin. The last thing she wanted was to force Maddie to justify herself.

'Don't mind me. I didn't mean anything by it. Talking about school has brought it all back. I was just trying, very awkwardly it turns out, to say that I miss him too.'

The arrival of the starters stopped the conversation in its tracks, much to Sofia's relief. She mustn't drink anymore, or she was liable to lose it as well. The whole meal was going pear-shaped before they'd even started eating, and she still had to say what she needed to say.

The salad Sofia had ordered was a riot of colours, with bright green lettuce and spinach cradling plump black olives and scarlet tomatoes, while strips of seared peppers crisscrossed the plate. Pomegranate seeds like rubies nestled in the crevices, pine nuts dotted the leaves and shavings of golden cheese drizzled with an olive oil and herb dressing topped the lot.

'Everything is so fresh here.' She forked up a mouthful. 'Mmmm. Even on a ferry we're getting fantastic food.'

Maddie popped another helping of *gavros*, the tiny whole fried fish she'd chosen as a starter, into her mouth, stopping only to dip them in the garlic mayonnaise first.

'Yeah, on a British ferry you'd be faced with a choice between a sweaty sausage roll and a dodgy-looking prawn sandwich, taking your life in your hands as you ate it.'

As the main courses and desserts came and went, Sofia glanced up at the clock on the wall. She'd barely listened to Maddie and Charlotte's conversation for the past half hour. She ripped open one of the packets containing lemon scented hand towels meant for those eating fish and rubbed it all over her hands and up to her wrists.

'Cleansing your sins?'

Maddie's voice brought her back round.

'Sorry?'

'You've been rubbing at the same bit for ages, sweetheart. And you haven't been listening to a word we've been saying.'

The waiter brought over three shot glasses of complimentary *raki* laced with honey and herbs, the drink they'd first had at the monastery that already seemed to Sofia like months ago, not days.

It was time to tell the truth.

She lifted her glass to the sky.

'*Yamas*!'

'*Yamas*!' her friends chorused back, as they all downed in one.

Sofia put her glass back on the table and stared out of the window to calm herself. The setting sun threw its orange rays back into the restaurant and covered her friends with a strange glow, lighting up their anxious faces.

The tears threatened to come even before she'd managed to get a word out.

'There's no easy way to say this…'

Chapter Ten

Sofia took a deep breath.

'I've lost my job. I've been made redundant.'

Maddie's arms went round her.

'Is that all? Oh, thank God, I thought you were dying.'

Charlotte got up from her seat and knelt down beside Sofia's chair to hug her too.

Something between a cry and a laugh came out of Sofia's mouth.

'But I told you I wasn't ill.'

Maddie stroked the bits of her back and arms that weren't being stroked by Charlotte.

'We thought you were lying to protect us.'

'Nope. Telling it like it is. I've been royally tossed aside by the company I've spent more than half my life helping to build. It's nothing really, don't mind me.'

The tears had beaten the strange laughter, and Sofia rested her head on the table and let them come.

Maddie's hand in hers gently pulled her up to a seated position.

'Oh, you poor baby. We know how much your work means to you. We're not saying it's nothing. We're just relieved you're OK.'

Charlotte wiped away her friend's tears with another serviette, which came away streaked with mascara. The black goo was also on the tablecloth. The staff were going to love them.

'It must seem like the end of the world today, but you'll find another job.'

Sofia tried not to let her lip buckle.

'I'm not sure I will … at my age.'

Charlotte banged her fist on the table.

'Rubbish! We won't have any of this ageist talk.'

'Char, I'm just being realistic. Taking on a new senior partner in a law firm would be very unusual at my age. It's different if you're already working there. No one's going to be bothered about your age.' She realised what she'd said. 'Well … until they are.'

Her friends waited until the next bout of crying was over. Charlotte was about to speak again. Her inquisition technique in such situations was well known. There was no point trying to shut her down.

'What excuse did they give for getting rid of you?'

'They're "*restructuring*". We've got a new top dog, a guy in his forties who wants to clear out the dead wood and bring in his own team.'

'What rubbish. You're very much live wood.'

'Thanks, I think.'

'My turn.' Maddie took her hand. 'Have they given you a big pay off?'

'Yes, but I don't care about the money. I've already got more than enough.'

'Lucky you.'

Maddie's murmured comment brought Sofia up short. Since Tony's death, Maddie had hinted that she wasn't exactly flush. He'd been nowhere near retirement age, and they still had a mortgage on the house.

'Sorry, that was thoughtless of me.'

Maddie poured the dregs of the bottle into her glass.

'No, it was nasty of me. I didn't mean to say it out loud. I know your work has always been such a big part of your life, of your identity.'

Sofia frowned.

'You're making me sound like some sort of self-obsessed crazy career woman with no time for anything or anyone else.'

'Not at all.' Maddie smiled. 'You always had time for fun.'

'Don't say had. It sounds like everything's over.'

Sofia leant on Maddie's shoulder.

'Maybe it is.'

'Right, you need to stop that sort of talk right away. Think of the thousands of women you've helped over the years. Women who otherwise might not have got a fair deal in their divorce settlements. There must be so many clients out there who are grateful to you.'

'Suppose so.'

Sofia sat back up in her seat and let the tears fall again.

'The person I most wanted to help was my mum. Seeing her go through all that crap with my dad and wishing there was someone who'd stand up to him on her behalf. Someone who could take that smug smile off his face for good. Him and his fancy personal lawyer, who also happened to be his bloody mistress, all ready and waiting to shaft us.'

A picture of the two of them together at some big legal awards do brought the bile rushing into her throat. Her father in a dinner jacket with one arm round his precious Cherie, the other arm holding up his prize for best something or other – destroyer of families if she'd had a vote.

Maddie put her finger to her lips.

'It's OK, love, you don't need to go there. He's not with us anymore. He can't hurt either of you now.'

'But she's still around, isn't she? Still in the house in Mayfair, with her stupid yappy dogs and her remodelled face.'

Sofia knew she'd suddenly inhabited the wounded teenager she'd been back then, but she didn't care.

Maddie nodded several times.

'Yeah, she sure is. Not sure it's the dogs' fault, but that's right, let it all out.'

Sofia couldn't stop more sobs. Her only focus was the freeze frame of her mother's stricken face when she'd arrived back at the family home one Christmas to find her father gone for good and the divorce papers on the hall table.

'I was in my second year at uni when he broke the news to her. He waited until I was far away, hundreds of miles away in Scotland, the coward. I was too young and naïve then to fight them.'

Sofia let out a bitter laugh.

'Ironically, I'd chosen to study law to follow in Daddy's footsteps and make the man proud. Later on, I fell in love with the law for its own sake, but to think that he was the inspiration makes me want to vomit.'

Charlotte ruffled her hair.

'You always were a fantastic arguer though. You could row with a paper bag. Still can, given the chance.'

Charlotte's little joke had pulled her back into her adult body.

'There's a little more to it than that, I assure you. But I made sure that I got a first and became the best damn divorce lawyer in town, eventually. It was too late for mum, but I like to think I helped other people.'

'You certainly did, baby. We've always been so proud of you.'

'I actually faced her in court a few times, you know. My dad had retired by then, but the satisfaction I got when I beat her in a case was like nothing else.'

Maddie stroked Sofia's back as if she was expecting a burp to come out.

'Yeah, you did mention it once or twice. We're not losing it quite yet.'

Sofia covered her eyes with her hands.

'It's the thought that it might all be over that's bringing it back.'

Charlotte put both her hands together as if in prayer.

'Nothing is ever truly over. It just changes into something else.'

Maddie put on a serious face.

'Oooh, listen to the Dalai Lama over there. You're not going to go all New Age on us, are you, Char?'

'I happen to be a very spiritual person, actually. But we're concentrating on Sof at the moment…'

'I know. And at least you can have a break before you decide on your next move, Sof. We did wonder how you'd got so much time off at once, and why we weren't being interrupted every few minutes by your office ringing. Now we know.'

'You do.'

Sofia reached for both their hands. They were on a once-in-a-lifetime holiday, and she wasn't going to let the memories of her father's betrayal spoil it for everyone.

'And I'm thrilled we have so long to spend together. We've not seen each other like this, as in every day, sharing meals and laughs, since we were at school.'

Maddie went to speak, but Sofia put her hand over her friend's mouth.

'Oi!'

'Before you say it, I'm aware these are not the simple days of school when the worst thing that could happen was a boy rejecting you or a big fat spot breaking out on your forehead. There are many reasons why we're here together now, and many things going on in all our lives, both good and bad, but one thing's certain, we need to make the most of the two weeks' holiday in glorious Greece that we've got left.'

Maddie put her hand up.

'What about motivational speaking as your next career… That's a huge thing these days, isn't it? You can talk the hind legs off a donkey that's for sure.'

'Cheeky cow.'

'Just trying to help.'

Charlotte swilled the last of her wine around in the glass.

'So, you're not going to try and fight the redundancy, or take them to an industrial tribunal?'

'There's honestly no point. I wouldn't want to be there after this, anyway, knowing I'm very much surplus to requirements. They've given me a very generous settlement, generous enough for me not to have to worry for quite a while. Maybe I do need to take a step back and think about what I really want, rather than what everyone else thinks I want.'

'"Tell me what you want, what you really, really want."'

'Please stop singing, Mads.'

'OK.'

'So, please let me pay for a few treats now you know everything, starting with this meal. It really does give me pleasure. Us enjoying ourselves is a poke in the eye for them … and my dad.'

'"Zig-a-zag ah!"'

'Final warning, Mads.'

'OK. And, of course, it means we can go to the posh, poncey places you like a bit more often.'

Sofia smiled a sad smile.

'Yes, there is that as well.'

'Fine by me.'

A couple of waiters had appeared behind Charlotte.

'I am afraid we must close the restaurant now, as we will be arriving in port in a few minutes' time.'

Sofia clocked that they were the only three people still there, sitting in the half dark. Out of the windows were the lights of another Cycladic island, another harbour, with dark hills rising up behind.

'Of course. Can I pay please?'

'Certainly.'

Sofia rolled up the mascara-stained serviettes and placed them on the next table while the waiter fiddled with the card machine.

Charlotte wagged her finger.

'Naughty.'

The Tannoy announcing the ferry's arrival and calling for all passengers getting off to make their way down to the hold was deafening in the restaurant.

'Ow!' Charlotte put her hands over her ears.

Sofia rose to her feet.

'We need to go and get our luggage. New island, new start, here we come!'

There hadn't been much to look at last night in the dark, and they'd all fallen into their beds, wrung out and more than a little drunk after their emotional meal on the boat.

Maddie pulled open the voile curtains on another gorgeous day, the sun already high in the sky and the azure sea shimmering and beckoning far below. She was pleased to see that their rooms were simpler this time round. Her one housed just a big wooden bed with white sheets and a blue bedspread folded across the end, a freestanding wooden stencilled wardrobe and a bench seat. The blue tiled bathroom was similarly basic, with a compact shower, toilet and sink, a far cry from the ultra-luxurious bathroom of the first hotel, with a shower which could have fitted the three of them in.

Outside the French windows there was no fancy terrace

with a plunge pool, just a balcony with a small table and two chairs, plus a fabulous view. She'd been too tired to close the olive-green shutters last night, so the sun had already laid its palm on her bed, slicing the sheet into sections of gold.

Stepping out onto the balcony was like stepping onto a filmset, and she gasped as she looked down. Unlike the previous island, there were plenty of trees below her, pines, firs and even oaks, and the sound of cicadas trying to attract mates was as loud as an alarm clock. It was hard to believe it when people told you that every Greek island was totally different from the next, but on the evidence so far, she was sold. They'd only travelled three hours, but this could be a different country.

The starkly beautiful, but barren hills of the first island, with its jagged edges of brown against blue, had been replaced by softer contours, topped with leafy green points. It was much closer in look to where she lived, a village outside Manchester, which still had both feet firmly planted in the countryside.

The metal of the bistro style chair she chose was hard against her back, and Maddie retrieved one of the cushions she'd seen piled up on the wooden bench seat to put behind her. She was warm enough in her short cotton nightie and flip-flops, but she wrapped a fine wool pashmina in pink paisley tightly around herself, given to her by her son for her birthday last year. It made her feel a little bit closer to him. Not that he wanted to be close to her.

Seated with her feet up on the railings, she was startled by a little bird who landed on the table beside her. Unafraid, his beady little eyes watched her closely. She wasn't sure why she assumed it was a he, but it just looked male and a trifle cocky.

'Sorry, I don't have any food,' she whispered, making a mental note to find something in a local supermarket.

Wildlife had been one of Tony's loves, and together they'd walk the hills of their beloved Pennines on their days off, identifying birds from their song and looking out for particular species to tick off in their *Birds of Britain* log, which she kept firmly tucked away from prying eyes. She could just imagine Sofia's reaction.

The bird in front of her still hadn't moved and was pecking at the holes in between the metal flowers of the table design. *Determined little thing, aren't you,* came into her mind.

'Hang on. I've just remembered a half-eaten packet of crisps in my bag. It's all I've got, but I'll go and get them.'

She grabbed the crisps and rushed back out, worried that her avian friend would have given up and flown away.

But no, he was still there, looking straight at her, the natural oil in his feathers glinting in the sun.

It would sound fanciful to the others if she said that the bird in front of her had a look of Tony about him. Obviously, he didn't actually look like him – he was a bird for goodness's sake – but there was something … probably his persistence, his unwillingness to give up on the hope of food until the very end.

She'd been reading a lot about reincarnation on the internet during the long and lonely evenings, and she liked the idea that a little bit of her husband could be flying or crawling around nearby. But it would make her sound crazy if she said it out loud.

Three crisps should be more than enough. Maddie broke them into pieces and laid them on the table.

The bird was straight in there, tucking into the crisps in full view rather than taking them off to his nest to eat in private. Once they'd gone, he stared expectantly at her.

'More? You're a greedy bugger, Tony. But then you always were.'

Maddie broke up another three crisps, which were whipped away in seconds.

'You can't be serious.'

Tony was advancing towards the packet with a determined hop. Maddie leaned over and shook out the last bits from it.

'OK, but don't blame me if you get too fat to fly, my love.'

A noise behind her made her sit up straight.

'Mads?'

Maddie prayed that Charlotte hadn't heard her talking to the bird and calling it Tony. Her friend was standing on the adjacent balcony, the image of a scene in an Impressionist painting, not that she could tell you which one.

A silk dressing gown in greens and reds, embroidered with delicate cranes was loosely belted at the waist, and Charlotte's elegant and already brown bare feet anchored her on the patterned tiles, while her long blonde hair hung loose in waves down her back.

She looked younger, and less stressed. Maddie wondered for a moment what it must be like to look that effortlessly glamorous first thing in the morning. Not that she'd ever know.

'Morning.'

'Who were you talking to earlier?'

'What?'

Maddie spun round and located the empty crisp packet on the ground. Tony was nowhere to be seen.

'I could hear you speaking to someone.'

'No. Probably just singing out loud.'

Charlotte knew what she'd heard hadn't been singing, but Maddie had looked so startled when she'd mentioned it, that she'd let it drop. Even if the woman was talking to herself, it was her business.

'OK, if you say so.'

Maddie was desperate to keep this new – she could even say fledgling – relationship between her and the bird a secret. It was a tiny link to her husband. Her smile at her own joke prompted an odd look from Charlotte. She really hoped Tony would be back tomorrow. She'd be ready for him this time.

'Have you got your phone out here with you?'

'No, I was giving it a break for half an hour. Call me controversial, but we're surrounded by all this glorious nature. Why do I need to stare at a screen?'

'Because Sof messaged to say let's all meet downstairs for breakfast in half an hour, and you wouldn't have known otherwise?'

'Fine. See you there.'

Her little moment of peace on the balcony was well and truly over. She'd have to wait until the next morning to see Tony again.

Chapter Eleven

The plainer rooms were echoed by a simpler breakfast, which was no bad thing thought Maddie. Too much choice always threw her; she preferred fewer options but good ones in everything from food to clothes.

The hotel owners were a husband-and-wife combo, Theo and Thea, who smiled a lot and looked just like each other. They were roughly the same height as Sofia, but much more rounded. Had they always looked like each other, she wondered, or was it something couples did subconsciously over the years? Did they actively choose similar haircuts, clothes and a way of smiling? Or was it all just coincidence?

Thea was waving her arms around in the large wooden-beamed room they'd been directed to and pointing to plates laden with food.

'Please, help yourselves. There is fresh bread, home-made jam, honey from our hives, hard-boiled eggs, pastries, a different home-made cake every day, cheese from our dairy, and plenty of fruit from the trees in the orchard. We like to serve only what is in season. There is no need to fly fruit around the world, when we have so much here.'

Their host pointed to a huge bowl of deep red glossy miniature globes.

'The cherries are wonderfully sweet this year. Here, try, please.'

They all took a cherry, and as the sweet juice flooded Maddie's mouth and stroked her throat, she moaned out loud, and knew she'd never look at a cellophaned packet of the stuff in a British supermarket in the same way again.

Thea took such pleasure and even pride in their reactions, a pattern that Maddie had noticed ever since she'd arrived in Greece, with everyone from ice cream vendors to restaurant owners. She couldn't imagine Barry from her local greengrocers getting quite so excited at people tasting his wares.

Thea turned to her husband, who took the conversational baton in a move Maddie could see was well-rehearsed. She must stop studying couples, torturing herself by watching how they slotted together and complimented each other. She needed to get used to being on her own and believing that just her was enough.

'I will make any drinks you desire. We have everything from fresh orange juice, made with our own oranges of course, to any coffee you like from the big machine.'

Theo pointed over to a gleaming chrome monster in the corner, obviously his pride and joy. Maddie already knew she'd feel mean if she asked for a tea.

'Do I have any takers?'

'I'd love both if that's OK, Theo. An orange juice with ice and a cappuccino.'

Sofia looked at Charlotte, who nodded back.

'Three of those please, or rather six.'

'Of course. Please, choose your food, find a seat on the terrace and I will bring them to you.'

The big wooden wraparound terrace had views in all directions, and Maddie was pleased to see the comfortable wicker chairs with padded olive-green cushions and low coffee tables, tailor made for long lazy breakfasts. There were people at a table further on, talking and laughing in what Maddie now recognised as Greek.

The view towards the town below appealed the most, so they could watch people going about their business as they ate.

Maddie flopped down on the first chair, her plate piled high with food.

'Let's sit here.'

'Fine.'

Sofia followed, took the chair opposite and lowered her voice to a whisper.

'It's a little bit ... rustic here, isn't it?'

They were all tired after travelling between the islands yesterday, but Sofia's comment had her on edge immediately.

'Just because everything isn't high end and in taupe doesn't mean it's not charming. I absolutely love it up here on the hill. We're surrounded by nature and wildlife. You can hear birdsong and see butterflies. For me that's way better than superyachts and disco bars.'

'Not sure what disco bars are when they're at home.'

Maddie stuck out her tongue at her friend.

Charlotte joined the group, and Sofia leaned in towards the two of them.

'I'm really sorry I didn't check properly, I was in a bit of a flap after all the work stuff, but the hotel doesn't have a swimming pool.'

Maddie shrugged her shoulders.

'So what? We've got the sea just down there.'

Theo appeared from behind Charlotte carrying a full tray of coffees and orange juices.

'I'm sorry to listen to your conversation, but your friend is right. Why would you need a swimming pool when you have the sea so close? It is nature's gift, and we Greeks believe that bathing in the sea is good both for your body and your mind.'

Maddie made a face at Sofia while Theo's attention was taken up with serving Charlotte.

'See! He agrees with me.'

'Mmmm.' Sofia's tight smile didn't convince her.

'And I hope I'm not speaking out of turn here'—Theo put the now empty tray under his arm—'but a swimming pool uses up so much water, which is a precious resource here on the island. We chose not to have one, and as our customers are mainly Greeks, they understand our philosophy. I hope it doesn't spoil your enjoyment of the hotel. Thank you.'

Sofia's face was like thunder when he walked away.

'I didn't realise I'd booked us in with some eco-warriors.'

'Sof! Don't be a bitch. They're lovely people. And I happen to agree with them.'

Maddie used her fingers to put a large piece of the cake of the day in her mouth.

'I'm sure this has walnuts in it. It's delicious.'

Charlotte typed something into her phone and put the picture next to Sofia's uneaten piece.

'Here it is! It's called *karydópita*, a spiced cake with lots of crushed walnuts added.'

'It's yummy. You must try it. Sof, aren't you eating yours?'

Sofia had turned her face to the view down the hill.

'No, you have it.'

'You're not sulking, are you?'

'Of course not. Just to let you know, the hotel on the next island has a socking great swimming pool, I'm pleased to say.'

'So, you are sulking.'

Sofia turned to face her.

'Will you be boycotting the pool at the next hotel? Or popping down to see if there's anyone left on Greenham Common when you get back? Or even bunking up with that guy ... Swampy, isn't it?'

'Now you're just being ridiculous. All I said was that I can see why the Greeks aren't fussed about swimming pools in the main. I much prefer being in the sea to being bathed in chlorine. I am entitled to my opinion. Someone's got out of bed on the wrong side.'

'Now, now, children.' Charlotte had her phone in her hand again. 'I've been looking at my travel guides, and there are some amazing things to do on the island. We should make a list straightaway.'

Maddie managed to catch Sofia's eye and was rewarded with a tiny smile before her friend turned away, nose in the air.

'My number one suggestion for today is going for a hike in the hills and trying to find "the stunning waterfall at the end of a little gorge" where we can also swim. After last night's meal and sitting on the ferry for three hours, I'm quite keen to stretch my legs. Anyone else? We can get a taxi to the car park.'

Sofia picked up her own phone.

'Taxi be damned. We're not going to be relaxing by a pool anytime soon, that's for sure. So, if we're forced to commune with nature, we might as well do it properly and hire a car for the week.'

This time, it was Charlotte and Maddie's turn to exchange glances. Sofia was what Charlotte's dad had described as 'an accelerate and brake merchant' when he was alive. Their friend's driving was notoriously bad, and her road rage was something to behold. They usually avoided being in a car with her behind the wheel at all costs.

'Are you sure you want to do that?' Charlotte asked in a voice that to Maddie held more than a tinge of fear. 'With driving on the wrong side of the road and all that?'

Sofia waved away her question.

'Yes, it's fine. I always drive in Spain whenever I visit my mother, and that's on twisty mountain roads, so I'm quite used to it.'

A vision of Sofia hurtling along mountain tracks like a maniac, her elderly mother bumping up and down in the seat alongside her, was too much for Maddie.

'Poor woman,' she murmured under her breath.

'What was that?'

'Nothing, just saying that it will save us a lot of money on taxis.'

'It's not about the money…'

'Not for you, maybe, but a tank of petrol is a darn sight cheaper than taxis.'

'It's only a few euros difference.'

'A few euros are a few euros.'

Charlotte spoke again in a register far higher than the one she normally used.

'So that's settled. Meet down here in an hour. Swimsuits under your clothes as there'll be nowhere to change. And don't forget a towel and sensible walking shoes.'

'Yes, boss.' Sofia banged her fist on her chest several times in what they'd been told was a Greek gesture of love. 'What would we do without you?'

'Fall apart, probably.' Charlotte smiled to take the sting out of her words as she looked between the two of them.

She couldn't cope with much more of them behaving like children. It reminded her of the last few weeks trapped with Doug after she'd found out his sordid little secret. A cloud hanging over the house, flare-ups over the most stupid things and sitting in front of a blank canvas hour after hour. She had to say something.

'But please, stop the bickering. It's doing my head in. If I'd wanted stress and tension all day long, I'd have stayed at home.'

Both Sofia and Maddie stared open-mouthed at Charlotte's departing back.

The hire car was already parked on the other side of the courtyard when the three of them finally finished breakfast and walked out via reception.

'Oh good, it's a Suzuki Swift.' said Sofia, 'I've driven one of those before.'

Maddie couldn't have identified what model the car was if she'd been held at gunpoint. Never having held a licence, a pushbike was her preferred mode of transport if there wasn't a bus coming. Tony had been a motorcycle fanatic, so riding pillion was far more comfortable for her than being a car passenger.

But even in the unlikely event of her having had an opinion on the car, she'd have kept her mouth shut. She'd agreed with Sofia in the loos that, after Charlotte's uncharacteristic outburst, they were going to play happy families. There was definitely something up there, but it was going to take some careful groundwork to get it out of their friend.

The car hire guy, dressed all in black, waved and held the keys up in the air.

'Which one of you is the driver?'

'Me.'

Sofia went to grab the keys off him, but he held them just out of reach for a moment, so she had to stretch up.

'Hey!'

'Sorry, couldn't resist.'

His smile reached all the way to his sparkling brown eyes as he stared with interest at Sofia and put out his hand.

'Konstantinos.'

Sofia looked down at the strong tanned hand holding her own.

'Sofia.'

'Pleased to meet you, or *hero poli* as we say in Greece.'

Maddie raised her eyebrows at Charlotte.

'Here we go again. Do you think she'll remember she's got two passengers before she drives off?'

Car hire guy (they were too far away to hear his name) brought out an iPad and asked their friend to sign something.

Then he brought out his phone. Maddie strained to hear their conversation.

'He's asking for her number, I'm sure of it.'

'Let's get over there.'

'Hi!' Charlotte raised her hand at car hire guy, who smiled at her and Maddie for all of a second before looking longingly back at Sofia.

'Are you sure you don't need me to show you how everything works?'

'No, I'm fine, Konstantinos.'

Maddie smiled at the disappointment which oozed out of the man at not getting the chance to be squashed up against his new client.

'Remember what I said!' Konstantinos held up his phone as another car, a bigger, flashier, black one pulled into the courtyard, which Maddie presumed was his lift back to the office rather than a sudden upgrade.

She pulled open the back passenger door of the Suzuki and indicated that Charlotte, with her long legs, should get in the front. It wasn't an entirely selfless gesture. Being closer to Sofia meant being closer to the action. Charlotte would have no choice but to navigate. At least in the back she could close her eyes occasionally and hope no one would notice.

'Made a conquest?' Maddie caught Sofia's eye in the rear-view mirror.

'He asked me out for a drink if that's what you mean,' Sofia snapped back, before remembering their pact, and smiling widely. 'He seems like a nice guy.'

'Very much your type, I'd say. Knocking forty and fit.'

'Yeah, he is cute. I'll give it some thought.'

Although it was true that on paper Konstantinos was everything she liked, muscular and smiley being her main prerequisites, the thought of a possible date with him didn't fill her with the joy of old. He could fill out a t-shirt, no problem, but she knew nothing about him. She would be seeing Adonis again in a week's time. She knew what she was getting there, and what she would be getting was pretty damn good. Her encounter with Giannis hadn't exactly been a triumph. Surely, she could wait a week. She'd leave Konstantinos on hold for the moment. It was always good to have a back-up plan.

The journey to the car park was mercifully short and Maddie breathed a huge sigh of relief when she could open the car door and escape. There'd been a couple of hairy moments involving stray cats, lorries and boy racers taking corners on the wrong side of the road, as well as plenty of swearing in Spanish from Sofia, but they'd made it in one piece.

'Don't forget your hats.' Charlotte was back in Girl Guide mode, her earlier outburst seemingly forgotten. 'And as we have to swim through the gorge to get to the waterfall, I think we should lock our valuables in the car and just take our towels.'

'What! Hang on a minute... Swim through the gorge? I never signed up for that.' Maddie couldn't keep the tremble out of her voice.

'It will be fine. Hundreds of people do it every day.'

Charlotte was using her best matron voice now. 'Chuck everything in the boot you're not taking and let's go.'

The woodland path to the waterfall was paved with dappled sunlight and tall trees, and for the next half hour, Maddie tried to distract herself from what was to come by looking at the shape of their leaves. A trickling stream ran beside them, full of boulders and smaller stones, and the soothing sound of water enabled her to slow her breathing, rather than panting like an overheated dog. Plants with delicate pink flowers hung their branches over the stream, and tall green reeds with heads that looked like corn grew in the shallows.

A yellow butterfly fluttered in and out of the reeds just ahead of her for most of the journey. She and Tony had loved butterflies. It must be a good omen.

Not having any phones was somehow freeing. Maddie truly believed that taking away the pressure to photograph anything or put it on social media meant a deeper connection with virtually any experience, but she knew it wouldn't be a popular theory with anyone under thirty-five, so she usually kept her opinion to herself at family gatherings. Not that there'd been many of those lately.

There'd been simple meals at her daughter's, with her as the lone guest, but not the big family meals of old. Elsie would be big enough to join them now, in her own highchair. Maddie stumbled a moment as she imagined the scene, her little golden-haired granddaughter making the usual mess that babies made. She'd be happy to be covered head to toe in banana mulch if it meant they were all together again.

When they reached the huge rocks that signified the start of the stretch of water which led to the waterfall, Maddie noticed groups of people stretched out on them drying themselves in the sun like giant insects. The myriad of languages being spoken created an unwelcome buzz after the quiet of the pathway. She didn't hugely want an audience for her waterfall feat, but it seemed like there wasn't much choice.

The walls of the gorge stretched up on either side of the channel straight into the sky where a slim slice of startling blue was visible against the grey stone.

'The rocks are so tall, and it's such a narrow river.' Maddie's heartrate increased tenfold. 'I can't even see the waterfall.'

'Don't panic.' Charlotte laid her hand on her arm. 'It's just around the corner. Hardly any distance. Sof and I will be with you all the way, one in front and one behind. We won't let you drown.'

'Drown?' Maddie's legs were about to go from under her. 'Surely, I'll be in my depth, right? It's only a little channel.'

Both her friends had shifty expressions on their faces but stayed mute while fiddling with their possessions. Charlotte pointed behind the nearest rock.

'Clothes over there and...' Charlotte studied the stretch of water in front of her. 'Let's get in over here where it's shallowest. Hurry up. There's no one swimming at the moment, so we'll have the waterfall to ourselves.'

Although the sun was hot on her face, Maddie's first exposure to the water was a shock.

'It's freezing!'

Charlotte turned back, already thigh deep.

'The stream's coming from much higher up these

mountains, so it's not like the sea. Just get in slowly. We're right here with you, so shout if you're worried.'

Maddie couldn't hold in the scream which burst out of her mouth when she tried to put her shoulders under.

'Everything OK?' Charlotte turned back.

'Yes, fine.' Maddie wondered if giving up at this point was an option. The yellow butterfly was still with the group, fluttering just above Charlotte's head, which gave her the strength to carry on.

For the first few strokes, all she could focus on was coordinating her limbs and trying to get enough air into her lungs. But little by little, she found herself able to look up and see trees far above her and enjoy the sun on her back. When they finally turned the corner, all three of them stopped still a moment and just trod water to take in the sheer majesty of the waterfall in front of them. They could barely see the top of the rock, it was so far above them.

'Look at all that water, cascading down hundreds of metres.' Charlotte was the first to recover her voice. 'It's been there for thousands, maybe millions, of years.'

Maddie and Sofia continued to stare, fixed to the spot, but Charlotte motioned them to move forward.

'We need to try and get behind the waterfall, where there should be a natural platform.'

All three of them swam round and found the rock ledge, heaving themselves up to sit in a row and watch the curtain of water fall in front of them, rainbow-edged droplets breaking off into the still air and flying free.

The roar of the water was loud enough to stop any possibility of conversation, but no one seemed moved to speak anyway. Maddie reached out and held hands with the others. An enormous feeling of peace washed over her, something she hadn't experienced for a very long time. She hoped the others felt the same. It was a precious moment out of time, the rest of the world pushed far away.

When the voices of the next swimmers floated over on the breeze and broke the spell, all of them plopped back into the water without having to discuss it, and gave the incomers a satisfied smile on the way out.

Back on the bank, rubbing some warmth back into her body, Maddie looked down into the dark green water.

'Would I have been able to touch the bottom if I got into trouble?'

'God, no,' Charlotte replied. 'No one knows quite how deep it is down there.'

'Oh.'

'But you were really brave.' Charlotte moved in for a hug. 'And we kept you safe, didn't we?'

'You did.'

Maddie gave her friends the first genuine smile of the day. It had been scary at times, but she was so proud of herself for doing it. Connecting with nature was always a big part of her and Tony's free time away from their busy jobs, and it made him feel closer for a few precious minutes. He'd be proud of her too, wherever he was.

Chapter Twelve

Venturing down the hill into town late the next morning took a hell of a lot longer than Maddie would have liked. There were hundreds of steps to negotiate, and just as she thought they'd reached the bottom, there was another flight to conquer. Sofia and Charlotte were skipping down them like baby goats. Maybe that was a bit of an exaggeration, but they certainly seemed to be doing better than her. She couldn't even imagine what it would be like going back up.

Still, she'd said out loud that she loved being at the hotel up the hill, so she could hardly moan about it now. At last, they seemed to have reached some sort of high street, if you could call a few shops and cafés a high street.

Charlotte pointed at one of the cafés, up yet another flight of stairs.

'OK, it's this one.'

'Right. It bloody well would be, wouldn't it?'

Charlotte ignored her and marched off, closely followed by Sofia.

The best café in town couldn't possibly be at street level, thought Maddie, oh no, it had to be on top of a shop. Dragging herself up the last few steps, Maddie joined her friends at a table at the open window overlooking the town beach. The checked floor blurred before her eyes as she grabbed a glass of water from the carafe on the table. They hadn't come to Grandma's Café for the décor, but for the promise of the best ice cream on the island.

Not everything or everywhere could be the best, but she agreed that claims about ice cream needed thorough investigation. Charlotte pointed up at the picture of a goat on the brightly painted board and the list of ice cream flavours underneath.

Sofia spoke for both of them once the penny dropped.

'Are you telling me it's goat's milk ice cream we've come here to try?'

'Yep.'

'Won't that taste all … goaty?'

Sofia's voice held more than a trace of disgust.

Charlotte studied the menu on the table closely.

'I don't know. Like you, I've never tried it before. But let's give it a go.'

'Or a go-oat.'

The other two groaned at Maddie's attempt at humour.

'Feeble.' Charlotte hovered the translation app over the menu.

'OK, *pagotó* is Greek for ice cream, and some of the flavours are … *fráoula*, strawberry, *kerási*, cherry, *achládi*, pear, and *fistíki*, pistachio…'

Maddie giggled at the same time as Sofia.

'What is wrong with you two today? *Fistíki* is a perfectly normal word in Greek, I'm sure.'

Maddie coughed to cover another giggle and couldn't meet Sofia's eye.

'Yesterday you were at each other's throats, and now we're back in primary school.'

Sofia's attempt at a straight face set Maddie off again.

'I'll have a large *fistíki* please.'

'Me too. A very large *fistíki*.'

The waiter's arrival at the table quietened things down for a moment. But as soon as Charlotte uttered the words, 'Three cappuccinos, one *pagotó fráoula* and two large *fistíkis* please', Maddie caught Sofia's eye and they both collapsed onto the bistro style table, unable to breathe for laughing.

'I wish I found everything quite so hilarious.' Charlotte's plaintive voice brought Maddie up short.

'It's not that usual for me, honestly, Char, I can assure you. It's all her fault.'

Maddie pointed at Sofia, who put up her middle finger.

'Children, please.'

While Charlotte poured herself a glass of water, Maddie gave Sofia the signal they'd agreed on earlier to kickstart the conversation they all needed to have.

'So, how are your boys, Char?'

'They're hardly boys now, are they? Although they're still our boys, aren't they, Mads, however old they are.'

'True.' Maddie wasn't keen to get too involved in that one. Talking about her son was for another day. It was Charlotte's turn to spill.

'But everything's OK there?'

Charlotte frowned.

'Yes, why wouldn't it be? Luke's still happy working in the City and living in his rented flat in Clapham with Ella, paying some extortionate rent, while Rueben and George have bought a little house together up the road in Berkshire and are working in IT.'

Sofia took over the baton.

'OK, good that things are good. But it must feel a bit lonely now they've both moved out?'

'It's a lot quieter, certainly, but I'm pleased they're both independent. You hear all these stories of kids still living at home in their thirties. As I'm sure you'll both remember, I'd well and truly left home by the time I was twenty-one. My parents were pretty old fashioned, and I was keen to live by my rules, not theirs.'

Maddie nodded.

'I'd gone at eighteen. Which seems incredibly young these days, but it didn't feel like it at the time. I think we grew up quicker then.'

She couldn't let herself go back to those early days, sharing with a group of workmates. Whenever Tony could get away from uni, the house had been full of laughter and long lazy mornings in bed.

Sofia's voice was less upbeat.

'I didn't even have a choice. After uni, I didn't have a family home to go back to anyway... My dad had seen to that.'

Maddie shot Sofia a *'we're getting off track here'* look.

Charlotte looked from one to the other with a puzzled expression. Where was this going? It was obvious it was some sort of pre-planned move.

'So, in answer to your question, yes, the kids are fine.'

Maddie looked over to Sofia for some moral support. Charlotte was stonewalling big time.

'How's it going with Doug these days?' Sofia smiled. 'Is it lovely and romantic now it's just the two of you alone in the house?'

They couldn't possibly have got anywhere near the truth, but she needed to answer carefully. Charlotte pulled a serviette out for each of them from the holder.

'We've done my kids, and now we're on to my husband?'

Maddie put her hands on top of her friend's when she placed the serviette in front of her, and Sofia added hers too. It was a silly thing they'd started at school, calling themselves The Three Musketeers and pledging their support for each other in times of trouble.

Charlotte looked down at the stack of hands and up at her friends.

They only wanted to help, but the sudden physical contact undid her plan to lock down her emotions. She couldn't bear Doug to come anywhere near her, but she'd never realised how much she'd miss his hugs and hand-holding, until they were gone. He'd made it very clear they were still on offer, but she needed distance until she'd made up her mind what to do. Against her wishes, her eyes filled with tears.

Maddie spoke first.

'Look, we know there's something wrong. You're not painting, you never mention Doug and you're a bit … snappy. It's just not you. Please talk to us.'

Charlotte left her hands where they were at the bottom of

the pile but let a couple of tears fall onto the back of one of Sofia's hands on the top.

It was useless to pretend everything was hunky dory. These were her best friends, and they were far from stupid.

'You're right. There is something going on, but … I'm just not ready to talk about it yet. I promise you that when I am, you'll be the first to know. You're just going to have to be satisfied with that for the time being. Please, can we talk about anything other than my husband?'

The arrival of the waiter with the ice creams and coffees prompted a quick unravelling of hands.

Maddie sighed. They'd pushed Charlotte as far as they could for now. She knew how it felt when people tried to force her to talk about Tony and how she was coping without him.

'Just as long as you know we're here for you, anytime. All for one…'

'And one for all' her friends chorused back, although Charlotte's voice was barely above a whisper.

'Now let's tuck into these fabulous-looking ice creams. The waiter already thinks we're insane.'

It wasn't a stretch for Maddie to get on board with the best ice creams on the island slogan. The goat's milk gave the ice cream a slightly savoury tang which complemented the pistachio flavour well.

'Mmmmm, these really are gorgeous.'

Charlotte's smile didn't convince either of them.

'Yes, the strawberry is lovely too.'

Sofia cast around for something to lighten the mood.

'Oh God, I never told you, did I?'

'Told us what?' Maddie was up for some double-headed role play, anything to cheer Charlotte up.

'I managed to flash Dimitris the pool boy at the last hotel! I gave him the Full Monty.'

Maddie grimaced.

'Poor guy. When? And how?'

'He was out there, cleaning the plunge pool early one morning. But he was so quiet, I had no idea he was outside. I hadn't bothered with the shutters, so I pulled back the thin curtain, naked as a baby, and we just stared at each other for a moment before I yanked it shut again and waited until he'd gone. I was worried that he'd think I'd done it on purpose.'

'How embarrassing.' Maddie would have been completely mortified if it had happened to her. The thought of any man other than Tony seeing her naked was a no-no. And that was never going to happen with her husband again in this lifetime.

'Even if it *was* deliberate, he wouldn't have been interested anyway.' Charlotte's dead pan delivery gave nothing away.

'What do you mean?' Sofia's look of confusion was comical. 'Are you saying I've lost whatever it was I had?'

Charlotte smile was real this time.

'No, silly. You're still gorgeous. But Dimitris is gay. That's what we were talking about that morning in the garden. I was telling him about my son's experience, and he was explaining that things weren't quite so simple in Greece, particularly on the islands. Plus, he was terrified of his mother finding out. She's very religious.'

Maddie winced.

'Yes, I can see Maria might be a bit tricky.'

'But now we've left the island, and we're probably never going to see them again … I do have some stunning gossip.'

The twinkle in Charlotte's eye was unmistakeable.

Sofia grabbed her friend's wrist.

'You? Gossip?'

'Yes, me.'

'What? What is it? Tell us, or we'll have to kill you.'

'His boyfriend, who I saw creeping out of his room at dawn was none other than … the hot priest from the monastery!'

'No!' Maddie wouldn't have picked him as Dimitris's lover in a month of Sundays.

Sofia grinned at the others.

'Wow, that is Grade A stuff, Char. The thought of those two together is … frankly quite a turn on.'

'Sof! Really.' Charlotte took a sip of her coffee. 'Obviously it's none of my business. I shouldn't be telling people his secrets, and I really do hope they can be properly together one day.'

'Me too, of course.'

Charlotte raised her eyebrows at her friend.

'No, I do. I love a bit of true love.'

Just as long as it involved other people and not her, it was a wonderful idea. She'd seen what true love could do, and it wasn't always the fairytale ending of books. It could bring destruction and heartbreak in its wake too, so it was best to steer well clear.

Sofia glanced at herself in the mirror. 'Plus, I'm pleased that it wasn't personal and that I've still got it.'

'Vain cow.' Maddie punched her friend on the arm. At least Charlotte had smiled for a few unguarded moments.

The stroll down towards the town beach was a lot less strenuous. To Maddie's relief, they'd all agreed that they'd not be going up and down those endless steps to the hotel more than once a day, and they'd brought their swimming stuff with them. The ice creams had been extremely filling, and an afternoon lying on the beach would do nicely.

'Let's walk along here first.' Charlotte pointed to where some small boats were anchored. 'It must be the old harbour, built before the big one we came into on the ferry.'

The old wooden fishing boats lined up along the quay were painted in bright blues, reds and whites. They were obviously still in daily use, as the empty crates and nets on the decks could testify.

One guy even had a small stall of fish laid out beside him. He sat back on his metal chair and took a long drag on a cigarette as they approached.

Charlotte's first thought was that if someone had requested a hot middle-aged Greek fisherman for a film, this one could have come straight from central casting.

Tanned, lined, handsome face, tick. Battered denim cap, tick. Muscles in all the right places, tick. Startling blue eyes, tick. Slow, knowing smile, tick. Her fingers were twitching. He'd be a great subject to paint. The shock of even thinking it brought a glow to her whole body. It was the first time in weeks she'd felt the urge to capture a person on canvas.

'*Kalispéra.*'

He was speaking to them. She took the chance to practise her very limited Greek.

'*Kalispéra.*'

'Ah, you are English?'

It had lasted all of one word.

'Yes, how did you know?'

He gestured at them.

'You look English.' He pointed at Maddie. 'And she, with her beautiful hair is the big clue. We do not have many people with hair this colour in Greece, *kókkinos*, red.'

'I see.'

The man got to his feet, towering over all three of them, cigarette still in hand.

'I am Thanassis.' He pointed to his stall.

'Are you interested in some fresh fish? Caught this morning. Only a few pieces left.' He put his fingers to his lips and kissed them. 'Stunning cooked with just lemon, herbs and olive oil on the grill, or baked in the oven with a little fennel.'

His gesture gave Maddie a funny feeling in her stomach. Tony had been the cook in their house, and to hear another man talk about food with such passion took her aback for a second.

Charlotte answered for them all.

'It looks lovely, but we are staying in a hotel, so we don't have the option to cook.'

'Shame.' Thanassis nodded his head in the direction of his vessel. 'I also do boat trips, complete with gorgeous *spitikó*, home-made food, and local wine. You will get to see the best beaches on the island, beaches you cannot get to by car or on foot. Plus, we can watch the sun go down together on our return journey.'

'Oooh that does sound lovely.' Charlotte spoke before she'd okayed it with the others.

Seeing the excitement on her friend's face decided Maddie and she nodded at Sofia who put her thumbs up and grinned at Thanassis.

'Yes, we're in. As long as the price is right.'

Thanassis named a price, which was actually far less than Sofia would have been prepared to pay.

'Agreed. We can give it to you now in cash if you like, if you knock off ten per cent.'

She'd cottoned on to the fact that many Greeks were happier with cash, so they didn't have to bother with all that tax stuff, and would give you a better deal if you asked.

Thanassis ground his cigarette underfoot and smiled his lazy smile.

'That sounds good.'

Sofia handed him a wad of notes.

'*Efcharistó*. OK, I will just clear up, prepare the food and meet you back here in half an hour?'

'Great.'

Charlotte stepped forward.

'Can I please take a quick picture of you for my blog?'

Now she'd experienced the elusive desire to paint, however briefly, she wanted to at least capture him on camera in case the muse visited her in the future. She'd been taking fewer and fewer shots for the blog as the days passed, and she'd told the others she'd put the best shots together and publish it as one piece after they got home, so they didn't need to worry about anyone tracking their journey, Doug included.

'Sure. No problem.'

Thanassis struck what he obviously thought was an engaging pose, but Charlotte knew she'd prefer the unguarded shots she took when he'd stopped posing and sat down again.

Sofia noticed that his eyes hadn't left Maddie's face after the comment about her hair. He was still staring at her friend as they walked away, although Maddie was oblivious. Sofia quickened her pace and linked arms with the others. Her plan for the next half hour involved shopping, and she wasn't taking no for an answer.

'Right, I noticed a shop up that way that looked like it had some good stuff, and we've got time to pop in before meeting Thanassis again.'

Ignoring the groans, Sofia pulling the others along, bumping shoulders with Maddie.

'The handsome fisherman's taken a liking to you, I'm telling you.'

'Don't talk nonsense.'

'I'm being serious.'

'And I'm seriously not interested. You seem to forget Tony's only been gone just over a year.'

'Exactly. Isn't it time to … spread your wings?'

Sofia was surprised at the flash of anger that overtook Maddie's face. She'd obviously touched a nerve.

'I think you mean spread your legs, don't you? And the answer's no. We're not all like you, Sof.'

Sofia pulled her arm away from her friend, breaking up the trio. Charlotte carried on walking. She had no desire to play referee, and it would give her a chance to have a quick flick through her photos.

Sofia stood facing her friend, Maddie's thunderous look mirroring her own.

'And what's that supposed to mean?'

'Needing a man's attention all the time.'

'OK, thanks for that.'

Maddie reached over and held Sofia's hand.

'Sorry, I didn't mean to be so blunt. But I just get really fed up with people trying to push their widowed, divorced or occasionally single friends on me. They assume that we'll all have huge amounts in common, and that I'll obviously want to bonk their brains out, as I must be desperate after all this time.'

She *was* desperate, but for Tony's touch, not anyone else's.

The pain in Maddie's face shocked Sofia anew.

'I'm sorry too. I can see that must be incredibly annoying. But all I said was that he seemed keen on you. I'm not suggesting you wrap yourself up in his nets together on the dock right this minute.'

'I know, but it's just such a sore subject. Let's drop it please.'

Sofia opened the shop door and winked back at her friend.

'He is cute though, isn't he?'

Maddie turned her face away, so Sofia couldn't see her smile.

'You're incorrigible.'

Chapter Thirteen

Once inside, the array of swimming costumes, bags and scarves on display had Sofia darting from one to the other like a bee collecting pollen in a field of flowers.

Maddie rolled her eyes at Charlotte.

'Here we go again…'

After they'd given their approval rating on yet more bikinis for Sofia's ever-growing collection, Maddie noticed that Sofia had returned with a selection of stuff that looked far too big for her.

'Girls…'

'Oh no.' Maddie knew what her friend was going to say before she said it.

'Oh yes.'

Sofia thrust one armful at Charlotte and one at her.

'You said you'd let me buy you a few treats to get over my sadness at being made redundant.'

Sofia framed her own chin with her hands to give maximum waif vibes.

'To cheer me up, I insist you both try on the bikini and sarong I've picked out for you.'

Sofia put up a hand.

'And before you start kicking up a fuss, you must have realised by now that every woman in Greece wears a bikini, whether she's nineteen or ninety. And they don't give a damn about what other people think.'

Maddie couldn't disagree with her there. She'd seen women of all shapes and sizes in bikinis on the beach, relaxed and happy in their own skins. She definitely wouldn't be the biggest, although she'd almost certainly be the palest. Dare she give it a go? The idea of going home with a lovely brown tummy really appealed. Even if she'd be the only one to see it.

She looked over at Charlotte who shrugged.

'Why not?'

Sofia clapped her hands with joy.

'Oooh goodie.'

Sofia's keen eye for fashion and sizing meant she'd chosen well, Maddie had to admit to herself as she tried on the dreaded bikini.

'Show me, show me, please.'

She supposed Sofia had earned her fun.

Maddie emerged from the changing room in a high waisted khaki green number which unusually didn't make her shy away from herself in the full-length mirror, and Charlotte's simple blue two-piece also suited her down to the ground. The matching sarongs in complementary colours and patterns – blue and white stripes for Charlotte, and leopard print in khaki and pink for her – would make great cover-ups.

Charlotte walked up and down in front of the mirror, her

hourglass figure complimented by the structure of the well-made bikini.

'I have to say, Sof, you've chosen brilliantly.'

Maddie smiled too.

'Yes, even I can cope with this. Thank you.'

Sofia's eyes were shining with an evangelist's zeal at the sight of them both.

'You look fabulous, girls! Too glam to give a damn!'

'If you say so.' Maddie turned to go back into the changing room.

'No, don't put your underwear back on!'

Sofia's shouted command had the shop owner looking over with a startled expression.

'My one condition is that you keep your bikinis and sarongs on and put your clothes in your bags. We've got the boat trip in precisely'—Sofia checked her phone—'five minutes. The weather's gorgeous, so what better time to test out our new gear than while exploring beaches with Thanassis?'

Maddie didn't miss the wink, but she couldn't be bothered to respond.

Rubbing a little more suntan oil onto her bare stomach, Maddie laid back down on the pristine white sand with a contented sigh. The beach really was all that Thanassis had promised and more.

At first, she'd been too self-conscious to take off her sarong under the fisherman's watchful eye and kept it firmly in place until he'd anchored the boat a way out of the bay. But when Thanassis held up the snorkelling equipment, she'd realised she'd be mad to turn down the opportunity to swim in the turquoise waters with the others for the sake of a piece of cloth.

All those brightly coloured fish darting in and out of the reeds on the seabed would have been just a story for her friends to tell her rather than the gloriously immersive experience it had turned out to be.

With her friends' encouragement, she'd also managed to push herself straight into the water from the edge of the boat without panicking about how deep it was below her. Swimming through the gorge to the waterfall the previous day had been terrifying, but she'd had to admit that it had given her a little bit more confidence in her own abilities.

Tony's death had brutally ripped up her plans for the future, their future, so trying a few new things was important, and it might help her stumble her way into framing a new future. Not that she wanted to sound like a self-help book in her own head, but it did make a lot of sense. Her temper was still a work in progress. But slowly, slowly, or *sigá, sigá,* as the Greeks wisely say.

She closed her eyes for a moment and relived the three of them swimming under the surface of the water, holding hands, Sofia in a barely-there red bikini she'd bought earlier, next to her in green and Charlotte in blue, and she wondered what the fish had made of the multi-coloured giant shapes swimming above them. It would make a fabulous painting, and she wondered whether she should ask Charlotte to have a go at '*The Snorkelling Trip*' to get her out of her artistic funk.

Not that she could ask her friend anything right this

minute, as after their hour of swimming and snorkelling, Charlotte was fast asleep, gently snoring away. The woman deserved a break. And she and Sofia still needed to get to the bottom of what was wrong. They'd nearly got it out of her at the café, but she'd stopped short of confessing.

Sofia seemed to be asleep too, but just in case she was faking, Maddie pulled her hat down further over her eyes so she could watch Thanassis doing his thing in peace without being observed or even worse, teased mercilessly.

Their chef had set up a little tent over his cooking station on the beach, and the coals on the simple BBQ grill had gradually turned from red to white, which she knew from Tony's tutorials meant the heat would be just right for the fish. Not that she'd been watching Thanassis the whole time she'd been lying there.

She picked up a handful of golden sand and let it run away through her fingers, feeling rather than seeing the silky particles as they rejoined the rest. They had the whole beach to themselves. There was no way anyone could get down the almost vertical rocks to the shore on foot; they would tax even a goat. The rugged coastline they'd seen on their trip round the top of the island was gorgeous but wild, more like Devon and Cornwall than Greece. Coming across little golden pockets of beaches tucked away behind vicious-looking rocks every couple of hundred metres had been a welcome surprise.

The sea spray had coated her face in a refreshing mist which was cool to the touch, as they'd bobbed along the coastline, riding the waves with ease. Thanassis, totally in control at the helm, had pointed out passing birds and once a very large fish, all while manoeuvring the wheel with one hand and managing to smoke a stream of roll-ups with the other.

The boat had rocked alarmingly when Thanassis had guided her into their last stop for a very late lunch on the beach, but his experienced hands had held on to the wheel until the boat calmed, even though he'd had to throw a half-smoked cigarette into the pool of water at the bottom of the boat, which must have pained him. She was just pleased he hadn't thrown the butt into the sea for some unsuspecting marine creature to choke on.

Boats were always female for some reason; she wasn't sure why. She'd have to ask Charlotte. It was the sort of useless information she could reel off at the drop of a hat.

But Thanassis certainly knew how to handle his prized possession. If pressed, she'd have to admit to a weakness for men with a practical bent. Tony had been a half decent carpenter, when he could he bothered. The shelves he'd put up were still going strong, even if he was long gone. His cheerful face, hammer in hand and the silly tool belt that he'd insisted on buying around his waist, flashed into her mind, but she pushed it away. She needed something else to focus on, and both her friends were asleep, so she had no option but to study Thanassis, did she?

Maddie watched him take the fish out of a battered box full of ice and put the first pieces on the grill. The three of them had been dozing side by side in the late afternoon sun for quite a while, and the first pangs of hunger had crept up on her unawares. A large rumble from her stomach coincided with the first waft of frying fish coming their way.

Sofia leant up on one elbow.

'Mads, is that you, or rather your stomach?'

'Guilty as charged.'

'It already smells amazing, even from here. Thanassis is a very versatile man, isn't he?'

'I'm not answering that one.'

She really wasn't in the mood for another row.

'For fear of incriminating yourself?'

'Stop your dirty legal talk right now.'

'Oh look, he's setting up a place for us under the trees in the shade. How considerate. It must be nearly ready.'

Thanassis waved his long arm in the air.

'*Paréa*, my friends. It's time. You can eat now.'

'Lovely.'

Maddie reached for her bag to take out her sarong, but Sofia shook her head.

'Let's just take our towels to sit on. We're on a beach in the middle of nowhere. Why do we need to cover up?'

'OK. You're right.'

'Yes, I usually am when it comes to fashion choices.'

Sofia pointed at Charlotte's inert body.

'She looks really sweet when she's asleep, doesn't she? It's smoothed out those worry lines we've seen far too much of on this holiday. We'd better get her up and at it.'

A gentle tug on both arms produced a strangled cry from Charlotte.

'Hey, sweetie. It's OK. It's just us.' Sofia put Charlotte's dislodged hat back on her head.

'Grub's up and the hunky fisherman is ready for us.'

Maddie wagged her finger.

'You know his name's Thanassis.'

'Whatever. Hunky fisherman will do for me.'

The three of them made their way over to the shaded area and spread out their towels on the ground.

Thanassis ambled over holding a skewer aloft with a piece of fish and offered it to Maddie. Sofia couldn't imagine him doing anything in a hurry. Which could have its advantages.

'You have the first taste. Let me know if you think it's done.'

Maddie held his hand steady with her own while she took the piece of fish and put it in her mouth. The touch of skin on skin gave her a little jolt. But it was driven from her mind by the taste of the fish marinated in a simple lemon and butter sauce.

'That's fantastic, Thanassis.'

He held her gaze for a long moment.

'Thank you. I will fetch the rest.'

'Don't mind us…' Sofia whispered at his departing back.

Maddie hoped her blush wasn't too noticeable now she had a tan.

'Stop it. He offered it to me first because he can see that I'm a food connoisseur.'

'Greedy pig more like.'

'Miaow.'

At first Thanassis made to sit a little way from them, but Sofia beckoned him over.

'Please, come and eat with us,' she shouted. 'You've done all the hard work.'

Several different types of fish, all crisp and as fresh as the moment they'd been taken out the sea, were accompanied by a large bowl of some sort of dip, which Thanassis laid on a piece of cloth in the middle of the towels.

'This is *skordaliá*, made from stale bread, potatoes, almonds, garlic and olive oil. Everyone has their own recipe, and I made this myself this morning. It comes from my *yiayiá*, my grandmother, and has been in the family for generations. It's usually served with cod, but it suits all fish.'

Sofia noticed that he seemed to be addressing most of his remarks directly to Maddie. Not that she minded; she was genuinely thrilled to see her friend getting special attention.

Thanassis pointed to a large plastic container at his side.

'And the salad is a mix of things from my garden. But the key is to use only the best olive oil. I am warning you, never ever buy cheap *elaiólado*. You will ruin the flavour of whatever you're cooking.'

Thanassis's deep voice bounced off the rocks and reverberated around the tiny bay.

'Got the message.' Sofia dived in for another piece of fish and dunked it in the *skordaliá*, while Thanassis went to fetch some more stuff from his makeshift kitchen.

'Mmmm. That tastes so much better than it sounds or indeed looks for that matter.'

Maddie scooped up more of the dip with her own fish.

'Rude, Sof.'

'You have to agree it's a bit beige. And it has the texture of wallpaper paste. Usually, Greek food is so colourful.'

'Yes, it does look a bit weird, but I agree it tastes fantastic,' Charlotte chimed in.

Maddie looked behind her.

'The taste is far more important than the look. You're too hung up on image, Sof. And I'm not just talking about food.'

'I like nice things, so sue me.'

'Shhh. He's coming back.'

She'd hate for Thanassis to hear any negative comments when he'd served them up such a feast.

They ate mainly with their hands, just using a fork for the salad, and paper cups for the wine. It came in a big plastic bottle without any labels or markings, and Thanassis filled their cups to the brim.

'This *krasí* is a rosé, made from my friend's grapes from the vines we grow up in the hills. It is good with fish.'

Maddie knocked back too big a mouthful and coughed several times, causing Thanassis to rush round and pat her on the back.

'It is probably stronger than what you're used to in a restaurant, but it is natural and *organikós*, how you say, organic, which is of course a Greek word by origin, as many words in your language are.'

Sofia and Charlotte were sitting a few feet away, and Sofia leant across to whisper to her friend while Thanassis was dealing with Maddie's coughing fit.

'Crikey, have we got another Mr Portokalos from *My Big Fat Greek Wedding* on our hands? Convinced that every word in English comes from Greek?'

'Well, he is right in a lot of cases,' replied Charlotte. 'There are an incredible number of words that have Greek origins. It is considered the cradle of Western civilisation, after all.'

'Thanks, Simone Schama.'

Maddie had recovered enough to take some more measured sips of wine and pronounce it delicious.

Thanassis kept on stroking her back long after she'd stopped coughing, which wasn't an unpleasant feeling.

Great big chunks of watermelon were a refreshing end to the meal. The simple lunch on the beach was one of the best meals Maddie had ever had in her life, never mind in Greece, and she had to tell him.

'Thank you, Thanassis, for such a fabulous meal.'

'You are very welcome. It is nice to be appreciated.'

'I don't think there's any doubt about that,' Sofia muttered under her breath.

Thanassis looked in her direction for a moment but smiled his lazy smile again.

'Now, please rest for a few minutes before you go for a last swim and we make our way back. You must not swim straight after food.'

Charlotte had a little smile to herself at Thanassis's serious tone when it came to eating and swimming, so unlike his usual laidback style.

'Of course, we will leave it a while.'

The sun was slowly starting to dip in the sky when the three friends began to reluctantly pack up their things. A doze on the beach had settled their stomachs nicely and the swim that followed had given them enough energy for wading back to the boat, which Thanassis had anchored a little way offshore.

The breeze had picked up considerably and was playing with the ends of their sarongs, lifting them up in the air.

Thanassis strode out in front, the grill balanced on one

shoulder and the largest of the food containers on the other. Everything else was already in the boat, including their bags. He'd left the heaviest stuff till last.

As he attempted to climb into the boat, a particularly strong gust of wind ripped the sail that protected passengers from the sun from its base and flung it over the fisherman's face.

Maddie saw the next few seconds as if in slow motion, as Thanassis half fell into the boat and the metal grill hit him on the side of the head.

'No!'

She screamed into the wind, and they ran as one body towards him.

Sofia reached him first and turned back to the others.

'Shit. He looks like he's out cold. And he's bleeding.'

Chapter Fourteen

Maddie waded through the shallow water as fast as she could and tried to breathe through the fear, but Charlotte still got to the boat before her and bent over the side to get a better look.

'Don't touch him! Wait for me.'

Sofia and Charlotte nodded and pulled back.

The sight of Thanassis lying on his back at the bottom of the boat almost took her feet out from under her, but Maddie knew she was the one who had to think straight and fast. The first aid courses she'd done at the care home always advised assessing the situation first and against moving the injured party.

Her friends were staring at her, waiting for their instructions. If Sofia was fashion and Charlotte was facts, she wasn't sure exactly when she'd been assigned life-threatening emergencies, but it was happening ... and right now. There was no way she was going to let another man die on her watch if she could help it.

Maddie half leant into the boat and managed to get close enough to Thanassis to discreetly check if he was still breathing. A trickle of bright red blood made its way down the side of his face as she waited. Her own heart stopped for a moment and started again when she felt his warm breath on her face.

'OK, he's still breathing. He's got a nasty cut on the side of his head, which needs seeing to, but first we need to get him into the recovery position. Sofia, you're the lightest. Get right into the boat and gently push him over onto his side.'

Sofia leapt on board and turned Thanassis's inert body a few degrees to the side. Maddie leant in again and doubled checked that there was nothing blocking his airway. Fishing about inside his mouth with her fingers was a weird sensation, but she had to make sure. She'd been present when a care home resident had swallowed his own tongue during a fit, and she'd watched someone else perform the same check. They didn't need a stray cigarette butt making things worse.

'He seems stable. But we need to get him to a hospital as soon as we can.'

Maddie turned to Charlotte, who was still as a statue.

'Can you try and ring emergency services, please? It's...' Maddie racked her brains, but her mind had gone blank.

Charlotte came to with a start.

'One-one-two. I know. I programmed in into my phone.'

'Thank God for your efficiency, Char. They'll be able to send out the coastguard.'

Charlotte pressed the buttons over and over again and held her phone every which way in the air, but the precious seconds dragged by. After a brief run along the beach, she returned, panting, to the boat and shook her head.

'There's no service here at all.' A white-faced Charlotte pointed up at the cliffs. 'It's because of those. I didn't notice it earlier as none of us were on our phones.'

Any hope of immediate rescue, or indeed any sort of rescue, was gone. Maddie took a deep breath. Think, Maddie, think.

It was going to be up to them, or rather up to her, to get everyone out safely. They couldn't let Thanassis spend a night out in the open. There was no guarantee he'd be alive in the morning without treatment for the head injury.

She had no idea if anyone was waiting for him at home and would alert the emergency services. He'd not mentioned a wife or girlfriend, but as a fisherman she presumed he'd keep weird hours anyway, so being out all night wouldn't arouse suspicion.

And they'd not bothered to let anyone at the hotel know where they were because they were supposed to be back by sunset at the latest.

'No one knows we're here, do they?' Charlotte's plaintive voice proved she'd caught on quick.

Maddie exchanged a glance with Sofia.

'Probably not, but we're going to have to figure it out for ourselves. The good thing is that this was the last stop on our tour, and the sunset won't be long, so we can't be far away from our little harbour.'

She was using the same voice she used with the care home residents, slow and low, but they had to keep Charlotte calm. They had more than enough to deal with without setting off one of the panic attacks their friend had suffered from in the past. To her knowledge, Charlotte hadn't had one in recent years, but the situation wasn't exactly stable.

'I do have an idea though.'

Charlotte's hopeful nod made her look away.

'I watched Thanassis start up the engine when we left the port, so I've got a reasonable idea how it works. Tony'—Maddie stopped to regulate her breathing—'had an old lawnmower with a similar engine … and the key is not to flood it.'

Maddie hadn't meant to say the last bit out loud.

Charlotte's look of terror had returned, but Sofia took over for a welcome moment.

'Sounds good, Mads. If men can master it, there's no reason why we can't. We are the superior gender after all. Let's give it a go, shall we?'

It had given Maddie precious time to think and check the depth of the water in relation to how low the engine would hang.

'I need to be inside the boat by the motor, but I'm concerned we've drifted in towards shore a little since we anchored, and it's too shallow here. So, first you two will need to push the boat a little further out to sea with me in it. Once we've taken up the anchor, I'll try the motor and then you two jump back in. OK?'

'Sounds like a plan.'

Sofia's cheerful voice buoyed her, even if it was fake, although Charlotte remained worryingly mute.

'Can you help me get into the boat now, please, Char? You're the tallest.'

Giving someone in shock a specific task had also been mentioned as a good idea on one of her courses.

Her friend's powerful leg up and over the side of the boat almost had her on top of Thanassis. She stepped over the man without looking too closely. She could see his chest still moving at least. The blood was congealing on the side of his face, and in a small pool at the bottom of the hull, but the most important thing was to get out of there while they still had a bit of daylight. There wasn't any time to dress wounds.

The back of the boat was a mass of nets and cages, but Maddie stumbled to the narrow seat by the engine where she'd watched Thanassis steer their course and turned to smile back reassuringly at her friends. She lowered the bottom half of the motor gently into the water and fixed the picture of Thanassis starting her up firmly in her mind.

'Here we go!'

The first pull of the power cord produced a feeble splutter which died almost immediately.

'Damn.'

She tugged harder on the cord and the engine started for a couple of seconds before fading again.

Maddie crossed the fingers on one hand while she pulled as hard as she could with the other.

'Third time lucky!'

A sudden roar jerked her backwards as the motor sprang into life under her.

Maddie offered up a silent prayer as her friends clapped and cheered.

'No time to celebrate! Quick! Jump in.'

She kept the fear to herself that the engine would flood or stall, thus stopping them getting away.

Sofia flung herself over the side of the boat like a fish who'd just been landed, which even made Maddie smile for a brief moment. Charlotte hesitated in the water for a heart-stopping few seconds, until Sofia held out her hand to pull her much taller friend aboard.

The boat bucked underneath them as Charlotte managed to clamber on board, and Maddie had to battle to hold the engine steady in the water.

'Balance yourselves out. One on either side of Thanassis. Grab a seat and after that, don't move, whatever you do.'

She glanced back to check her friends were in the correct position.

'And we're off.'

It took her a few moments on the tiller to work out which way was right, and which was left, but after one dramatic lurch that brought forth a scream from Charlotte and made Maddie fear they might actually capsize, the boat steadied under her hands.

As they pulled out from the bay into open water, the promise of a dramatic sunset touched the sky with delicate corals and pinks.

Under any other circumstances it would have been beautiful, but it just brought home to her how tight the race was against the clock. They didn't know these waters, so once they lost the light, they could be in an even worse position than they'd have been on the beach. Her tactic was to hug the shore as much as possible, without going too close to the rocks.

It worked while she could still make out the outlines of the rocks, but it wouldn't last much longer. She wondered how much battery the others had on their phones, although a phone torch wasn't going to help much once they'd completely lost daylight.

Why had they opted for somewhere so remote? There were no other boats out at this time of night and very few signs of life along the coastline. But there was no point thinking about the what-ifs. She'd had enough of those after Tony's death. There'd been endless nights agonising over what she could have done differently. Looking back wasn't going to help the fisherman who'd shown them a wonderful day out.

A groan from the bottom of the boat had them all looking over at Thanassis, although Maddie quickly turned her face seaward again.

'Stay where you are. Please don't go to him. It'll unbalance the boat.'

Sofia shouted into the insistent breeze.

'He's opened his eyes, and he's trying to speak.'

Maddie kept her own eyes on the horizon.

'OK, that's a good sign. What's he saying?'

'Hang on. It's a name... Eimear. He's saying Eimear.'

'God knows who that is. He's probably got concussion.'

Maddie scanned the shoreline and the land above where a few lights were coming on up the hill.

'Surely we can't be far away now.'

Charlotte held up her phone for the umpteenth time and waved it around.

'Oh my God. I've got a signal! At last.'

Maddie heaved a big sigh of relief.

The voice of an operator asked for the details of their emergency.

'Char, tell them we have a head injury and possible concussion on board. And also, we'd really appreciate an escort back to the old harbour, as we have no idea where we're going or how much petrol's left.'

She'd kept that particular fear to herself. She had no idea where Thanassis stored his petrol, and they were in no position to search for it. The thought of running out in the middle of the sea at night didn't bear thinking about.

Charlotte's voice on the phone was back to its usual efficient self.

Five minutes later, with the sun going down in a blaze of glory in front of them, the lights of a coastguard vessel flickered on the water and a boat steamed towards them.

The male voice on the Tannoy was loud and clear.

'We have you. You're safe and only two minutes away from the port. Please, follow us.'

Maddie thought her eyes were deceiving her, because as she rounded the harbour wall, it looked like a whole throng of people were waiting on the pathway. The most welcome sight was the waiting ambulance and the blue-suited paramedics on the dock.

She steered the boat towards the gap between two similar vessels and cut the engine.

It took some major concentration to nose the boat into the space, but the moment she did, a huge cheer went up and the crowd surged forward. As her eyes adjusted to the gloom,

Maddie realised there were also several policemen holding people back. They must have interrupted some sort of major celebration in the town, maybe a wedding or a birthday party.

Two men came through the cordon, grabbed the ropes to secure the boat and unfolded the gangway to allow the paramedics to board.

One of paramedics was speaking, although it was hard to hear what he was saying above all the noise.

'Can you stay where you are please, until we have removed the patient from the boat.'

The three of them stayed still and silent as Thanassis was carefully taken off the vessel on a stretcher and placed in the back of the ambulance.

Maddie couldn't stop herself giving him a little wave as he was carried away. She hoped they'd given him a fighting chance.

A policeman helped each of them off the boat in turn, as the crowd's clapping and cheering got louder and louder.

Maddie could barely keep upright after being in one position for so long, and she ached in places she didn't know she had, plus the noise was overwhelming. She just wanted to climb into a very hot shower.

'What on earth is happening?' she asked the policeman in a shaky voice.

The young man waved his hand encompassing the crowd.

'It is for you. They are clapping for you. All of you. Thanassis is well loved on the island, and you three have saved his life.'

It was too much. They'd just done their best to help. They'd done what anyone would have done in the circumstances. Saving this man was a good thing, but she hadn't been able to save the man she loved. The memory of holding Tony in her arms and giving him CPR on the kitchen floor waiting for an ambulance was one she'd never be able to erase. She'd failed at the biggest test she'd ever faced, and the last thing she wanted was to be hailed a heroine now. The flashes of phone cameras left her dazed for a moment.

She turned back towards her friends, who looked as shellshocked as she felt. Sofia and Charlotte moved forward to link arms with her on either side.

'Ow.'

The muscles in her arms that had held the engine steady and absorbed all the stress screamed in pain.

'OK?' Sofia whispered in her ear.

'Fine, just need to get out of here.'

'Agreed. All for one…'

'And one for all,' Charlotte finished the sentence.

Beside the ambulance, the smiling faces of Theo and Thea swam into view in front of their vehicle stamped with the hotel's name.

Maddie fought back tears for the first time since she'd seen Thanassis fall into the boat. The peace and quiet of the hotel on the hill had never been more desirable.

'Can we just go, please?'

Thea took her hand.

'Of course.'

Before the ambulance doors closed on Thanassis's inert body, Maddie caught a glimpse of a young woman with rich auburn hair, sitting holding Thanassis's hand, tears streaming down her face.

As if she could feel someone looking, the woman raised her eyes and stared back at her for a moment. Maddie shivered in the warm air at the expression on the woman's face. It was as though she'd just seen a ghost.

Chapter Fifteen

A steaming hot shower and a couple of painkillers washed down with a double brandy had made Maddie feel a tiny bit more human.

The three of them were now closeted together in Theo and Thea's private living room at the back of the hotel, away from the prying eyes of the other guests, who'd obviously heard about the dramatic rescue at sea, judging by the lowered voices earlier on their way through reception.

Thea seemed to understand without being told that none of them wanted to answer any questions tonight, for which Maddie was very grateful.

The hotel owner's gentle face with its sweet smile appeared in the doorway as if Maddie had conjured her up.

'Do any of you want something to eat? We have some *moussaka* in the kitchen which I made earlier, but there is far too much for us to manage alone.'

Maddie would bet money that Thea had put an extra-large

portion in to warm as soon as the coastguard had told them their guests were on their way back to the harbour. But who was she to argue with the Greek obsession with feeding people in every single situation, good or bad? She was happy to eat in almost every imaginable mood herself.

'That sounds lovely, Thea, if it's not too much trouble. I'd love some.'

Thea's eyes lit up.

'There are also *horta*, greens, to go with it.'

'Count me in.'

Thea looked around at the others.

'Anyone else?'

Charlotte came out of her own daze.

'No, thank you, Thea.'

Sofia was stood at the fireplace, studying the many black-and-white family photos on the walls.

'Nothing for me either, thanks.'

As soon as Thea had left the room, Sofia took the seat next to Maddie.

'I'm not even going to ask how you can eat at a time like this.'

'It sounds yummy.'

Charlotte lowered her voice.

'You do know that *horta* are those wild greens they pick themselves up in the hills, boil and then serve cold doused in olive oil?'

'You're talking as if they were poisonous.'

Maddie was pleased that Charlotte's attention to detail was back in force after her wobble on the beach.

'Not exactly poisonous. Just weird and slimy.'

Thea's return with the food silenced Charlotte. Maddie attempted to get up out of her chair and reach the little table where the couple obviously ate their meals, but Thea shook her head.

'No, no, sit. I have brought you everything on a tray.'

'You shouldn't have, really.'

The smell coming off the individual pot of Greece's national dish was enough to send Maddie's senses into overload. There were glasses of both red wine and water on the tray and even a small vase with a couple of pink flowers.

'What a feast, thank you.'

As soon as Thea had left the room, Maddie broke the bechamel crust on the top of the dish with her fork to get to the aubergines and rich tomato-based mince beneath, and moaned with delight as the first mouthful hit home.

'You're missing out here, girls. You'll have to wait until breakfast now.'

Sofia sighed.

'It does smell nice, I'll admit.'

'Here, have a taste.' Maddie offered the next mouthful to her friend, who swallowed it with gusto.

'That is delicious.'

'Char?'

Her friend's horrified glance at the communal fork was answer aplenty. Maddie ate in silence, offering Sofia the odd mouthful and alternating the deep meaty taste of the *moussaka* with the tang of the iron-rich *horta*, a winning combination in her eyes, despite Charlotte turning her nose up.

After finishing the wine, Maddie sat back in the chair and closed her eyes for a moment. What a day!

Charlotte nudged Sofia, who was head down in an album of photos, seemingly stuck on a page of what looked like young Greek farmers working bare-chested in the fields. She indicated at Maddie.

'She's drifted off…'

'Not surprised. She deserves to sleep. Although we'd better get that tray off her before everything crashes to the floor.'

Sofia attempted to remove the tray, but Maddie called out and held on to it even tighter.

'OK, leave her a moment.'

The sight of a sleeping Maddie holding on for dear life to the tray almost moved Sofia to tears. Her voice cracked as she stroked her friend's hand.

'She was amazing today, wasn't she? Absolutely fantastic. The way she just got on with it and told us exactly what to do. So brave.'

Charlotte's lip wobbled too.

'I think if it was just us two, we'd probably still be stranded on that beach. And Thanassis would be one hell of a lot worse off.'

'Yeah, for sure. But we don't want to give her too big a head, do we?'

Sofia leaned in closer.

'Just testing to see if she's really awake,' she mouthed.

A loud snore rattled the glasses on the tray and erased any doubt.

Charlotte yawned.

'We should all get some sleep. But we can't leave her here like this.'

'Agreed. I'll grab the tray, and you pull her up.'

At a very late breakfast the following day, Thea informed them that Thanassis was doing well. He was being kept in hospital for twenty-four hours for observation, but the wound to his head was only superficial and he was expected to make a full recovery.

Thea crossed herself as she told them the good news and banged her fist on her chest. The man was obviously wildly popular on the island, as evidenced by the waiting crowd.

Something floated to the front of Maddie's mind.

'Who was the woman in the ambulance with him?'

'Ah, that's his daughter, Georgia. She's a good girl. She will look after him. She's leaving the kids with her husband and staying at his place until he is better.'

'I'm glad he's got someone there for him.'

Maddie stopped short of asking whether he was married. It would look like nosiness on her part. It didn't sound like he was, but maybe his wife was out at work all day.

As soon as the coffees arrived, Sofia took out her phone.

'I've found something fun we can do today.'

'What is it?'

Sofia smarted at the unnecessarily wary tone in Maddie's voice. She'd seen the look that passed between her and Charlotte, but she let it go. She'd show them she was perfectly capable of organising something that didn't involve shopping or luxury hotels.

'I'm driving you two to this amazing restaurant at the very tip of the island for lunch. It's in the middle of nowhere and it has amazing reviews. Apparently, it's totally out there and the owner is a real character.'

'I'm driving', 'middle of nowhere' and 'out there' were the three phrases that stuck in Maddie's head for all the wrong reasons, and she could tell by Charlotte's rapid breathing she felt the same. But maybe hanging around the town would only keep bringing back what had happened the night before, plus she had no desire to keep bumping into people who wanted to thank her for saving Thanassis's life. It would all die down pretty quickly, so maybe an away day was a good idea.

'OK.'

'OK?' Sofia frowned. 'It would be nice if you were both a bit more enthusiastic. I thought Char might like a break from all the organising.'

Sofia's pout reminded Maddie of Elsie, her granddaughter, when she was refused sweets. Not that she'd seen that cute little pout much recently. But that way madness lay.

Charlotte reached for another cherry from the bowl on the table.

'Thank you for the thought, Sof.'

'I'll need you to navigate, please. It's supposed to be pretty hairy to get to.'

Charlotte exchanged a worried look with Maddie while Sofia spooned sugar into her coffee. But they both knew it was a done deal.

'I know what you're doing above my head. You should both lighten up.'

For the first hour, the road up into the hills and down the other side had them all commenting on the cute houses with the pastel paintwork, the inviting cafés with tables outside under coloured parasols and the variety of animals in the fields.

'I just spotted another horse.' Sofia turned her head. 'Look, over there.'

Charlotte coughed loudly.

'Can you maybe keep your eyes on the road, Sof? Just saying.'

'I'm perfectly capable of driving and sightseeing.'

'Right.'

'Are you disputing that?'

'No. Right! The turning on the right.'

Sofia swung into the turning on the wrong side of the road with the brakes screaming.

'You weren't making it clear.'

Charlotte just stared straight ahead.

Another ten minutes on and the road had started to hug the coast and narrowed to a single track with passing places. The turquoise water on their left was some sort of inlet, and only a strip of shrub and rocks separated them from the edge of the road and the sea. If anything came the other way, they'd be in big trouble, thought Maddie. She wasn't convinced about Sofia's reversing skills so close to the water.

Sofia seemed a trifle nervous herself.

'Are you sure this is right?'

Charlotte shrugged.

'My map reading's certainly right. This is the way it says. You're the one who "*organised*" it.'

'OK, let's carry on for a bit.'

Maddie kept quiet and let the others fight it out.

She could see that the tarmacked section they'd travelled on thus far was about to run out completely, and that there was a stark line where it turned into a track.

Charlotte pointed through the windscreen.

'Are we still carrying on? That just looks like piles of stones on top of each other.'

Sofia leant over the steering wheel to follow where Charlotte was pointing.

'I'm sure it's fine.'

'If you've got a four by four.'

'Stop moaning.'

Sofia's attention was caught by something at the side of the road. She brought the car to a sudden stop which had Maddie's forehead positioned inches from Charlotte's headrest.

'What the hell, Sof?'

'Sorry. Look. Someone get their phone out! That goat looks like it's standing on the other one's back.'

Maddie stared hard out of the window and tried to supress a giggle.

'It really does.'

Charlotte pressed the button to wind down her window and snapped away.

'Of course, it's an optical illusion. The first one is standing on a rock.'

'Durr. Yes, we know.' Sofia took another look.

'But it is funny, isn't it. I can see you're laughing, Char, don't deny it. Your shoulders are giving you away.'

The acrobatic goat antics had broken the tension in the car more effectively than any words possibly could, thought Maddie with relief.

'Are we close now?'

'It says five minutes on the sat nav, but...' Charlotte eyed Sofia. 'It's all on that unmade road.'

'Hold on to your hats then. I'll go slowly.'

The bump down onto the unpaved road was a dramatic change in comfort levels, and Maddie listened with concern at the car's engine protesting as Sofia attempted to avoid the worst bits.

'Nearly there!'

A funny old shack finally appeared at the end of the track, bereft of cars or any sign of life.

'So, this is it?' Charlotte raised her eyebrows. 'This is the cool restaurant we've been looking for?'

Sofia pulled into an unkempt parking area at the side, which appeared to have several parts of old tractors as decoration.

'Don't judge a book by its cover.'

Charlotte snorted.

'We're talking *Misery* I presume? Or maybe *Silence of the Lamb Chops*?'

'Funny.'

The three of them got out of the car and walked round to the back of the property, which appeared as deserted as the rest.

Discarded lobster pots and fishing rods were leant up

against the roughly painted blue walls, and a steep flight of stairs led to an upper floor with a few rusty windows and a roof that had seen better days.

Charlotte indicated up the stairs.

'I don't think they'll be giving The River Café cause for concern any time soon.'

'I don't even know what or where that is'—Maddie put her foot on the first stair—'but you have to admit Sof, it looks pretty dead.'

Sofia raced past them both and got to the door first.

'Where's your spirit of adventure, Mads?'

'Left behind on a deserted beach for the time being.'

As soon as she reached the top of the stairs, Sofia knocked on the door and tried to peer in through the cloudy pane of glass at the top.

'There's someone in there. I'm sure of it.'

Charlotte tucked herself in behind Maddie.

'Make sure they haven't got a knife in their hand.'

'Don't be ridiculous. It's got a whole heap of five-star reviews. The only reason someone would have a knife in their hand is if they were preparing a feast.'

Sofia tried the door handle.

'It's unlocked. Let's go in.'

Maddie turned to Charlotte.

'We'd better give her some back-up.'

'We're not in a cop movie.'

'No, but we don't know what we're going to find.'

Sofia pushed gently against the door, which creaked open to reveal an extremely old lady dressed in black sitting in a rocking chair by a large fireplace.

Charlotte's scream was loud enough to alert the neighbours if there had been any.

'Is she dead?'

Sofia shook her head but didn't immediately cross the threshold.

'I don't think so, but I suppose we'd better find out either way. We might have to call the police.'

Holding hands, the three of them advanced into the large low room towards the inert woman.

'Hello, *yassas*!'

Sofia's call produced little reaction from the woman. They edged closer inch by inch. When they were almost within touching distance, a noise behind Charlotte made all three of them gasp.

An aproned middle-aged woman with a knife in her hand and a fierce glare stood there watching them.

'What the hell are you doing to my mother?'

Sofia recovered her voice first.

'Nothing, honestly. We've done nothing to her.'

Charlotte reached out a hand to touch the sleeve of the woman's cardigan.

'We were just a bit worried that she might be ... dead.'

'Dead?' The woman's rich laugh ricocheted around the room.

'That is funny. She certainly sleeps like the dead. My mother is ninety this year, but I can assure you she is very much alive.'

The elderly woman's head suddenly jerked up at the noise of her daughter laughing. She stared in horror at the three women ranged in a semi-circle around her, before her daughter stepped in front of Sofia.

'She doesn't speak any English, and she can't see that well. *Entaxéi, Mamá*. Everything is OK.'

The younger woman slapped her thigh with one hand, the knife still in the other.

'*Nómizan óti ísoun nekrós, Mamá*. They thought you were dead!'

The old woman gave them all the once-over and started to cackle, echoing her daughter. Her cheery face had Sofia joining in, followed swiftly by the others. For a long moment, the five women laughed together, great belly laughs, which left them all gasping for breath.

'I'm sorry...' Sofia stroked the old woman's arm. 'We're all sorry. We made a mistake.'

The old woman looked up at her daughter in confusion.

'*Lypoúntai, Mamá*. They are sorry.'

A smile broke out on the older woman's face, and she pointed to her chest.

'*Eímai Anastasia*.'

Charlotte pointed at her own chest.

'*Eímai* Charlotte; *eínai* Sofia and Maddie.'

The old woman smiled again, and held out her hand to her daughter, who rushed to her side and kissed her on the top of the head.

'And I'm Daphne. Pleased to meet you. Have you come here to eat?'

Sofia stepped forward.

'Yes, that was the idea. Is it possible? I don't think you take reservations, do you?'

Daphne waved the idea away with her hand.

'No, none of that nonsense. And there's no menu. You get what I'm cooking for my mother, my husband and me.'

'OK, sounds lovely.'

Sofia wouldn't have dared argue at this point. Daphne pointed to somewhere at the other end of the room.

'Go and sit on the balcony and I will bring you all wine.'

Ducking behind the huge fireplace, which was virtually the width of the room, Charlotte was amazed to see a whole wall of windows at the end of the space, not visible from what they'd assumed was the car park, which let the light flood through. The view was straight out onto the water and beyond.

A covered balcony, accessed through huge French doors, boasted four solid wood tables and chairs painted a vibrant blue. From where they were, the balcony appeared to be suspended in mid-air.

'Wow, look at this.'

The three of them walked onto the whitewashed decking of the balcony and made straight for the railings, eager to take in more of the view. To the left were the tree-studded hills on the other side of the inlet and a few boats, and beneath them was water so clear they could see individual stones and fronds of greenery.

Sofia pointed to the right and covered a laugh with her hand.

The others clocked the sturdy flight of stairs up to the balcony and beyond it a paved area with a solitary truck parked.

Maddie burst out laughing too.

'So that's where we were supposed to come up to the restaurant, from the dockside. Not through their living room, invading their privacy and terrifying Anastasia with our screaming?'

Charlotte smiled.

'That's about the size of it.'

Daphne appeared on the balcony with a tray and indicated that they should sit at the table at the very front, the best seat in the house.

'White wine, homemade bread and *taramasaláta* like you will never have tasted it in England. None of your bright pink stuff, full of dangerous food dye.'

Daphne made an *'I'm about to vomit if I think about it anymore'* face.

'Proper Greek *taramasaláta* is white, not pink.'

With that, she turned on her heel, earning a salute from Sofia.

'We've been told. Tuck in.'

The tangy dip combined with the homemade bread rapidly vanished.

Charlotte kept a close eye on Sofia's wine intake, as they still had the return journey to endure.

A giant grilled squid on a platter followed the dip, served with a simple Greek salad and a lemon and butter sauce.

Daphne pointed downwards.

'It was swimming there just a few hours ago. My husband is a fisherman, so I know everything is the best, otherwise he would throw it back.'

Maddie idly wondered if he knew Thanassis, but she didn't want to out the three of them as the lifesaving crew, so she kept quiet.

Just as she was thinking she couldn't possibly eat another

thing, a big pot arrived and its lid was removed with a flourish.

'And this ... is my famous chicken and herb dish with potatoes.'

'Bloody hell.' Sofia patted her stomach as soon as Daphne had disappeared. 'I'm so full already I can hardly move. I wish I hadn't eaten so much of that fabulous bread.'

'Even I'm struggling,' Maddie sighed.

'I feel like Dawn French in that Vicar of Dibley episode where she had to eat four Christmas dinners.' Charlotte got up and walked around for a few moments before coming back and staring at the food. 'It does looks gorgeous though. You know we're going to have to eat it, right?'

The others nodded.

Charlotte dished out equal portions with more wine and water and issued the command.

'Three, two, one... The last one to finish pays.'

Sofia took a large gulp of the wine.

'Soooo unfair, it's always me.'

Ten minutes later and task completed, Sofia laid her head on the table.

'I feel like one of those geese fattened up to make foie gras. Please tell me it's over.'

Charlotte patted her friend on the back.

'Sit up, she's back.'

'Here is your dessert!'

Sofia barely managed to hold in the groan as Daphne held aloft a large cake.

'This is *melópita*, Greek honey cake, made with ricotta. It is from Sifnos, the island where I was born. I came to this island for love.' Daphne hit her chest with her fist. 'But this is my home in a cake. Please enjoy.'

After Daphne closed the balcony door, Sofia looked from one to the other.

'I'm sure it's wonderful, but I seriously can't.'

Charlotte nodded.

'I don't think I can either.'

Maddie felt all eyes on her.

'You're not seriously expecting me to eat a whole cake, are you?'

Sofia put up her hands.

'Well…'

'Don't be ridiculous. Even I'm not attempting that. Now, who has the biggest bag?'

Charlotte's confused look made Maddie want to laugh.

'Me, why?'

'Everyone's going to eat a tiny slice, to leave some crumbs, then we wrap the rest in serviettes and smuggle it out in the bag.'

Charlotte looked at her precious bag and back at the cake.

'I suppose it would work.'

'It has to, unless you're volunteering to stuff that lot down.'

'No way.'

Safely back in the car with the cake stowed in the boot, Maddie gave both her friends a pat on the shoulder from the back seat.

The previous day had really taken it out of her. To be so close to losing Thanassis had been terrifying. She didn't even want to think what sort of state she'd be in if he hadn't made it. It would have been the end of her holiday, for sure. After what she'd been through with Tony, there was no way she'd be able to smile and carry on if the man had died. Today's trip, complete with its bickering, laughs and yet another stomach-bursting meal, had been the perfect way to ride out the aftershock.

'Today certainly took my mind off yesterday's drama. Thanks, girls.'

Chapter Sixteen

After an early night followed by a day of luxury on the posh sunbeds at the out-of-town white-sand beach, Charlotte was back in charge as activity leader, much to Maddie's relief.

Thea had informed them at breakfast that Thanassis was now out of hospital and recovering well back at home, which was reassuring. Maddie just hoped the whole episode was over and done with and they could enjoy their last couple of days on the island without any more attention from the locals before they moved on to their final destination, the island where Sofia's friend Grace lived.

Tonight, they were off to a *panigýri*, a traditional celebration with simple food and wine, according to Charlotte, which raised money for village activities and was usually linked to the church. They'd been warned to only bring cash.

It was right up in the hills, and they'd convinced Sofia not to drive, so she could enjoy herself, although it was as much for their benefit as hers. Country roads in the dark with Sofia at the wheel really didn't appeal so taxis both ways had been booked.

Currently crowded together in Charlotte's bedroom, they only had ten more minutes to decide what to wear before it was time to go. Sofia had insisted that Maddie and Charlotte each pick two potential dresses, and she'd make the final decision on what they'd be wearing.

Maddie had pulled her sensible navy linen shift dress from the wardrobe, and at the last moment added a hot-pink number with tiny shoestring straps as the second option. It clashed horribly with her red hair, although she'd read in a fashion mag in the hairdressers that clashing was a good thing.

She was slated to go last, and Sofia had already changed into a red mini dress and matching heels, which of course they'd had no say over. Charlotte was in a slinky silver number that the queen of fashion had deemed the winner from the two choices on offer. The dress could be mistaken for a nightie in the wrong light thought Maddie, but she had to admit it looked great on her friend.

'Come out, come out!'

Sofia's voice was loud even inside the bathroom. Maddie smoothed down the navy shift dress and prepared to step back into the room. Dressing up really wasn't her thing. She was happiest in jeans and a t-shirt, and for work she had a series of drip-dry lilac tunics and matching trousers, so she never even had to think about what to wear in the mornings. The pink dress was definitely the odd one out in her meagre wardrobe of dark colours, the showgirl in a room full of office workers. She'd picked it up on a whim in her local charity shop, with the tags still on. She wasn't sure she'd ever find the right occasion to wear it.

Sofia's reaction to the navy dress was muted to say the least.

'Mmmm. I suppose we *could* dress it up with some funky jewellery and shoes, but frankly it's a bit school parents' evening or applying for a bank loan, isn't it?'

'Charming. Not that you've probably experienced either.'

'Try the other one on.'

'Yes, Ma'am.'

Back in the safety of the bathroom, the chiffon fabric of the pink dress felt soft against her skin when she put it over her head, but the small mirror above the sink only allowed her to see down to her shoulders, so she had absolutely no idea if it suited her.

'Are you coming out?'

'Yes, stop going on.'

Sofia's face had a very different expression this time round.

'Wow! That is stunning. You look gorgeous, good enough to eat. That's what you're wearing. And no arguments.'

Maddie caught sight of herself in the full-length mirror and had to look away and look again.

The dress was absurdly flattering; it hugged her in all the right places and skimmed over the awkward bits. Instead of clashing with her hair, it made a feature of it, and for once she didn't want to apologise for being born with bright red curly hair. She could appreciate her lightly tanned skin also added nicely to the effect. She didn't look like herself at all.

Charlotte made a good attempt at a wolf whistle.

'That is definitely the one, lovely.'

'Wait.'

Sofia ran out of the door but was back in seconds with some low-heeled gold sandals, and a long gold chain.

'Try these with it.'

Maddie had to agree that it all went perfectly together.

'Thanks, Sof. You've done a great job.'

Her friend blew her a kiss.

'Just making the best use of the utterly fabulous raw materials.'

A message pinged on Sofia's phone.

'Taxi's here. No changing our minds now.'

The winding road to the top of the hill made Maddie very glad they'd insisted Sofia didn't drive. The twists and blind corners were still hair-raising, even more so as the driver chatted on his phone the whole time with only one hand on the wheel, but at least she was confident he knew the roads.

He finally pulled into a layby before a narrow road that led up to the church and beyond. Groups of people on foot were making their way up the final hill in the dark, using their phones as torches, and talking and laughing loudly.

'This is as far as I can take you. You must walk from here. Too many people.'

Sofia handed over the cash and the three of them joined the back of the crowd. The atmosphere was friendly, people nodded and smiled at them, but the only voices she could hear were Greek. The idea that they were having an *'authentic experience'* would please Charlotte.

At the top of the hill, people streamed past them into the venue, while they stood and took it all in. A vast outdoor stone terrace was set with long tables and benches, around a stage with a live band. Strings of lights in the trees round the edges illuminated the scene with ease. In front of the stage was an empty space which Maddie presumed would be for dancing. The noise level was already high, as friends and family greeted each other with extravagant hugs and kisses and nabbed a table as their own.

'What do we do?' Sofia looked at Charlotte.

A man approached them before she could reply and pointed them in the direction of a series of long tables to one side.

'*Eíste Anglídes?* Are you English?'

They all nodded furiously.

'It is simple. You line up here for your food and drink and then sit wherever you like.'

'Thank you.' Charlotte took charge as he walked off to greet a new arrival. 'I did know that though.'

'Of course.' Maddie smiled at Sofia as they joined the end of the queue.

A whole army of women in aprons stood behind big bowls of Greek salad, huge chunks of bread and vast metal vats of a meat that Charlotte couldn't quite identify, next to yet more vats of home-made chips.

She pointed at one of the vats of meat and tried out her very basic Greek.

'*Ti eínai aftó?*'

'*Katsíki*' was the reply, which didn't help her a whole lot.

The woman's neighbour nudged her in the side.

'Goat. It is goat.'

Charlotte turned to the others with a grimace.

'It seems to be all there is.'

The memory of the cute goats at the cheese farm was uppermost in her mind. She'd looked at the photos she'd taken many times to study the animals' movements in possible preparation for a series of oil paintings when she got back home. Every single face was different, and they all had their own distinctive markings. How could she possibly eat one?

Maddie smiled at the woman serving and then back at Charlotte.

'It's fine. It's not as if any of us is vegetarian. You wanted the real thing. It doesn't get much more real than this.'

They watched the person beside them in the queue, who was handed a disposable plate with a hefty portion of everything on it, except the meat. Then the man proceeded to point at a particular piece of goat's meat, which was weighed on a scale, wrapped in a piece of greaseproof paper with an amount in euros written on it, and passed along.

After picking out their meat, tiny amounts for Sofia and Charlotte, and a nice big chunk on the bone for Maddie, they moved along to the drinks station, which was manned solely by men, who'd been completely absent from the food stations. Whichever way you looked at it, and particularly for their age group, Greece was still a patriarchal society, but they weren't here for a political debate.

'*Krasí, býra í neró?*'

They'd all learnt the basics for wine, beer and water by now, and opted for white wine and water, which was handed over in big plastic bottles.

'Surely we won't drink all this ourselves?' Charlotte gripped her bottle of wine like it was a dangerous weapon.

Maddie smiled at her friend.

'Never say never.'

They'd reached the end of the line where two men stood with a tin full of cash. The total was nothing compared to a meal in a restaurant.

'The villagers provide all the food and drink themselves, donating their own animals and salad ingredients, so that every penny goes to the community,' Charlotte piped up as Sofia handed over the joint money.

Maddie clamped the bottle of water under her arm as both hands were full.

'Yes, you've told us that already.'

'So sorry if I'm overloading you with information.'

Maddie bumped shoulders with her friend.

'Don't get on your high horse. We love your facts. Now, where shall we sit?'

Sofia had already made straight for a table that consisted mainly of men under the age of forty. One of them immediately budged up to make room for her, and Maddie and Charlotte slotted in on the other side.

The serious business of eating and drinking stopped any conversation for a while and Maddie noted that even Charlotte had finished every bit of her tasty goat.

Gentle music floated through the night air as the plates were cleared from the tables by the aproned women, and people showed their appreciation for the food by clapping and cheering.

The three of them hollered along with the rest.

Sofia nodded at the bottles on the table.

'Pour the wine, Char. We've still got two bottles to get through.'

Charlotte filled up two paper cups with wine but only put water in her own cup. She didn't want a repeat of Sickgate in Thea's lovely hotel. Drinking so much that night had taken her somewhere she wasn't quite ready to go. The time for action was getting closer, and the need to make decisions was hurtling towards her like an oncoming storm. Telling her friends exactly what was wrong wasn't an option until she allowed herself to fully examine how she felt. She either needed to make friends with the gremlin sitting on her shoulder or push it off. The thought of Doug as a gremlin made her smile for a moment.

'Char, watch out! It's going all over the table.'

Sofia's voice pulled her back to the present. Her friend grabbed the first cup of wine and swigged it down, demanding an instant refill seconds later, which went the same way.

'Wouldn't it be easier to drink it straight from the bottle?'

Sofia stuck out her tongue.

'You're not on the wine express yourself then?'

She'd asked for that. Charlotte stuck out her own tongue.

'No, I'm not planning on decorating my hotel room with a goat special tonight.'

Sofia did a thumbs up. They could barely hear each other over the noise.

The band, who'd played a series of low-key numbers to accompany the food, had upped the tempo and were now in full swing, belting it out, fiddles ablaze.

They just sat and watched people tackle the first few

dances, which looked incredibly complicated, although Sofia couldn't stop her body moving in time with the hypnotic beat. It was impossible to keep still as the music pulsed into her over and over again.

Sofia's neighbour got up and held out his hand. She'd found out earlier the group were all doctors, on holiday from Athens, rather than locals, although one of their party had grown up here. He'd introduced himself as Apollo, another god, appropriately named if his physique outlined in black T-shirt and jeans was anything to go by.

'Do you dance?'

'I do, but not well.'

His seriously white teeth made Sofia wonder if he was really a dentist rather than a doctor.

'I can teach you the basics.'

And I can probably teach you a thing or two as well went through Sofia's mind, but she stayed quiet. It had been tricky getting hold of Adonis yet again. There was a big wedding on at the hotel, which he needed to oversee, and he couldn't speak to her until tomorrow. She had to be patient. Geographically speaking, she was getting closer to him. She'd see him again in a couple of days' time.

'*Páme*. Let's go.'

Sofia smiled and waved back at the others as she was pulled onto the dance floor.

Charlotte poured some more wine into both her and Maddie's cups.

'Do you fancy cutting some moves?'

'No, not really. I hate making a fool of myself.'

'Maybe I'll have a go later, when I've drunk a bit more.'

Maddie sat back and enjoyed watching the handsome young man dancing with her friend. There was lots of touching and laughter as he showed Sofia what to do. The dance involved a sort of conga line which wrapped round and got faster and faster in time with the music. As it reached its crescendo and the music faded out, the people dispersed.

Sofia returned to the table, laughing and breathless.

When the last person left the dance floor, Maddie caught the eye of a man sitting on the opposite side of the terrace and gasped.

Without breaking eye contact, he got up and moved slowly towards her. As he reached their table he smiled his slow smile, a small plaster on the side of his head the only sign anything had been wrong.

He put out his hand and bowed low.

'Will you dance with me?'

Her first instinct was to say no. But Maddie realised she very much wanted to.

'Yes, thank you.'

As she got to her feet, the tempo of the music changed yet again, and several couples made their way onto the dance floor. It was no fast wiggle this time, it was a slow dance number, not what she would have chosen at all. Her heart banged in her chest, but she couldn't really back out now.

Thanassis held her close, and her body gradually relaxed against his, as the music made its way through her from her feet upwards and she gave in to the sensuous beat.

Maddie closed her eyes for a moment, the woody smell of his aftershave flooding her senses. The guilt fell away briefly. It was nice to be in a man's arms again. Not the man that she would have wished for, but Thanassis was a more than adequate substitute.

His hot breath was in her ear, their faces an inch apart.

'I did not dream you would be here. I was coming to see you tomorrow anyway, at the hotel, to say thank you.'

'There's really no need.'

Thanassis pulled his head back a moment and looked at her with the blue eyes that seemed capable of seeing into her soul.

'Of course there is a need. You saved my life.'

'Hardly.'

He pulled her in even closer.

'Don't be modest. You were very brave.'

The heat between them was undeniable. Even Maddie could remember what chemistry looked like. Or more importantly felt like. And it had been a while. The bare skin at the vee of his open linen shirt touched her shoulder a moment as he moved against her, and she held in a sigh.

Around them, outside their little bubble, she became aware that people had started to murmur, and the noise was increasing by the second. Over Thanassis's shoulder, she glimpsed the disapproving face of his daughter in the crowd, her set mouth saying more than words ever could.

She pulled back out of his arms.

'What is it?'

Thanassis looked around him.

'Ah, I see, people have put two and two together. They know it is you, my saviour.'

A slow clap reverberated around the space, taken up table by table, which sent a shiver down Maddie's spine.

'I'm really not comfortable with this.'

'No, I understand. I will take you back to your friends.' He leaned into her one last time, his breath soft in her ear this time. 'But before I do, my daughter goes back to her own home tomorrow, thank goodness, and I am a free man again. Will you let me take you out, just the two of us?'

Her head was all over the place, never mind her body.

'I'm not sure that would be a good idea.'

His bright blue eyes fixed her to the spot.

'Do you trust me?'

Without thinking too hard, she nodded.

'Then I will call at the hotel for you tomorrow afternoon around five. Wear your swimming stuff.'

As he handed her back to her friends, a huge cheer broke out, ringing in the night air. Maddie acknowledged the crowd with a bow, but her head swam as she sat down hard on the bench.

Sofia put her hand out to steady her friend. They needed to get out of there. Maddie had been pushed to her limits already and Charlotte wasn't going to get her dance tonight.

'The taxi is waiting at the bottom of the hill. Let's go.'

Chapter Seventeen

Sofia decided not to mention Thanassis and the smoochy dance straightaway at breakfast. Maddie had only just arrived. She and Charlotte would let her have something to eat first. Her friend hated having her hand forced, and she'd tell them what had happened in her own time. Obviously, they needed – and deserved – a full debrief, but the direct approach wasn't the right one here.

A slightly jaded-looking Maddie joined them both by the cake of the day and moved a big slice onto her plate.

'Morning.'

Sofia took a deep breath.

'And a very good morning to you too. It's another lovely sunny day.'

Maddie gave her a puzzled look.

'Okaay. Have you been overdosing on HRT on something?'

'Rude. I'm just thrilled that we're all here on holiday together, enjoying ourselves and exploring the local attractions.'

Sofia tried very hard not to emphasise the words *enjoying* and *exploring*.

'Sof, if you want to know something, just ask. Don't give me the tour guide bullshit.'

She'd obviously blown it, so she might as well go for bust.

'OK, did you enjoy dancing with Thanassis? Did you kiss him? And when are you seeing him again?'

Charlotte had stopped spooning yoghurt and fruit into her bowl to listen as well.

Maddie did a double take.

'Woah. Calm down. Can I at least get a coffee first?'

Sofia stopped tapping her foot on the floor.

'Suppose so.'

Caffeine-d up, Maddie was more willing to talk, and her audience of two were chomping at the bit to listen.

'So, to answer your questions, yes, I did enjoy dancing with Thanassis. No, I didn't kiss him. And yes, we are going out late afternoon for a thank-you drink.'

Sofia made with the big eyes.

'Just the two of you?'

'Yes, just the two of us. You're not suggesting you come along to watch, are you?'

'No! I'm not that desperate for "male attention".'

Although if Adonis failed to ring tonight, she'd consider axing him for good.

Maddie took another sip of her coffee.

'If you say so…'

Sofia went to put another spoonful of sugar in her coffee, most of which went on the table.

'But if you're going to be whisked away later…'

'I didn't say whisked away; those are your words... It's just a drink between friends.'

'Whatever. But it means we need to do something fun together this morning before you abandon us.'

Charlotte spoke before Maddie could fire back.

'No one is abandoning anyone. It's lovely that Mads and Thanassis are getting the chance for a quiet drink away from prying eyes. There's a lot to process after the accident.'

'Thank you, Char.'

'Why don't we head out to the town in the hills with the marble streets? I wanted to see it before we left anyway. There's a circular route where you walk from a historic village with some ancient ruins to the town and back. We can stop for lunch on the way and it's only around six kilometres in total.'

Sofia and Charlotte looked over at Maddie with raised eyebrows. Charlotte had noticed that Maddie kept up with them a lot more easily now. There was none of the panting, and not nearly as much of the moaning as there'd been on the first island.

'Only six kilometres?'

'It's nothing, honestly. And she'—Charlotte pointed at Sofia—'needs to use up some of that excess energy. What's been wrong with you the last couple of days? You can barely keep still. Restless isn't the word.'

'You know it's rude to point.' Sofia threw down the last of her coffee. 'There's nothing wrong with me.'

'Hmmm. Anyway, meet down here in an hour and bring—'

'Sensible shoes, a hat and a bottle of water.' Sofia's eyes met Maddie's.

'Yes, we know, mum.'

'Don't call me that. It makes me sound old.'

Sofia reached over to stroke Charlotte's arm.

'As if. We love you looking out for us and our potentially wrinkly skin.'

Maddie looked down at her own hands.

'Potentially wrinkly? I think I'm there, big time.'

Sofia leapt up from the table and started walking away.

'No! Never! I won't listen.'

Charlotte made a face behind her friend's departing back and bent down to whisper to Maddie.

'She's in a right tizz. I'll try and find out more later when you're out.'

Maddie replied with a thumbs up, but her mind was elsewhere.

The beauty all around made it easy not to think about how far they still had to walk, and Maddie was grateful for the break it gave her from the thoughts buzzing around her head. The constant butterflies in her stomach weren't helping either. She'd made out to her friends it was just a casual drink with Thanassis, but deep down she knew it was something more. She wasn't quite sure what exactly, but she'd find out in a few hours' time. Not that she was looking for any sort of relationship with the man, but there was a connection there that couldn't be denied. It made her feel she'd agreed to something naughty, which although exciting, was tinged with all sorts of guilt.

'Look at that!'

Sofia pointed skywards.

A brightly coloured bird flew over their heads and settled in one of the trees at the side of the path. There were trees as far as she could see, all the way down to the water far below, a splash of blue in a forest of green interrupted only by the oleander shrubs dotting the hillside with pink and white splodges.

The wild nature of this place was much more her cup of tea than the barren hills and stark landscapes of the previous island, beautiful though it had been in its own way.

Charlotte pointed ahead.

'We're nearly there.'

Someone really needed to give the woman a little flag to hold aloft.

A few houses with whitewashed walls and pots of red and pink geraniums on their steps appeared in front of them, but the properties were still very spaced out. Their gardens boasted rows of vegetables and the odd fruit tree, along with plenty of old machinery and even the odd car now and again, rusted right through and used as a chicken coup or a mini greenhouse. While she was admiring the flowers growing in a particularly wrecked model, a feeble cry stopped her in her tracks.

A tiny ginger kitten was stuck under the bottom of a blue painted gate, trapped by its bigger, stronger grey sibling who was holding it down with both paws.

'Get off her, you bully.'

Maddie wasn't sure why she was convinced the little ginger kitten was a girl, but she would have happily put a bet on it.

The grey kitten skittered off into the undergrowth, but his sister stayed where she was on her back, mewling.

'Hey, sweetie, are you OK?'

Her advance towards the kitten was halted by a big tabby that shot out of a bush the other side of the gate and licked the ginger kitten on the head while staring straight at Maddie.

'OK, I've got it, mum. It's easy to do. You take your eye off them for a minute, and they start fighting.'

And if you get it wrong, so wrong there's no way back, one day they might turn on you too.

Slowly, the grey kitten padded towards his sister again, intent on renewing his attack, but this time he received a boff on the nose from his mum for his trouble. Two other kittens, one black and one ginger, crept out from under a bush and attempted to suckle from their mother. After an irritated flick of the tail, the mother accepted her fate, lay down and let the first two have their fill. They were joined straightaway by the warring siblings who took up their positions side by side, agreed on something at last.

Moments later, a sleek ginger cat strolled up to the gate and stood guard over his brood, eyeballing Maddie, who moved back a couple of paces.

The picture of family unity brought tears to her eyes. Her little family had no dad to diffuse arguments or watch over her babies. Not that they were babies anymore, but they had been, once. What was the matter with her? Crying over a few stray cats? The dance with Thanassis at the *panigýri* had forced her to think about what was missing from her life. Something she avoided doing wherever possible.

'Mads?'

Sofia had turned back to see what was up.

Maddie put her finger to her lips.

'Shhhh. Come and see.'

Her friends were as taken with the kittens as she was, and they all watched them feed, fight and play for a good twenty minutes before moving on.

Maddie was just relieved no one had noticed her red eyes.

Charlotte had her phone out again in the name of research.

'There's supposed to be a fantastic ice cream shop just along here. It even has halva as a flavour.'

'What's halva when it's at home?'

Maddie looked at Sofia.

'No, me neither.'

'But I'm up for trying anything that has the words ice cream in it.'

'Agreed. Let's go, or *páme* as they say in Greece!'

A shower and a swift lie down after the walk brought five o'clock ever closer. Dressed in a pink linen shirt and denim shorts, with her hair up in a ponytail, Maddie went down to reception with five minutes to spare. She didn't want it to look like she'd tried too hard. The others were already sitting in the reception area, ostensibly reading magazines.

'Hello? What are you two doing here?'

Sofia made a good show of reluctantly tearing herself away from an article in the magazine.

'Oh, hi. Just relaxing down here rather than in our rooms.'

'Really?'

Maddie snatched up Sofia's reading matter and turned the page, smiling all the way.

'And you're fluent in Greek now, are you? That was quick. You ought to apply to the Guiness Book of Records. Or are you just keen on pictures of celebrities no one in England's ever heard of?'

Sofia attempted to grab back the magazine, but Maddie was too quick for her.

'How long were you planning to keep up this farce?'

Charlotte put down her own magazine and sighed.

'OK, we were worried about you. We just wanted to make sure you were going to be safe on your date.'

'It's not a date! How many times do I need to say it?'

Her voice level had attracted the attention of Thea in reception.

'Everything OK?' she shouted over.

'Fine,' Maddie shouted back, before lowering her voice again.

'I don't know what this thing with Thanassis is. But I wish you two would let me be a grown-up and make my own decisions.'

Sofia got up and pulled Maddie in for a hug.

'Of course you're a grown-up, but we also know that this is the first time you've spent any time alone like this with a man – I'm not calling it a date – since Tony died.' Sofia held up her hands. 'We just want to make sure you enjoy it and are not stressing out about it.'

'Thank you both for your concern, but I'm not stressed … much.'

Her friends really did care, and although they felt like

overprotective maiden aunts at this point, she couldn't imagine being on this journey without them.

The noise of a motorbike pulling up outside put their squabble straight out of her mind as her stomach curled into a knot. The bike sounded just like Tony's. For one insane second, she imagined him walking into the hotel, dark hair all over the place as usual, winning smile in place.

But it was Thanassis, in a red T-shirt and jeans, who appeared in reception, two helmets hooked over his arm. Maddie clocked his bafflement at being confronted with three women rather than just the one he'd come for, but he recovered well, which was a big tick in her book. He approached their group with a blistering smile.

'My three guardian angels, all together. What a lovely surprise!'

Maddie stepped forward and took the helmet he was offering her.

'Don't worry. They're not coming with us.'

'Shame.' His eyes twinkled. 'But we don't have room anyway.'

His attention was solely on her. The others might as well have been invisible. It must be an unusual feeling for Sofia, thought Maddie, as she tried to avoid catching the smell of Thanassis's aftershave again. Not that he was Sofia's type, far too old, but she was always the one out of the three of them who men looked at first.

In a tight long-term friendship, everyone had their assigned roles, and Sofia's was definitely the man magnet. Not a role Maddie or Charlotte had ever craved, but Thanassis obviously hadn't got the memo. His eyes were on her again. It was nice to be appreciated, but it wasn't going anywhere.

'Are you OK on a motorbike? Have you been on one before?'

'I can honestly say hundreds, if not thousands, of times.'

His relief was palpable.

'Ah good, as it is a lovely way to see some hidden parts of the island. Parts that most tourists never see. And we won't be bothered by anyone wanting to talk to you about what happened.'

'Works for me.'

Maddie blew a kiss back to her friends as Thanassis linked arms with her.

'Goodbye, angels. Be good, and don't wait up.'

Sofia waited until they'd gone out the front door.

'He definitely wants to explore her hidden parts, no matter what she says.'

'Very definitely.'

'Char! That's not like you.'

Charlotte smiled at Sofia's shocked reaction.

'I'm a bit bored of being like me all the time. We could all try swapping personalities for the day tomorrow. I'll make endless raunchy remarks, Maddie can take us on a very long tour of ancient monuments, and you can spend some time communing with the elderly. What do you think?'

Sofia stared at Charlotte open-mouthed. She wasn't sure what to think. She and Maddie still hadn't got to the bottom of what was wrong with their friend after her wobble in the ice cream café a couple of days ago. But this sort of talk was very unlike Charlotte.

For Sofia, knowing with certainty how her schoolmates were going to react in any given situation was a big attraction of the friendship between the three of them, since the rest of her life had so little structure, especially now her job had been snatched away from her.

The idea that cool, calm Charlotte might suddenly become the wild one was disturbing. She'd get onto Maddie tomorrow and make it a priority to get their friend talking. It was definitely a two-woman job.

'Sof?'

'Yes.'

'I'm only kidding. Don't look so worried. Now it's just the two of us, shall we go outside onto the terrace for a drink and a proper chat?'

Sofia's heart sank. She was all too familiar with Charlotte's proper chat technique. It looked like she was going to be put under the microscope first.

'Aperol Spritz?'

'Yes, lovely.'

Seated on the terrace with the view down to the town and the beach beyond bathed in sun, Sofia forced herself to relax and wait for the first question with a semblance of ease.

'Are you looking forward to moving on to the next island?'

At least Charlotte was starting with an easy one.

'Yes, it will be lovely to show you both a place that I've come to know and love.'

'What's it like?'

'A mixture between the two islands we've visited so far. There's a sophisticated main town with loads of bars, restaurants and great shops, but it's also got good beaches and plenty of hiking country.'

'Sounds great.'

This was all a bit too easy. Sofia braced herself for the next one.

'And why did you choose it for us out of the other two hundred and twenty-six inhabited islands you could have picked? Is it because you're desperate to see Adonis again?'

And there it was.

'What? Why are you saying that?'

Charlotte gave her straw a ferocious suck, depleting the level in the glass instantly.

'This one's a bit different, isn't he?'

'I don't know what you mean.'

'I think you do. Tell me a bit about him. We know virtually nothing.'

'Er, OK. He's the manager of a very high-end hotel, which takes up too much of his time. He was born on the island, although he did his degree in hospitality in Athens and Paris.'

'I don't need his CV. What about personal stuff?'

'He has a younger brother and sister and he's an uncle to loads of kids.'

'Better… Has he ever been married?'

'No.'

Sofia finished her drink quickly. She'd need more alcohol to cope with this.

'Another Aperol?'

Charlotte also had an empty glass.

'Yes please, but Theo's in my eyeline so I'll order it. You stay where you are.'

Bang went any opportunity to escape to the bar, even for a moment.

'So, where were we? Ah yes, Adonis. Never married and no kids?'

'No, absolutely not.'

'And exactly how old are we talking?'

'I'm not sure…'

'OK, now you're lying. You might as well tell me, or I'll just look him up later.'

'Where's that drink?'

'Sof…'

'Fine. He's forty-eight.'

'Interesting. That's quite old for you.'

'Rubbish. And it's still a fourteen-year age gap.'

'Does that worry you?'

'What worries me more is that he's so damn hard to get hold of. It would be virtually impossible to have a relationship with a man like him. Not that I'm looking for one, but he's a workaholic.'

Sofia hadn't meant to say any of that out loud. Charlotte had pierced her armour with ease.

Theo put their new drinks down on the table and received a big smile from both of them.

'They've really looked after us well here, haven't they?' Sofia took the first sip. 'I know I was a bit funny about there being no swimming pool at first, but it's been so relaxing.'

'OK, stop changing the subject.'

Sofia sighed. She'd tried a few of the tricks in her arsenal to avoid difficult conversations, but there was no getting away from her friend. Charlotte was wasted as an artist.

'Interesting that you'd like to speak to him more than you do now.'

Sofia held on to the edge of the chair to stop herself fleeing. Why had she handed that piece of ammunition to Charlotte? Bad mistake.

'But I'll leave that for another time. I still need an answer to my previous question. I repeat, does the age gap bother you?'

'Well, it never has before. As you know, I like younger guys. They're fitter, usually a lot more easygoing, and willing to try new things … and I don't just mean in the bedroom.'

Charlotte shook her head.

'No, I get it. While women in their sixties seem to blossom and grow, a lot of men in their sixties, not all, but some, seem to get grumpier, more set in their ways, and one hell of a lot more predictable.'

Sofia could tell that last comment was a lot more personal than general. Maybe this was a way of getting Charlotte to talk about her issues and steering away from her own for a while. She was convinced it was tied up with Doug. But before she could open her mouth, Charlotte waved away the possibility with her hand.

'But we're getting off the subject. So, why do you think the age gap is bothering you this time when it hasn't before?'

'I'm not sure. But I do know I need the loo.'

Surely Charlotte wouldn't follow her in there.

'Wait! Please don't run away, Sof. We'll change the subject in a minute. I'm not trying to interrogate you…'

Not much you aren't. Sofia was up and out of her chair.

'I just think you need to look at why it bothers you this time round. You're very jumpy, and you've just admitted that you get annoyed if Adonis can't talk to you when you want to talk. You're used to calling the shots, and it's not quite working out with this one. Maybe you like him more than you're letting on.'

Sofia had truly had her fill of talking about Adonis. His promised phone call was already late.

'Shall we go into town later for a meal by the port? I don't think we're going to see Maddie again for quite a while.'

Charlotte accepted defeat gracefully.

'Fine. Meet you down here in an hour.'

The moment she got into her room, her phone buzzed with a message.

> Sorry. Can't talk. Major problem. The flowers for the wedding weren't good, so I'm hosting a special dinner tonight for the family at the hotel to apologise. Ax

What did she care about some unknown bride's flowers? Sofia fired off a text of her own.

> Sofia from the other day here. Do you fancy a drink in town later?

> At last! Sounds great. Come to the Corfu Hotel bar any time after nine. Konstantinos x.

She'd give her friends jumpy and restless. And Adonis could swivel on it.

Chapter Eighteen

There wasn't really an alternative to grabbing Thanassis round the waist and hanging on for dear life as he manoeuvred his motorbike round the many bends in the roads on the other side of the island.

It was a position Maddie was more than familiar with after being married to bike fanatic Tony for so many years. She appreciated Thanassis's efforts to take them as far away from her hotel and his home as possible to a place where, hopefully, they wouldn't be recognised. It was just weird being so close to him, feeling the muscles in his back move under her body and inhaling his smell. It was a mix of aftershave and exertion, not sweat exactly, just the smell of a man, a smell she'd not encountered this close up for a long time.

It combined with other, less familiar, scents along the roadside, such as wild garlic, curry plant and now the tang of sea salt, to produce a heady mix. As the bike began its descent, the first glimpse of the sea made her want to scream into the still air. It took her right back to when she was a little girl and the once-a-year trips she took with her mother to stay in a bed-and-breakfast in Blackpool owned by her Aunt Maisie.

They'd go on the bus and whoever saw the sea first would shout the word 'bananas!'. She had no idea why it was bananas; it was just one of those silly family traditions that she shared with her mum. There had only ever been the two of them, her dad had never been in the picture, and although money was always tight, they'd had a lot of fun together.

Leaving her beloved north to spend her secondary school years on the outskirts of London had been a wrench, but her mum couldn't turn down the offer of a better-paid job with free accommodation. And she'd never have met Tony, or indeed Sofia and Charlotte, so it had worked out for the best.

The woman who'd given her life had been gone three years now, but her laughter still echoed down the years.

Maddie turned her head to whisper the word bananas and blew a kiss at the sky. Pushing ninety, her mum had been worn out by illness and happy to go when the time came, so different from Tony, who had everything to live for. But there was no point dwelling on it. Today, she'd promised herself she'd embrace the present, not the past.

Thanassis brought the bike to a stop a few minutes later, in front of a tiny golden bay, where a shimmering turquoise sea lapped at the edges of the sand, and cliffs on either side protected the beach from the worst of the elements. The road had narrowed to a track which no car could make it down, and they were alone. She barely knew the man, but strangely she didn't feel remotely nervous.

They set up camp on the sand, on a waterproof blanket Thanassis had apparently stowed in his pannier, along with several bottles of beer, and bread, meat and grilled vegetables wrapped in paper.

They hadn't discussed food, but as ever, Maddie found she could eat. She chinked bottles with the cook and unwrapped her booty. Straightaway Maddie fashioned herself a sandwich, which she held up for Thanassis's approval.

'I've made a real doorstopper.'

'Doorstopper?'

'It means chunky.'

Maddie started demonstrating with her hands but had a sudden attack of shyness when she realised he was looking at the shapes she was making in confusion.

'Never mind.'

'It is *choirinó*, pork, with slices of peppers from the garden, roasted in olive oil. And of course, home-made bread.'

Maddie took a big bite.

'It's gorgeous, thank you.'

A peaceful few minutes looking at the sea while eating reminded Maddie how little men talked compared to women. She, Sofia and Charlotte, wouldn't have been able to stop themselves commenting on everything in front of them. It was nice for a change.

Thanassis reached into his pocket and brought out a tobacco pouch.

'Do you mind if I smoke?'

'Of course not. In fact…' Maddie deliberately stamped on her sensible side. 'Can I have one?'

'A roll-up?'

'Yes please, I used to smoke them back in the day.'

She hadn't had one for years, but it was that sort of day.

'With your husband?'

Thanassis's fingers were working at making the cigarettes while he spoke.

'Yes, with Tony.'

Thanassis put both cigarettes into his mouth, lit them and handed one to her. It seemed perfectly natural to take it off him, and the slight dampness at the end when she took the first drag brought Charlotte's horrified face to mind.

'And your husband, Tony...' Thanassis turned to look at her. 'He is dead, yes?'

'Yes.' She didn't mind telling him for some reason.

'I know this. I saw it in your eyes that first day down at the port.' Thanassis turned back to look out to sea. 'The pain is something you can recognise instantly if you see it in the mirror every morning.'

Maddie stared straight ahead, rather than at the man sitting next to her.

'You too?'

'Yes, my wife, Eimear, died five years ago.'

Thanassis did the sign of the cross on his chest.

Maddie put her hand on his arm. The soft dark hairs were warm to the touch.

'I'm so sorry.'

'For you too.'

The sea began to blur in front of her eyes. She blinked and sneaked a peek at him.

'It's coming back to me. You said her name out loud several times the other night ... while you were barely conscious.'

Thanassis turned to her with a smile.

'Did I? I suppose it is not so strange. I think of her every day. One day, not too soon I hope'—his smile was like the sun after the rain—'we will be reunited.'

'It must be nice to believe that. I really don't know, but I would love to think it's true.'

Maddie turned her head away, so Thanassis didn't see her eyes. But she didn't need to tell him she was near to tears.

'Don't be sad. Why don't we talk about them a little? It is hard to talk to people who don't understand.'

Maddie nodded. It was hard. So hard. Some people got upset themselves, and others just looked embarrassed and made excuses not to meet up again.

'You go first.'

'OK. Eimear was nineteen when I met her. She was a tourist, like you, from Ireland. It was her first time abroad, and she had all these big plans to travel the world. But we took one look at each other and that was it. We both knew.'

Maddie sneaked another look at the man beside her. His eyes were closed, but he had a great big grin on his face.

'And that also explains why your English is so good.'

Thanassis shrugged.

'I suppose. Eimear never left. It was a lot for her to give up, but my life was here on the island. We've been fishermen in these waters for four generations, and tradition is strong in Greece. But she fell in love with the island as well as me, and the people took her to their hearts.'

His clear blue eyes stared into hers a moment.

'What about your Tony?'

'It's not so different. We met at school.' Maddie held back a sob. 'We were both sixteen.'

The memories of the tall, gangly boy came flooding into her

mind. 'We both went for the last piece of cake in the cafeteria, and he let me have it. That was Tony, generous to a fault.'

Thanassis smiled.

'I don't like mean people.'

'Me neither. Everyone thought we'd split up because we were so young. He went off to university because he needed a degree to be a teacher, which was always his dream, and I started work in social care. But we managed to meet up most weekends and we never found anyone else we thought was a better fit.'

Thanassis took another long drag on his cigarette.

'Eimear had all this beautiful red hair, very much like yours, which is another reason why I was drawn to you.'

'Ah, and that's why your daughter thought she'd seen a ghost when we brought you into the harbour. And why she was giving me a strange look at the *panigýri*.'

Thanassis sighed.

'She is very protective of me. She still misses her mother dreadfully and is so sad that Eimear never got to see our beautiful grandchildren.'

The crack in his voice told Maddie that her companion was near to tears himself.

'My son, Alex, works as a chef in Dublin where Eimear was from and where her relatives still live. They have been so welcoming, but I miss him all the time. My daughter, Georgia, is married to a local man, so she looks out for me. Do you have children?'

'Yes. My daughter, Becca, runs two bakeries in the north of England. She's married, but no children yet. While my son…'

Maddie couldn't go on any further.

Thanassis put his hand over hers. A hand with rough skin. A working hand.

'What is it?'

'My son and I have fallen out. Or rather I have fallen out with his wife…'

There was no point in varnishing the truth now.

'I said some things I bitterly regret. Which means I haven't seen my beloved granddaughter, Elsie, for three months. No one else knows. And it's killing me.'

Maddie couldn't keep the tears at bay any longer. Thanassis carefully took the cigarette from her hand and stubbed it out on the sand before he held her sobbing figure in his arms, the stunning beach and the glorious sea all but forgotten.

When she could speak again, she reluctantly pulled out of the comforting embrace, but not before Thanassis had wiped away her tears with his thumbs.

'You must fix this. Family is everything. We have lost so much. You cannot lose them.'

'I know.' Maddie's throat was so sore she could barely swallow. 'I just don't know how.'

'Find a way. Your friends will help you.'

Maddie stayed silent.

'They don't know?'

She shook her head.

'Please tell them. I'm begging you.'

'I will. I promise.'

'Good. And you know you cannot break a promise made to a Greek.'

Thanassis stood up, pulled his T-shirt over his head and stepped out of his jeans. Maddie found it hard to tear her eyes away from his muscular body, not honed in a gym, but by years of hard physical work out at sea, as evidenced by the tan lines halfway up his arms and across the tops of his thighs. She must stop gawping.

'And now we must go for a swim to wash away those tears and let all that salt go back to the ocean.'

Maddie let her shorts drop to the ground and rushed to unbutton her shirt. She'd treated herself to a second bikini in red, now she remembered how much easier a bikini was compared to a swimsuit.

Thanassis reached for her hand, and together they ran into the sea, deliberately splashing each other until they were in deep enough to push off the bottom. For a blissful moment, Maddie forgot everything other than the sensation of water on her body as she put her head under and surrendered to the pull of the sea.

After a swim to the nearest rock and back, luckily still just about within her depth, two strong hands grabbed her round the waist and held her up in the air for a moment before flinging her back into the sea.

'Hey!'

A grinning Thanassis came up for air, hair slicked back, and resembling a big seal.

'Right, you're for it.'

Maddie reached over and used all her strength to dunk his head under and hold it there.

A spluttering Thanassis came up for air and grabbed hold of her again, picked her up and marched out of the sea with her in his arms before carefully laying her down on the sand.

For a moment their eyes met as he stood over her, but

Maddie was the first to look away. Thanassis was still on his feet when she looked again.

'Another beer?'

'Great.'

Maddie pulled herself into a seated position and took the beer he offered. He sat down next to her and raised his beer to the sky.

'*Yamas!*'

'Cheers.'

The peaceful silence as they drank gave her a chance to recover. But there were still things about him she wanted to know.

'Can I just ask… Five years on, have you not met anyone else?'

Thanassis's blue eyes held more than a hint of a smile.

'Look, I haven't been a *papás*, a priest. There have been a few women. But nothing serious. When you've had the best, it's hard to settle for anything less.'

'I know… Believe me, I know.'

She mustn't start crying again.

'And you?'

'It's only been just over a year. I'm still so furious at Tony leaving me like that, I don't think I could look at another man, maybe ever.'

'Surely you are not planning on a life without … love?'

Maddie laughed.

'Neither of us is looking for love. I think you mean a life without sex, don't you? And the answer is yes, very probably.'

Thanassis turned onto his side and leant up on his elbow.

'That would be a terrible shame.'

'Would it?'

'I think so.'

The sun behind him made his eyes hard to read, but Maddie knew what she'd see in them. She'd known the second she agreed to go for a drink.

Thanassis covered the distance between them in a heartbeat and pulled her underneath him with ease. The first touch of his lips made her whole body shiver. After a moment's hesitation she kissed him back with an intensity which surprised even her.

His hands in her hair told her he wanted to set it free, and she pulled the hairband out and threw it onto the sand. She reached back to undo the clasp on her bikini top and cast that off too.

As she lay down again, he moved slowly from her mouth to her liberated breasts, paying attention to each one in turn, causing her to groan out loud.

His fingers gently pulling down her bikini bottoms made her think for a second how much trickier all this would have been in a costume, but only for a second. The sensations that overwhelmed her when his tongue reached its ultimate goal pushed everything else from her mind while the world exploded into a million colours.

When she opened her eyes again, Thanassis was positioned above her, his blue eyes as dark as she'd ever seen them in the diminishing light. He reached down to kiss her mouth again and lit a fire in her body that she'd learnt to live without. She was hardly an inexperienced teenager. She was a woman of sixty-two who wanted this, badly.

His voice was soft but held a touch of steel.

'Are you sure?'

Maddie nodded. She waited impatiently while Thanassis reached into his jeans for a condom, Neither broke eye contact as he lowered himself into her inch by inch. She was the one who moved against him first to set up a rhythm that had them both moaning with pleasure.

The feel of bare skin on bare skin was something she'd missed more than she realised. And the way a man's body melded with hers. Being here with Thanassis was so familiar, yet so different. Their entwined bodies changed shape without discussion, so deep was their understanding of each other's needs.

The sound of the sea in her ears and the feel of the sand under her naked body were magnified a hundred times as she emptied her mind and focussed solely on the sensations ripping through her flesh over and over again.

The lazy tempo switched to an urgency that wouldn't be denied. Her mind flooded with colour again as she screamed out into the night air at the same time as Thanassis moaned out loud and their arching bodies stilled as one.

Laying back on the sand, side by side, silence settled over the bay. Thanassis reached behind him for his jeans, made and lit them both another cigarette, and passed hers over without speaking.

In front of them, the sun threw out the last of its deep-orange rays before slipping slowly beneath the surface of the water.

She'd finally got her sunset over the sea, the one she'd missed out on while she was desperately trying to manoeuvre a boat into port with Thanassis's unconscious body on board.

And what a sunset it was. The whole evening had been magical. Without analysing it too deeply, something inside her had shifted for good. Her terrible secret had been revealed, to Thanassis of all people, and she'd allowed herself to be just flesh and blood for a couple of hours, an insignificant speck on a beach on a tiny island in the middle of the sea.

She was fairly certain she and the man who'd brought her body gloriously alive would never meet again – her mind would stay forever faithful to Tony – but the guilt she thought she'd feel about giving in to what her body wanted and needed mercifully wasn't there.

They'd go back to their own lives, their own families, but it was fine. In fact, it was a damn sight more than fine.

Chapter Nineteen

Sofia peered into their hotel bar and spotted Charlotte nursing a glass of something at the back of the room. Her friend was staring down at her phone with such a sad look on her face that Sofia wanted to scoop her up and hug her. Which would be pretty tricky, given Charlotte was probably twice her height – well, maybe not twice, but that's what it sometimes felt like.

Before she joined her friend, Sofia wanted to nip to the cloakroom. Her own evening hadn't exactly been a winner either. Rushing away from an early dinner with Charlotte at the port to meet Konstantinos, the car hire world's answer to a young George Clooney, hadn't been all she'd hoped for.

The bar he'd suggested turned out to be full of his friends, who were all a similar age to him and mostly incredibly loud and drunk. He'd greeted her happily enough and spent some time kissing her thoroughly in front of his mates, which seemed more for their benefit than hers. He tasted of rum and coke, not a drink she liked much anyway.

When she'd popped to the unisex loo, he'd been waiting outside as she washed her hands, indicating with his eyes that they should go back into the cubicle together. She'd certainly had toilet sex as a teenager, but it was a very long time ago and she had no wish to repeat it. Even back then it hadn't been anywhere near her favourite location. The back seat of a car or the woods had been way better.

A proper bed, clean sheets and preferably a bottle of champagne, or at least wine, were on her wish list now. She'd made it clear to Konstantinos that she had no desire to be shoved up against a U bend, and suggested they went back to his.

His reluctance to leave his friends was almost comical – almost – but his eagerness in the cab had her worried for the cab driver, who was so intent on checking out the action in the rear mirror that they'd almost veered into the path of an oncoming car.

Once at Konstantinos's flat, obviously shared with several other blokes if the number of beer cans in the kitchen and crumpled clothes on the sofa was anything to go by, she'd begun to have major doubts. Charlotte was sitting on her shoulder, telling her she was only sleeping with this guy to spite Adonis for not having enough time for her.

In a couple of days, she'd be leaving the island. She was probably as old as this one's mother, if not older. It never usually bothered her. Age was just a number as far as she was concerned, but a crummy flat was a crummy flat.

When he'd emerged from the kitchen with two opened beer cans and thrust one at her, she'd known it was time to go.

His feeble protestations at her leaving hadn't convinced

either of them, and she'd bet he'd been back at the bar in the town with his cronies before she could say 'very bad idea'.

Sofia reapplied the pink lipstick that had been inexpertly kissed off and studied herself in the harshly lit mirror of the hotel's cloakroom. She wasn't unhappy with what she saw, and her tan was coming along nicely.

Adonis had messaged again, a photo of himself looking sad and alone at the dinner table, but she'd kept up radio silence. She'd decided to give the man one last chance, but she'd bloody well make him work for it. Hopefully, he'd occasionally be able to tear himself away from his beloved job to spend some time with her once they got to the next island.

But right now, it was time to do some investigative work on Charlotte.

Her friend was still in the same position she'd been in earlier, staring morosely at the phone.

'Hi.'

The phone was quickly turned over, but not before Sofia saw the name DCB as the author of Charlotte's most recent text.

It didn't ring any bells. But it could be code for someone. Charlotte's eyes were somewhat glazed when they finally turned her way.

'Hello. Where did you slope off to?'

'I told you I was going for a walk before I came back to the hotel.'

'Hmmm. Not sure I believe that.'

Charlotte's voice was slightly slurred. Surely, she hadn't been sitting there drinking on her own ever since they'd gone their separate ways.

'Any sign of Mads?' Sofia looked up at the clock. It was past eleven. 'Shouldn't she be back by now? It's been six hours. What on earth are they doing?'

'That's why I was down here having a drink. I couldn't relax in my room. Motorbikes always scare me.'

'Me too a bit.'

Charlotte's face dropped even further. This wasn't helping anyone.

'But Mads is used to being on the back of a bike. It's not like one of us being asked to saddle up.'

'But she's not the one in the driving seat, is she? What do we do if she doesn't turn up? Would we even find out if they'd had a crash?'

Charlotte was clearly having a major attack of the glumps.

'Let's not get ahead of ourselves. It's hardly four in the morning. We've only just lost the daylight.'

Charlotte downed the last of whatever was in her glass.

'Suppose. Do you want a drink?'

'Yes, please. I really fancy a Cointreau with ice.'

Charlotte attempted a smile.

'Very retro.'

'I don't care. I like it.'

'OK, you stay there. I'll get them.'

'What are you drinking?

'Brandy.'

'Okaaay.'

As Charlotte got up, Sofia caught a whiff of neat alcohol on her breath. It was worse than she'd thought. Thea and Theo had told them to help themselves at the bar if the couple had already gone to bed. And it looked like Charlotte had taken them at her word. They were supposed to make a note of what they took in a little book. She'd better check later that her friend had fessed up.

Charlotte's phone was lying on the table. And it was ringing. On mute, but Sofia could see it was DCB again, calling rather than texting this time. She wasn't spying; it was there for anyone to look at.

When Charlotte came back with the drinks and put them down on the table a little too forcefully, a bit of the Cointreau slipped over the side and onto the wood.

'Have you got a hankie, Char? That stuff's like sugary glue. God knows what it's doing to my stomach.'

Charlotte pulled out a tissue from her bag and did some ineffectual mopping up. The phone was still ringing on silent.

'Give the hankie here.'

Sofia got a small glass of water from the bar and cleaned up the mess. She indicated down at the phone.

'Everything alright? Whoever it is, is very persistent.'

Charlotte was all too aware of who it was: her scumbag of a husband.

She was saved from answering by the arrival of Maddie coming through the door and the sound of a motorbike roaring off into the distance. Their friend's hair was all over the place, but she had a radiant glow that Sofia recognised immediately. She looked nothing like the woman who'd gone out earlier that evening.

Both of them put down their drinks and rushed to her side.

As soon as they reached her, Maddie burst into tears and the three of them ended up in a group hug. It only lasted a few moments before she pulled away.

'Don't worry about me, honestly, I'm fine. These are happy tears. I've had a wonderful evening, strange but wonderful.'

Questioning Maddie would have to wait until a later date. She was obviously safe and well. Charlotte was much more of an issue. Sofia put her arm around her recently returned friend.

'Come and sit down over here with us. Would you like a nightcap?'

Maddie shook her head.

'I'm pretty bushed to be honest. I'd really like to go straight to bed, if you don't mind.'

Sofia urgently mimed drinking and crying at Maddie when Charlotte turned her back for a second. She didn't know if Charlotte actually had been crying, but she needed Maddie to understand something was seriously up. Luckily, she caught on fast.

'On the other hand, why not? Let's all sit and have a drink together.'

'A Cointreau for old times' sake?'

'Yeah, lovely. Char, Sof and I will bring these over, you go and sit down.'

Charlotte nodded and weaved through the chairs, knocking against two or three on her path to their table by the window.

'See what I mean.'

Sofia pulled Maddie close and lowered her voice.

'I can see you've been shagged senseless, and don't bother denying it. Good luck to you…'

'Sof!'

'Shhh. But there's something seriously up with her over there. She keeps getting texts and phone calls from someone called DCB. Any ideas?'

'No. Never heard her mention anyone with those initials. Could be one of her double-barrelled posh Surrey friends I suppose... But not sure what could be so urgent.'

'OK, let's tread carefully.'

Back at the table, after a mouthful of their liqueurs each to Charlotte's three gulps of brandy, the phone vibrated again.

Sofia couldn't stand it any longer. She put her hand on her friend's arm.

'Char, we're worried about you. Who is this DCB?'

Charlotte picked up the phone and switched it off. She turned to face them both with her head held high.

'It stands for Doug Cheating Bastard.'

Both Maddie and Sofia just sat and stared at her for a long moment. Sofia had barely ever heard Charlotte swear, let alone speak about her husband like that.

Silent tears ran down Charlotte's cheeks as she gripped the table with both hands. The ends of her fingers were already turning white.

'I can't breathe. I need some air.'

Maddie recognised the onset of one of Charlotte's panic attacks. It was hardly surprising, given what she'd just revealed, but they needed to get her up out of her seat and calm her down before it turned into a full-blown one. She nodded at Sofia.

'Let's take her outside. Some fresh air might help.'

Gently they took an arm each and guided Charlotte out onto the terrace and into a comfy chair. The night was warm, but Thea had thoughtfully left out a big wicker basket with soft blankets for guests to use, and they laid one over Charlotte's lap.

'Look at all those stars.' Maddie pointed upwards in a bid to distract her charge. 'Without pollution it's incredible how bright they shine. I'm sure that's Orion up there, look?'

She had absolutely no idea, but she was hoping it would prompt Charlotte to say something as she hadn't spoken for several minutes.

'It's much more likely to be Cassiopeia.'

Bullseye.

'I knew you'd know.'

Charlotte's ragged breathing had calmed to a more normal level.

Maddie turned to Sofia.

'Can you get her a glass of water, please?' She lowered her voice to a whisper while Charlotte stared fixedly at the sky. 'And bring our drinks over, but not hers. I think we're going to need them.'

Sofia nodded.

Charlotte had managed to drink most of the water, and the colour had come back into her face while they waited, Maddie was pleased to see.

She and Sofia had grabbed a chair and a blanket each too, and the sound of the sea far away below them was magnified in the night air.

They weren't going to push Charlotte to talk as she so obviously needed to, but they were giving her the space to do so. Maddie moved any plans to tell her friends about her estranged family and the mess she'd made to the back of her mind. It could wait.

Charlotte murmured something, which Maddie strained forward to hear.

'OK, Char?'

'Not really, but I want to talk.'

Maddie leant over to hold one of Charlotte's hands and Sofia took the other.

'We're listening.'

'Doug has been having an affair for two years… I found out not long before we came away.'

Sofia leapt up out of her seat.

'No! The bastard. The complete and utter bastard.'

A stare from Maddie made her sit down again.

'Go on, Char.'

'He says it's … over with her for ever. I'm the one he loves, and he doesn't want our marriage to end. I've got these three weeks to decide what I want to do.'

Sofia was on her feet again and pacing the terrace.

'Leave him of course. How could he betray you like that? I bet it's some young thing in the office, isn't it? Keen to get her hands on what she sees as a good bet.'

Charlotte's tears started to fall again.

'It's not, though. That's the thing. She's our age, even a couple of years older than us.'

Sofia stopped in her tracks. The bleakness in Charlotte's eyes was terrifying.

'You've both met her. It's the office manager, Natalie.'

'Not that mousy woman we met at your party last summer?' Sofia came to stand next to Charlotte. 'You introduced her as your friend.'

Charlotte stared down at the blanket as more tears fell, and the dark blobs stained the fabric.

'I thought she was my friend…'

'Oh sweetheart.' Sofia walked behind the chair and started to massage her friend's shoulders. 'What a bitch she must be to be able to look you in the face as if everything was normal.'

'To be honest, I don't blame her as much as Doug. At least she's single. He's the one who's married with a family.'

'I want to kill her. And Doug. I want to kill both of them.'

Maddie indicated towards Sofia's chair.

'Can you sit down, Sof? I know you're angry on Char's behalf, but I'm not sure how much this talk of murder is helping.'

Charlotte's voice was weak, but she managed a smile.

'Thank you for wanting to kill them … I think.'

Sofia sat as she'd been told and tucked the blanket in firmly around her.

'Sorry. I know I always go off like a rocket about cheating because of what my dad did to my mum, but I really am sad for you.'

'I know. I'm sad for me too.'

Maddie's hand was still entwined with her friend's.

'Two whole years! Did you have any idea?'

'No, not until I walked in on them at work…'

Charlotte's voice trailed away.

'What? At it full pelt over a desk?' Sofia couldn't stop her mouth.

'Yes, as you say, Sof, *"at it full pelt over a desk"*.'

Maddie shook her head.

'What a cliché.'

'Yes, it showed a distinct lack of imagination on Doug's part. He could at least have gone for the stationery cupboard.'

Charlotte's attempt at a joke broke Maddie's heart. She squeezed her friend's hand hard.

'Why didn't you tell us before? We could have helped you through that first shock.'

'I just wanted some time to process it all myself first. We were coming away together, and I knew at some point I'd want to talk about it, and that you'd both be there for me when I did… Which you are.'

Sofia held on to the arms of the chair to stop herself getting up again.

'But we've been in Greece for nearly two weeks. How did you hold it in all this time?'

Maddie smiled at Sofia's indignation.

'The same way you managed to keep quiet about your being made redundant for a whole week?'

Sofia smiled back.

'Fair enough. You've got me there.'

'There's a right time and a right place for everything.'

Charlotte had turned to her with trepidation in her eyes.

'Also, Mads, I didn't want to go on about my problems with my husband, who is still very much alive, although a cheating bastard, when I know how much you're struggling. You made a comment last week about me at least still having a husband…'

'I'm truly sorry about that. It was a stupid thing to say. Please don't think I'd ever want you to keep stuff back about your marriage just because Tony isn't here anymore. He'd be horrified.'

'He would, wouldn't he. Lovely Tony.'

'Look, he wasn't a saint, but I never had to face what you're facing. Whatever we can do for you, we're here.'

Sofia took another big swig of her Cointreau.

'Are you sure it's over with Doug and this … cow.'

'He says it is. I suppose I have to believe him.'

'Why? And could you ever trust him again?'

Doug being revealed as just another cheat had shaken her to the core. Sofia wasn't sure she could ever trust a man again, even one who hadn't been caught in flagrante.

Charlotte's sigh was heavy, weighed down by a hundred thoughts.

'I honestly don't know. I asked him to leave me alone while I was on holiday, to give me time to think, but he's upping the ante, texting and ringing all the time, telling me how much he loves me, how much he's missing me and how lonely he is at home.'

'I bet. Now he's been found out.'

Maddie reached out and applied pressure to Sofia's knee.

'Not sure that's helpful, Sof. Do the boys know?'

'God no. As much as I'm furious with Doug, he adores them and has always been a good father. They probably never need to know if, and I say if, I stay with him. But obviously if I don't, they'll have to know something. I genuinely hope his relationship with them will carry on much as normal.'

'That's incredibly decent of you.'

'What's the point of causing more pain? Even though the boys are in their thirties now, they'll still be devastated if we do divorce. I'll fight to keep things as amicable as possible if we go down that route, but it won't be easy.'

Maddie thought about her own desperate situation and

how quickly things had fallen apart in the aftermath of Tony's death. It had only taken her a year to alienate half her family.

'True. It will be tough for them if you do decide to split for good. It's not the same as a death, I know, but it's an ending too. A divorce brings its own fallout for everyone else involved. I've seen it with my friends and their kids.'

Maddie snuck a glance at Sofia, who put her hands up.

'You know my position. No second chances.' She couldn't stop the crack in her voice as she carried on speaking. 'But ... it is sad in some ways that I didn't have any sort of relationship with my dad after his affair. It did change things forever. If you can somehow keep it friendly, Char, you'll be doing well.'

Sofia's brave face struck at Maddie's heart too. So much pain caused. And the legacy of her father's betrayal meant Sofia had never fully trusted another man since, not that she'd dare say that out loud. Plus, it was Charlotte they were dealing with tonight.

Their friend drank the last of her water and hugged them both in turn.

'Anyway, thanks for letting me talk. I think I've drunk myself sober, but I've got a long way to go before I decide anything either way. I know you're both here for me. But I don't want to spoil things for everyone and bring us all down. We're off to the next island in the morning, which means another week to relax and enjoy ourselves, so please, let's do just that.'

Chapter Twenty

Tony was nowhere to be seen, was Maddie's first thought, as she stepped out onto the terrace. She'd saved him some bacon from yesterday's breakfast, and she'd got used to the little bird greeting her each morning, and to watching him while he ate. They were leaving today, so it was her last chance to have a chat with him.

Was he angry with her for sleeping with Thanassis? Had he flown away in disgust? She was powerless to stop her eyes filling with tears. This was ridiculous. Maybe it was time to give the social media reincarnation posts a rest. She left the bacon on the table in case Tony had overslept too and walked back into her room. There would be no regrets about her wonderful night.

Charlotte looked none the worse for wear, Maddie was pleased to see when she went down for her own breakfast. Either it was real, or she was making a supreme effort to act normal. Hopefully the act of telling them about Doug had lightened her load just a tiny bit. Her friend still had some major decisions to make, but maybe they could be a sounding board now it was all out in the open.

It looked like the others had almost finished their meals, but she'd not even started, after coming down an hour later than usual. She'd slept like a log. It was certainly true that exercise helped you drift off, maybe not the sort of exercise they prescribed in gyms, but it had worked. It was the best night's sleep she'd had for months.

She allowed herself a secret smile as she reran some of the memories from the previous night through her head. Thanassis's soft mouth gently kissing hers, sharing a cigarette naked on the beach, and Thanassis poised above her, locking eyes.

Sofia appeared silently beside her, breaking her concentration.

'Thinking about which cereal to try, are you?'

'Mmmm.'

'Are you, my arse. You know we'll get it out of you somehow, don't you?'

'Very probably. But for now, we're focussing on Char.'

Maddie helped herself to some yoghurt and fresh fruit. It was time to turn the tables a little.

'And what about you? Are you excited about seeing lover boy later today?'

'Lover boy? That sounds like something out of a cheesy romance from the seventies.'

'Well, are you?'

'Not that he'll ever have any time to spend with me, but yeah, I suppose so.'

Theo was heading their way to take the coffee orders.

'Rubbish. You're vibrating with excitement, like an overexcited debutante on heat.'

'Charming.'

Theo had reached Maddie's side.

'And we'll leave it there for both of us for the time being.'

Sofia smiled a tight smile.

A lazy morning on the terrace, sipping coffees and keeping off any tricky subjects suited everyone, although Sofia's fidgeting was starting to annoy Maddie. They'd packed and vacated their rooms after breakfast and Theo was all set to drive them to the ferry for the three o'clock sailing. The weather had got significantly warmer even since they'd arrived two weeks ago and the sun was beating down, forcing them to sit in the shade under the crocheted parasols that Thea had made herself. Maddie had swapped notes on technique with her, not that she'd get much use out of a fancy parasol back home, but it would be fun to try and make one. It was better than sitting doing nothing in the evening. She might even think about joining a knitting club, now that it was apparently cool to knit and crochet.

Sofia's glance at her phone for the umpteenth time prompted Maddie to speak.

'Looking at it's not going to get us there any faster.'

'Just don't want to miss the ferry.'

'Mmmm, sure.' Maddie stretched out her legs in front of her, so they were in the sun.

'Wow, it's hot today, isn't it?'

Weather talk was always acceptable to fellow Brits, and she might as well try and distract Sofia.

'Do you both remember the summer of 'seventy-six'?

Charlotte sighed.

'I sure do. It was baking hot in those classrooms. It was the end of our first year at the school, wasn't it, and we'd already become fast friends?'

'That's right. I remember.' Sofia smiled. 'On the hottest day of the year, most schools in the country had sent their pupils home, but ours insisted on staying open for some bizarre reason.'

'Yes, and the older kids decided to go on strike, and one by one the classrooms emptied onto the school field, and everyone just sat down and waited in protest at being kept in the heat like cattle,' Maddie added.

'I can remember being a bit frightened of leaving the classroom, as we were the youngest. I was terrified about what my parents would say,' Charlotte replied.

Maddie shot her fist into the air.

'But we did it, didn't we? The whole school was out there on that field. It was a real example of pupil power.'

Sofia laughed.

'The teachers really didn't know what to do, did they? I remember our teacher, Miss…'

'Grange,' Charlotte added.

'Yes, that's it, Miss Grange, she was quite young, probably not much older than our kids are now…' Maddie turned to Charlotte. 'Poor thing. She was pleading with us to stay inside, but we weren't having any of it.'

'And the headmaster came out onto the field and gave a speech, sweat dripping off his brow, not sure if it was heat or stress.'

'Probably a bit of both.'

'I just remember a lot of flirting, the boys taking off their ties and everyone lying around on the grass chatting.' Sofia had her eyes closed.

'Yes, you would.' Maddie tapped her friend on the leg and smiled as she opened her eyes.

'It went on for hours, but what happened in the end?'

'Eventually they forced us back inside,' said Maddie. 'There was a big assembly where we got a massive telling off. But at least no one had to do any work that day.'

A phone alarm sounded in Sofia's bag.

'At last. That's us. We need to go and say goodbye to our hosts.'

Many hugs later and armed with huge doggy bags of the cake of the day, a tangy *lemonópita*, which Thea thrust at them for the boat journey, they were finally loaded into the hotel van.

'She does know the boat ride's only an hour and a half?' whispered Charlotte, looking down at the huge portion. 'We've not long had breakfast.'

'But this time, it's a much smaller boat, and there'll be no flash restaurant, so you might be glad of it,' piped up Sofia.

The van pulled out round their black hire car, still parked in front of reception.

'Not delivering it back to Konstantinos personally?' Maddie tried to make her face into the picture of innocence. Charlotte had filled her in on Sofia's mysterious disappearance the previous night, which had become a tiny footnote after what had been revealed next.

'No, he's perfectly capable of picking it up himself.'

'I see.'

'You don't. You really don't. But I don't want to talk about it.'

'Fine.'

The drive to the port was completed in silence, each lost in their own thoughts. Maddie was leaving behind the island that had made her feel alive again, if only for a night; Charlotte the place where she'd been honest for the first time about her problems; and Sofia was just grateful for her near miss with car hire guy. She'd probably have had to scrub herself with bleach.

It was indeed a much smaller boat that greeted them. Maddie was pleased that they weren't sailing from the tiny port round the corner as she had no desire to relive the memories of the rescue all over again or even bump into Thanassis.

'OK?'

Sofia gave her a quizzical look as they boarded. Her face must have been showing something of how she felt about one of the strangest weeks of her life.

'Yes, good, thanks.'

She'd replied on autopilot, but it was true she felt lighter. There were still some major hurdles to get over, plus the great big elephant in the room – the estrangement from her son and his family – but at least she'd made a start.

Once they'd climbed two sets of stairs to the main salon, Charlotte led them towards a door.

'It's a lovely day. Let's go and sit outside. We can pretend we're on a mini cruise.'

More coffees and some of Thea's delicious cake later, they all rushed to the front of the boat as they approached the harbour of the next island, cameras at the ready. It was all new for Maddie and Charlotte, and the turquoise domed churches which dominated the town were interspersed with more white cubed houses going up the hill and plenty of grander buildings in an Italianate style.

It was on a much bigger scale than the previous island, but there was still plenty of green on the tops of the hills.

The water churned beneath them as the boat edged into position, and the call came for passengers to disembark.

Sofia had been scanning the dockside for several minutes and let out a yelp when she spotted something or someone in the distance.

'Yes! I wanted to keep it a secret until now, but we're staying at Adonis's ultra posh hotel for one night before we move on to ours for the rest of the week, my treat. And he's here to pick us up.'

Sofia moved faster than either of them had ever seen her move before. She was off the boat and onto the dock before they'd got to the edge of the platform, and straight into a man's arms.

She'd taken a flying jump and wrapped her legs around the man's waist, and he was hugging her back for all he was worth.

'If I did that, I'd probably kill someone.' Charlotte smiled at Maddie. 'Or at least have them flat on their backs on the concrete.'

'She's certainly keen to see him.'

'You can say that again.'

They reached the happy couple, tongue deep in a very involved kiss.

Maddie feigned a cough.

'Er... Hello?'

Sofia broke away from the man, eyes shining.

'Oh hi. This is Adonis, and Adonis, these are my friends Maddie and Charlotte.'

'Hello.' He put out a hand and shook theirs in turn. 'Pleased to meet you.'

As good-looking as any of the men Maddie had seen her friend with, this one was definitely a man, rather than a boy.

She managed to give Sofia a thumbs up as he loaded their bags into the car with ease.

At the hotel, the luxury level of which Maddie had never experienced in her life, if the trip through the marbled reception and gilded lift were anything to go by, she and Charlotte were shown into a twin-bedded room with views out to sea and its own balcony.

Adonis's quiet authority as he'd moved through the hotel was impressive, thought Maddie. His popularity with the staff was obvious by the way everyone smiled and greeted him. All except for one young woman on reception who gave their party a distinctly frosty look when she thought no one was looking. It seemed to be directed at Sofia, and Maddie hoped it didn't mean trouble for her friend. Maybe the woman was just having a bad day.

The room they'd been shown into wasn't like any twin room Maddie had ever seen, each bed was the size of a large double, and the pastel linens on the bed and the delicate carved glass light fittings screamed expensive but tasteful.

'I hope you will be happy here.' Adonis had brought up their bags personally, although there seemed to be numerous lackeys around who could have done it. His English was excellent, and Maddie found his slight hint of a Greek accent on certain words cute. She could see the attraction of this one, no problem.

'Please settle in and order anything you like from room service on me. I must get back to work now, but I will see you very soon I hope.'

'Thank you,' Maddie and Charlotte spoke almost at the same time.

Adonis raised his hand.

'It's nothing.'

Sofia had been standing quietly by the door, and before he left the room, he pulled her in for a thorough kiss, which had Maddie and Charlotte not knowing where to look.

Sofia bumped down on the nearest bed.

'So … what do you think?'

Maddie bumped down next to her.

'Obviously, he's gorgeous, and unusually he seems lovely with it. What's not to like? I can see why you were desperately keen to get here.'

Maddie raised her eyebrows while Sofia looked down at her hands.

'It's just a casual thing, honestly.'

If she kept saying it over and over again, maybe it would make it true, like a spell. Was it because she had no job to go back to, that it felt a bit different this time? She was standing on the edge of a cliff, and she mustn't let herself step over.

Charlotte stared out of the French doors at the sea below.

'He does seem really nice, Sof.'

'Thanks.'

Maddie looked down at the bed she was sat on and across at the neighbouring one.

'One …two. Where are you going to sleep?'

'Funny. Adonis has a room at the top of the hotel, as well as a flat in town.'

Charlotte joined them on the bed.

'Are we going to see anything at all of you this week? It's supposed to be the three of us together.'

She tried to stop her voice from sounding pathetic. Now she'd told her friends about Doug, she felt even more vulnerable, rather than less. It was like the façade she'd so carefully built up over the last few years was crumbling around her, and she wasn't sure what she'd find beneath it.

Sofia put her arm round her.

'Of course. Don't be silly. Adonis works all the hours God sends. It's a miracle he was able to pick us up today.'

'Yes, that was kind of him.'

The buzz of Sofia's phone was loud in the room. She kept it firmly turned away from them both while she read the message.

'Just got to pop out for an hour. I'll be back later, and we can all go for dinner. I've got a special place in mind.'

Before they could do more than nod, Sofia was out of the door and off.

'Claiming his reward for the valet service if I'm not mistaken.' Maddie reached for her sponge bag and headed into the bathroom big enough for four.

'Don't be mean, Mads. She looks really excited.'

'That's what I mean.'

Charlotte picked up the room service menu from one of the ornate side tables.

'Let's take him at his word. Do you fancy a cocktail on the balcony?'

'Sure do. You choose. Let's order two of each so we don't have some poor guy traipsing up and down.'

'Good plan.'

With two Cosmopolitans each in front of them, and the whole of the main town laid out below, Maddie and Charlotte spent some peaceful moments watching the divers on the swimming platform and the boats pulling in and out of the port.

Charlotte spoke again first.

'Oh, look at all the cats being fed by that house. There are some binoculars on the side. I'll get them.'

A gang of twenty cats had converged on the feeding bowls at the sound of a rattling tin, and Charlotte and Maddie took it in turns to watch them fill their bellies.

'Would you ever have another cat?' Charlotte sipped at her cocktail and surveyed her friend.

'I'm not sure. We had Bill and Ben for so many years. They weren't related, but they died within a week of each other at the ripe old age of eighteen. I do miss having a cat, but they are a tie, aren't they?'

'I remember them. A black one and a tabby, wasn't it? They can be a tie, but they're also great company.'

'True. You were always more of a dog person, weren't you?'

Charlotte gulped back a tear.

'Yes. I was heartbroken when Sophie went. She was only

eleven and a half, but dogs don't live anywhere near as long as cats, especially big dogs.'

Maddie was still looking at the cats through the binoculars.

'I'm really not sure what I want to do with the next phase of my life, now Tony's gone. So, would taking on another animal be fair?'

'Don't be ridiculous. You'd be fine. Cats don't need that much input. It's not like having a dog. I don't think I'd have another one now.'

There was no way she could commit to having an animal when she didn't even know where she'd be living in six months' time. Would she still be in her spacious Victorian house, surrounded by all her things, a newbuild box somewhere with a pared down life, or even a stunning modern flat?

'Not for a long time, anyway. I'd like to do more travelling first. But maybe a little itty-bitty cat for you?'

'You make it sound like I could keep it in a matchbox and take it out every now and again and play with it. Are you worried that I'm lonely?'

'No…Not exactly. I know you've got your family, work and friends. But a sweet little face looking up at you every morning would be nice.'

She was putting herself in Maddie's position. Living on her own was one of the things that scared her the most if it didn't work out with Doug. She'd never done it. She'd gone straight from her parents to university halls, followed by living with a group of friends, and then him.

Maddie handed over the binoculars again.

'You might be right. I'll give it some thought. And while

Motormouth is off having fun, how are you really feeling about DCB at the moment?'

Charlotte put down her drink.

'That's a conversation swerve and a half. I will admit I do find it a bit difficult when Sof goes off on one of her rants. Obviously, she was deeply affected by what her dad did, but like most things, my relationship woes aren't so black and white.'

Maddie kept her own counsel. It was important for Charlotte to say what she really thought without comments either way.

People always told her she was a great listener and so non-judgemental, but what that really meant was that she knew when to keep her trap shut in the main.

'Also, I wouldn't say it to her face, but Sof has never really been in a long-term relationship with all its ups and downs. Yes, she had that very brief marriage to Rupert, but he was just a temporary dad substitute, and she knows it. Since then, it's been a parade of gorgeous, but ultimately unsuitable men. So, I think it's hard for her to know what it would be like to jack in a thirty-year marriage.'

Maddie restricted herself to nodding.

'Obviously she'd understand it with her head, but I'm not sure she'd really feel it.'

Maddie didn't really want to get sidetracked onto Sofia's issues now she'd got Charlotte on her own.

'Agreed. But as it's just the two of us, how *is* it going?'

Charlotte put her head in her hands.

'I'm all over the place. One minute I'm furious with Doug, the next I can't imagine living without him.'

'Even after what he's done?'

Charlotte stopped speaking and Maddie worried she'd skated too close to the edge this time.

'Again, it's not that simple.'

The tears glittered in Charlotte's eyes when she looked up again.

'What do you mean? What is it?'

What could possibly justify Doug's behaviour was the question on the tip of her tongue, but she kept it back.

'I can see now that as the boys grew up, we started drifting apart. My career had taken off, big time, and I think Doug felt threatened by that.'

'But doesn't he run a successful business?'

'To be honest, it's never been quite as successful as he made out. I've been the main breadwinner for years now.'

'Wow. I had no idea.'

'No one has. I keep the truth away from people to protect Doug.'

'Ah, the fragile male ego. I think we've all dealt with that.'

'I might as well be completely honest. In the past couple of years, it's gone from bad to worse. I've put in money to keep the business afloat, but at the same time our relationship has been going slowly downhill.'

Maddie stroked her friend's arm.

'Ah, I'm so sorry.'

'When the boys finally left home, a lot of joy went out of our lives, well, *my* life really. Instead of listening to what two vibrant young men had been up to all day, over dinner, I had morose Doug telling me about the latest disaster at work.'

Maddie would be thrilled to hear about Tony's work day,

morose or otherwise, but voicing that would stop Charlotte in her tracks.

'Yes, I can see that would be tough.'

'I started to pull away from him, Mads. I made out I was painting day and night and spent a lot of those nights in the spare room. And then I'd wait until I heard him go out of the house before I got up.'

'It sounds like the whole thing was very stressful.'

'It was. But I think I was also in denial about how bad things were. Of course, our sex life went to pot.'

Maddie swallowed the last of her second cocktail. She had to be grateful that everything had been fine and dandy on that score right up until Tony's death. He may be gone, but she had a whole trove of romantic memories to dive into.

Charlotte's voice had dipped to a whisper.

'I turned him down a few times, so he stopped asking. It felt easier that way. And then it just became the norm.'

The tears when they came were silent, and Maddie took her friend into her arms and let her cry on her shoulder.

'Shhh. Let it all out.'

After a couple of minutes, Charlotte pulled away and leaned back in her chair again.

'So, you can see why I bear some responsibility for the whole thing as well. I made it clear I didn't really want him at a time when he was under immense stress.'

Maddie couldn't let that one lie. She'd heard it so many times before, women blaming themselves for everything that went wrong in a relationship. It took two people to let things go sour.

'But you were stressed up to the eyeballs as well by the

sound of it. You were shoring up the business, working your arse off, dealing with your empty nest and no doubt the lingering effects of the menopause, which doesn't help anyone's sex life. You're being too hard on yourself.'

'Maybe. But can you see why it isn't exactly how it must appear to Sof?'

'I can. Ending a long and mostly happy marriage is a huge decision. And one that is yours, and only yours, to take. There's no judgement here. If you stay together, I'll back you all the way, and Sof will just have to get used to it.'

She'd never be able to look at Doug in the same way again, but that wasn't helpful to say right now.

'Hello? Where are you?'

Sofia's voice in the bedroom brought an abrupt end to the conversation.

Charlotte put her finger to her lips.

'Not a word of what I've just told you, please.'

Maddie banged her chest in the Greek gesture of love.

'Of course not. Hey, Sof, we're out here.'

Chapter Twenty-One

'Everything sorted?'

Maddie went straight in with a question to stop Sofia asking any of Charlotte, who'd had more than enough for one evening.

'Sorted?'

'We assumed you had to go and'—Maddie put her fingers into air quotes—'"sort something"?'

Sofia tried to hide her smile.

'You can talk. We never got any of the juicy details about your evening with Thanassis, the hot fisherman.'

'No, and you're never going to.'

'Spoilsport.'

Sofia looked down at the empty glasses on the table.

'Have you two had a nice time, chatting?'

Charlotte smiled up at her.

'Lovely, thanks. We took Adonis at his word and ordered cocktails.'

Sofia clapped her hands together.

'Good. I'm starving now though. Shall we go out?'

'Sorting things can give you a right old appetite, I'm told.'

Sofia ignored Maddie's remark.

'I've got a car waiting downstairs to take us to the next part of my treat.'

The car dropped them off at an isolated beach with a small white-boarded restaurant and tables right on the sand.

There were candles on every tabletop and plenty of couples staring into each other's eyes. They were shown to a spot right on the front row facing the water, with nothing between them and millions of gallons of sea but a strip of sand.

'What a romantic setting!' Charlotte stared out to sea. 'Shame it's just us three.'

Sofia reached out for both their hands.

'It's not a shame at all. Let's be proud to be three women here together. It's a celebration of our friendship and our love for each other, if that's not too sickly greeting card for you.'

'It is a bit.' Maddie smiled at both her friends. 'But it's a gorgeous idea. Fifty years is one hell of a long time to know each other. We've outlasted husbands, countless relationships and numerous court appearances. And that's just you, Sof.'

'Hilarious.'

'But seriously, I want to thank you two for supporting me so much over the past year. I know I've been a crabby cow at times, but you've always been there at the other end of a phone for me, no matter what. Tony would have been very proud of the two of you.'

Sofia grabbed a menu and fanned herself with it.

'Don't set me off before we've even ordered a drink.'

'Or me.' Charlotte leaned forward and grabbed Sofia's hand.

'I want to thank you too, Sof, for organising this whole trip. I'd certainly never have got it together, but it's come at just the right time for me...' Charlotte's voice trailed away. 'And now you both know why.'

Maddie squeezed Sofia's other hand.

'Me too. More than you know.'

Maybe tonight would be a good time to tell them about the rift with her son.

'Me three.' Sofia squeezed back. 'I need you two now like I've never needed you. I've only got to work out what to do with the rest of my life. Simple.'

'We're all at a strange place in our lives, aren't we?' Maddie smiled at her friends. 'And we've all got some big decisions to make. Without going all philosophical on you both, life's been a little bit crazy recently, but there's plenty of life in the old dog yet.'

Sofia did her outraged face.

'Who are you calling an old dog?'

Settled happily with a large carafe of white wine and some water, Sofia put her hand on top of the pile of menus before the others even had a chance to look.

'We can share some starters, but we must all have the dish that they're famous for here, *kléftiko*. I insist.'

'What's that when it's at home?'

Maddie was getting better at recognising the names of Greek food, but this was a new one on her.

'It's pieces of succulent lamb, marinated and slow cooked

with peas, potatoes, herbs and plenty of local cheese, all wrapped up in a parchment parcel and tied with string.'

'Mmmm, sounds wonderful. I'm convinced.' Maddie licked her lips.

'I have to warn you, it's pretty filling. So shall we just have some courgette fritters with *tzatzíki* to start?'

Sofia took her hand off the menus at last.

'Fine with me.' Charlotte unwrapped her serviette and placed her knife and fork on the whitewashed table, painted with blue and green starfish. 'You've got me salivating too.'

The main courses were brought out to them by three different waiters holding a dish each, and laid down with plenty of ceremony.

They pulled open the strings holding the parcels together at the same time, and the smell that rose up caused them to moan out loud.

'This looks'—Maddie forked up the first mouthful—'and tastes, amazing.'

'Are these special potatoes, Sof?' Charlotte piled the melting cheese on top of one.

'Yes, they're really waxy, so they don't fall apart. They grow them here in the centre of the island.'

'And this white cheese?'

'Different islands, and indeed different families, all have their own variations on the basics, and the cheeses vary. You can use *feta*, *graviera*, which is a yellow cheese, or indeed any local cheese you like.'

Charlotte smiled at the enthusiasm in her friend's voice.

'You're sounding worryingly like me.'

'I was just so blown away by this the first time I had it, that I wanted to know all about it.'

Sofia put on a posh voice.

'It's said to be named after sheep-rustling bandits called the Klephts, engaged in fighting Ottoman rule. They would cook their ill-gotten gains on coals in an underground pit to avoid detection and to stop the smell escaping.'

'Oooh, crafty. That's fascinating.'

Sofia's side helping of facts was obviously doing it for Charlotte, mused Maddie.

'Can we carry on eating this delicious food now, before you two start on the overthrow of the Ottoman empire?'

Sofia stuck out her tongue at Maddie.

'I'm just so pleased you both love it too.'

The end of the meal coincided nicely with the sun slowly going down over the water. They'd been offered a shot of *mastika* liqueur to finish off the evening, which went well with a bit of people watching. Entwined couples and groups of friends strolled along the shore in the twilight, and someone, somewhere in one of the properties backing on to the beach, played a guitar, slowly and mournfully.

Charlotte lifted her glass to her friends.

'What a lovely evening you've given us, Sof. It really has been a treat. To friendship. *Yamas!*'

'*Yamas!*'

'*Yamas!*'

'I'm so pleased this evening was an improvement on last night, Char. I'm still reeling from Doug's doings.' Sofia caught Maddie's grimace at her words. 'Not that I'm going to be bringing it up again. It's my turn for confession time...'

Sofia drained the glass. 'My evening wasn't great either. Yes, I did meet up with Car Hire Konstantinos…'

'I knew it.' Maddie slammed her glass down on the table.

'And he turned out to be a particularly unreconstructed male, who thought that bonking in the bogs of a bar might be fun…'

'You didn't do it?' Charlotte's expression was a classic.

'No, I didn't. Nor did I want to spend much time in his scuzzy flat. So, my virtue is safe for another day.'

Maddie raised her eyebrows.

'Virtue?'

Sofia grinned and Maddie knew what was coming next.

'What sort of evening did *you* have, Mads?'

'OK, I might as well get it over with. I'm never going to see the guy again, and I'm not giving you the details…' She wagged a finger at Sofia. 'And I mean it, but, like the famous cocktail … yes, I had sex on the beach with the Hunky Fisherman, and it was lovely.'

'Woah! Good on you, girl.'

Sofia poured each of them a mouthful of wine from the tiny amount left in the second carafe.

'We've got to celebrate you breaking your duck. Cheers!'

The three of them clinked glasses again.

It so wasn't the right time to reveal that she'd also told Thanassis about her family rift ahead of her best friends, thought Maddie. This was an evening just to kick back and forget their problems, not bring them out and dissect them.

Stumbling back into their hotel room after midnight, she and Charlotte kissed Sofia goodnight and thanked her once again.

'Will we see you at breakfast?'

'Probably. Adonis has to be up and at it early.'

Sofia put up her hands.

'Don't say it! And remember we're going to that eighties' night at the club tomorrow where you'll meet my friend Grace again, who might even be doing a spot of DJing.'

Maddie flopped down on the nearest bed on her stomach.

'I thought you said DJing for a minute.'

'I did. Night, night, sleep tight, don't let the bed bugs bite.'

'I really hope there won't be any in a hotel of this class.' Charlotte's voice drifted off as she slumped down on the other bed, making the others laugh.

'Night, lovelies. See you in the morning.'

Maddie just waved a hand in Sofia's direction. She'd used up all her talking.

The following morning, they breakfasted in style on the enormous hotel terrace decorated with palm trees and statues, and were waited on hand and foot. The food was spectacular, but Maddie couldn't help comparing it with Thea's simple repasts made with love. She knew which she preferred.

'We're being taken to our new hotel after you've both finished here.' Sofia leapt up out of her seat to pick up a dropped serviette, but a waiter got there first and was treated to a smile.

'You won't get the five-star service we're getting here…'

'Good.' Maddie said under her breath. She'd had enough of lurking waiters who appeared at every turn.

'But the setting is stunning.'

Sofia was true to her word, and the much more manageable family-run hotel to one side of the port gave them vistas all round the town and out past the harbour to the majesty of the Aegean.

Again, they had three rooms in a row, this time on the ground floor, with little blue tiled terraces jutting out over the water, and sturdy ladders to climb down into the sea if you wanted to indulge in a spot of early morning swimming. There was also a substantial pool to one side of the hotel, which Sofia was keen to point out.

Adonis's cousin, Petros, and his wife, Artemis, were their hosts this time, a sweet couple in their thirties with a couple of toddlers at their heels.

'This is so cute.' Charlotte waved at her friends on the terraces either side. 'I think it's my favourite one so far.'

Maddie's heart was still with Theo and Thea's unpretentious warmth, but this came a close second.

Sofia shouted from her terrace at the end.

'You two need to get unpacked, pronto, as we're going on a cliff walk from here to the next village and back to get our stamina up for clubbing tonight.'

Sofia skipped back into her room after making her announcement.

'Are we?' Maddie pulled a face at Charlotte. 'She's like the Duracell bunny. Spending time with Adonis seems to be making her even more hyper, rather than calming her down.'

'There's no point resisting. And it might be fun.'

She'd hardly describe it as fun exactly, but the breeze blowing in off the water as they followed the coastal path to the unnamed village was refreshing in the heat, Maddie had to admit.

There were plenty of things to look at out at sea, everything from cruise ships to fishing boats, not that she wanted to dwell on those too much. And looking down occasionally gave her glimpses of hidden hollows with the golden skirts of their beaches fanning out into the water. Maybe they should try another boat trip, preferably without a major incident at the end of it. Surely Adonis would know someone who could take them. Everyone on a Greek island had a relative who did something useful.

Maddie was aware she was keeping up with the others a lot more easily now. She'd deliberately cut back on the drinking too, after realising quite how much she was putting away compared to Sofia and Charlotte.

It didn't take a genius to work out the two things were probably connected. She was glad they hadn't said anything about the booze or tried to stop her. That would have probably encouraged her to drink even more, just to put two fingers up to being told what to do. The only person who could change her life was her, something it had taken a long time to work out. The peace of the islands had given her the space to think, along with a helping hand, or rather two helping hands, from a passing fisherman.

She smiled at her own joke, before promising herself she'd get back out on the moors when she returned home. A memory of striding out over rough grass with her son, little Elsie strapped to his chest in a sling, hit her right between the eyes. How much her granddaughter must have changed in the last three months. What sort of grandmother was she if she didn't fight for the right to be involved in her life?

She was probably never going to be best mates with her son's wife, Hayley, but surely, she could put her anger and grief aside to be civil and make it work somehow?

A bus trundled past them, packed with holidaymakers heading for one of the big beaches at the other end of the island.

'How much further?' Maddie shouted ahead to Sofia.

'Not much.'

She could swear she'd seen a secretive look pass between her and Charlotte, who was directly behind.

'Where exactly are we going?'

'You'll see.'

Another couple of kilometres in and they seemed to be no closer to any villages. She was hot and thirsty and fast getting fed up.

'Where is this bloody village? What's it called?'

Both Sofia and Charlotte looked at the ground.

'Only a tiny way to go now.' Sofia pulled off her mini rucksack. 'Let's have another water break.'

'Oh yes, let's.'

The three of them drank in silence for a few moments before Sofia pulled out her phone.

'Let's get some nice shots of you two. You can use this in the blog, Char. Stand there.'

Maddie forced a smile as she put her arm around Charlotte.

'That's it! Cheese, or *tiri* as we say here!'

'We? Is she becoming Greek after one night with lover boy?'

Charlotte tried to suppress a laugh.

'Shhh. Just do as she says so it's over quicker.'

Sofia clicked away and moved backwards to get an even better shot, far too near to the edge in Maddie's opinion.

'Careful, Sof. Not so close.'

The next second she'd disappeared from view completely. Only sea and sky were visible where a diminutive dark-haired woman had stood a second earlier.

They ran as one to the edge.

'Sof!'

Charlotte had her hands over her eyes, so Maddie had to be the one who peered over to confront the worst.

Instead of seeing a body flayed over the rocks, blood everywhere, Sofia was on her bottom on a wide ledge only a couple of feet down, laughing her head off. Maddie's heart stopped slamming in her chest.

'Someone give us a hand up, will you?'

Charlotte reached for her friend and hauled her back up to the path, with Sofia still laughing.

The three of them collapsed onto the ground together and even Maddie was helpless in the face of her friend's mirth. They sat and giggled while several walkers gave them strange looks.

Maddie was the first to recover.

'Have you damaged anything?'

'Just my pride. I'll probably have a sore bum for a couple of days.'

'You were lucky.'

Maddie put on the voice she used with the care home residents.

'That was a silly thing to do, wasn't it?'

'Yes, Miss.'

'You're not going to do it again, are you?'

'No, Miss.'

'OK, and a more difficult question. Just where the hell is this mystical village?'

Sofia's expression became shifty and there were more looks at Charlotte before she pointed to a collection of white buildings only a couple of hundred metres away.

'Over there.'

'Doesn't look much like a village to me. More like a hamlet, or just a ham.'

As they approached, Maddie could see the white stone walls around the property, and something moving in the gardens.

'What is this place?'

Sofia and Charlotte pretended not to hear her.

'Hello?'

'You'll find out soon enough.'

The road curved away from the buildings and along the cliff for the next few metres, so Maddie was none the wiser.

Sofia had brown stains all over the back of her expensive white linen shorts which she'd be absolutely furious about, was Maddie's main thought as they rolled up to the entrance.

'Surprise!'

Chapter Twenty-Two

The name Bright Light Cat Sanctuary answered her questions. As did the preponderance of the creatures rubbing round her ankles the second they were inside the gate.

The door opened and a tiny dark-haired woman with wild curly hair rushed out to greet them, embracing Sofia in a tight hug.

'Angeliki!' Sofia's voice was so loud that Maddie had to cover her ears.

'Sofia!'

The answering call from the other woman was even louder, and the two of them eventually disentangled after more cheek kissing and exclaiming, before Angeliki turned to greet them.

'Welcome.'

Maddie made do with a handshake as did Charlotte. Sofia was still beaming with joy.

'I take it you two know each other?'

'Yes, Angeliki is a friend of Grace's, and I hope she's become my friend over the last year too.'

'*Vevaíos!* For sure we are friends.'

Sofia made the heart sign with her fingers.

'I didn't expect to find you here today though. It's a real bonus.'

Sofia patted her friend on the shoulder once more before turning to the others.

'Angeliki has a veterinary practice in the town. She's very dedicated and works all hours.'

The vet did a mock curtsey.

'Thank you for that. I volunteer here for the odd shift and do some of their urgent operations as well as regular sterilisations of the cats to keep the population down. Can I show you all around?'

'That would be great.' Maddie frowned. 'Why do I detect a slight Scouse accent?'

'Because I trained and lived in Liverpool for ten years.'

'That'll be it then. Great city.'

'Yes, I would love to go back some day. But my work keeps me so busy… Come, this way.'

On every fence, low wall, little patch of terrace, or corner of the extensive gardens was a cat.

Charlotte bent down to stroke a big tabby, who immediately rolled onto its back, purring in ecstasy.

'How many cats have you got here in total?'

'Usually between sixty and seventy, but sometimes up to ninety. The woman who owns the property, Annike, bought these buildings years ago for a song, thank goodness, when she moved here from Norway.'

'How on earth does she manage all this?'

Maddie swung her arm in a big arc, trying to ignore the

little black cat who was looking hopefully at her from the top of the wall. It was pretty obvious what Sofia and Charlotte's plan was: make poor, lonely Maddie fall in love with one of the cats and take it home with her.

'She has an army of volunteers.' Angeliki pointed at figures out in the gardens. 'Some are from the island, but others come here from abroad for the free accommodation and simple food they get in return for their help. They're mainly young women, or occasionally couples travelling together who decide to stay a while.

'It's very popular with the Irish, but it's not just youngsters; we have a huge age range. The volunteers are up early, and they have the afternoons to themselves. As long as you're not looking for hotel style bedrooms, you like eating communally, and of course, most importantly, you love cats, it works.'

'What a lovely idea. I wish I'd known about something like this when I was young. Tony and I could have…'

Maddie stopped herself saying more. She'd done with the could haves. A cute black and white mother cat suckling her babies distracted her for a moment, and she stared fixedly at the ground to the right of the little family. When she looked up again, Sofia's expectant eyes were trained on her.

'I know what you two are doing…'

'What?'

'Never mind. Let's get on with the tour.'

Angeliki gave them all a puzzled look before continuing.

'Of course, not all Greeks love cats. Some people see the feral cats as little more than vermin and even try to'—the vet closed her eyes a moment—'poison them.'

'No!' Maddie couldn't stop herself.

'That is why we strive to keep the population down where we can, and offer subsidised sterilisations at the surgery, plus fundraise all over town. As you can imagine it costs a lot in food and bills. Annike is amazing. She gives all the cats names, and she can pick each one out in a pack, no trouble. No cat turned away is the motto of the sanctuary.'

The stunning scenery and the sight of so many contented cats lolling in the sun or scratching away at special posts had wormed its way into Maddie's heart whether she liked it or not.

'And of course we do our best to rehome as many cats as we can, both here and abroad. Visitors come to the sanctuary, fall in love with a particular cat and we arrange the transportation back to their country.'

Maddie knew if she looked up, both Sofia and Charlotte would be focussed on her. She wasn't going to fall for their little games.

The tour of the grounds was almost over, when Maddie spotted a ginger cat with only three legs in the middle of a pack. The plucky little thing was keeping up with the others and even elbowed a bigger cat out of the way to get to the food.

'What's happened to her or him?' Maddie tried to keep her voice casual.

Angeliki reached in and picked up the little cat with one hand.

'A she. Cinnamon, or *Kanela* in Greek, was hit by a car six months ago and left to die at the roadside, which often happens with feral cats. And if you've seen anything of Greek driving, you'll know why it's so common.'

Charlotte and Maddie nodded vigorously in unison.

'Someone brought her to me, and I managed to save her life, but I couldn't save her leg. We didn't know how she'd cope when she came here, but she's a real fighter.'

The cat's solemn green eyes stared up at Maddie. It was crazy to even entertain the possibility of taking a three-legged cat all the way back to Manchester, wasn't it?

'Would you like to hold her?'

Maddie took a deep breath. A lot rested on her answer.

'OK.'

She took the cat from Angeliki's arms and turned her back on the others for a private moment. The white underfur on the cat's belly was supersoft to the touch and after a tentative stroke she was rewarded with a loud purr from her charge.

They locked eyes as the tiny cat stretched out its back legs, the little stump on one side barely moving. The animal's blinking eyes were giving her cat kisses the entire time she held her. Maddie's own eyes filled with tears. She couldn't cry, not now, not with everyone watching. One of her tears escaped and fell onto the cat's fur, making her jump, but she carried on purring like a trooper.

The decision had been made as soon as she'd agreed to hold her. This brave little scrap of a cat was coming to live with her. Not one of the more perfect specimens that played around her feet. It had to be this cat. They'd both been knocked about by life, but neither of them was going to give up.

There'd be some red tape to go through, and it wouldn't happen straightaway, but she'd give this cat her best life, the life she deserved. She'd keep her Greek name, *Kanela*, to remind her where she'd come from. Her friends had known better than she did what she wanted or needed.

When she turned back, the three women standing in front of her all had tears in their eyes as well.

'You crafty buggers. It's worked... Where do I sign?'

Angeliki led her over to the office to start the formal adoption process before leaving for her work in the town.

'I'm so pleased you've picked her. I know you'll look after her.' Angeliki lowered her voice and looked around at the cats beneath their feet. 'Don't tell the others, but she's my favourite. Such a strong girl.'

After plenty of photos of *Kanela* in every single pose imaginable, and a tearful goodbye to the little cat, it wasn't just Maddie who needed the excuse of the 'quiet hours' between three and five in the afternoon for a lie down. It had been one emotional morning.

She was still looking at shots of *Kanela* on her phone while they waited for the car to take them to the club. They'd all agreed to wear the same dresses they'd worn to the *panigýri*, but Maddie had absolutely no plans to dance with stray fishermen tonight.

The Star Bar turned out to be high up on one side of the main town, a big performance space surrounded by old stone walls and open to the skies, with a bar attached.

Sofia took them up to the counter and looked from one to the other and then to the barmaid and back several times as if waiting for something. It was Charlotte who clocked it first.

'Oh my God, it's Suzie Sessions, isn't it? My brother had her poster up on his wall for years. He was obsessed with her.'

Sofia smiled.

'Yes, I think most teenage boys were obsessed with Suzie in the eighties. I got a bit of second-hand glory because I looked and acted a bit like her, being small, dark and mouthy, or as we say, spirited.'

'You still do look alike.' Maddie smiled. 'What's she doing here of all places?'

'She owns the bar. Married a Greek years ago and stayed. Got two grown up sons.'

'Hey, Sofia!'

Suzie came down the bar to greet their friend.

'Didn't realise you were back in town.'

'Yes, and I've brought my friends this time, meet Maddie and Charlotte.'

Suzie waved from behind the bar and Charlotte did a particularly vigorous wave back while Maddie restricted herself to a smile and a nod.

'Hi, girls. First drink's on me. What would you like?'

Sofia dived in on their behalf.

'Three Mythos please.'

'Coming up. Is Grace on her way?'

'Yes, she should be here in a minute.'

Suzie handed over three ice-cold bottles of the Greek beer they'd all come to love, condensation dripping in rivulets down the green glass. Charlotte wouldn't dream of drinking beer at home, but here it seemed the natural choice.

'Take these, and I'll catch you later.'

Charlotte reached for one of the beers and leant so far over the counter she was practically lying on top of it.

'Thanks so much, Suzie. Love your music. Always loved your music. My brother really, really loved your music. Such a pleasure to meet you.'

Suzie handed the bottles over to the others with a small smile.

'Good to hear.'

Maddie shepherded Charlotte to her seat.

'A little starstruck are we?'

'You don't understand. She was all my brother talked about. And like most teenage boys, he barely spoke in those days. We even persuaded my parents to let us go to see a gig of hers in Reading of all places. And you know how strict my parents were.'

Maddie raised her eyes to the sky.

'Don't remind me.'

The lying she'd had to do to release Charlotte from their clutches had involved them both developing an intense interest in art classes, followed by sleepovers at hers, which really meant clubbing for most of the night with Sofia, whose mum had been fine with it, even turning out to pick them up at all hours. Luckily, Charlotte had always been a fantastic artist, so it wasn't a problem to produce a few pieces as proof of their passion for both of them.

'Honestly, I can still remember Suzie's gig. It was amazing. It's so weird to find her here, on a tiny Greek island. I can't really believe it.'

'Okaay. Maybe she'll let you take her pic later to show your brother. I don't think many of this lot'—Maddie pointed at the crowd pouring into the bar—'will have a clue who she is.'

Charlotte was still staring in Suzie's direction.

'I wonder why she gave it all up? She just disappeared after a few hits. Never made another album.'

'For love, it sounds like.'

'How romantic.'

Charlotte really hoped that the love that had tempted Suzie was still alive and kicking. To give up your country as well as your unique skill was huge. Her talent for art might have deserted her for the moment, but she hoped and prayed she'd find it again soon. She couldn't imagine going through the rest of her life without painting.

The next time Sofia looked over at the bar, Grace was there talking to Suzie.

'Grace! Over here!' Sofia gave an ear-splitting whistle.

Maddie put her hands up to her ears.

'Thanks for that, Sof. I thought it was going to be the music that hurt my ears, not you.'

Once Sofia had hugged the life out of her old friend, she reintroduced her to the others. Maddie had met up with Sofia's tall, blonde uni mate, Grace, a couple of times over the years, Sofia's first wedding being one occasion, and at a couple of parties, but she'd not seen her for ages, and not since she'd lost Tony.

Grace had also been widowed herself a few years ago, she recalled, but according to Sofia, was now happily hooked up with an ex special-forces soldier called Will. She certainly looked well on it.

Both she and Charlotte were hugged in turn by Grace.

'Hi. I remember meeting you both ages ago, but as madam here has basically had hardly any time off work in the last ten years, it's been a while. But now all that work nonsense's over…'

Sofia bumped against her friend.

'Don't say that! It's not over.'

'OK, on hold. Anyway, it's great to see you both here on the island. Welcome and *Yamas*!'

'*Yamas*!'

Maddie and Charlotte smiled back and clinked bottles with Grace.

'I'm not naïve enough to think I'm the only attraction on the island. I'm sure you've both met a certain someone called Adonis.'

Sofia put her hands on her hips.

'Grace! Why are you trying to wind me up the second I've got here?'

Maddie winked at Grace.

'We certainly have noticed Adonis. Sof was desperate to get here. On the previous island she was all twitchy and restless like you wouldn't believe. She even turned down a perfectly hunky car hire guy with the looks of a Greek god, and you know that's not like her…'

Sofia slammed her beer down on the table.

'Oh great, you're ganging up on me now.'

Grace put her arm round Sofia's shoulders.

'We're just excited that this one's lasted more than one night. I was here when you met him almost a year ago, remember. And you've been back for more quite a few times since, haven't you?'

'Back for more sounds sleazy. Look, I keep telling you all that it's just casual. He's a nice guy, and we get on well. There's nothing more to it than that. Why won't you believe me?'

Sofia wasn't sure how convincing she sounded. It was almost as if she was trying to convince herself. She couldn't bear the thought of being in thrall to a man. Look where it had got her mother, years of torment and regret, feeling she'd failed and wasn't good enough. There was no way she was going to let a man make her feel like that. Keeping things light with Adonis was the key, even though her body ached knowing he was so close.

Charlotte patted her friend on the arm.

'I believe you.'

Maddie exchanged a look with Grace before she spoke.

'Mmmm, me, not so much.'

The music from next door had been getting louder and louder as they talked. Grace stood up at the sound of an announcement in both Greek and English.

'OK, I'm on in a few minutes. I'll see you in there.'

After they'd waved her off, Maddie downed the last of her beer.

'So, I wasn't dreaming about you saying she's a DJ. I thought I'd made it up.'

Sofia finished her bottle too and stood up.

'She's still a teacher by day, but she's always loved music. She does a soul session at the eighties' nights every now and then to keep her hand in.'

'Fantastic. Go Grace!'

Charlotte took a last lingering look at Suzie manning the bar before they moved through to the music venue.

'Oh! That's why it's called the Star Bar!'

Maddie looked up at the hundreds of stars twinkling above them, now darkness had fallen.

'I have to admit that's pretty special.'

Grace was already on the raised dais with a much younger blonde guy, who was coming to the end of his set.

They quickly found seats at a table next to the large dance floor and ordered more beers from the floating waiters.

When, minutes later, the first beats of McFadden and Whitehead's 'Ain't No Stopping Us Now' pulsed into the night air, Charlotte was straight out of her seat.

'Come on, you two! We have to dance to this. It was our anthem back in the day.'

Maddie and Sofia let themselves be led onto the dance floor, and the moves came back to them in a rush.

The warm air, the stars, and the sight of people of all ages and nationalities giving it their all was a truly memorable experience, mused Maddie. She'd never dream of going to a club in Britain, but here it really didn't seem to matter.

After dancing through the whole of Grace's set, which brought the memories flooding back, all Maddie could think was how much Tony would have enjoyed it.

It was like she'd taken two steps forward and one back. Every song recalled a moment frozen in time in a way that hit her more deeply than a photo ever could. As the beat pulsed through her, the final song brought an overload of memories from a soul weekender they'd gone on with friends in Norfolk, a precious few days away together while Tony was at university.

Everything from being pushed squealing around the on-site

supermarket in a trolley, to dancing next to each other in unison with hundreds of others, and shutting themselves away in their room for a snatched few minutes alone all through the day and night made her head whirl.

She couldn't bear to let the music pulse through her any longer. She left the others to it, found their table and ordered more beers for everyone. The blonde male DJ was back and had changed the music to more of an Indie vibe. Sofia and Charlotte were still going strong, and she watched them for a long moment, trying to calm her racing mind.

'All a bit much?'

Chapter Twenty-Three

Maddie nodded. She hadn't noticed Grace sit down next to her.

'You could say that. It's the memories that overwhelm you.'

'I get it. I really do. Music has a way of reaching right into your soul and twisting it over and over again.'

Maddie passed Grace a beer.

'Cheers.'

'Cheers to you too and thank you for a wonderful set. It's the story of my youth. I was always a soul girl.'

'Me too.' Grace indicated towards the dance floor where their friends were still jumping up and down frenziedly. 'Not as keen on this Indie stuff.'

'Me neither.'

Maddie turned to face Grace.

'You obviously heard from Sof about Tony. It's what's making me ultra-sensitive to everything tonight.'

'Yes, I was very sorry to hear about your husband.'

Maddie put her hand over Grace's for a moment.

'And I was sorry to hear about your husband too. Phil, isn't it?'

'Yes, that's right.'

'I think it's important to keep their memory alive, don't you? I hate referring to Tony in the past.'

'I agree. The girls and I often talk about Phil. There's usually some laughter in there now as well as tears.'

The others would be back in their seats soon. This was her opportunity to speak to someone who really understood.

'Be honest with me. Does it really get any better?'

Grace took a careful sip at her beer.

'It does get better, gradually, but it never goes away fully. There are no easy fixes, but based on my experience, you do learn to live with it. Family is key. Friends are invaluable, of course, but you need those ties with your family to be unbreakable too.'

Maddie swallowed some beer a little too quickly and coughed.

'You have children, don't you?'

Maddie nodded, unable to speak for a couple of seconds.

'Yes, a son and a daughter.'

'Any grandchildren yet?'

Maddie forced a smile.

'A little girl called Elsie.'

'So, you know how lovely it is. My new little grandson, Dexter, my eldest daughter's child, has brought so much to my life.' Grace's mouth turned down. 'And although they live on the other side of the world, we're making it work. And there's going to be another baby soon if everything goes well for my other daughter back in England. I can honestly say that four years on, I'm in a totally different place from where I was when Phil died.'

The talk of grandchildren brought tears to Maddie's eyes, but luckily Grace was staring into the distance. She wasn't about to admit to this lovely woman that she'd mucked it up royally with her own granddaughter, but she needed to find a way of telling her friends and soon.

'I took a chance coming to this island a year ago... I urgently needed something to change in my life.' Grace's focus was on her again. 'I was stuck in the same cycle of grief and anger over Phil leaving me, and nowhere near the acceptance that all the books drone on about.'

Grace could be describing her story. She may have only signed up for a three-week holiday island hopping, but it had made her examine her own life under a microscope.

Maddie nodded her understanding at Grace's impassioned words.

'Forcing myself out of my comfort zone has been so good for me in more ways than I could ever imagine. So, if you get the chance to do that, then please take it.'

Grace's eyes were shining.

'I never thought I'd find love again, and I certainly wasn't looking. I was sick and tired of people trying to set me up and telling me it was time to move on.'

'Yeah, I get that. It's bloody annoying.'

'I didn't even like Will much when we met, but he grew on me.' Grace couldn't stop the smile from taking over her whole face. 'It's probably too early for you, but don't discount the possibility of love finding you. He has made me so happy.'

Grace touched her arm.

'Sorry, how selfish. I shouldn't be going on about how happy I am in front of you.'

'No, it's fine, honestly. I'm genuinely pleased for you. I can't get my head round it for myself quite yet, but it's nice to know it's out there.'

'It doesn't need to be a big deal. We're not talking marriage or even living together. Just some male companionship occasionally can be nice. And don't rule out a holiday romance either. Sof tells me you spent some time with a hunky fisherman on the last island?'

'Oh my God. I'm going to blush. She's awful, isn't she?'

'But we love her.'

'We do.'

'I understand. The first time you do anything, even go on a date, it's hard, so hard.'

'Hopefully…'

Maddie gasped.

'Did I actually say that out loud? I thought it was just in my head.'

Grace nodded, unable to speak for laughing, which set Maddie off too.

Sofia arrived at the table and flopped down between them.

'What's so funny?'

Maddie couldn't meet Grace's eye.

'Nothing.'

Sofia looked from one to the other.

'It can't be nothing. You've both got tears in your eyes, you've been laughing so hard.'

Maddie passed her friend a beer.

'I know you hate being left out. But let's just say it's nothing for you to worry about.'

Sofia took an angry swig at the beer, and Charlotte's appearance at the table stopped any further conversation, as all three of them stared at her.

Her long blonde hair was plastered to her head, and the sweat was running in rivers down both sides of her face while her silver dress was stuck to her body in big damp lumps.

'That was fantastic! I used to adore The Jam. Paul Weller went to my friend's school and they used to practise in the school hall.'

Sofia passed over another beer.

'Eeeew. Don't get too close to me, please. I'm meeting up with Adonis later, once he gets rid of all the annoying hotel guests hanging around the bar. Why can't they all just have an early night?'

Maddie and Grace exchanged glances. Usually, it was the men waiting around for Sofia, not the other way round.

Charlotte leant over and rubbed her cheek slowly against Sofia's.

'Yuk! Get off.'

Maddie waved down a waiter. Charlotte was already pretty trollied, so they might as well catch up.

'More beers, children?'

Grace looked down at her phone.

'I could squeeze in one more. Thanks.'

Another energetic bout on the dance floor had the four of them high kicking in unison to 'New York, New York', with Charlotte and Grace as the glamorous blonde bookends, hair shining brightly under the lights, and she and Sofia the flashes of red and brunette in between.

Back in their seats and halfway down their new beers, Charlotte giggled and leant over to Grace.

'I know. You can be our fourth musketeer! You'd have to be called D'Artagnan though, because he was the one who joined last.'

Maddie marvelled at Charlotte's grasp of facts even when three sheets to the wind.

'That's a great idea.' Sofia smiled at Grace. 'Remind me of the other names, Char.'

'Um, Athos, Porthos and Aramis.'

'Oooh, bagsy Aramis. I had an old boyfriend who wore that aftershave. Just a whiff of it could get me going.'

Maddie laughed into her beer.

'I'm sure Alexandre Dumas would be proud.'

'Who's he?'

'The author of the original book.' Charlotte smiled. 'Aramis originally wanted to be a priest.'

Maddie nudged her friend.

'Perfect for you, Sof.'

'Shut it!'

'Aramis was very charming though, so that suits you.' Charlotte paused a moment. 'Hang on, let me think. Athos was brooding and noble, so you can have him, Mads, and I'll be Porthos who was known for his strength, but also his vanity. I can get very touchy about my hair.'

'Impressive.' Grace nodded in Charlotte's direction.

'Oh, she knows loads of stuff.'

Maddie raised her beer towards the others.

'So, all for one...'

The shout when it came even attracted attention from the committed dancers.

'And one for all!'

Sofia put her arm around Grace.

'That's it now, you're bonded with us for life.'

Grace drank the dregs of her beer.

'Thanks for a lovely evening, you lot. It's been like going out with a gang of mates back home. I've not danced and laughed so much in ages.'

'One for the road?' Maddie raised her hand to attract the waiter's attention.

'Not for me, thanks. Will's arriving any minute and we've got an early start tomorrow. He's taking me on some special boat trip to celebrate one year of us meeting.'

Sofia looked over at the entrance.

'Ah, that's so sweet. And ... here he is.'

A tall, dark, handsome man strolled over to their table and Maddie's stomach contracted at the way Grace's eyes lit up when she saw him. He had the same sort of physique as Thanassis, broad shoulders and muscles honed by hard work, definitely not an office boy. His slightly apprehensive look as he approached them was at odds with his imposing presence.

'Hello ... girls, I think you prefer to be called, so Grace tells me. "Ladies" is out these days. I'm Will.'

Charlotte stood and held out her arms.

'Hey, Will. Come closer. Don't worry, we won't eat you.'

Charlotte's hug must have been extremely sweaty, thought Maddie, as Will smiled manfully and moved swiftly on to her. His relief when she stuck to a handshake was palpable.

His grip was firm, and close up, he was even better-looking. She managed to give Grace a thumbs up when Will's back was turned.

He got to Sofia last, picked her up and twirled her round like she weighed nothing.

'Sof, we'll catch up soon, yeah.'

'You bet.'

Before he put her down, Maddie noticed he'd whispered something in her ear. She wondered what that was all about.

The couple waved goodbye but were barely out of the door before Sofia spoke.

'This is top secret, but I can't keep it to myself anymore.'

Maddie guessed what was to come.

'Well, you have waited a whole five seconds.'

'Funny. Will is going to propose to Grace tomorrow at the little beach where they went on their first date together.'

Charlotte was about to get stuck into her next beer but stopped mid-air.

'Ah, how romantic.'

Maddie reached for another bottle too.

'Does Grace actually want to get married again?'

Sofia did a double take.

'Have you seen the way she looks at him?'

'I'm not disputing that she loves him. But marriage?'

Sofia frowned.

'Don't spoil the mood. There's more.'

Sofia leaned in further, although no one could possibly hear what they were saying over the music.

'He's been planning it for a while. There's going to be a wedding as well. They have to do the formal bit at the town hall first, but he's fixed it for them to get married on the beach below their house at sunset the day before we leave.'

Charlotte slumped down onto one elbow.

'Aaaahh. How cute.'

'Grace hates fuss, so it had to be something simple, just a few friends. They're off to Australia the day after anyway for an extended trip to see her daughter and grandson, so that will double up as a honeymoon. Her other daughter and her wife are flying there too as a surprise.'

Charlotte was now resting her head on the table and mumbling softly.

'I always wanted a beach wedding. Mine was terribly formal, in a church... Horrible big meringue of a dress. My parents organised it all. No one asked me what I really wanted.'

Sofia exchanged a worried glance with Maddie, before clapping her hands together.

'Well, you'll be part of this wedding now as we're all invited, and ... I'm going to be the one and only bridesmaid! Grace promised me that if she ever got married again, I'd be her bridesmaid. I don't think she thought it would happen in her wildest dreams, after Phil died, but she can't change her mind now. I've never been a bridesmaid before.' Sofia pointed at her friends. 'And you're both a little bit to blame for that.'

Charlotte sat up.

'I did ask you! We had the dress and everything. It wasn't my fault your appendix burst the day before the wedding. Not yours either I know...'

'Oh yes, I think I'd sort of blanked that out... I missed the whole thing didn't I, stuck in hospital?'

'You did, and we were all worried sick about you. You were mentioned in the speeches.'

'Aaah, that's nice.'

Sofia turned her attention to Maddie, who put her hands up.

'You know we eloped the day Tony graduated. We didn't have anyone there, let alone bridesmaids. It was just the two of us.'

Maddie closed her eyes for a moment, remembering the happiness on Tony's face in the registry office when he'd said I do.

'I didn't want my mum to have to worry about the cost of a wedding either.'

Sofia smiled at her friends.

'Fair enough. You're both excused.'

'Thank God for that.' Maddie leant forward. 'Since you're quizzing us, why weren't you asked to be a bridesmaid at Grace's first wedding?'

Sofia sighed.

'Grace's bossy mother insisted that she only had small children as bridesmaids. No adults allowed. Parents had a lot more say in those days.'

Charlotte nodded.

'That's so true. I'm not sure I made any of the decisions about my own wedding. My parents were desperate to get me down the aisle as soon as possible after the engagement was announced in case I let the *"oh-so-suitable"* Doug escape.'

Sofia patted her friend's leg. This wasn't getting them anywhere.

'I'm sure you made a stunning bride, Char. And I know

Grace felt bad about not defying her mother too. Which is why she made the promise. I'm so excited for them … and for me.'

Maddie took another swig of beer.

'Let's hope that Grace says yes tomorrow then…'

'Stop it, grumpy pants.'

'I am honestly thrilled for Grace if that is what she wants. And for you, Sof, getting the chance to be a bridesmaid after all these years.'

Sofia's smile was as wide as a Cheshire cat.

Maddie couldn't stop her mind going back to what Grace had said about strengthening ties after loss. She'd done the exact opposite and alienated a big chunk of her already tiny family. She couldn't keep it to herself any longer. There wouldn't be a better opportunity, and she'd drunk enough to be able to say it out loud.

'But … if we're talking secrets, I think the time has finally come to tell you mine.'

She could get through this without breaking down, of course she could. Two instantly serious faces stared back at her.

'I told you that my son was angry with me after Tony's death, about feeding him the wrong food and all that, and that things had been tricky.'

Maddie took a deep breath.

'It was actually worse than that, a lot worse. There was one humungous row at their house when we'd all been drinking. I'm not proud of this, but I called his wife a vicious controlling cow and accused her of stopping him from coming to see me since Tony's death.'

Charlotte's gasp was easily heard above the music.

'I know. It was wrong, and I shouldn't have done it. I felt pushed into a corner... The upshot of all this is that I've been banned from their home. I haven't seen Elsie for three months ... and I miss her so much.'

The tears when they came were hard and fast. Both women had rushed to her side and were stroking her back. At least it was out there now. She hadn't deliberately wanted to keep it from them, but the whole thing was a sorry mess.

Sofia had tears in her eyes too.

'Oh Mads. We knew something was horribly wrong. That's so sad.'

'Sad ... and stupid. I've been such an idiot.'

Sofia knelt down in front of her and took her hands.

'Stop that. You're not an idiot. Don't be so hard on yourself. You were an angry, grieving widow who let her tongue get the better of her.'

'And it sounds like your son had had a right go at you as well.' Charlotte attempted a smile. 'Vicious controlling cow is probably not what you'd want to hear your wife called, but he kicked the whole thing off with his accusations about too many bacon sandwiches.'

'Full Englishes, if we're being accurate.'

Maddie's heart rate returned to something approaching normal, as the relief of finally telling the truth kicked in. It didn't show her in a good light, but at least she'd been honest.

Sofia pulled her up to a standing position.

'We've all had enough. Let's grab a taxi and go back for a quiet chat at the hotel.'

Gathered on Sofia's terrace with cups of herbal tea and the sound of the sea gently lapping at the wall below them, Maddie could still hear the music ringing in her ears.

Sofia reached out and touched her friend's knee.

'All right, Mads?'

'Slightly deaf, but other than that, bearing up.'

'Now you've told us everything, the question is what are we going to do about it?'

Maddie hadn't thought that far. Just saying it out loud had completely drained her.

'What can we do about it?'

'My inkling is that your son is probably as upset about all this as you are.'

'I'd like to think so. But he's not going to take my side against his wife.' Maddie's laugh was strained. 'You know what they say, happy wife, happy life.'

Charlotte put up a hand.

'No, that's true. If you want my opinion, I think you're going to have to be the one to apologise first.'

Maddie sighed.

'Yes, I'd worked that out for myself. And I can't let it go on any longer. Thanassis more or less told me the same thing.'

'Thanassis?' Sofia's shock showed on her face. 'He knows?'

'It all came out that night on the beach. I didn't intend to tell him. I was just looking for the right time to tell you two. But it's easier to tell someone you barely know.'

Charlotte elbowed Sofia in the side.

'Yes, the main thing is working out a solution now. Let's not get hung up on who knew when.'

Sofia held her side a moment.

'Of course. Why don't we try and put together an email, the three of us?'

Maddie shrugged.

'Well, it can't possibly make things any worse, so why not?'

'OK, let's write it out first. Char, you've got the best handwriting. There's some notepaper in the room and a pen on the side.'

'Yes, Ma'am.'

After half an hour of crossings out, sighing and even a smattering of laughter, they finally had a draft that Maddie was happy with.

'Can you read it out one more time, please, Char.'

'OK, here goes. *"To my darling family. Please can we find a way of sorting out our problems and moving forward with our lives. I am missing you all so much, and Elsie must have grown and mastered so many new things since I last saw her. I accept that the whole blow up was my fault, and I am truly sorry. I apologise unreservedly for my rude remarks to Hayley…"'*

Maddie did a mock vomit.

'Do we have to keep that bit in? I know I went over the top, but there was a little bit of truth in it.'

'Yes' was the deafening response from both her friends.

'OK, I get it. Carry on.'

'Where were we? Ah yes… *"apologise unreservedly for my rude remarks to Hayley and hope she can forgive me. I wasn't in the best place when I said those things. Losing your dad has been the most horrible experience of my life, but I don't want to make things any worse by losing contact with you all and not being part of Elsie's life. I miss him every day, as I'm sure you do. Your dad would be so sad that things have come to this. I'm not saying this to make you feel bad, but because you know it's true. He never got to meet Elsie, who he would have absolutely adored, so I want, and need, to be there for her, on behalf of both of us. He's a part of her too. I really hope that you will let me back into your lives one day, hopefully soon, and we can start all over again. All my love, Mum."'*

'Do you think that will do the trick?' Maddie looked up at the others, who both seemed to have something in their eye.

Charlotte wiped her tears with a tissue.

'If it doesn't, they've got hearts of stone.'

Sofia fetched her iPad from inside the room.

'So, if we're all agreed, let's send it now. It won't take me a minute to type it out. Do you know your login and password?'

'Don't I need to send it from my own computer?'

'Nope, as long as you've got the details.'

In her mind, Maddie was waiting until she got home to send it. Maybe give it another read through. Fiddle about with it a bit.

'I'm not sure about sending it tonight.'

Sofia fired up the device.

'There's no point in waiting. That child will be walking in a minute. Let's get on with it now. They're two hours behind in England, so it's already eleven in the evening there. He probably won't see it until tomorrow, depending on how regularly he checks his personal emails.'

Maddie looked at Charlotte for reassurance. As the cautious one, she might back her up.

'I agree with Sof. You've got nothing to lose. It can't make things any worse, and it just might improve the situation.'

'OK, I accept that I'm outnumbered two to one. Here, I'll write down the details.'

Sofia typed like a madwoman, pressed send and leapt up out of her seat as her phone buzzed in her bag for the second time.

Maddie indicated down at the bag.

'Got somewhere to be, have you?'

'I have, as a matter of fact.'

'Don't forget clean pants and a toothbrush.'

'Ha ha, I actually have things at the hotel and at Adonis's flat.'

'Have you now? Very organised.'

'I can hardly wander around Adonis's hotel looking like a wild animal.'

The disdainful look on the face of the attractive receptionist sprang into Maddie's mind. She wouldn't need much of a reason to disapprove of her friend.

'Of course not.'

'Leave her alone, Mads. I think it's romantic. Grabbing any available minute she can with her man.'

'Yes, it is sweet. I'm probably a teeny bit jealous.'

Maddie pulled her friends in for a hug.

'Before you go… Thank you both for helping me with the email. I feel a bit sick at the idea that it's already gone and it's winging its way across seas and countries at this very moment…'

Sofia snorted.

'I don't think it quite works like that, but carry on.'

'I don't know what I'd do without you both. So, thank you, my lovelies.'

Maddie held on to the others for a few seconds more until

Sofia wriggled out of the group embrace as yet another message buzzed on her phone.

'Got to go. Car's waiting. Let's do something fun tomorrow. A morning at the pool now we've got one. Or check out some of the beaches?'

She was through the door before they'd even had a chance to reply.

Charlotte chuckled.

'She's keen, isn't she? Never seen her like this before. I don't feel at all sleepy after my night boogying. Fancy another herbal tea?'

'Yeah, let's go crazy. Thanks.'

Maddie looked out to sea at the lights of the little boats far in the distance. Several of them were almost definitely fishing boats. She didn't know if Thanassis came this far afield on his travels, but he'd certainly be proud of what she'd done tonight. Confessed everything to her friends and set about doing something about it. Whether it would work or not was another matter, but at least she'd tried.

Chapter Twenty-Four

After the revelations of the previous night, everyone was happy to just top up their tans and laze around the pool until lunchtime.

Sofia had eventually appeared when breakfast was almost over, and the phrase *bright eyed and bushy tailed* could have been written to describe her, thought Maddie. They only had a few days left on the island; a few days left of their holiday full stop. How Sofia would cope without Adonis on tap didn't bear thinking about.

But Sofia wasn't the only one who would struggle when their time in the sun was over. They all had things to face when they got back. Maddie wasn't going to let the thought of going home to an empty house spoil their time together if she could help it, plus she'd promised herself she wouldn't check her phone every five minutes to see if there'd been a reply from Dan. At least she had the promise of a new cat. It wasn't the same as being reconciled with half her family, but she had to hang on to something, otherwise she'd go crazy.

They were all sunbathing in brand new bikinis with tasselled edges in their signature colours of red, blue and green, Sofia's last gift. Maddie's swimsuits had been consigned to the back of the suitcase long ago. It now seemed perfectly natural to wear a bikini all day long, even round a hotel pool where it wasn't just Greeks on holiday.

Being a lot more comfortable in her own body was just one of the ways the trip had helped her. And she had Thanassis to thank for some of that ease. Their night on the beach wasn't something she'd be repeating in a hurry, however wonderful it had been. But he'd shown her that it was possible to live without one eye permanently on the past. The present had good things to offer too.

The never-ending cycle of grief for Tony's absence wasn't quite as daunting anymore, and the warmth of the Greek people, the culture, the food and, of course, the sun had all contributed their share. If only she could sort things out at home. Maybe if she rested her eyes it would help…

What felt like moments later, she was well and truly woken up by Sofia leaping up off her sunlounger and racing round the pool shouting 'Yes, she said yes!' several times.

'We're talking about Grace, I presume?'

'Of course. Who else would we be talking about? She's just texted from the beach. The wedding's on, with yours truly as the one and only bridesmaid!'

'You will go the ball, Cinderella.'

Sofia wrapped her arms around herself and did a twirl, which had Charlotte grinning.

'Ah, how lovely. Give her our congratulations.'

'Will do.'

Maddie leant over to take the biscuits served with coffee that Sofia had rejected. She was starting to get peckish. Lunch couldn't be far away.

'Don't eat them!'

'Why on earth not?'

Sofia's eyes sparkled.

'Because we've all been invited to a late lunch at Adonis's brother's house in the hills. It's so hard for him to get away from the hotel in the evenings, his busiest time, so it's been arranged for four o'clock. His sister's going to be there too, so I'll meet both his siblings, their partners, and his nieces and nephews for the first time. Luckily, the scary mother won't be there, so I'm getting the easy ones first.'

Maddie popped a biscuit into her mouth and disposed of it in a second, followed by another.

'Sounds lovely. I'm starving.'

'Char?'

'Well, I'm not starving yet, but I'm sure I will be by the time we get there.'

Maddie studied the way Sofia was tapping her fingers on the little side table.

'Are you nervous?'

'Of course not. Why are you saying that?'

'You seem a bit … strung out.'

'OK, I suppose I am a little. I don't usually get to meet the families as you know. But this is Greece. You can't get away without meeting the family. But it doesn't mean anything.'

Like hell it didn't. She was well aware that this was a test that she'd need to pass. Not the ultimate showdown with the family matriarch, but a test nevertheless. Why hadn't she picked someone who was constantly on the move, like a pilot or a ship's captain? Not someone firmly anchored to his family and his job on a small Greek island.

Maddie and Charlotte exchanged a glance.

'I know what you're doing.'

Maddie reached over to touch her friend's leg.

'I don't want to put a downer on the proceedings, but have you thought about what you're going to do when you go back to England in precisely … three days' time?'

'Stop it!'

As well as not having instant access to Adonis, the great big gaping hole where her work had been was something Sofia couldn't think about right now. Being away with her friends had been just the tonic she needed after being unceremoniously dumped. But it wasn't real life. It was a sun-drenched fantasy, but she was determined not to let it end before it had to.

'As you rightly say, we still have three days left to enjoy ourselves. Let's not talk about what happens back in England until we get there. Can we all make a pact, please?'

Charlotte sat up on her sunlounger.

'Fine by me.'

The idea of facing Doug again and having to rake over everything in person wasn't a pleasant one either. It would decide the future of their marriage. Being so far away from her husband and his mistress had been refreshing. She wasn't going to bump into Natalie over the pastries in the local mini market on a tiny Greek island, the way she very well might in their upmarket village deli back in Surrey. In fact, she had even met the woman there for coffee a few times in a gesture of friendship towards Doug's colleagues. Just the memory made her feel sick.

If she did stay with Doug, and it was a big if, either they'd have to move, or Natalie would. The house had got too big for just the two of them anyway. And realistically the boys lived near enough that they didn't need to stay the night when they visited. What was the point of having unused bedrooms that needed regular cleaning? The holiday really had given her the freedom to step away from her life and think a bit more deeply about her situation rather than just blindly carrying on.

Maddie sighed.

'Sorry, that was my fault for bringing it up. OK, I agree, no more talk about what's waiting for any of us back home until we get on that plane.'

Sofia grabbed her sun hat and phone.

'Agreed. It's a casual do at the brother's house, but we'd better all jump in the shower now and get ready. The car will be here in forty minutes.

Maddie lay back on the sunlounger again.

'Not sure I need that long to beautify myself…'

'Well, as long as you're ready on time.'

'Of course. I wouldn't want to be late for your future in-laws…'

Sofia batted her on the leg with the hat.

'You're going to pay for that. I'll get you back, don't you worry.'

The drive into the hills with the sea at their side was stunning as the heat of the day started to fade a little. They were right on the edge of the narrow roads that wound their way up and round, never losing sight of the sun sparkling on the turquoise water below as the houses petered out and the odd goat occasionally appeared in their path.

Maddie was thankful Sofia had accepted lifts for them all in one of Adonis's courtesy cars, rather than insisting on driving herself in the state she was in. It was a relief not having to worry about whether they'd be going over the side any minute.

A whitewashed house with thick stone walls, deep-blue painted window frames, and a covered terrace on the side appeared at the end of a winding drive. It stood on its own, and even from this angle, it was obvious that the views over to the sea would be spectacular.

Adonis had said he was meeting them there, and he was the first person Maddie saw when they pulled up at the house, at the head of a substantial reception committee several people deep. She reached over and squeezed Sofia's leg.

'They're going to love you.'

'Let's hope so.' Sofia bent to pick up the flowers she'd brought as a gift. 'Not that it really matters if they don't, as I probably won't see most of them ever again. Damn! Why can't I get this door open?'

'Just wait a moment.'

The driver rushed round and pulled open the door that Sofia was wildly yanking at from the inside.

'That's better. It's obviously broken.'

Maddie and Charlotte rolled their eyes at each other.

Adonis rushed forward to take Sofia by the hand as soon as she got out of the car.

'Hello, darling. Welcome, everyone. Come into the shade and we'll do the introductions.'

An hour in, and several carafes of wine later, the whole party had relaxed somewhat, observed Maddie. They'd feasted on *taramasaláta*, *kolokithokeftédes* – the courgette fritters they'd all taking a liking to – smothered in *tzatzíki*, and *dolmádes*, local vine leaves stuffed with rice and mince, all accompanied by chunks of homemade bread. And they hadn't got anywhere near the main courses yet.

Adonis was very much in big brother mode, making sure everyone got the chance to speak and keeping the conversation a delicate balance between Greek and English so that no one felt left out. Maddie could see what made him such a talented hotel manager.

Their host, Kostas, and his wife, Ariadne, plus Adonis's sister, Lydia, and her husband, Christos, kept sneaking glances at Sofia all through the starters, giving Maddie the impression that their brother bringing a woman to a family dinner wasn't a regular occurrence.

Their children, Maddie still hadn't quite worked out who belonged to who, seemed to range from teenagers to those in their early twenties, and were far more brazen in staring at Sofia when they thought no one was looking, as well as grabbing their fair share of wine when their parents were talking.

Several cats weaved in and out of everyone's legs, and Maddie couldn't stop herself giving them the odd titbit from her plate.

'Ah, you are a cat lover?'

Lydia, the sister, had spotted her spoiling the animals.

'Busted.' Maddie smiled but rushed on when she saw the woman's confusion. Busted didn't really translate.

'Sorry. Yes, you're right. I love cats, can't resist their little faces. In fact, I'm going to adopt one from the cat sanctuary up past the main town.'

'Ah, yes, I know it. You do not have any cats to adopt where you live in England?'

The woman's frown told her she couldn't for the life of her understand why someone was taking a cat all the way back to England. Put like that, it did sound a bit crazy.

'It's complicated.'

'I see.'

She obviously didn't, but was willing to let it go.

'And you and Sofia, and your friend…'

'Charlotte.'

'Ah yes, Charlotte, were all at school together. Is that right?'

'Yes.'

Her internal warning system told Maddie to tread carefully. She'd been briefed by Sofia that Greeks were happy to ask you even the most personal questions at the drop of a hat. How old you were, how much you paid for your house, and what you earned were apparently standard enquiries. What was considered nosy in Britain was fine here.

'And you were all in the same year? Which would make you all the same age?'

It was asked with a smile, but Maddie's eyes searched out Sofia further down the table.

Sofia's eyes and ears were on high alert, and she'd caught the words school and same age and seen the determined expression on Lydia's face. There was no way she wanted her age revealed this early on, which Maddie would know, but she needed to make it crystal clear. Why were they so obsessed with how old she was? It was like they were sizing up a racehorse they were thinking of buying. The atmosphere cooled a few degrees. Her eyes met Maddie's, and she gave a brief shake of the head. Moments later she was relieved to see her friend get up from the table.

At the signal from Sofia, Maddie went for the first thing that came into her head.

'Sorry, but I need the toilet. Can you tell me where it is, please?'

'Of course.' The smile didn't waver, but Maddie could tell that Adonis's sister was annoyed she'd failed in her mission. Whether she was the sole interrogator or briefed to speak on behalf of everyone else was hard to tell.

When Maddie returned, she was relieved to see that the main dishes were being brought in by Kostas and Ariadne, which was a spectacle in itself. Kostas put the first one on the table.

'Help yourselves everyone. In honour of our guests, we have beef and aubergine stew, *moskári me melitzanes*, a chicken stew, *kapamas*, and a lamb stew with *avgolemono*, which is a delicious creamy egg and lemon sauce.' Ariadne put the dishes in the centre of the table and made to go back to the kitchen.

Maddie caught Charlotte's eye.

'Surely not more food?' she mouthed.

Ariadne returned with two bowls, even bigger than the rest.

'To go with it, we have island potatoes mashed in olive oil, and *maroulosalata*, a lettuce salad to take away the richness of the stews. Please, eat!'

The food was genuinely fantastic, and to Maddie's relief, thankfully there was no more talk of ages or cats. The chatter around the table got louder and louder as the meal wore on, and they were encouraged to sample everything on the table. By the time the *loukoumades*, small Greek doughnuts, plus a separate jug of chocolate sauce on the side, came out, Maddie was so full she couldn't believe that anyone would even attempt one.

But Sofia's pleading eyes forced her to take a couple of the sweet treats and swallow them down with some water.

Just when she thought it was all over, and most people at the table had lapsed into a semi-conscious state, the shot glasses and the *raki* came out and were passed round.

Sofia stood up and toasted their hosts.

'Thank you for your hospitality and a truly stunning meal. The best we've experienced in Greece.'

The satisfied smiles of Kostas and Ariadne showed it was very much the right thing to say.

'It has been so lovely to be welcomed into Adonis's family and to meet you all. *Yamas*!'

Everyone joined in with the shouts of *Yamas!*

Just moments later it seemed, Adonis pointed at the two cars which had appeared in the driveway. He stood and hugged his brother and sister and their partners in turn.

'Thank you so much *ta agapiména mou adérfia*,' which Maddie guessed meant 'my lovely siblings'. 'But I must go back to work.'

There was a collective groan.

'I'm so pleased you have met Sofia and her friends.'

This was followed by cheers and clapping.

'And now, sadly we must leave you to the washing up.'

Lydia flicked her brother with a serviette.

'Pah, that was always the case. Mummy's little treasure never had to do the washing up.'

She reached up to kiss him on the cheek.

'Don't leave it so long next time. You work too hard.'

Adonis gave Sofia a thorough kiss before getting in his car.

As soon as they'd cleared the driveway in their own car, Sofia undid several buttons in the front of her dress.

'Aaah. I don't think I can ever eat again.'

Charlotte slumped back against the seat.

'Me neither.'

Maddie patted her own stomach.

'Even I'm stuffed.'

Charlotte slapped her friend on the thigh.

'Don't hear that very often, Mads.'

'True.'

Charlotte turned towards Sofia.

'They seemed really nice though, didn't they?'

Maddie spoke before Sofia had the chance to reply.

'Yes, if slightly obsessed with knowing how old you were, Sof.'

Sofia put her hands over her eyes.

'Don't. I'm so relieved it's over.'

'Adonis knows the truth though, doesn't he?'

'Of course, he knows the truth. They're a picnic compared to what the mother's going to be like. Mothers never like me, and I'm sure Greek mothers will like me even less. That little treat is set up for tomorrow.'

'Oooh.'

'It's just because I'm going home in a couple of days. I'll be back, but Adonis wants me to meet all the important people in his life before I go.' Sofia suddenly looked out of the window. 'Will one or both of you come with me, pleeeeease…?'

Maddie shook her head.

'That won't look at all weird.'

'I did run it past Adonis. He's organised a car to drop me off to have coffee with her in the morning because he can't take any more time off work. He said if I wanted to bring one or both of you that would be fine.'

'Okaay. Char?'

'You're better with old people, Mads. The three of us turning up might freak her out. So, I'm happy not to go.'

'OK, I can see I won't get out of this one.'

Sofia leant over and hugged her friend.

'Thank you. Thank you.'

'Please don't squeeze my stomach. It might explode.'

'I know, let's stop in the town on the way and do some shopping. We can walk a bit of this food off.'

'OK, but the coffees are on you.'

'It's a deal.'

Charlotte was thrilled to see a couple of art galleries in the main town on their walk as well as several art supplies shops. There hadn't been anything like this on the other islands, and she wasn't that interested in buying clothes; she had more than enough.

She stopped outside one gallery with a stunning window display. It called to something inside her, far more than a collection of dresses and tops ever could.

'You two go on. I just want to pop in here. Let's meet in an hour in the main square. Decide on a coffee shop and message me the location.'

'OK, if you're sure.'

Sofia barely looked back. Nothing and no one was going to get in her way when it came to shopping.

Charlotte went through the door of the gallery, housed in an old building, which felt as familiar to her as entering her own house. The spacious room opened right up at the back and was hung with brightly coloured abstracts.

At one end, in a light-filled glass conservatory, a woman sat painting at an easel.

The smell of the oil paints made her head swim. She'd missed this so much. Why had she allowed Doug to take this from her as well as her sense of place in the world? Her art wasn't his to toy with. Charlotte watched in silence for a long while until the woman beckoned her over.

'You are also an artist?'

Her accented English made Charlotte think she was Scandinavian.

'Yes, how did you know?'

'You looked so at peace. And you stayed still for so long.'

Charlotte looked up at the glass roof with the dazzling blue sky beyond and out at the white houses climbing up the hill.

'What a gorgeous place to paint.'

'It really is. I'm Astrid, the artist in residence here.' The woman pointed to a set of stairs in the corner. 'I live in the flat above, with a roof terrace overlooking the sea. It is simple, but it has everything I need.'

'I'm Charlotte. Pleased to meet you.'

Charlotte's head was blown by the idea of actually living and working in such a lovely place. It was something she'd never considered. She had to find out more. If she was late for coffee, so be it.

Maddie was now officially bored stiff by the number of shops they'd visited and dismissed after a few minutes. Unusually, Sofia couldn't find anything she liked. They were back on the street once again.

'Nothing in there either?'

'No. It's to wear to meet Adonis's mum. It's got to be just right.'

The wrong image could send everything crashing down before they'd even started.

'But you've got loads of clothes with you. Your suitcase was massive. I made do with hand luggage.'

'Nothing I've brought is suitable. It's got to be tasteful and a bit conservative with a small c.'

'Really? Why can't you just be yourself?'

'Because I know this woman will be all judgy. Did you hear Lydia calling him "mummy's little treasure". I want to make a good impression.'

'For someone who's saying it's only a casual thing, you seem very bothered about what his mother will think. I don't have to dress up as well, do I?'

'Don't be ridiculous.'

Maddie pointed at a shop with a big gold C on the front.

'What about this one? It's got the sort of expensive things you like in the window.'

Sofia took her arm and rushed her past.

'Oh no, we can't go in there, even if the clothes are amazing. That's Celine's. She's a horrible French ex of Will's who tried to ruin things between him and Grace.'

'Well, I can't fault you on loyalty.' Maddie blew her friend a kiss. 'Which is a nice thing. But what about this next shop? My body's crying out for coffee.'

Sofia eyed a white dress in the window with a high neck, a pleated skirt and a thin gold belt round the middle.

'Yes, that might work. You don't think white's too young?'

'No.'

Maddie really thought it might make her friend look a bit

like a majorette, but if she didn't get some caffeine in her soon, she'd collapse.

The dress looked a hundred times better on Sofia that it did on the model in the window, something that invariably happened, observed Maddie. Apart from one foray in front of the mirror to show her the dress, her friend spent ages faffing in the changing room, but to her great relief they were eventually out on the pavement again with a bag bearing the posh logo of the shop and heading for the square.

Seated at the chicest coffee place in town with views through the streets to the sea, a waiter approaching their table made Sofia pick up a menu and open it.

'Shouldn't we stall him and wait for Char? She's late.'

Maddie picked up her phone.

'I did message her to tell her where we are, but I can see she's not read it. I'll message again, but you know what she's like when she's talking art. I'm beyond desperate for a cappuccino after that shopping marathon, so let's order.'

On the walk back to the hotel after lingering over their coffees in the square, Charlotte was full of her meeting with Astrid and opened her bag to show them the selection of watercolours, brushes and paper she'd bought.

'I can't wait to get going on a couple of pictures while I'm here. Just simple stuff, but it's a start.'

Sofia and Maddie smiled at each other. It was lovely to see their friend so happy.

They'd only been settled on Sofia's terrace for around half an hour, watching the boats, when the phone rang in the room.

Sofia raced to answer it, but moments later called out for her friend.

'Char, it's for you.'

'Me?'

Grasping the receiver with an unsteady hand, Charlotte held the phone away from her ear, letting Sofia listen too.

'Charlotte Trent.'

'Yes.'

'Your husband is waiting in reception.'

Chapter Twenty-Five

Charlotte slammed the phone down and slumped onto the nearest seat.

Sofia loomed large above her.

'What the hell? What's he doing here? How does he even know where you are?'

Charlotte just shook her head. It was too much to deal with, even without Sofia's questions.

The shouting brought Maddie in from outside.

'What's happened? You've gone very white, sweetheart.' She knelt down by the chair and held Charlotte's hand.

'Bloody Doug's in reception.' Sofia paced up and down. 'I've got a good mind to go down there myself and give him a piece of my mind. How dare he invade her space like this? I'll give him two-year affair!'

'No!'

Charlotte's wan face took on a determined look as she rose from the chair.

'You will not go anywhere, please, Sof. I need to sort this out myself.'

Maddie stroked her friend's back.

'Too right. Sof, don't leave this room. Be useful and get a glass of water, please.'

Sofia's snort told them what she thought about being grounded.

Maddie lowered her voice.

'Are you sure you're up to this?'

'Yes. It had to happen sometime; it might as well be now. Don't worry, I won't bring him up to my room. I'll take him to that little café down by the port where it's nice and quiet.'

Sofia's anger was slightly muted by the time she returned with the water.

'Sorry about my outburst, but the way Doug has treated you just makes me see red.'

Charlotte gulped down the glassful before speaking.

'I know, Sof. But I've got to deal with this in my own way. He must have bullied the name of the hotel out of one of the boys. I gave them the details in case they needed me urgently.'

Maddie had a sudden pang at the thought that no one needed her anymore, urgently or otherwise, but quashed it quickly.

'Are you ready to go down?'

Charlotte nodded.

'OK, we trust you to follow your heart. And if you need us, just message and we'll be straight on it.'

'Yes, we can kick his ass with the best of them.'

'Hopefully, that won't be necessary, Sof.'

Maddie pulled Charlotte into her arms.

'The best of luck, my love. Group hug.'

Charlotte held on tight to the two of them, before turning on her heel and heading for the lift.

The sorry sight that greeted her in reception was almost comic, if it weren't also a little bit sad. Doug looked like a typical Englishman abroad in an old movie, red faced and dishevelled. He still had his straw hat on, and his chinos and polo shirt were crumpled beyond belief.

She had a moment to herself before he saw her. She tested out her feelings and realised that the predominant one was confusion.

His face when he did see her was like than of an expectant child who'd done something momentous, like learn to use the potty.

'Darling!'

He was up, out of his seat and rushing towards her before she had time to respond. The other guests stared in fascination.

Charlotte submitted to a sweaty kiss on the cheek. It would look very strange to turn away. She wanted the least fuss possible until she could get him away to a quieter spot.

'Hi.' Charlotte opted for a cool smile. 'Why are you here exactly? Is everything OK with the boys?'

'The boys?' Doug looked around as if they might magically appear. 'Yes, they're fine, why?'

'I couldn't understand why else you would get on a plane in such a hurry and come all this way to Greece if it wasn't something to do with one of them.'

'I've come to see you.'

The little boy lost look that had once worked wonders on her was fast losing its power.

Doug groped for her hand which she kept firmly by her side.

'The thing is, I've realised I can't live without you any longer.'

Had he only just realised? Here in the lobby? Analysing his words stopped her from feeling anything.

'We need to talk.'

'I agree. We really do need to talk. Let's go to a little café I know where we won't be overheard.'

'OK, whatever you think best.'

Walking side by side and slotting into their usual rhythm was disconcerting. She was almost as tall as Doug, and she'd spent weeks with women with much shorter legs than hers, who kept begging her to slow down.

'It's really beautiful here, isn't it, darling?' Doug waved his arm around to encompass the little restaurants which stretched out all along the strip next to the water, and the boats beyond.

'Maybe we'll have to come back out here for a proper holiday sometime? Would you like that?'

Doug's hopeful face tugged at her heartstrings just a little bit. But she ignored the question and led the way to the end of the promontory, where, she was relieved to see, nearly all the outside tables were unoccupied.

She made straight for the one right at the end. It faced out to sea and to the islands far off in the distance. Doug finally took off his hat and offered her the choice of seat. He had always been hot on manners; she couldn't fault him on that. Not that it was good manners to shag the office manager.

Once seated, Doug gave her his best smile.

'Lovely to have a bit of privacy, isn't it?'

'Mmmmm.'

The approaching waiter stopped any further conversation.

'What would you like, darling?'

His use of the word was already grating on her.

'A bottle of Mythos, please.'

'You don't normally drink beer...' Doug's face was a picture.

'I don't normally do a lot of things, but here we are.'

'Two Mythos please.'

With their beers in hand, Doug went to speak again at the same time as her.

'Charlotte...'

Only her friends called her Char. He'd always preferred her full name.

'Doug.'

His eyes were on her.

'No, please let me go first.'

Charlotte nodded.

'Again, I want to tell you how sorry and ashamed I am of my behaviour. And you finding out the way you did was unforgivable...'

'We both agree on that then.'

Doug's startled face at her comment made her want to laugh.

'But it's you I love, Charlotte, not Natalie. You're the mother of my sons, the woman I come home to every night, the woman I've cared for and who's cared for me for over thirty years. Surely you don't want to just throw our marriage away?'

'I think it's you who's put in most of the groundwork on that one.'

Doug put up his hands.

'Fair enough. I deserved that. Is there anything I can say that will persuade you that the affair with Natalie was a moment of madness?'

'But that's just it, isn't it? It wasn't a moment. It was a solid two years of lies and deceit. With a woman I thought was a friend.'

The anger built inside her as Doug carried on talking.

'Natalie was a terrible mistake. She was going through such a hard time, Charlotte, and she was distraught at having to put her mother into a care home. She's got no one else. She turned to me for help…'

'Don't you dare defend her!'

Doug's body jolted against the table.

'You were hardly giving her the type of help they recommend at The Samaritans, were you? Where does it say if a workmate is depressed then lay them back over the desk?'

Her shouting had attracted looks from the only other occupied table. But she didn't care. Doug's shocked face swam into focus.

'Charlotte, sweetheart.'

'Don't sweetheart me. Anyway, it's not Natalie I'm really angry at, it's you.'

Doug attempted to stroke her arm, but she flung his hand away.

'Again, I deserved that. But I've never seen you like this before.'

'Maybe because, hopefully, you've never had an affair before?'

'Of course not. This is the one and only time.'

A lock of his hair fell over his eyes in a way she used to find cute.

'You do believe me, don't you?'

'Who knows what to believe?'

'How can you say that? This is so not like you.'

'What? Helpful, accommodating Charlotte, you mean, who's there for everyone? Who volunteers for committees, is always dressed appropriately and pretends to other people that her art is some sort of hobby so you can look like the main breadwinner? I'm sick and tired of that Charlotte.'

The hurt in Doug's eyes was almost too much to bear. They'd had more than thirty years of a marriage that had been happy in its own way before things went south. She didn't need to stick the knife right in and twist it round.

'Sorry, that breadwinner comment was nasty. But being away has helped me to understand that I'm not really that Charlotte anymore. It's just taken me a while to realise it.'

'I liked that Charlotte.'

Doug's sad little voice stiffened her resolve.

'Well, I'm sorry to tell you she no longer exists.'

Charlotte put her hand on his arm this time.

'Can we be totally honest with each other for once?'

'Sure.'

'Have you really been happy these last few years? Because I don't think I have.'

Doug took a long swig of his beer.

'There's been such a lot of pressure, with the business failing and everything. It's hard to separate us out from that.'

'I know you've had a tough time of it these past few years. But I genuinely believe that people in happy marriages don't have affairs. Or at least not affairs that last two years.'

Doug's head went down towards his chest.

'I'm not having another go at you, honest. I'm just being realistic. I don't know how I would have felt if it had been just a one-night stand. I'm not saying I'd be any more thrilled about the idea, but two years is a bloody long time.'

'So, what are you saying? That me flying all this way to beg you not to break up our life together has been a waste of time?'

Charlotte put her hand over his.

'It's not been a waste of time. Because we needed to face this anyway, with or without Natalie's interference.'

The more she talked, the more Charlotte solidified things in her own mind. The affair with Natalie was just a symptom of their problems, not the cause.

'What do you mean?'

'When the boys left, something changed inside me. My years as a caregiver were over, which is all normal and natural; you want them to go off and live their own lives, rather than being emotionally reliant on you.'

She was laying it out for herself as much as him.

'So, at that point you realised I wasn't needed anymore as well?'

'This time, Doug, it's not about you. It's about me.'

He was looking at her as if she was speaking a foreign language.

'We grew apart, but neither of us wanted to acknowledge it.'

'But we've been married for so long. There are bound to be ups and downs. Surely we can try again?'

Charlotte had to harden herself against the pleading note in his voice. Doug downgrading a two-year affair to nothing more than a marital blip gave her the strength to carry on.

'Ups and downs yes. But this is something more. I'm telling you I'm the one who's changed, not you.'

'I thought you loved me, for better or worse.'

'Let's not look too deeply into the marriage vows at this point, Doug. I'm pretty sure adultery is mentioned somewhere.'

She'd even got a little smile out of him. His sense of humour had always been a tick in the pro column.

'As I was saying, I'm the one who's changed. I don't want the four-bedroom house in Surrey anymore, the Friday night takeaway and the pub quiz every Monday.'

'But we were always on the winning side. You were our secret weapon. You know almost everything.'

He'd forced a smile out of her too.

'Flattery won't get you anywhere, either.'

'So, what do you want?' The fear on his face was palpable. 'There's no one else is there? Someone who's made you feel differently?'

'No, there bloody isn't. Incredibly, a woman can have the urge to change her life without there being a man on the horizon.'

'OK, keep your hair on. What exactly is your plan then?'

'For once, I don't have a plan, that's the whole point. I want to explore new ideas, travel more. I met a woman today who was working as an artist in residence in the town here, who was inspiring.'

'A woman? You're not…'

'No, Doug. I'm not rushing off to be a lesbian either. Typical of a man to think that. Would that make you feel better?'

Doug's face made her think it definitely would.

'Don't answer that. I just want to experience new things.'

'And we couldn't do this together?'

Charlotte was torn for a moment, seeing the devastated look on his face, but there was no going back.

'No, it's something I have to do on my own.'

'Are you saying it's definitely over between us?'

Charlotte took a deep breath and looked into his eyes, the bright blue eyes she'd looked into every morning for as long as she could remember.

'I am. With a heavy heart and a lot of sadness, I am.'

The tears that formed in his eyes and slipped down his cheeks were mirrored in her own. They held hands over the table and stared at each other until the tears dried.

Charlotte was the first to shatter the silence.

'You probably don't think it now, but you'll end up thanking me in years to come.'

Doug's laugh was brittle.

'Can't see that happening, but at least I know there's no point hoping any longer.'

'We'll sort everything out between us when I get back. I'm going to take the last two days of my holiday as planned. I presume you have somewhere to stay tonight?'

Doug gave a short, miserable nod.

'We'll tell the boys together…'

'Oh my God, the boys.'

'I promise I won't slag you off to them, and I'll explain it's a joint decision. You are a great dad.'

'Just not such a great husband…'

'Don't play the pity card.'

The twinkle was back she was glad to see. It was faint, but there somewhere.

'Fine.'

'And we'll look at selling the house and all that boring stuff.'

Doug put both his hands on the table, as if to steady himself.

'We'll always have our boys to tie us together. And I genuinely hope that we can stay friends.'

Charlotte had a sudden vision of Doug as a young man dashing through the rain to meet her at the station and twirling her round, drops of water flying everywhere.

Her voice caught in her throat a moment.

'Look at me, Doug. Friends?'

He reached for her hand again and stared deep into her eyes.

'Friends it is.'

Chapter Twenty-Six

Maddie and Sofia were waiting for her when she walked back into the hotel, their worried little faces at odds with everyone else in the bar.

She joined their table, and the waiter was at her side in a moment.

'Three brandies please.'

Charlotte sat back in the chair and reached for their hands.

'It's done.'

They waited in silence, hands entwined, until the arrival of the drinks. Charlotte lifted her glass towards the others.

'*Yamas!*'

The *Yamas!* in response was decidedly muted, and she could see that Sofia especially was desperate to know the outcome of her talk with Doug. Charlotte took a good swipe at the brandy before she spoke. She wasn't sure how her news would be received by Maddie, given she was voluntarily calling time on her husband, but it was too late to worry now.

'It's over. I'm getting a divorce.'

Sofia punched the air.

'Yessss!'

Maddie put her finger to her lips.

'Calm down, Sof. The end of a marriage isn't usually something to be celebrated.'

'It is in this case.'

Maddie turned to Charlotte.

'How are you feeling, love?'

'Everything under the sun. Sad, relieved, exhausted, you name it, I'm feeling it. But the overwhelming emotion is relief, so I know deep down I've down the right thing.'

'Good for you. It can't have been easy.'

'Weirdly, when it came down to it, it was surprisingly easy. I shocked myself at how quickly I knew it was over once I'd spent a few minutes with him.'

Charlotte waited a beat for her racing heart to calm.

'I wasn't sure up until that point if I'd really have the strength to end things for good, but all the anger and hurt bubbled up inside me and came pouring out like a once dormant volcano. I suddenly knew what I had to do, for my own sake, no one else's.'

Sofia gave her friend a thumbs up, earning herself a frown from Maddie, who threw her brandy back in one.

'Shall we get out of here? There's a fantastic ice cream place up one of the back streets that I've been meaning to try. It has a smoked hazelnut flavour that all the reviews rave about. It will give us all a walk, too.'

'That sounds lovely. I'm a bit talked out to be honest. It will be nice to think about something else.' Charlotte turned to the others and stifled a yawn. 'Thank you both for being here for me. I think I'll be up for an early night tonight.'

'That suits me.' Maddie nudged Sofia. 'Especially as I've been volunteered to meet scary Greek momma in the morning.'

'I'll pick you up here at ten.' Sofia grinned. 'I'm not planning on an early night. I've only got three left with Adonis.'

After checking in on Charlotte the next morning, Maddie left her friend to have a long lie-in, turning the sign on her door to Do Not Disturb. While having a leisurely breakfast alone, she couldn't resist opening her emails yet again, but there was still nothing from her son. It had only been just over a day, but it didn't bode well.

The sound of a car outside told her that Sofia had arrived. She put down her coffee cup and brushed the crumbs off her navy linen shift dress. It was the best she could do in the circumstances.

The driver opened the car door to reveal Sofia looking the very image of a visiting European princess, dress and make-up immaculate. It was completely over the top for a visit to an old woman in Maddie's eyes, but she was wise enough not to mention it. Even at a quick glance, she could see Sofia was strung taut as a wire.

'You're ten minutes early! I've only just finished my coffee.'

'Well, you can never be too sure with the traffic.'

'Okaay. And you're feeling OK about today?'

A big nerve was twitching in Sofia's forehead.

'Perfectly calm. How's Char?'

'I've left her to sleep.'

'Good. It's what she needs.'

She'd quite like to go back to bed too. There'd already been an unsettling moment with Aphrodite, the attractive receptionist who seemed to hang on Adonis's every word, as she prepared to leave the hotel.

Normally Adonis was with her, but he was already up and in his office. As she'd approached the desk, the woman had looked left and right to check no one was around and beckoned her over.

'Your car is waiting, madam.'

'Thank you.'

As she turned to walk away again, she clearly heard the whispered words, *'he will never be yours.'*

When she turned back again, the woman's face was the picture of innocence, a false smile plastered on her lips.

She wasn't going to give her the satisfaction of querying her words, even though her first reaction was to punch her. There was no proof she'd said it, which the woman had made damn sure of. It would sound pathetic reporting it to Adonis, and as if she cared too much. She gave the woman a glacial stare before walking out.

She wasn't about to mention it to Maddie either. They had enough to deal with as it was.

They pulled up at a traditional white house, with old oil cans filled with red geraniums all round the perimeter. For a moment, it reminded Sofia of the steps up to Giannis, the paddleboard instructor's flat, and she swallowed hard. It was important she made a good impression here, and that evening had hardly been perfect. But she wasn't going to take it as a bad omen, yet.

An elderly woman appeared at the door, with another woman behind her that Sofia recognised as Lydia, Adonis's sister. She was glad she'd brought reinforcements too. Not that it was a battle, but it was nice to have Maddie with her.

It was Lydia who stepped forward first to welcome them and invite them to come through for coffee in the garden.

'My mother speaks very little English, so Adonis asked me to come along to help, so you can communicate.'

Sofia could feel the mother's eyes on her the whole time. They were about the same height, but the older woman was all in black, still in mourning for her long-dead husband. The black against the white made them look a little like pieces on a chessboard. *Let the games begin* was the phrase that came to mind. Sofia smiled a big smile in the woman's direction but got very little in return. A smile wasn't exactly difficult to translate. She pointed at her chest.

'Sofia, *hero poli*.'

The woman pointed at her own chest.

'Cassandra.'

There was no pleased to meet you too. She had a vague memory from school that Cassandra was the Greek goddess who foresaw terrible things. And from the look on her face, Sofia's relationship with Adonis was one of them. She'd just have to grin and bear it. A quick coffee and they'd be gone again.

Out in the garden, they were directed towards some spectacular bushes bursting with yellow flowers. Not being a gardener, Sofia hung back slightly and left the others to it. She'd killed more house plants than she'd had hot dinners. Thank goodness Maddie was asking Lydia and Cassandra plenty of green-fingered questions, and at one point she even detected a hint of a smile on Cassandra's face. But it didn't last.

Once the coffee was brought out with some biscuits introduced by Lydia as *melomakarona*, and apparently full of orange, cinnamon and cloves, Sofia took the chance to moan in delight at their taste, which earned a surprised glance from Maddie.

Normally, she'd never dream of eating biscuits, but needs must. There wasn't a flicker from Cassandra, just the same eagle-eyed stare.

Even Lydia must have been feeling the strain, as she dropped her spoon on the ground and had to go inside for a new one.

When she returned, Sofia ate another biscuit to try to win some brownie points, but when she checked to see if Cassandra approved, she was stunned to see tears in the old woman's eyes.

'*Aftí eínai megáli.*' It came out of her mouth in a whisper. '*Óchi paidiá ya ton Ádoni mou.*'

'*Mamá!*'

'*Óchi paidiá!*'

The second *Óchi paidiá!* was a definite shout.

Sofia had learnt enough Greek on her visits to know the words, *megáli*, old, *óchi*, no and *paidiá*, children.

It was pretty obvious what his mother was saying. She was too old to give Adonis any children.

'I'm so sorry.' Lydia's face was red. 'I must apologise for my mother's rudeness.'

'It's nothing.' Sofia tried to smile. On top of being a foreigner, she was also past her childbearing years and not of the Greek Orthodox religion. Pretty much a full hand for Cassandra. The old woman was openly crying now, and Lydia passed her a handkerchief.

'Stop it, *Mamá. Stamáta!*'

Lydia turned back to her.

'I know you understand what she has said to you, and it is not acceptable. But you must understand that Adonis is her first born and *Mamá* is from a different generation and very religious. Adonis is the clever one and has always been a workaholic. But all these years she has prayed that he would find a nice Greek girl and settle down.'

Sofia nodded. She prayed herself that Maddie would be able to keep quiet at this attack on her. Her friend losing it wouldn't help either.

'She is just a little shocked at his choice, when there are many women here on the island who would love to take your place.'

Aphrodite the receptionist would be at the head of the queue, no doubt. They were welcome to him, if this is what they'd have to put up with, was Sofia's first thought, but she tried to look at it from his mother's point of view. It was certainly a big wake-up call. Her decision to keep things casual with Adonis was looking like the right one.

'I don't want to upset your mother any further, so maybe it is better if we go. I will call for the car.'

'Thank you. I will take her inside for a rest.'

But as soon as Lydia tried to help her mother up out of the chair, she moaned and slipped out of her daughter's arms, falling to the floor on her side.

'Mads! Help her.'

Maddie was there in seconds and knelt down to the old woman. Luckily, she'd fallen onto grass rather than the tiled patio. Lydia was frozen in the same position, a gap between her arms where her mother had been.

'Sof, bring me those cushions to put under her head and feet. And Lydia…'

'Yes.' The woman came out of her trance.

'Can you get me a glass of water, please?'

Lydia ran inside as if her life depended on it.

Sofia placed the cushions in the appropriate places and watched as Maddie felt the woman's brow and checked her heart rate.

'Is she going to be OK?'

'I think the old dragon's just fainted, but let's wait a moment.'

The woman stirred and moaned out loud at the sight of two women she barely knew hovering above her.

'It's OK. *Eínai entáxei.*'

Maddie had her care home voice on, but Sofia was so thankful she was here. When Lydia returned, Maddie instructed her to help sit the woman up and got her to sip the water.

'I think your mother will be OK, but let's get her into bed. I think you should call the doctor out to check her over, but my feeling is that she's fine.'

'Are you a nurse?'

'No, I work in a care home, but I see this all the time. When older people get overexcited, they can easily faint.'

'Thank you. Thank you so much.'

Sofia waited outside while Maddie and Lydia took the old woman into the house. She'd already called for the car. It would only add to the problem if she was in there as well. It was a shock to be hated by someone you barely knew; she'd only ever experienced it in court when a ruling went in favour of her client and against their spouse. But it certainly put her relationship with Adonis in a new light. There was no way she could fight that level of animosity.

Maddie appeared outside just as the car was pulling in. They climbed in in silence.

At the end of the road, Maddie slapped the seat in front of her.

'Bloody hell!'

'I know. Thank God you were with me.'

'I thought people were exaggerating about Greek mothers and their sons.'

'There's certainly no way I'm planning to get between that particular Greek mother and her son. Do you think she'll be OK?'

'Yes, she was fine by the time I came out. She actually smiled and thanked me for helping her.'

'Well, you're not the one who's corrupting her little boy with your mature womanly wiles.'

'True.'

Sofia's phone rang, and she fished it out of her bag.

'Speak of the devil. Sis has obviously updated her big brother.'

Sofia listened for a few moments, nodding vigorously, before blowing a kiss down the phone and ending the call.

'He says his mother has behaved very badly, and he'll make it up to me tonight.'

Maddie raised her eyebrows.

'Stop it!

Sofia smoothed down her skirt.

'And the old bat seems perfectly fine now.'

After regaling Charlotte with the full horror of their morning, they opted for a casual lunch of calamari and Greek salad in the hotel, sitting out on the terrace.

Just as they were clearing their plates, there was the buzz of a phone.

Both Sofia and Charlotte reached for their bags but shook their heads moments later.

'Not me.'

'Nor me.'

Maddie grabbed her bag from the stool beside her. They'd been told way back on the first island that it was bad luck to put handbags on the floor as your money would drain away, so in most places little stools were provided to put the bags on.

She remembered with a racing heart that Sofia had set an alert to tell her if she had a new email.

Her son's name flashed up as the sender.

'Oh God, it's Dan. I don't know if I can face opening this.'

Sofia patted her leg.

'Do you want one of us to do it?'

'No, I'd better do it. If it's bad news, I need to know first.'

'OK.'

Her heart was in her mouth as she pressed on the newly delivered email. Its contents had her in tears within the first few seconds.

The words became so blurry that she had to hand it over to Sofia.

'Read it out loud, please.'

Sofia fished her glasses out of her bag.

'"*Mum. I've been hoping you'd contact me ever since that terrible day. We miss you like hell too. Things were said on both sides that never need be repeated. You're right that dad would be so sad and disappointed in all of us, and we owe it to his memory to try and build bridges. Elsie says hello and that she's looking forward to seeing her Granny M very soon. She can't actually speak yet, obviously, you haven't missed that much, but we can interpret baby talk. Love you. Dan.*"'

Sofia's eyes were full of tears now, too.

'And look, there's a video of Elsie, waving.'

Maddie took the phone and sobbed all over it, until Sofia took it back off her and passed her a serviette.

'You don't want it to go rusty. What a strange day. And we're only halfway through it. Talk about dramatic!'

Sofia had been deeply hurt by the way Cassandra had

treated her. Normally, she would never put up with that kind of behaviour from anyone, but the woman's age, and – more importantly – the fact that she was Adonis's mother, had gagged her more effectively than anything could. Combined with Aphrodite's bitter little comment earlier, she'd be glad to get out of here.

Maddie was still grinning from ear to ear.

'I'm so happy. I could kiss both of you.'

'Let's settle for a round of beers.'

Maddie stayed attached to her phone for the next half hour as the others dozed in the sunshine. Sofia came to with a start at a flurry of buzzing.

'More messages?'

'Not exactly.'

Maddie shook Charlotte's leg.

'Listen you two. I hope you don't mind me bailing, but there's a flight out of here tomorrow morning on the little plane, which connects with Athens and then on to Manchester. Dan's going to pick me up from the airport.'

Just saying the word Dan made her friend smile, thought Sofia, so how could she be so mean as to make a fuss, especially when Maddie had stepped in so magnificently this morning.

'Of course not. You go ahead.'

'Yes, you need to make things right as soon as you can,' Charlotte added her approval.

'Thanks, you two.'

Sofia frowned.

'You'll miss the wedding, though.'

'Oh yes, the wedding. Please give my love to Grace. I'm sure if you explain the circumstances, she'll understand.'

Given their little chat at the eighties' night about family, Maddie was convinced of it.

'Don't give it another thought. Char and I will boogie under the stars and drink ourselves stupid on your behalf. Plus, I'll even organise a car to take you to the airport.'

'Thank you.'

'But there is one condition…'

'I know I'm not going to like this.'

'Tonight, we go for an early gyros in town and then the three of us have a last swim together on a very special beach at sundown.'

'I might be missing something here, but it doesn't sound too bad.'

'Char?'

'Yes, I'm in.'

'Meet back here at five with your swimming stuff.'

Stomachs pleasantly full of gyros, they'd enjoyed the walk along the headland in the opposite direction to the cat sanctuary and had dropped down to a large sandy beach. The first fingers of the orange sunset had appeared in the sky, but there was still plenty of light left.

Maddie went to put her bag down on the sand, but Sofia stopped her.

'It's not this beach. It's the one over that little hill where the white church is.'

'Can't we stay here? It's lovely.'

'No, you've got to see the next beach. It's so pretty.'

Maddie and Charlotte followed Sofia up the steep path, past the *Mamma Mia!*-worthy church and down the steps on the other side.

'Oh good, we're the only ones here.'

Sofia jumped down the last few steps and onto the sand.

'Why's that good?'

A suspicion started to form in Maddie's mind.

Sofia handed them both a cold beer from her cool bag.

'Down in one first!'

'Sof, why is it good that no one's here?'

'Because this is the point at which I reveal you don't need your swimming stuff at all. It's a nudist beach!'

Maddie sighed heavily.

'Sofia Barnes! You little rat!'

She and Charlotte dutifully downed their beers in one alongside Sofia. Maddie spluttered as the contents of the bottle went down too fast, and Sofia patted her on the back.

'I just thought it would be a lovely end to our holiday together, with you leaving in the morning, Mads. It's a mark of how far we've come. So, are you both brave enough?'

Charlotte was already pulling her dress over her head.

'I ended my marriage yesterday. I think I can cope with a bit of water on my body.'

'Mads?'

'Oh, why not? I'm going home tomorrow to see my son and granddaughter for the first time in months. No one knows who I am anyway.'

'That's the spirit.'

Once the discarded clothes and shoes were piled up on the beach, Sofia reached over to hold hands with the others.

The white bits of their bodies showed up starkly against their impressive tans as the sun dipped towards the water. Flames of peach and tangerine danced in the sky above their heads as Sofia pulled the others forward.

'Let's run in together. One last time. All for one...'

'And one for all.'

They hit the sea at the same time and each of them broke into a grin as they waded into the warm water as far as their thighs.

'Last one in buys the cocktails at the little bar on the way back.'

Sofia dived under like a seal, while Charlotte and Maddie gently lowered themselves in and both turned to float on their backs.

'Looks like we're sharing it, Char.'

'Fine by me. Sea water against bare skin does feel pretty good. Who knew?'

Sofia surfaced again and turned onto her back too.

'It's been a wonderful holiday, hasn't it?'

Maddie splashed some water at her friend.

'Yes, you did well, little one.'

'Don't call me little one!'

Maddie's shriek of laughter was cut short by Sofia pulling her under.

Chapter Twenty-Seven

Looking at her friends sitting across from her at breakfast, Maddie was struck by how changed they were from the women she'd met at the airport in London on a grey Thursday morning only three short weeks ago.

The pale, stressed faces that had been holding on so tightly to their secrets were gone. In their place were relaxed smiles, enhanced by golden tans. She glanced across at the mirror, where a healthy-looking redhead with freckles all over her face smiled back. She barely recognised her either.

The secrets that had weighed her down too hadn't disappeared in a puff of smoke, but at least there was hope and love in her son's response. Living without Tony would still be an uphill battle, but stepping out of her life for a while had done so much to move things along.

'Penny for them?'

Charlotte's kind face looked into hers. Her friend had confided last night that she'd been worried to tell her about her decision to end things with Doug, given Maddie's own loss, but Maddie hoped she'd been able to reassure her that Charlotte Trent was the only one who really knew what the inside of her marriage looked like and what was right for her.

'I was just thinking that we all look a damn sight better now than when we were standing in that departures hall.'

Sofia glugged down her glass of freshly squeezed orange juice with ice.

'Too right we do.'

'We were all at a crossroads back then, and we didn't even realise it.' Maddie pointed at Sofia. 'And don't even think about singing that Beyoncé song…'

'As if!'

'I know you were.'

'"*I am alone at a crossroads…*"'

'Stop. I'm trying to be serious here. And you know the actual title of the song is "Listen", don't you, which is highly appropriate in your case.'

'If it's good enough for Queen Bey…'

'As I was saying before I was so rudely interrupted, we were all at a crossroads in our lives. But together, we've helped each other make tough decisions and act on them. Your friendship means more to me than you'll ever know.'

Sofia sniffed.

'Enough. I can't do tears before coffee.'

'OK, I'll stop being nice. It's obviously disturbing you.'

Charlotte wiped her own eyes with a serviette.

'I think it's lovely. And I feel the same. I'm not sure I'd have been as brave at confronting Doug if I hadn't known you two were back here waiting for me, whatever I decided.'

Sofia covered her hands with her eyes.

'You've set me off now.'

Charlotte delved down into her beach bag.

'And to say thank you to you both … and as you're leaving this morning, Mads, just a little something from me, to remind you of our time spent together.'

Charlotte handed them two tissue-wrapped parcels.

Sofia ripped the paper off hers straightaway.

'Wow!'

She held up the watercolour of the terrace at Adonis's hotel, framed against a clear blue Greek sky, with the town ranged below it and the flowers on the tables picked out in bright pinks and yellows.

'This is amazing, Char. So gorgeous. Adonis will be chuffed when I show it to him.'

Maddie had pulled the paper off hers too and was sat staring at the picture with tears in her eyes.

Sofia reached for the frame.

'Show me. What's it of?'

Maddie slowly turned the picture round on her lap and a vision of Thanassis as they'd first seen him stared back. He was sat on the metal chair next to his fish stall, smoking a cigarette with his boat behind him. His brilliant blue eyes held a note of promise, and his battered cap was slightly off at an angle.

'Stun…ning. You've captured him to a tee, Char. You're really good at this.'

'Thanks.' Charlotte looked over at Maddie with concern. She still hadn't spoken. 'I couldn't sleep last night, after getting about fourteen hours the night before, so I got up and painted these. They're only simple watercolours, but it felt so good to be painting again.'

She leant over to touch Maddie's knee.

'Mads, what do you think of yours?'

Her friend's teary eyes were smiling at last.

'It's absolutely gorgeous. It's just so lifelike it gave me a shock.'

'That's the biggest compliment you can pay an artist. I tried to paint something big enough to mean something, but small enough to fit it in your case.'

'This certainly means something. I'd leave clothes behind to get this in.'

Sofia snorted.

'You did, didn't you? Leave your clothes behind?'

'Funny.'

Charlotte tried out a cheeky smile. 'I was thinking you could put it up somewhere in your house and maybe look at it every once in a while. No one will ever know it's anything but a painting of an anonymous fisherman. Only we'll know when we visit what it really signifies.'

Maddie gave the picture a last stroke before wrapping it up again.

'You crafty mare!'

'You're welcome.'

Maddie clasped the picture to her body.

'OK, my car will be here in a few minutes' time, so the only thing left to discuss is you, Sof.'

'What do you mean?'

'This thing with Adonis. How can you pretend to yourself it's not serious?'

Sofia's hand froze on her coffee cup.

'Because it's not.'

'Rubbish. He's in love with you.'

'Where did you get that from?'

Maddie could see Sofia's neck going red as she spoke.

'The way he looks at you, the fact that he's introduced you to his family…'

'Yes, and look how that went!'

Maddie smiled at the memory.

'I admit his mother didn't seem to be your biggest fan, but she doesn't know you like we do.'

'The woman fainted on the spot at the thought that I might defile her precious son. How can I compete with that?'

'The very fact that you're even talking about competing with her makes me think that you're more than a little bit in love with him too.'

Why was her friend saying such rubbish out loud? Yes, she'd like to carry on seeing him, but love was out of the question.

'That's crazy.' Sofia turned away from her friend. 'Char, you're the voice of reason, what's your opinion?'

'You do seem very good together. He obviously adores you. Not that I'm an expert on relationships'—Charlotte gave a sad little smile—'including my own. But what I will say is that sometimes it is hard to see what's obvious to everyone else.'

Sofia put her hands over her ears.

'No! I'm not listening anymore. Let's get back to the weeping and wailing at your departure, Mads.'

Maddie carefully wrapped the picture of Thanassis in one of her dresses and put it back in the case.

'If you want to ignore what we're saying, it's up to you. Just think on it, Sof.'

The sound of a car arriving prompted Maddie to get up and pull her friends in for a last hug.

'We ought to make this an annual event.'

'Yes!' Sofia punched the air. 'Girls on tour. Summers in Greece.'

Charlotte kissed both of them on the cheek.

'I'm up for it.'

'And now…' Maddie pulled away. 'I really must go.'

They stood waving until the car had disappeared round the corner and Maddie was lost from sight.

Sofia wiped a final tear from her eye.

'A morning by the pool before we get ready for the wedding?'

'Sounds great.'

Given that Sofia had allegedly decided on what to wear days ago, she was taking an awful lot of time to get ready, thought Charlotte.

Grace had asked her bridesmaid to wear something simple in red to match the flowers, and had specified bare feet all round. As planned, the couple had signed the civil papers the day before. Neither of them was religious, and both had been married before, so a church wedding was out.

Technically it meant they were already married in the eyes of the law, but according to Sofia, for them the ceremony on the beach was the real wedding.

Charlotte had opted for a slinky pale green number, and

after a quick hair wash, a dollop of mascara, and a slick of lipstick, she was ready.

She'd been sat on Sofia's terrace for a good twenty minutes now.

'Sof! What are you doing in there?'

'Coming!'

Sofia stalked onto the terrace like it was a catwalk.

Charlotte's breath caught in her throat. There were simple red dresses, and there were simple red dresses. Stopping six inches above the knee, this one clung to every curve on her friend's body, the sensuous fabric swooping low at the back but attached to a collar at the neck. The contrast between the rippling silk and Sofia's tanned, lithe body was an arresting sight.

'That dress is bloody sensational!'

'Char, you never swear.'

'I do now. I've certainly never seen it before, either. I thought you were going to wear something from your already substantial wardrobe.'

Sofia's shifty look confirmed to Charlotte it was new.

'I bought it secretly on the shopping trip in town, although I made out to Mads that I'd only got the dress for my visit to scary Momma.'

'I bet it wasn't cheap.'

'Er, no. I'd be embarrassed to tell her how much it cost, which is why I hid it. But as she's not coming to the wedding, I won't ever have to.'

Charlotte rubbed the silk between the fingers of one hand.

'Those stunningly simple dresses are always the most expensive.'

'I had to have something special, not only for Grace and Will, but because it's my last night with Adonis for a while.'

Sofia's face fell.

'Don't worry. As soon as he sees you in that, he'll want to kidnap you and lock you away somewhere in the hotel vaults, rather than let you leave.'

'Okaaay, not at all creepy then.'

Charlotte laughed and reached for her silver shoulder bag.

'We can take our shoes off when we get there.'

The path down to the beach was strung with fairy lights, and the small crowd that had gathered waved and cheered every new arrival. Silver chairs either side of an aisle made of sand were hung with bunches of red roses mixed in with white gypsophila. They could see Will in the distance, waiting at the end of the aisle, talking to his best man, who could only be his son, so alike were they.

Beyond Will was just blue sea, all the way to the sky.

Sofia had been asked to meet Grace at the house first, and she touched Charlotte on the arm.

'Will you be OK on your own for a few minutes?'

'Don't be silly. I have been socialised. I've only got to walk about fifty metres down there. Go and see to Grace.'

Sofia peeled off to her left and gently knocked at the door of one of the white houses above the cove.

'Come in!'

Grace stood in her white lace underwear in the kitchen. She

turned at the sound of the door being opened and appraised her friend's outfit.

'Woah, hot stuff.'

'Hot stuff yourself! How did you know it was me? I could have been anyone. And you're in your knickers.'

Grace moved to enfold her in a hug.

'I saw you coming up the path.'

'Why aren't you dressed? They're all waiting.'

'I only need to throw the dress over my head. I wanted to have a moment alone with you first. You're so much a part of my story.'

'Aw!'

Grace pulled Sofia in further and kissed her on the top of her head.

'Let's have a quick drink to us.'

Two full champagne flutes were waiting on the table. Sofia picked up the nearest one and handed the other one to her friend.

'To us!'

The two women downed the icy liquid side by side.

'Us.' Grace put down her glass. 'Also, I wanted to give you something.'

'What is it?'

'Hang on a moment, Miss Impatient.'

Grace handed over a slim wrapped box, which Sofia ripped into and pulled out a thin gold bracelet studded all round with tiny red stones.

'Oh, it's gorgeous. Can I wear it now?'

'That's the idea.'

Grace fixed the bracelet around Sofia's tiny wrist.

'I couldn't imagine having anyone else as my bridesmaid.'
'I'd have been furious if you did.'
'Exactly.'
'But now, madam, it's time to get dressed.'

Sofia pulled Grace's simple white linen shift dress shot through with silver from its hanger.

'This is lovely.'

'It has a special meaning for us. It was the dress I wore to Will's space party, right here in this house. The first time we danced together, the first time I felt my body respond to his—'

'OK, let's stop it there. You need to actually put it on, unless you're planning to walk down the aisle in your underwear. Poor Will's going to think you've deserted him.'

'He's made of stronger stuff than that.'

Grace's dreamy smile wasn't getting them anywhere.

'Dress. On.'

'What a bossy bridesmaid.'

Sofia slipped her arm through Grace's as they checked themselves for a final time in the large, blue-framed mirror above the table.

Grace smiled at their reflection.

'White and red. The good girl and the naughty girl.'

'Which is which?'

'Hard to tell. I think we're all a bit of both.'

Sofia handed her one of the posies of red roses casually tossed on the table and grabbed the other one for herself.

'Are you finally ready?'

'As I'll ever be.'

The walk down the aisle was a riot of cheering and clapping. Sofia smiled at Charlotte, but her heart missed a beat when she saw Adonis staring straight at her. He'd said he wasn't sure whether he'd be able to get away in time, but here he was, his blond good looks standing out in a sea of dark heads.

Their joint present to the happy couple, which Grace had no idea about, was the honeymoon suite at the hotel for the night, before they left for Australia tomorrow. The couple's luggage had been smuggled out and taken to the hotel earlier. Angeliki was looking after Karen the cat, so she was in on it too.

They'd nearly reached the top of the aisle, and Will still had his back turned away from his bride. Angeliki and her boyfriend, Nick, were level with them now on their right as they paused for Grace to blow a kiss to her friend.

Sofia took Grace's posy and moved to the chair set aside for her at the front, just as Will turned. She wouldn't have wanted to miss that first look at Grace for anything in the world. The love it contained was boundless, and glancing back at her friend told her Grace returned his love a millionfold. She had absolutely no doubts about this marriage going the distance.

The simple but heartfelt ceremony with its personalised vows, as the guests watched the sun go down, moved everyone to tears and she locked eyes with Adonis as the celebrant invited Will to kiss the bride. There was certainly fire between her and her Greek lover – she couldn't wait to get him back to their room later and tear his clothes off – but how could there be anything else? It just didn't add up.

The age gap between them, his crazy mother, a jealous receptionist, and the full stop on him ever having children of his own were just some of the major stumbling blocks, plus he was from a different culture, a whole different country. Adonis's life was here, on a Greek island in the middle of the Aegean. She was essentially a tourist he occasionally had fun with. She had fun too, a lot of fun. But it was time to think about the next stage in her life. There was no place for her here.

The drinking and dancing on the beach to music from around the world went on long after darkness had fallen. All the neighbours had been invited to the wedding, along with a few friends and colleagues.

Crates of iced champagne and beer were refilled the moment they ran low, and a mass delivery of delicious gyros kept everyone from keeling over halfway through the revelry, alongside an enormous tower of red and white cupcakes.

It was just as Grace had wanted it, mused Sofia: intimate and unfussy. Her friend and her new husband only had eyes for each other the whole evening, as it should be.

Every time she'd sought out Adonis, he'd seemed to be staring at her too. Between them, they knew a large proportion of the guests, but finally they stopped chatting to other people and got together for a slow dance. Just the touch of his hands up and down her back had her desperate to get back to his flat for their last night together.

The happy couple stumbled over just before midnight to thank them both for their generous gift and were now about to depart in one of the hotel's luxury limos.

Grace leaned into her as they hugged goodbye and whispered in her ear.

'Don't let this one slip through your fingers.'

Will's arm round his new wife's waist pulled Grace away before Sofia could explain the impossibility of the situation.

Sofia caught up with Charlotte as they lined up along the path to wish the newlyweds well. She'd been keeping an eye on her friend throughout the evening, but Charlotte seemed perfectly at ease, talking to complete strangers and dancing with Angeliki's amiable boyfriend, Nick, who turned out to be quite a mover.

Sofia threw her arm round her friend's shoulders.

'Have you enjoyed the wedding?'

'I've loved it. I haven't stopped chatting and boogie-ing all night.'

'And you're sure you don't mind me leaving with Adonis now Mads has gone off? I'll be back for breakfast.'

'Of course I don't mind. Actually, I'm not going to be on my own.'

'Oh?'

'Don't worry. Not planning on a one-night stand. I'm off to a bar with Angeliki and Nick. They're going to drop me back later.'

Sofia's worry about leaving her friend on her own vanished with the dusk. She could finally enjoy the rest of the night with Adonis without feeling guilty.

'Great.'

Grace and Will blew kisses to everyone as they made their way up the path. Sofia got a real kiss and a thumbs up from her friend.

The moment the car drove off, Adonis grabbed her hand.

'Sofia, we need to talk. And I mean really talk this time.'

Chapter Twenty-Eight

'Can't the talking wait until we get back to the flat? We don't want to spoil the mood.'

Sofia leant over, pulled him to her and kissed his face all over, until she got to his lips. The deep moan that escaped from Adonis's mouth told her she'd bought herself a little time.

His hands were all over her, one moment pushing the fabric of her dress up her thighs, and the next delving down her bare back beyond the edge of the dress until he reached her skimpy briefs.

A sudden glance up told Sofia that the driver was watching their every move. She'd started this, but the man worked for the hotel, and she was sure that Adonis wouldn't want it all round the staff room. She certainly wasn't going to finish it on the back seat of a car.

She pulled her dress down to a more modest level and coughed loudly. Adonis came out of his trance and followed her gaze to the mirror.

They held hands until they reached the flat and then ran up

the stairs together, barely shutting the door behind them before he had pushed her up against the wall. She wrapped her legs round him and moved against him just once, but it was more than enough.

Her expensive dress was thrown on the floor, followed by her underwear, as he ripped off his own trousers and shirt and they half-staggered half-fell together onto the rug. Weddings always turned her on.

It was over in moments, but Sofia knew there was plenty more to come. She leant over to lick the place on his neck that drove him crazy. But instead of responding like he usually did, he pushed her gently away and sat up.

'I mean it, Sofia, we're going to talk.'

Picking up his trousers from the floor, he slowly climbed into them and passed her a dressing gown from a hook on the door. Seeing him topless, muscles moving everywhere, was hardly calming her down, but she could see she wasn't going to sidetrack him a second time.

'Let's talk up on the roof terrace. I'll bring the wine and glasses.'

The tiled floor was cool under her feet. The lights twinkling below them all the way to the port usually gave her a lift, but it was a feeling of dread that was uppermost in her mind as she made her way to the little table and chairs in the corner. Keep it casual had always been her motto, and don't let anyone mess with your head, or worse, your heart; it always ends in tears. She'd managed to keep the L word at bay for so many years. Why break the habit of a lifetime?

Adonis poured out two glasses of white wine and passed

one to her. The dry grapefruit flavour was soothing on her throat, but she kept on full alert.

'Will you let me say what I need to say, and promise not to change the subject, or deliberately try to turn me on beyond endurance?'

There was a smile at the end of the sentence, but Adonis was deadly serious. She knew enough about him to know that.

Sofia nodded.

'You can't leave the island tomorrow.'

For one second, Sofia was tempted to ask if there was a sudden ferry strike or a storm forecast, but she kept quiet. Levity wasn't required at this point.

Adonis leant over, took her hand and kissed it.

'I am scared to tell you how much I love you, Sofia *mou*. My Sofia. I miss you so much when you go away, and I count every moment until you come back.'

Tears filled her eyes, but she turned away so he wouldn't see her crying.

'I want you to stay here with me, where you belong.'

His hand was still on top of hers.

'I know how much your father let you down, but I would never do that. You can trust me; I hope you know that.'

His light touch on her cheek brought them face to face again.

'Don't cry, my darling. You are everything I want and need. I just hope I can make you believe me. Forgot your father and what he did to your mother. This is our story.'

The double mention of her father had her reaching for the wine glass.

'I was hoping, now that your work has changed, you would consider staying?'

The love in his voice stopped her from lifting her head again to meet his eyes.

'The whole thing is impossible.'

'Sofia *mou*...' His hand on her chin was soft. 'Look at me a moment, please. What is so impossible?'

His eyes glittered in the dark.

'Your mother hates me.'

Adonis slammed down his glass.

'I don't care what my mother thinks. I am a man, not a boy. She will get used to it in time.'

'But she's right that I can't give you children, or her any more grandchildren.'

'I am so sorry you had to hear that nonsense.'

Adonis reached forward to kiss her on the forehead.

'Listen, my love. I have never wanted children. I knew as a young man that it wasn't on my wish list. I love children; it's just never been something I've desired for myself. I'm forty-eight, if I'd wanted children, in Greece I could easily be a grandfather by now. It's seriously not for me.'

'Me neither.'

Adonis stroked the inside of her wrist, which wasn't helping with her concentration at all.

'See, we are well suited. I've got my nephews and nieces for whenever I feel the need for the company of young people. Which isn't that often. They're exhausting.'

Sofia nodded her agreement.

'But those nephews and nieces are also my mother's

beloved grandchildren, so she's just being greedy. She has plenty already. Next point on your list of negatives?'

It was like they were at a formal meeting with an agenda. She was keen to get on to any other business as soon as possible. She could tell that he was smiling without looking at him, but she had to put it all out there.

'I'm so much older than you. You will get bored with me.'

'Sofia *mou*, one thing I can say, hand on heart, is that I will never get bored with you. And remember, men usually die first anyway.'

'Please don't talk about you dying, I couldn't bear it.'

She hadn't meant to say that out loud.

'You're so sweet. Is there anything else that's worrying you?'

'There is one more thing…'

'Yes?'

'At the hotel the other day, Aphrodite whispered to me that you would never be mine.'

Adonis hit his head with his hand.

'Ah, that silly girl. How dare she say that to you? I will get rid of her.'

'No! Don't do that. Or not straightaway, anyway…'

Sofia raised a smile.

'Why would she say something like that?'

'This is embarrassing, but she has … pursued me.'

'And you've given her no reason to think she might catch you?'

'No!'

'Nothing?'

His tiny hesitation rang alarm bells.

'I want there never to be any secrets between us.'

Sofia debated for a microsecond telling him about Giannis the paddleboard king but dismissed it without a second thought. This was a fresh start. Her past conquests would stay firmly locked in the safe.

Adonis spoke again.

'Aphrodite tried to kiss me once at a Christmas party for the staff. I did not respond, I swear. She is not my type.'

Sofia began to feel a tiny bit of sympathy for the woman.

'Is that all?'

'That is all, Sofia *mou*. So, have I answered all your points?'

He was making it all sound so reasonable that she found herself seriously considering this man's wish for her to stay and make a home with him. Other men had tried, and she'd been tempted once or twice, but she'd always backed out at the last minute.

'If – and it's a very big if – I did stay, what on earth would I do all day? You work so hard.'

'But you understand this, as you like to work hard too.'

It was true. And she hadn't even begun to tackle the problem of what came next now she didn't have her work to throw herself into on her return. She'd have to do something, or she'd go crazy.

She sneaked a look at Adonis, who had his eyes closed for a moment, thinking hard. He looked so cute she was tempted to reach out and stroke his face.

'Could you start a business here? You have such a sense of style. You always know what to wear and how to advise others.'

'Thank you. I didn't realise you'd noticed.'

'Don't be modest, Sofia. It doesn't suit you. I always notice what you are wearing. I prefer it when you wear nothing'—Sofia could see his white teeth through the gloom—'but we mustn't get distracted.'

'Mustn't we?'

'Naughty.' Adonis poured out a little more wine. 'I actually have a business idea that I have been wanting to put to you for a while.'

'I'm listening.'

'Have you noticed that most of the top hotels have boutiques in them now? They offer specially curated collections of everything from clothes and bags to swimwear.'

'Yes, not only have I noticed, but I've also bought things in them too.'

'I have wanted to put one in our hotel for a while now. I think we are as you say in Britain "*missing a trick*". We have a captive audience, but it would have to be very high end and exclusive, and not many people have the skills I need to get it right.'

'So, it's just my work skills you want?'

'Stop pouting. I want everything, Sofia *mou*. You would not be serving these women, and men as well hopefully. You would be doing the choosing because you have impeccable taste. You would have a sales team under you to direct as you wish.'

Her mind was ablaze with what she could do, given the right space and the freedom to choose her stock. She could travel to other islands, track down small suppliers, offer handmade couture, and even provide a mending and altering service, something she always felt was lacking, even in top hotels.

'Well?'

'It's certainly a lot to think about. It's all a bit overwhelming at the moment, but I promise I'll give it plenty of thought.'

She trailed her fingers through his hair and across his chest.

'Can we stop talking for a while now?'

'Of course, my love. It is a big decision. Take your time.'

Adonis took her by the hand and led her back down to the bedroom with its huge, white-painted bed and crocheted blue cover.

Their lovemaking was gentle and filled with tender emotion, the sweetest she'd ever known between them.

Sofia woke in the early hours with a pounding head and a racing heart. She stared at the man next to her, gorgeous even in sleep.

What was she thinking? She'd got swept up in a fantasy. She'd led him on and got him to believe his dream of being with her on the island was achievable.

His mother would never forgive him. Was it really fair to rip him away from his family? She'd seen close-up what rupturing a family could do. She had a perfectly good life and a home waiting for her back in London. It might be a bit lonely at times, but she had her hard-fought freedom, and she wasn't ready to give it up. It had worked well for her all these years, and it would again.

She got dressed in the dark and found a piece of paper and a pen.

Couldn't sleep. Too many thoughts in my head. I will ring you. Sofia x.

It was a coward's way out, but it was too much to grapple with all at once. She'd go back to Britain with Charlotte as planned in the morning and take it from there. They could carry on as they always had, meeting every couple of months.

It was light by the time she'd carefully closed the flat door and gone down the steps in her bare feet, slinging her shoes over her shoulder. The two hundred metres to the hotel were completed in the peace of a new morning. Only the fishermen were awake, shouting over to each other as the boats pulled out of the port and onto the open sea.

They'd been given keys to the hotel's main door, and she tiptoed in and went to her room, where she spent a dry-eyed restless few hours, longing for breakfast to begin and end, and for the car transporting them to the ferry to come and take her far away from the emotional maelstrom.

Over their breakfast coffee and cake, Charlotte was full of tales from the post-wedding partying and luckily didn't notice straightaway that Sofia wasn't her normal bouncy self. But it didn't last long.

'Is everything OK, Sof? You're very quiet. Are you sad at leaving Adonis behind?'

The idea that she was sad about leaving him, rather than rejecting the whole other life she'd been offered, would just about cover it without having to reveal the truth. Plus, it was true: she *was* sad about leaving, but Charlotte didn't need to know what she was saying no to.

The minutes until they could board the ferry seemed like

hours, and even when they were finally on deck, they had to wait for all the cars and lorries to load, so it was hardly the quick getaway she'd hoped for.

At long last, she was standing with Charlotte at the front of the boat with the engines running, more than ready to watch the island disappear into the distance.

Just as they were about to leave, a commotion on the dock demanded her attention. A man in a black BMW had abandoned his car in the middle of the dockside and was pushing his way through the waiting crowd. He ran towards the boat like a madman.

Sofia's heart turned over when she saw who it was.

Charlotte leant further over the rail.

'Isn't that Adonis?'

'Oh, is it? Yes, you're right.' Sofia knew her nonchalant act wasn't fooling her friend.

Of course he'd know what time her boat left. Any hopes of quietly slipping away had disappeared completely.

'Sofia *mou*. Over here!'

Both women turned their head in the direction of his voice.

'You cannot leave.' Adonis spread his arms to the sky. 'I love you, and I can't live without you.'

Charlotte had heard those very same words from her own husband just two days earlier, but they'd failed to move her. Sofia had one big decision to make. She studied her friend, who had gone bright red, and gently pulled Sofia's head round to face her.

'OK, we only have a few moments to do this. You must answer me truthfully.'

Sofia's eyes strayed again and again to the figure standing below her on the dock.

'Do you love him?'

Sofia nodded miserably.

'Could you make a life here on the island with him?'

Again, the sad nod.

'Then stay, Sof, for once in your life, stay. Don't leave like every other time. Gather up every ounce of courage you have and be brave, my friend.'

Charlotte pushed Sofia's suitcase towards her.

'Go on. Get the hell off this boat.'

Sofia hugged her friend tight.

'Will you be OK on your own?'

Charlotte smiled into the sun.

'I'm going to have to learn how to be on my own, but I think – no, I know – I'm going to be OK. I've spent thirty years with the same man, and now I'm going to explore being me again. You, on the other hand, have spent thirty years on your own, and now it's your time to explore real love. It could be your last chance. Go. And that's an order!'

The whistle sounded to warn any visitors to get off the boat before it departed, and Sofia dragged her case down the steps and off the ferry onto the dockside.

Adonis stood waiting quietly a few feet away. The look of joy on his face when he saw her was something she'd treasure forever.

Sofia dropped her case and ran into his arms. The crowd waiting on the dock and the passengers on the boat erupted in cheers.

Her lips met his, as he hugged her so tight she could barely breathe. But she pulled out of his embrace to look him in the eye. She needed to say it.

'I love you too, Adoni *mou*. I've loved you almost from the moment I met you. I love you more than I've loved any other man in my life, ever. I was too scared to admit it until I saw you standing there, fighting so hard to give us a chance, a future together.'

Adonis went to speak, but she put her finger to his lips.

'We both know it's not going to be easy, but as long as we face everything together, anything is possible.'

She leaned into him and whispered in his ear.

'What I can promise you is my love for the rest of our lives.'

Adonis's soft lips on hers stopped any more talking.

Sofia let the demons fly out of her heart and up into the bluest of blue skies.

For the first time in her life, she really was going to stay.

Epilogue

Six Months Later

Sofia took her seat at the table reserved for three and made sure the bottles of alcohol she'd requested were chilling in their buckets of ice.

The stunning view outside the restaurant's wall of windows was of London decked out in all its finery to celebrate the upcoming festive season. The lights and baubles on the trees and shop fronts below twinkled in the pin-sharp winter sun.

Not surprisingly, she'd arrived first, but then she'd only had to walk down a flight of stairs after her successful meeting on the top floor, rather than travel down from the north by train, like Maddie, or drive from Surrey, like Charlotte.

She'd just agreed a deal to franchise a range of exclusive shoes and bags for the hotel, one of many deals she'd struck over the past few months, travelling all over Greece from big cities to tiny islands. Today's negotiation in her former hometown was the last piece of the jigsaw for the new season collection.

The food she'd ordered to celebrate with her friends was waiting under covered platters on the table. The chef had been a bit taken aback at first, given the restaurant's reputation for fine dining, but Sofia had insisted. And she'd paid them handsomely for the privilege.

Maddie and Charlotte arrived together, in a flurry of kisses and cold cheeks. The group hug was long and full of feeling, which threatened to spill over into tears before they'd even spoken.

'Sit, sit!'

Sofia indicated that the other two should take the seats in the window, the ones with the best view.

'It's so lovely to see you both. We've got so much to catch up on.'

They'd spoken on the phone numerous times, but it was the first occasion Sofia had managed to meet up with her friends in person since they'd waved goodbye to each other in Greece.

'Wow. Look at that.'

Maddie pointed out St Paul's Cathedral in the distance and turned back to Sofia with a frown.

'Why are you giving us the best seats in the house? You haven't gone off him already, have you? Poor sod. Surely you haven't left the man stranded in the middle of the Aegean?'

'No!' Sofia sighed. 'Of course I haven't gone off Adonis. He's the love of my life, something you both knew way before I did.'

They both nodded and looked a little too smug for her liking.

'Good.'

Charlotte went to lift the covers off the food.

'What's this?'

'Wait a minute, Miss Nosey. It's a little thank you to you two for nudging me in the right direction. Are you hungry?'

'Starving.' Maddie rubbed her stomach.

'Nothing changes.'

Maddie laughed.

'I'd say a hell of a lot has changed since the holiday.' She took Charlotte's hand and squeezed it. 'This one has been on a painting residence in California for three months, whatever that is, and you live on a Greek island now…'

Charlotte squeezed back her friend's hand and smiled.

'And you, Mads, are reunited with the family you thought you'd lost.'

Maddie grabbed her phone.

'Elsie's walking! She took her first steps yesterday, and I was there. Look!'

After cooing for ages over Maddie's cute granddaughter, Sofia turned back to Charlotte.

'The gallery looked amazing, Char. On the beach at Carmel, wasn't it?'

'Yes. It was lovely. But I have to be honest, not quite as lovely as Greece though.'

'Aw, I'm pleased. The paintings you produced were absolutely stunning. You know I've bought one for the hotel, don't you? It should arrive next week.'

'I do, you naughty thing.'

Maddie snorted.

'I don't have the money to be "naughty", but I did buy the set of postcards off the website.'

Charlotte smiled at her friend.

'That means just as much, honestly.'

She reached for both her friends' hands.

'I've really missed you two, especially after our special summer holiday. As you know, the house sale's gone through, and the divorce is nearly done and dusted. Strangely, I'm getting on better with Doug now than I have for years.'

Charlotte held up a hand.

'And before you say it, Sof, I know there's no going back, and I'm happy about it. I've got news too. I told you I'd spotted a quirky two-bed coach house by the river, a couple of miles away from my old home. Well ... the owner accepted my offer yesterday, so you're both welcome to come and stay as soon as it's through.'

Maddie reached for the ice bucket.

'Dying of thirst here. Aren't we allowed to celebrate that? Char owning her own home for the first time ever?'

'Of course, we are...' Sofia pulled the serviettes from the ice bucket and removed the covers from the platters.

Bottles of ice-cold Mythos, drops of moisture glistening on the green glass, were accompanied by the traditional frozen glasses, and the food was revealed as a whole host of meze, everything from warm *spanakópita* and calamari to *taramasaláta, dolmádes, tzatzíki,* a big Greek salad, bread and olives.

'Surprise!'

Maddie reached for a piece of *spanakópita*.

'Yum. Let's get stuck in.'

Sofia pushed back her chair and stood up.

'Can you please let me do a toast first?'

Maddie smiled and dropped the slice of pie back on her plate.

'I suppose so. But hurry up.'

'Grab a bottle each, girls.'

Maddie and Charlotte rose as one.

'I just want to thank both of you for helping me to see that what I wanted, and needed, was right under my nose. Adonis has made me so happy, and I love living on the island with him, and his crazy family, who are getting a little bit more used to me, thank God. Even his mother's softened a bit and actually smiles at me now and again. Oh yes, and I love my new job.'

Sofia lifted her bottle towards her friends.

'Here's to more island hopping for us. Next summer's a definite. And every summer after that.'

Maddie punched the air.

'Amen to that!'

The three of them clinked glass on glass.

'*Yamas!*'

Sofia took a large gulp and raised the bottle again, glancing between her friends, as all three of them broke into a smile.

'All for one...'

'And one for all!'

DON'T MISS *STILL GOT IT*
YOUR NEXT MUST-HAVE ESCAPIST READ

'THE BANTER? HILARIOUS. THE CHEMISTRY? OFF THE CHARTS. AND THE HEARTWARMING MOMENTS? PERFECTION.'

Grace Foreman never expected to find herself widowed before she turned sixty – but when she packs her bags for a summer on a gorgeous Greek island, the last thing on her mind is a holiday romance. Grace would rather take a chance on a tan … or maybe a new summer wardrobe…

But then Grace meets ex Special Forces soldier Will Lancing – and although Grace isn't looking for love, she soon finds out she's *still got it* when it comes to playing the dating game…

AVAILABLE IN PAPERBACK, EBOOK AND AUDIO!

Acknowledgments

I want to say a big thank you to anyone who has read this book. It's my second, and number two in The Greek Getaways Collection, although, like *Still Got It*, it is also a standalone novel.

Huge thanks go once again to the wise and kind Broo Doherty, my agent; to Charlotte Ledger, Publisher at One More Chapter, for taking a chance on me with a three-book deal; and to Helen Williams, my editor, for her thoughtful analysis and enthusiastic support.

Thanks also for the input from editor Laura McCallen, and back up from Kara Daniel and Sofia Salazar Studer.

This book is set on three different Greek islands, each one an amalgamation of many of my favourite locations in The Cyclades and beyond, including Antiparos, Ikaria, Syros, Ios, Paros, Naxos, Samos, Astypalea and Amorgos.

Greece is always my go-to destination, and I hope the books help you escape there too. My Greek is coming along, very slowly.

Again, thanks to my beta readers, David Young, Louise Gannon, Yasmin Pasha, Elke Tullett, Pat Chappell, Hazel Easterbrook, and Jane Goodwill, who all give very useful feedback, most of which I agree with!

Although we're now scattered further afield, Yamas, or

cheers, to those of us from the Creative Writing MA at St Mary's University, Twickenham, who still meet regularly to chat about all things book over many drinks: Sarah Kirwan, Sarah Nelson, Clare Rees, Joel Bradley, Robbie Westacott, Ezra Harker Shaw, Adam Sharp, and Molly Gartland.

And to other friends and family who have also shown their support in various ways, from the TV Girls and the School Mums Posse to my brother and sister, Paul Smith and Helen Chandler, plus Greek friends Elina and Ilias, Ann and Vassilis, and Maya and Dimitris.

And of course, love always to David, Scarlett, and Fergus.

The author and One More Chapter would like to thank everyone who contributed to the publication of this story...

Analytics
Imogen Wolstencroft

Audio
Fionnuala Barrett
Ciara Briggs

Design
Lucy Bennett
Fiona Greenway
Liane Payne
Dean Russell

Digital Sales
Laura Daley
Lydia Grainge
Hannah Lismore

eCommerce
Laura Carpenter
Madeline ODonovan
Charlotte Stevens
Christina Storey
Rachel Ward

Editorial
Rosie Best
Kara Daniel
Catherine Jackson
Charlotte Ledger
Federica Leonardis
Laura McCallen
Jennie Rothwell
Sofia Salazar Studer
Helen Williams

Harper360
Emily Gerbner
Ariana Juarez
Jean Marie Kelly
emma sullivan
Sophia Wilhelm

International Sales
Ruth Burrow
Bethan Moore
Colleen Simpson

Inventory
Sarah Callaghan
Kirsty Norman

Marketing & Publicity
Chloe Cummings
Grace Edwards
Katie Sadler

Operations
Melissa Okusanya

Production
Denis Manson
Simon Moore
Francesca Tuzzeo

Rights
Ashton Mucha
Alisah Saghir
Zoe Shine
Aisling Smyth

Trade Marketing
Ben Hurd
Eleanor Slater

The HarperCollins Contracts Team

The HarperCollins Distribution Team

The HarperCollins Finance & Royalties Team

The HarperCollins Legal Team

The HarperCollins Technology Team

UK Sales
Isabel Coburn
Jay Cochrane
Leah Woods

And every other essential link in the chain from delivery drivers to booksellers to librarians and beyond!

ONE MORE CHAPTER

YOUR NUMBER ONE STOP FOR PAGETURNING BOOKS

One More Chapter is an award-winning global division of HarperCollins.

Subscribe to our newsletter to get our latest eBook deals and stay up to date with all our new releases!

signup.harpercollins.co.uk/join/signup-omc

Meet the team at
www.onemorechapter.com

Follow us!

@onemorechapterhc

Do you write unputdownable fiction?
We love to hear from new voices.
Find out how to submit your novel at
www.onemorechapter.com/submissions